AFTER THE ENDING

THE ENDING SERIES BOOK ONE

LINDSEY POGUE
LINDSEY FAIRLEIGH

Cover Design by Molly Phipps
We Got You Covered Book Design

L2 Books
101 W. American Canyon Rd. Ste. 508-262
American Canyon, CA 94503

978-1-723814-80-8

OTHER NOVELS BY THE LINDSEYS

THE ENDING SERIES

The Ending Beginnings: Omnibus Edition

After The Ending

Into The Fire

Out Of The Ashes

Before The Dawn

World Before: A Collection of Stories

NOVELS BY LINDSEY POGUE

A SARATOGA FALLS LOVE STORY

Whatever It Takes

Nothing But Trouble

Told You So

FORGOTTEN LANDS

Dust And Shadow

Borne of Sand and Scorn

Wither and Ruin (TBR)

Borne of Earth and Ember (TBR)

NOVELS BY LINDSEY FAIRLEIGH

ECHO TRILOGY

Echo in time

Resonance

Time Anomaly

Dissonance

Ricochet Through Time

KAT DUBOIS CHRONICLES

Ink Witch

Outcast

Underground

Soul Eater

Judgement

Afterlife

ATLANTIS LEGACY

Sacrifice of the Sinners

Legacy of the Lost

For our unbelievably supportive family and friends,
who encouraged us when we announced
our crazy decision to write a book.

For Dennis and Brian,
who give us the space to live in two worlds,
even if one isn't real.

"Friendship is unnecessary, like philosophy, like art…It has no survival value, rather it is one of those things which give value to survival."

-C. S. Lewis

PROLOGUE

March 15, 1 AE (from the journal of Danielle O'Connor)

If someone had told me three months ago that 90 percent of the people in the world were about to die, I would've laughed. If someone had told me the survivors would develop unbelievable Abilities, I would've called them crazy. If someone had told me I'd find love with the least likely person, I would've rolled my eyes. And if someone had told me that, after everything, the people I cared about most would be torn from my grasp, I would've walked away.

I wish I could walk away now.

DECEMBER

1

DANI

Cringing, I glared at the stinging, red paper cut on the tip of my index finger and muttered, "Damn hand sanitizer." I'd always been a fan of good old-fashioned soap and water, and I was irked that my dissertation advisor had forced the slimy, astringent goop into my hands when I'd left his office.

Unfortunately, the compulsory germ-killing reminded me of Callie, my pathetically sick roommate. I'd driven her to the campus clinic first thing that morning. She'd been sitting on our couch in pajama bottoms and a purple pea coat, mumbling, "I'm going to the doctor right now…just give me a second…," and staring at the floor. I'd immediately hustled her out to the car and zipped her to the doctor.

"It's just a bad case of the flu, I'm sure," the doctor had claimed, barely perceptible worry tightening her eyes.

Callie's ashen coloring had been troubling, but not as much as the doctor's instruction to take her to the hospital if her condition worsened…like the other sick students…dozens of them. I couldn't believe a flu outbreak was forcing so many healthy people into the hospital. It wasn't like we lived in a third world country or something.

The handful of students missing from my morning study group only intensified my concern—a handful is a lot when there are only eleven students to begin with. As I cleared the last crosswalk on the way back home, being careful to avoid the puddles left by the morning rain, I wondered if the outbreak would end up being as deadly as the Spanish flu was nearly a century ago.

I shook my head, dispelling my unusually grim thoughts. *It's just the flu*, I told myself for the hundredth time. *She'll be fine. They all will.*

As I entered my turn-of-the-century brick apartment building, I distracted myself with thoughts of how incongruous the classy exterior was with the 1980s-remodeled interior. The décor was tragic—pastel and gold foil abstract art hung on the walls, and the carpet was a tacky combination of mauve, coral pink, and faded turquoise…and that was just the beginning. The apartments themselves included worn blue carpet—no doubt covering handsome hardwood—stained linoleum, and appliances with chipped plastic. *Such a waste…this place could be exquisite. But, at least the rent's low…*

I walked to my ground floor apartment, unlocked the door, and shifted my computer bag to brace myself for the impending "happy Jack attack." Except when I opened the door, it didn't come.

"Jack?" I called out, curious.

Following his whimpered response, I found the 120-pound, adolescent German Shepherd staring forlornly at Callie's closed bedroom door.

"Hey, Sweet Boy," I said, crouching down to scratch his shoulders and to let him sniffle my neck. "She probably just wants to sleep. Want a *treat?*"

Jack wagged his way into the kitchen while I quickly peeked into my roommate's bedroom. Inside, Callie snored softly as she slept. *She's fine.*

After rewarding Jack's amazing abilities to sit ("sit"), shake hands ("nice to meet you"), and play dead ("bang"), I plopped down on my bed and opened my laptop. Jack hopped up and settled in next to me, causing a bed-quake.

Cam, my adorable boyfriend, wouldn't get home from work for another half hour. Rubbing Jack's velvety ear, I decided to write a nice long email to my best friend, Zoe—she had neither answered when I'd called during my walk home nor responded to my texts. The woman worked like crazy, and we hadn't chatted in days. Besides, writing to her would kill time *and* help me avoid doing anything productive on my birthday. *Genius.*

Date: December 4, 4:30 PM
From: Danielle O'Connor
To: Zoe Cartwright
Subject: Birthday Heresy

Zo! I can't believe we're apart on a birthday. It's practically heretical! Thank you SO much for the amazing drawing...it's totally perfect. I can't believe how many details you remembered from that night. Cam was super impressed too.

Anyway, how was your date with Mr. 58 (or was it Mr. 85)? You promised to give me juicy details, but alas, I've heard nothing from my wayward Zo. It was the blond guy, right? Or was that the last one? Gah...I can't keep up. Give me an ooey-gooey, nitty-gritty description of EVERYTHING. Please.

On a totally different note, the flu is getting pretty bad over here. Is it bad in Salem too? This morning I took Callie to the doctor, and Zo, I'm really worried about her. She's so pale and weak. Actually, she looks just like you did when you had that H1N1 virus a few years ago. Cam's been making soup for her...he's so sweet. Besides, his cooking is a gazillion times better than whatever I'd conjure up. My food might make her feel worse...

So...I'm sure you want to know about tonight's birthday plans. Cam (sigh, drool) is taking me to his restaurant and then to that Irish pub—you know, the one where you had too many Long Islands and danced on the table... Anyway, Cam said he invited "everyone we know" to the pub. But, considering that over half of Seattle seems to be sick, I'm guessing less than a dozen people will show. Whatever...I'm just excited to get out and have some fun.

Oh...gotta go...Cam just got home and is harping on me to get changed for dinner. I guess soggy jeans aren't classy enough. I'll give you a recap tomorrow, assuming I'm not too hungover to open my eyes.

Dani

We'd been at the pub for several hours when Jamie's pink, designer stiletto jabbed my shin. "Did you hear about that student who *died* today?" she asked.

My food and alcohol-induced semi coma receded momentarily, allowing me to process her eager words. Always the drama queen, that Jamie. She never knew when to keep her mouth shut, so we constantly butted heads.

Sighing, I grumbled, "What are you talking about?"

"Ohhhh…so you *don't* know." Jamie's eyes narrowed with vindictive pleasure.

Not for the first time that night, I mentally cursed Cam for inviting her. "Evidently not," I replied dryly.

"Yeah." Her chest heaved with delight as she explained, "some undergrad died of the *flu*. You know, the one that *everyone* has right now. You do at least know about *that*, right? So now people are dying from it. Doesn't Callie have it too?"

Hateful bitch, I thought viciously. I'd never really liked Jamie, and my concern about Callie clouded my judgment, along with the three vodka tonics and the glass of Champagne. "You're a hateful bitch," I retorted.

The statement earned shocked stares from several of the young Seattleites sitting around the corner booth, including Cam. But I wasn't done. For days I'd been worrying about Callie, and stupid Jamie had just implied the worst. *She'll be okay. It's just the flu.*

With a sickly sweet smile I cooed, "Callie's doing much better, thanks for asking. But *you*, Jamie…you're looking quite pale. Are *you* sick? Or, have you just had too much to drink? You *do* at least know about your reputation as a lush, right?"

A growing silence encompassed our table. As I opened my mouth to continue, Cam interceded. "Let's get a drink, D," he said through gritted teeth.

I was quickly ushered out of the booth by his firm grasp. His unusual forcefulness was more than a small turn-on, and suddenly, I was really looking forward to returning home with him.

By the time Cam and I left the pub, the confrontation with Jamie was nearly forgotten. We entered our apartment, eager to reach our bedroom, and noticed that Callie's bathroom light was on. When I went to turn it off, much to my shock, I found my roommate curled up on the linoleum floor. The air was thick with the rank smell of vomit. *Oh my God…*

I fell to my knees beside Callie and turned her onto her back. She was burning hot and coated in sweat. Jack, curled up next to her, kept nuzzling her cheek and watching her face for a response. There was none.

While we'd been out eating, drinking, and being generally merry, Callie had vomited what looked like all of her insides into the toilet. I stared at my friend's non-responsive form, unable to move for several long seconds. And then I started panicking.

"Callie! Callie, wake up!" I implored, nudging her gently. She didn't respond. I shook her harder, watching her sway like a rag doll. She looked so pale, so young. "Cam! We have to take her to the hospital!" I screeched.

When I looked behind me for Cam's unfailing support, I found him on the phone. He was repeating our address. *Oh...9-1-1...I should've thought of that.*

"Thanks," he said, ending the call. "They'll be here in fifteen or twenty minutes," he told me.

"But, she's...," I began but didn't know how to finish. *Sick? Comatose? Dying?*

"I know, D, but they said it's an unusually busy night," Cam told me, filling two glasses with water from the kitchen tap. "They'll get here as fast as they can."

When the paramedics finally arrived, Cam had to pry me from my prostrate position beside my unconscious friend to give the emergency crew enough room to help her. We followed the ambulance to the hospital and watched as Callie was rushed through the emergency room and into a restricted area. *FAMILY ONLY*, read the sign taped to the door. All we could do was sit...wait.

As I looked around, my mind returned to a mostly-sober state. I wasn't in an emergency room waiting area but a stifling, body-packed cage. People crowded in on all sides, milling, mumbling, mourning. They all looked sick. Hundreds of them. *Shouldn't the hospital be taking care of these people? What if they infect me? Infect us?*

Cam was sitting beside me, holding my hand. He looked just as ill as everyone else in the crowded room. *What if he* is *sick? Like Callie...oh God...like the guy who died...*

The air grew perceptibly hotter and viscous. Clammy chills consumed my body. *Stay calm...stay calm...stay calm...*

Hours passed, and then I saw her. I recognized the silky blonde hair and pink stilettos. Jamie. *You're a hateful bitch,* my words replayed in my head.

I watched as they wheeled her through the stuffy room, unconscious. Just like Callie. I'd been honest in my earlier assessment of her; she really had looked ill. *You're a hateful bitch.*

Jamie disappeared through the same metal doors as Callie had. FAMILY ONLY. Medical staff and unconscious patients were the only people who'd passed through them. So far, only the medical staff had returned.

Desperately, I looked at Cam, hoping he could somehow give me the air my lungs couldn't seem to capture. But he appeared ready to pass out, completely unaware of my emotional flailing.

Zoe, I thought, *I need you!*

2 SENT TEXT MESSAGES:

TO: Zo

Callie's in the ER. She's in a coma. Cam and I came in with her a little after 2AM. Been here for hours, but the docs still haven't told us anything. Wish you were here.

December 5, 6:00 AM

TO: Zo

BTW, I'll call Grams in a bit to check on everyone back home. How are YOU feeling? Me? I'm freaking out…

December 5, 6:04 AM

2

ZOE

Rushing into the small, outdated bungalow, I threw my messenger bag on the russet suede couch with excessive force. I was instantly irritated that Sarah, my roommate's closest friend, was there…again. Eating *my* food. *Why am I not charging her rent?*

"Where's Jordan?" I snipped, unwinding my black cashmere scarf and charcoal knee-length pea coat, and tossing them over the back of the couch.

"She's in the shower. You hungry?" The curly-haired free-loader twirled noodles on her fork, utterly oblivious to my annoyance.

I took a deep breath, trying to calm myself before speaking. "Thanks, but I'm rushing off to the bar for my night shift." I eyed the plate of spaghetti in front of her. "Someone's gotta buy the food around here," I added.

Hurrying down the hallway to my bedroom, I slammed the door behind me. I barely had time to remove my sweater before my cell phone vibrated in my pocket. Sighing, I answered, "Hey Dad."

"Hi honey, how are you?" He muffled a cough on the other end of the line.

"Getting ready for work. Other than that, I'm fine." I unzipped my knee-high, black calfskin boots and flung them into the corner. The brisk air was a reprieve, cooling my legs, which had been fermenting in their leather confines.

"I thought you just got *off* work?"

"Yeah, well, I'm *always* working. That's the joy of having two jobs."

"Oh yeah. I forgot." He cleared his throat.

"How could you forget? I've been working at the gallery *and* Earl's for like…ever."

"Well, that's the joy of getting old," he teased, but he sounded exhausted.

"You sound horrible, Dad." I pulled off my brown pencil skirt and laid it across the bed.

"Gee, thanks. You sure know how to make your old man feel good," he bantered.

"Yeah, well, someone's gotta worry about you." Trying to lighten the conversation, I asked, "What kind of mischief have you gotten into lately, anyway? I haven't talked to you in a while, so don't tell me 'nothing,' 'cause we both know *that's* not true."

He chuckled and sighed, "Nothing, I promise…Well, there was—"

I laughed, interrupting his admission with feigned exasperation. "I knew it! What'd you do now, Dad?"

"I *tried* to re-landscape the backyard—" He was cut short by a coughing fit.

I grimaced. "Are you sure you're okay? You really *do* sound bad." I grabbed some jeans out of the closet and shook them out.

His cough persisted, and I grew increasingly worried. "Dad…"

"I'm fine. It's just a lingering cold. Charlene's sick too. I probably caught it from her when I was helping weatherproof her windows last week."

I was immediately sidetracked by the knowledge that he was spending time with his beautiful, *single* neighbor. I wished, more than believed, he might be coming out of his shell. My dad hadn't dated much since my mom's death. According to my older brother, my dad had never really been the same in general. However, his scatterbrained lack of focus was all I'd ever known, and even at the age of fifty-seven, he still needed me to look out for him.

"At Charlene's, huh? How…interesting."

"Oh, stop it. You know we're just friends." Joking aside, his voice was agitated, as it normally was when I tried to encourage him to date.

"She's been after you for how many years now? I think it's time you gave her a break, Pops," I said, switching to speaker-phone and tossing my cell onto the bed.

"I was just helping her out."

"Oh, trust me, *I know*." I hopped around, tugging on my faded jeans and almost falling over.

"Knock it off, Zoe." His fatherly voice always emerged when I goaded him in the areas of love and affection.

"You're right. She wouldn't know what to do with herself. Probably not a good idea," I said bitterly. He continued scolding me, and I tuned him out as I pulled a green Earl's t-shirt over my head and gazed into the mirror.

Envisioning my usual gallery attire paired with the conservative hairstyle I still wore, I wasn't surprised I was habitually single. *I look like an uptight school marm*, I observed regretfully.

Pulling my dark hair from its bun, I watched it cascade past my shoulders and settle just above my waist, uncreased despite the twisted knot it had been in all day. I tried to imagine what I would look like with Dani's wild curls and rolled my eyes. Wondering was pointless. My hair was boring and straight, but at least it contrasted nicely with my light skin and blue-green eyes.

My dad had blue eyes, but not quite the same color as mine.

They were paler, and his hair was so much lighter. *I must look more like Mom...*

"Zo? You still there?"

"Yeah, I'm here."

"Anyway, it's nothing," my dad said.

"It's been over twenty years, Dad. Are you gonna be alone the rest of your life?"

His voice softened the way it always did when he was attempting to reassure me. "Don't worry about me, hon. I've got you kids." He cleared his throat. I couldn't help but scoff at the idea of having us "kids" as suitable companions. He and Jason were still trying to rebuild their relationship, and I was on the other side of the country.

"Speaking of you kids..." My dad's voice brightened. "Jason called me yesterday. He's doing well and likes Washington more than Colorado. Said he's moving up in rank real quick." He paused for a second, and when I didn't say anything, he continued, "Eleven years as a Green Beret and he's finally getting where he wants to be."

"I didn't know he'd left Colorado," I said quietly. I couldn't believe my brother hadn't told me he was being reassigned...or whatever.

"Oh...I'm sure he's been busy and doesn't have much time to talk. He probably assumed I'd fill you in." My dad prattled on, but I was more focused on the realization that Jason and I had drifted even further apart.

Sarah's sudden coughing fit in the living room pulled me from my thoughts. Upon hearing one gag after another, I promised myself I'd make time to get a flu shot soon.

1 SENT TEXT MESSAGE:

TO: D

Tried calling you, but got your voicemail. Is Callie doing better? Dad's sick too. Can you ask Grams to check on him? I'll call you after work.

December 5, 5:15 PM

Date: December 5, 2:24 AM
From: Zoe Cartwright
To: Danielle O'Connor
Subject: :(

D,

I tried calling you again, but you're probably asleep. I hope Callie's doing better. I'm sorry it took so long to get back to you. I've been super busy covering shifts at the gallery AND at Earl's. I hadn't realized how many people were sick until last night...one of my co-workers died. Can you believe it?! Maxine was so healthy and young...it's all so scary. It feels like I was just joking around with her yesterday, and now she's gone.

Speaking of gone, you should probably know Jason's apparently stationed over in Washington now. Of course, he didn't tell me himself; I had to find out from my dad. I bet Jason doesn't even know you're in Seattle.

Oh, and of course...HAPPY BELATED BIRTHDAY! Did you even get to celebrate? Sorry I couldn't be there, but we'll make up for it when we see each other for Christmas. I promise. I'm gonna get some sleep before I have to wake up and head to the gallery... again. Happy late 26th!

Hasta la vista,
Zo

After putting it off for a day and getting no sleep thanks to Jordan's fitful night of coughing and vomiting, I finally took the time to go to the doctor for a flu shot.

Walking into the clinic, I felt like I was entering a prison. The walls were white and sterile, and fluorescent lighting illuminated the bland space. Glass barriers separated the sick from the healthy. Patients stood in zigzagged lines throughout the waiting room like inmates, their medical paperwork in hand instead of eating trays and handcuffs.

Near the door, a security guard handed out surgical masks. Eyeing the mass of people, I groaned and grabbed a mask before getting in line. My attention was immediately captured by the two women in front of me; they were talking about the Center for Disease Control.

"Well last night the CDC *finally* addressed the issue nationally," said the red-haired woman. She clearly thought their involvement was overdue.

"It's about time." Her brunette friend sounded relieved.

"They aren't even sure if the vaccine works yet. The Virus is spreading so quickly…it's like they can't keep up with it."

"I heard they think it's airborne—not that it's surprising."

The redhead nodded. "I know. And they want us all to stay indoors. Real practical." Her face soured in disgust as she surveyed the crowded room.

I followed her eyes, taking in the number of people with pallid skin and runny noses. My skin crawled as I thought about the orgy of germs I'd walked into. The idea of being in a room swarming with the ill, breathing the same recycled air as the rest of the throng, made my stomach curdle. *Great.*

Just as I was debating the quickest exit out to the open air, a platinum blonde shuffled through the door. Her skin was unnaturally tanned, her face caked with makeup, and she had bubblegum-pink fingernails. Taking a second look, I noticed the heavy make-up was a desperate attempt to cover the cold sores around her mouth and the dark half-moons under her eyes.

Blondie stopped dead in her tracks. She took one look at the line drawn out before her and started complaining. "This is ridiculous," she spat and marched her way to the front of the line.

"Hey! You have to wait in line like the rest of us!" a waiting patient called out.

"Miss, you need to get to the back of the line. There's no cutting." My eyes zeroed in on the guard touching the girl's shoulder. *Shouldn't he be wearing gloves or something?*

His eyes widened as he listened to an announcement in his ear piece, then he started speaking again. "If you've had H1N1 before, form a line over here please!" He pointed to the far left wall. "If you're showing any flu symptoms, please stay in the original line."

I found myself smiling at his words. *Thank God*, I thought as I moved to the shorter line. *Maybe I'll get to work on time after all.*

"Oh, that's me," Blondie simpered and smiled at the guard. He eyed her closely as she hurried to my line. The exertion proved too strenuous, and she began wheezing almost immediately.

My phone vibrated, distracting me from the commotion. It was Sarah.

"Hello?"

"Where are you?" she whimpered.

"At the clinic attempting to get a flu shot. Why?" I waited for a moment. The phone was silent, and then I realized Sarah was crying. "What happened?" My heart was racing, and I tasted blood on my tongue as I chewed the inside of my cheek.

"Jordan's dead," she sobbed. "I didn't know if you knew."

I didn't know…I hadn't even realized she was so sick. I'd never been close with Jordan. We'd worked together at Earl's and had been roommates for two years, but we'd always been too different to be good friends.

"Did you hear me, Zoe? It's so loud there—"

"Yeah, I heard you." I stared blankly at the floor. "Where are you?"

"I'm at your house. I took Jordan's key. Is that okay?" she asked timidly and sneezed into the phone. The question was trivial, but it was sweet that she'd asked all the same.

"Zoe Cartwright?" called a nurse.

When I didn't respond to Sarah's question, she choked out, "Zoe? I'll leave if you want me to."

"No, no, it's fine. I'll be home soon."

I hung up and followed the nurse into the doctor's office. I had to wipe away a stray tear as I remembered the time one of the many douchebags I'd dated left me stranded at some dive bar at two o'clock in the morning. Jordan had come to my rescue, and we'd grabbed a late night coffee before heading home.

1 SENT TEXT MESSAGE:

TO: D
Jordan's dead…
Date: December 6, 8:45 PM

3

DANI

Zoe's roommate is dead. With a shuddering sigh, I leaned back against Cam. His arms wrapped reassuringly around me, interlocking just under my breasts. If only there was something sexual in his touch. If only we had the energy for such distractions. His body burned against mine, like he'd spent hours sitting too close to a fireplace. Staring out the wide living room window into the grim winter drizzle, I watched as our combined body heat slowly fogged up the glass.

"D, let's go to bed." Cam's too-hot breath brushed my neck as he spoke, worrying me.

"You go ahead," I said, meeting his reflected gaze. "I'll be in soon. I just need to do a few things first."

Exhaling heavily, he held me more tightly.

I patted one of his hands and murmured reassurances. "I'll be quick. I promise."

Cam kissed the top of my head, breathing deeply. "Mmm…D, how do you still smell so good?" He took another deep breath. "Even after two days. You smell…mmm…more like you. If I weren't so tired…" He trailed off with a husky chuckle. The distinct thread of desire wasn't enough to push either of us into action.

He released me and moved away. "Don't blame me if I'm already dead asleep by the time you crawl under the covers."

Dead asleep. Ha. Ha. I looked at him over my shoulder and gave my least-amused, most-withering expression. He laughed as he retreated to our bedroom.

I examined my reflection in the night-darkened glass and, studying my diminutive height and build, pale skin, and long crimson curls, gave myself the same death stare. *Nope, not scary at all.* My flushed cheeks and feverishly glowing eyes, however, were a little unsettling. I felt like crap and looked like it.

With a sigh, I plucked my phone from the window sill and called my grandma.

"Hello?" the elderly Irish woman greeted with her usual musical lilt.

I let out an unexpected sigh of relief. "Hi Grams, it's me."

"Oh, Dani-girl. I've been meaning to call you to see how the rest of your birthday went, but one thing after another kept popping up, especially with all the sick folks. So, how are you, girl? How's that boy of yours? Did you have a good time on your birthday?" Her raspy voice eased some of my anxiety, but there was just too much sickness and death to settle my nerves completely.

"We're both fine and…my birthday was…lovely," I lied. "How are you?"

"Oh…don't you be worrying about me. These old bones have weathered worse storms. Did you get the package I sent you? I overnighted it yesterday."

"Uhhh…I don't know. I'll check the mail room tomorrow. What's in it?"

"Medicines and herbs—things to keep you healthy." She paused for a moment. "Mind you, fetch that package first thing in the morning, you hear?" Her steely tone welcomed zero argument, making me cringe. *Things must be bad down there.*

"Yes, Grams," I replied. "Do you think you could check on Tom? Zo said he's sick. I think she's really worried."

"Of course."

"Thanks. Zo'll be relieved knowing you're looking out for him."

Grams breathed deeply before saying, "Now, I'm sorry, but I really must cut this short. Promise me you'll take extra special care over the next few days, you hear?"

"Yes, Grams, I promise. You'd better do the same, *you hear?*" I mimicked, receiving a gravelly laugh in response.

"I do love you, Dani-girl," she stated earnestly, nearly turning my sudden good humor to tears.

"I love you too, Grams."

After the goodbyes, a heavy weight settled on my shoulders, like all of my anxiety and fear had solidified and were threatening to crush me. I thought I might understand what Atlas felt like…just a little.

I quickly scrolled to Zoe's name and pressed call. While I listened to five rings without an answer, I stared at the black Celtic knot tattooed on my wrist, knowing Zoe had the same on her hip. Her recorded voice greeted me after the sixth ring. "You've reached Zoe Cartwright. Please leave me a message and I'll call you back…maybe."

Sighing, I waited for the beep and said, "Zo…I need to talk to you. Like now. Call me." I ended the call and quickly logged onto my computer, pondering the email I was about to write.

How much should I tell her? Should I tell her that Callie's going to die like Jordan? Or that Cam and I are definitely sick? Should I lie to her like I did with Grams? Maybe I'm wrong. Maybe Callie will make it. Maybe Cam and I aren't really sick. Maybe none of it's real.

A twisted version of myself added, *maybe telling her will make it real.*

Date: December 6, 9:30 PM
From: Danielle O'Connor
To: Zoe Cartwright
Subject: What the hell is going on?

Zo,

I just spoke to Grams. She said she'd head over to your Dad's soon. I'll let you know as soon as I hear anything. Don't worry about my birthday—it's really not important right now. There's too much other crap going on for it to matter.

I'm SO sorry about Jordan. I don't even know what to say... only that I'm sorry. Was it the flu? I just assumed...

Cam and I just got home from visiting Callie in the hospital again. One of our pseudo friends, Jamie Jenks (I think you met her), also died this morning. I said some stuff to her—bad stuff—at the pub the other night. Sometimes it's like I just lose control of my mouth. And now she's dead. At least Callie is only in a coma. The doctor isn't sure if she'll come out of it. I called her parents, and they're on their way. Her dad said the government is trying to blockade all of the state borders for quarantine or something. Not that it matters, everyone already has the damn virus.

And Jason is stationed near me? No, I don't care. Seriously. I'm just surprised I didn't already know we were living in the same state. Whatever. Is he coming home for the holidays? I sort of hope not. Every time I even mention your brother around Cam, he gets his sour, jealous face. I can't blame him. I sometimes wonder if it's just a natural male reaction to Jason. He's just too...I don't know... everything. Whatever.

But honestly, I feel pretty crappy, so I'm off to bed. Don't worry…I'm probably just feeling the aftereffects from the big night out and from spending too much time in hospital waiting rooms. I'll let you know about your dad as soon as I hear back from Grams.

Dani

Callie's dad cleared his throat for the dozenth time before saying, "It happened early this morning and, well, we know how close you two are…were…and we just thought you should know." The horrible, wrenching strain in his voice pulverized my heart just a little bit more.

The two-bedroom apartment suddenly felt vacuous without Callie's bright energy. She'd always filled the rooms with singing and excitement. Her touches were everywhere, from the spicy orange scent of her favorite candles to the photos of the Seattle skyline she'd taken over the years and had placed on the living room and hallway walls. It was *her* sun-faded couch that I currently sat on and *her* olive-green angora throw that was currently warming my legs. All of these things were *hers*, or had been, but I didn't want any of them—I just wanted to see Callie again.

"Thank you for telling me." I sounded hollow. *How can she be gone?* "You're welcome to stay in her room if you'd like…if it's not too hard…I mean…I…I'm so sorry…"

Mr. Roberts coughed. "Thank you, but no. That won't be needed. We're staying at the hospital, unfortunately. We're not feeling well." *Oh no…*

"Okay, Mr. Roberts, feel better. Just let me know when you'd like to come get her things."

He choked out, "Of course."

The call ended with mutual well-wishes. I tossed my phone on the cushion next to me and hoisted my aching body off the couch. I felt like I'd been trampled by a herd of wild horses. As I hobbled over to kneel beside Jack at Callie's bedroom door, I wondered how my joints weren't creaking audibly.

When we'd returned home from the hospital the previous night, I'd closed off Callie's room. Jack kept sitting at her door, trying to lean his furry body through the hollow, fake wood. Except it suddenly felt like the heavy stone entrance to an undisturbed tomb.

Steeling myself, I opened the door, finally letting Jack enter the room containing the last vestiges of one of his best friends. I hung back in the doorway, and Callie's scent washed over me—sustaining and suffocating. *She's never coming back.*

Some strange urge drove me further in, forcing me to stare around at all of her belongings—things she would never use again. *She's never coming back.*

Standing still, I focused on a blank spot on the wall in an attempt to stop the room from spinning. I was losing it. Emotional control was slipping through my fingers like desert sand. *Why isn't Callie here right now?* I collapsed on the floor on hands and knees, fighting back sudden nausea. *She's never coming back.*

Jack stopped his sniffling exploration and rushed to my side, licking the backs of my hands. I wrapped my arms around him, clinging to his warmth…his vitality.

"Hey Jack," I breathed after a few minutes. "I'm okay, Sweet Boy." It was a lie, but it didn't really matter. I unclenched my fingers from his scruff and stood on shaky legs. "Let's get outta here."

Jack leaned against my right leg as I rushed out of the room and eased the door closed. Click. *I can't go in there again.*

Date: December 7, 9:00 AM

From: Danielle O'Connor
To: Zoe Cartwright
Subject: Losing Hope

Zo,

Callie's gone. I just...this is so surreal. I can't think about it anymore. But I can't NOT think about it either. What happens now?

When I talked to Grams, she told me she hadn't been able to find your dad. But she promised to search around town. She also told me she wasn't feeling well. Sorry. Wish I had better news.

Yeah, so, it looks like Cam and I have the flu, too. Cam's been throwing up in the bathroom most of the day. We'd go to the hospital, but there isn't any point. The emergency broadcast said to stay away from all hospitals and doctors' offices. I honestly don't know what to do. Too much emotional crap. I need to go pass out now.

Dani

I woke with a jolt, immediately feeling like I'd taken a dozen shots of rum. I crawled over Cam's sweaty body and barely made it to the bathroom before vomiting. Jack settled on the linoleum beside me, his head resting on his front paws while he watched me.

The bloody, violent heaves seemed to last forever and left me a shaking, cavernous husk. My insides were raw, like I'd swallowed lighter fluid, lit a match on my tongue, and let the flames scorch my body from the inside out. Though I attempted to drink a few sips of water before rejoining Cam in bed, the most I could manage was to rinse out my mouth.

When I finally returned to our bedroom, Cam was awake and

curled up on his side facing the doorway. "D, I woke up, and you were gone. I'm so tired. Stay with me?" he rasped.

"Of course," I soothed as I unsteadily slid over his body and into bed. "Go to sleep, my Cam. I'll be right here. I love you," I whispered, snuggling behind him. But he was already in a deep sleep, and I was trying not to vomit, again.

Hours later, the world resumed its lurching motion and forced me to return to my worship of the toilet. My stomach muscles heaved and contracted endlessly, nearly making me pass out from exhaustion.

Using the wall for support, I eventually made it back to the bed. As I dragged my worthless limbs across Cam's body, I became aware of Jack's incessant whining and froze.

Beneath me, Cam wasn't breathing. *Cam? CAM! NO!!!*

"Wake up, Cam," I begged, rolling him onto his back and sitting astride his limp form. "Come on, baby. Wake up, please!" I touched his face tenderly—kissed his lips, his eyes, his cheeks. I could smell him, so I knew he must still be there.

"This isn't happening. You can't do this to me! You can't leave me! Please, Baby, just wake up! PLEASE!"

But every part of him was limp, lifeless.

"DAMMIT, CAM," I screeched, banging on his chest with my weak limbs. "You have to wake up! You can't leave me like this! You promised me…you said we'd grow old together! You PROMISED!" I gave one last scream before collapsing on top of him. All of my sounds turned to sobs.

"Please, Cam, wake up," I croaked.

He's dead.

While I lay on his body, my mind flashed through all of the things we should've shared. We'd planned to share. We'd wanted to share.

I saw Grams, acting as my father and mother, walking me down the aisle. Toward Cam.

I saw our children—a little boy and baby girl—both with dark red hair.

I saw family vacations with Zoe and her shadowed husband and child.

I saw our children grow up and marry and have babies of their own.

I saw myself grow old and wrinkly with Cam after a life filled with love and companionship, like he'd promised.

And I watched him die as an old man.

All of my future hopes faded away as, in my mind, his aged, lifeless body transformed into the Cam growing cold beneath me. Young Cam. *My Cam.*

He's dead.

Slowly, I became aware of Jack whining and tugging on my pajama pants. I felt like a sleepwalker as he led me off the bed and out of the room. I didn't look back at Cam's body as I shut the door.

He was gone…dead.

Jack nudged, pushed, and tugged me into the living room, where he stared at me with pleading black eyes, willing me to do something.

I collapsed onto the couch with arms and legs sprawled haphazardly. I gladly would've passed out, except something was jabbing into my thigh. As I moved the offending lump, I realized it was my laptop.

I needed to talk to someone. But I couldn't go back into the bedroom to get my phone. Cam's body was in there. *Definitely not. Can't.*

I also couldn't just stay on the couch and die, however appealing giving up sounded. Staring at the computer on my lap, I decided I could handle emailing Zoe, drinking a glass of water, falling asleep on the couch…and, depending on my luck, maybe dying.

I trudged into the kitchen with Jack close behind me. The water burned like whiskey at first but transformed into liquid heaven after the fifth sip. I had to remind myself not to drink too quickly.

I set my refilled glass on the counter before dragging a giant bag of dog food from the pantry. Too weak to pick it up, I tore it open and let the contents spill onto the linoleum. Jack wagged his whole body in excitement at the mountain of food.

"There you go, Sweet Boy—just in case I don't make it," I told him, scratching his neck. My throat clenched, but I was too exhausted for tears.

Jack wagged and whimpered, unable to decide on the appropriate response.

Sitting back on the couch, I stared at the wall and sipped water as I waited for my computer to boot up. I begged my mind to stay empty.

Date: December 9, 8:30 PM
From: Danielle O'Connor
To: Zoe Cartwright
Subject: (no subject)

Cam's gone.

He stopped breathing. He just stopped being. I mean, one minute I left him sleeping in our bedroom, and the next minute he was just...gone.

He's dead, and I loved him. He's lying in our bed—dead—and I still love him. But shouldn't I not want to face a world without him? Shouldn't I want to die? I don't know how I feel right now. I feel nothing.

I'm sorry...I haven't read any emails or answered any calls for days. I haven't even spoken with Grams. I've just been...passed out. I'm really tired, so I'm going to lie down on the couch and hope I wake up. I miss you. I miss you so much that it makes me feel...something. Love you, Zo.

Dani

4

ZOE

On any given night, the idea of getting into bed with my perfectly worn flannel sheets would've been welcomed. I would wrap myself in blankets and bake in the divine, sweltering heat. But I couldn't. Though I could feel the monstrous chill closing in around me, nipping at my ears, nose, and neck, the covers were suffocating. They were too warm, too tight. I couldn't get comfortable. Only moments after slipping under the covers, I threw them off.

I'm fine. Everything's fine, I lied to myself. *Just get a glass of water, and go back to sleep. It's just a fever...it'll be gone tomorrow.*

I struggled to get up. My head throbbed, my body ached, and my sweats felt like sandpaper against sunburn—abrasive and raw. I loved my pajamas, yet I couldn't tear them off fast enough. Naked, I welcomed the chill of the night on my unshielded body.

Suddenly, the cool air felt like shards of glass cutting me. *Shit! What the hell's wrong with me?* My body was too sensitive. My skin felt like heavy leather being pulled as I moved—stiff and unable to mold to the form of my body. *I have to do something.*

It was below freezing outside, and I was lying in bed, naked and sweating. I tried not to think about Jordan's death, but I couldn't help but wonder, *Am I dying?*

My mouth started watering, and I attempted to swallow the bile rising up my throat, but it wouldn't stay down. Lurching over the edge of the bed, I reached for the trash can as my stomach convulsed. I vomited until I felt hollow. Eventually, even the dry heaves ceased, and I wiped my sweaty brow with the back of my hand. Shaking, I stared at everything I'd puked up and waited for my breathing to steady.

I hobbled to the bathroom and locked the disgusting trash can inside. Retrieving a large mixing bowl from the kitchen, I settled on the couch and turned on the television. Although its luminescence burned my eyes, Bob Ross's calm, soothing voice talking about "happy little trees" and "whatever your heart desires" made me think about painting instead of pain. At least for a little while.

1 SENT TEXT MESSAGE:

TO: D

Why aren't you picking up your phone? Are you OK? Stupid question, I know. I can't believe what happened to Cam. I'm so sorry D. Please just call me.

December 10, 11:45 AM

Dani's email riddled me with fear. Every hair on my body stood on end as a sense of despair took root deep inside me. The panic and alarm I'd hidden away in the crevasses of my mind finally escaped their restraints. I couldn't catch my breath as hysteria wrapped itself around my throat like a boa constrictor. *She's not answering. She can't be dead! What about Jason? Dad and Grams?*

I could hear Sarah retching in the bathroom. Of course I'd get sick too. *Am I better? I'm feeling better, but…*

Remembering that my dad was alone and that Dani was worse off than I was, I used my rising conviction to levy my fear.

I tossed my phone away in haste, completely forgetting that my ex, Dave, had texted me to make sure I was okay. I'd also forgotten that I had missed his call and that I was scheduled to work a gallery opening.

Frantically, I shuffled through my room, snatching anything and everything lying around. My body still ached, but I ignored it. I put no thought into what I grabbed, filling my bag on autopilot.

I have to stay in control, I told myself as I took a deep breath. *Dad needs me. Dani needs me.*

I tried to change my flight home for Christmas, but I couldn't get through to the airline. I would've settled for driving across the country, but I didn't have a car. *Dammit!* Then I remembered…the bus station. I just needed to get there and buy a ticket. Then I could get to them. *Hopefully it'll be soon enough…*

Date: December 10, 11:35 PM
From: Zoe Cartwright
To: Danielle O'Connor
Subject: Freaking Out

Where are you, D? Why haven't you contacted me? You'd better be alive! I'm trying to hold it together, but I can't do that if you're MIA.

I went to the bus station to buy a ticket home. It's shut down. To make it worse, the airline's phones have been busy since yesterday. Things are pretty bad here. Everything's closed, including Earl's and the gallery. I haven't been able to get a hold of you or anyone else. The only people I've seen around Salem aren't particularly in the best frame of mind—most are skittish, talking to themselves or smelling like they haven't showered in a week. I even saw a blonde chick from the clinic...she was filthy and wandering aimlessly around downtown like she didn't know where she was. It's really bad.

I'm beginning to feel trapped here in the middle of this frozen, crazed wasteland. Everything's falling apart, and there's nothing I can do about it.

I've called you at least 7 times. I'm so worried about you, Dani. Please call or write when you can.

I love you,
Zoe

Folded into the overstuffed chair in my living room, I stared absentmindedly out the picture window, mesmerized by the white flurries floating to the ground. My phone slid from my grasp, and my eyes followed it as it landed among the magazines and laundry strewn on the carpet. *Jordan was always the tidy one.*

I shivered. Wearing only boxers and one of my dad's old t-shirts, I felt like my toes were ice cubes. I held a mug of cold tea and stroked the old, worn fabric of my shirt, wishing it still smelled like my dad.

It had been a week since I'd heard from him, and Jason hadn't called me back either. Dani's last email had crumpled any hope I'd had left that things would get better. *I'm losing everyone.*

"You're cold." Sarah's voice was timid and quiet behind me.

"I'm always cold," I muttered. I often berated myself for making the stupid decision to move to the East Coast, forcing myself to endure the freezing winters. *And now I'm far away from everyone I care about...*

Sarah cleared her throat.

Momentarily removing myself from oblivion, I looked at her. She held out a burgundy fleece blanket, and I wondered how pathetic I must appear. Too exhausted to be stubborn, I accepted her offering and managed a weak smile. "Thanks, Sarah." I set the blanket haphazardly on my lap, refocusing my gaze on the darkened world outside.

Before I could slip back into the empty, paralyzing void, I felt Sarah's delicate hands on my lap, repositioning the blanket to cover me. The warmth of the thick fleece soothed me, and my eyes began to sting as the salty tears I'd been fighting finally emerged. Lacking the energy to hold them in, I let them fall. My chin trembled, and my chest was burdened with swells of loneliness as my doubts began to consume me.

Wiping my cheeks, I looked at Sarah again. Her curls were wild and unbrushed, and her clothes were dirty. She had dark circles under her eyes, and her lips were chapped—a pet peeve that I would've done something about in another life. I'd forgotten she was sick too. *And she's taking care of me.*

"You don't have to do that." My voice was unintentionally distant and cold, but I lacked the will to do anything about it.

Sarah stood abruptly. Her features were pinched with worry, and her eyes were red and swollen. Nostrils flaring, she tried to compose herself before speaking. "Sorry, I didn't mean to...bother you."

She turned to leave, and hot guilt coursed through me. *She's just being nice. Don't be a bitch*, I thought. I shook myself, trying to dispel the mental numbness, and grabbed Sarah's hand gently.

She turned. "Thank you for letting me stay here, Zoe." Her words were filled with emotion and gratitude. "It means so much to me. I don't want to be alone." Her cracked voice broke my heart. "I know you don't want me here, but I—"

Tears were streaming down her face faster than she could wipe them away. She sat down on the couch and began sobbing into her hands, her body shaking violently.

Seeing Sarah's anguish was too much. I wanted to scream. Rising from my chair, I went to sit beside her. I pulled her into my arms and wrapped the blanket around us. She coughed, reminding me she was infected, but it didn't really matter anymore.

"I'm glad you're here," I whispered to her and knew it was true. *At least I'm not utterly alone.*

After drifting in and out of sleep for what seemed like hours, Sarah and I were startled awake by the shrill ring of my cell phone. I jumped up and rushed to retrieve it from the floor even though my joints were stiff from being curled up on the couch. *Please don't hang up!*

Fumbling with the phone, I was finally able to answer it with shaky fingers. "Dad?" I cried in a trembling voice.

"Zoe, I can't talk long—"

"Dammit Jason, where the hell've you been?!" I shrieked. "Have you heard from Dad? I can't get ahold of him and—"

"Listen to me, Zoe. You need to get to Colorado. I need you to head to Peterson Air Force Base near Colorado Springs; it's safe there," he said between uneven breaths.

"How am I supposed to get to Colorado? I don't have a car; the bus station's closed—"

"Zoe, focus! Find a way to get there and do it as soon as you can." His words were rushed and clipped.

Jason's scared.

"Answer me, Zoe!" he snapped.

"Yes, I'll get there. I promise. I'll find a way." The garbled sound of movement on the other end told me I had only a second before Jason ended our conversation. "Wait! What about Dad and Dani?" It was silent. "Jason? Are you there?"

"Dani's alive?" His voice was grave.

"I don't know. Cam's dead, and she was really sick the last time I—"

"Where is she?" he asked.

"She's at her apartment in Seattle, but—"

"I'm headed there now. I'll check on her and meet you at Peterson. Do you understand?"

"Yeah. I'll be there as soon as I can." My mind was whirling with questions. "Don't you need her addr—"

"Text it to me. I'll be in touch. Just pack what you need and go."

"Jason, I'm—"

But there was a click and the line went dead. My brother was gone.

Adrenaline pumped through my veins, bringing me out of my stupor.

Still sitting, Sarah stared up at me curiously. "What's going on? Who's Jason?"

"My brother," I said distractedly. *Pack and go,* was all I could think.

I looked around in a frenzy, though it didn't take long—there weren't many places to look in the tiny, two-bedroom home. *Think, Zoe. What do we need?*

"Zoe?" Sarah prompted.

Running to my room, I tried to explain, "Um, he said there's a safe place for us to go, but it's in Colorado. We've gotta figure out a way to get there."

"But how?" Sarah was standing in my doorway, wide-eyed and expecting an explanation.

"I don't know. We could steal a car." I dumped the contents of my already packed bag onto the bed.

Sarah wrapped the blanket more tightly around her. "Do you know how to do that?"

"I have no idea, but I'll figure something out. Who knows, maybe we'll find one with keys."

Socks, iPod, phone charger, underwear, towel...I searched through my room, hoping I wouldn't forget anything important. In my haste, I didn't think about the house or what I was leaving behind. All I could think about was getting to Jason in Colorado.

Before Sarah could question me any further, someone started pounding on the front door. Startled, we looked at each other. I brought my index finger to my lips and cautioned Sarah to stay quiet before I tiptoed to the living room. Upon hearing a dog whining on the front porch, I moved slowly toward the peephole and peered out.

"What the—"

1 SENT TEXT MESSAGE:

To: D
Jason called. He's coming for you. Hang on, D!
December 11, 2:30 AM

5

DANI

I *can't breathe*, I thought frantically. I was being constricted, pressed into something warm and hard and sort of lumpy. And I wasn't lying down anymore. And I thought I might die if I didn't get a drink of water.

"Go make yourselves busy," a woman ordered. I didn't recognize her voice. "Now!"

The footsteps I heard sounded like a somber stampede. The front door opened, and after several long seconds, shut quietly.

I still couldn't breathe. At my pathetic whimper, the squeezing instantly relented. Suddenly, I was lying back down on the cushy couch, staring up into a man's angular, tear-streaked face. With its chiseled features and eyes like brilliant blue topaz, he could have been an ancient, grief-stricken warrior.

Jason.

I'm dead, I admitted. *Jason never cries. He probably doesn't know how to cry.*

His eyes widened, showing more whites than usual, before he scooped me back up and crushed me against his camouflage parka. I sat limply in his arms as he held me like I was a little girl freshly awake from a nightmare.

"Jason," I grunted. "I...can't...breathe."

"Sorry." He loosened his hold just enough to keep me from suffocating and murmured, "I thought...Dani...You didn't look alive..."

With the newfound ability to breathe, I imagined sitting there forever. I was nestled safely in Jason's arms and listening to him whisper softly while I remembered what it was like to be alive. *I'm not dead.*

Briefly, I tried to recall how I'd come to be on the couch, feeling like a decrepit corpse. The memories seemed trapped, guarded by a fragile sheet of ice. I prodded the mental block gently and recoiled at the turmoil that immediately burst to life in my chest. Thankfully, the pain faded as I shoved the memories back under the thin barrier.

After a few minutes, Jason regained his composure. He picked me up and carried me into the bathroom with my dog trailing close behind.

"Thanks. I can take it from here," a blonde woman told him briskly, and I was transferred to her deceptively strong arms. "I'm Chris." She smiled, reassuring me like a mother to a sick child, as she set me carefully on the tile floor. "I'm going to help you wash up," she explained, already peeling off my soiled pajamas. "You'll feel like a new woman when I'm done with you."

The ruined clothes were promptly tossed into the wastebasket beside the toilet, and with equal efficiency, I was deposited into the steaming bathwater. Only after I was clean did I acknowledge the acrid stench coming from the wadded-up pajamas in the little garbage can. *My pajamas. Oh...that's disgusting...*

Embarrassment washed over me. Jason had held me in those foul clothes. Not only had he smelled everything my body had expelled during the two days I'd spent passed out on the couch, but he probably had it all over him.

Sometimes, the smallest, least important thing could light the fuse leading to the mounds of emotional dynamite piled in my head. With mortification as the spark, waves of despair and horror exploded in my chest. *Cam! He's dead...*

Sitting in the bath, I began to cry. Chris let me work through it, holding my hand as I poured out gallons of grief. She seemed to be pulling the gut-wrenching feelings out of me, cleansing my heart and mind just as she was cleansing my body. It felt like I cried for an eternity.

Eventually, sporting fresh pajamas and damp hair, I was again settled in the living room, but this time on an unfamiliar couch.

"This isn't my couch," I said to no one in particular. I watched Jack as he stared forlornly at the clean kitchen floor. Someone had swept up the mountain of kibble and locked it away.

"Yes, well, yours was...unsuitable. We swapped it with one from an apartment down the hall. It's not like they'll be needing it anymore," Chris explained, setting a glass of orange juice and a generous plate of breakfasty goodness on the coffee table in front of me.

I stared at the food but didn't touch it, even though my stomach grumbled in need. Cam usually made me breakfast. "What d'you mean? Why won't they need it?"

Chris halted her efforts to arrange a fuzzy blanket around my legs and looked at me with sharp, sky-blue eyes. Her expression melted into sympathy before she spoke. "Because they're dead, hon. Most people are. I thought you knew."

"I...," I tried to speak, but my throat caught after the first sound. I shook my head.

Satisfied that I was covered and warm, Chris moved to the other side of the coffee table to sit in a large recliner—another item from the furniture shopping spree in my neighbor's apartment.

"It was that damn Virus...we all had it...weeks ago," Chris said, gesturing around the room even though it was empty of anyone but us. "Several days back, everyone in the world seemed to be infected. Now pretty much everyone's dead. The rest are like you and me—Survivors. But as far as we can tell, we're in the extreme minority."

"I don't understand," I said, confusion creasing my brow. "This is impossible."

"Not impossible. Just improbable...and really, really awful." She pointed to the plate of eggs and potatoes on the coffee table. "Eat up, hon. You've got to get your strength back before we leave."

Obediently, I moved the plate to my lap and asked, "Who's 'we,' and where are 'we' going?" I took a tentative bite of scrambled eggs and wondered if it was the best thing I'd ever eaten. Suddenly terrified of being left behind, I added, "Am I part of 'we'? And what about Cam?"

Chris opened her mouth to answer just as Jason stepped out from Callie's room and into the hallway leading to the living room. He gestured to the bedroom, "Why don't you get some rest in there, Johnson? It's been a long day." It wasn't a question.

Chris hesitated, shooting an anxious glance in my direction.

"Don't worry about Dani," he reassured her, "I'll take care of her." A slight smile accompanied the warmth in his voice.

Chris stood and stalked across the living room, pausing when she reached the beautiful, imposing man. She was surprisingly menacing for such a motherly woman.

I busied myself with eating but still paid close attention.

"Don't try any of your usual shit with her," Chris hissed. "She's been through hell. I know you're incapable of resisting a pretty girl, especially a vulnerable one, but I swear..."

"What? You think you can take me?" he asked frostily.

She glared at him for a long moment before stomping to the bedroom and slamming the door.

Quietly, I finished the food. I attacked the glass of orange juice next, alternating between sipping through the neon green straw and staring at the floating flecks of pulp. Jason took Chris's seat, and I focused twice as hard on the juice.

"Dani?" His voice was thick with concern.

With the straw still between my lips, I responded, "Hmmm?" My heart froze when I glanced up, and the straw fell from my mouth.

Every inch of Jason exuded wary remorse like he'd done something horrible and was afraid to tell me. Or was about to.

"You're not taking me with you, are you? You're just gonna leave me here," I accused with surprising steel.

"What? Don't be ridiculous. Of course I'm taking you with me."

I released a relieved breath. "Oh…well I just thought…I guess I don't really know what I thought…" *He's taking me with him! I won't be left alone!* "Thanks, Jason."

"Yeah, of course," he said. "But the thing is, you need to know…" He hesitated, searching my eyes across the three-foot distance between us. "You need to get some rest. You look exhausted."

I was confused, knowing he'd been about to say something entirely different. Regardless, I said, "I need to talk to Zoe."

"The phones went down a little bit ago."

"I'll email her," I countered.

"After you've rested." He sounded like he was used to being obeyed.

"I'll do it now."

"No. Later."

Impatiently, I set my empty glass on the table and tossed my arms up in exasperation. "Are you serious? Why are you being such a…"

His eyes narrowed. "Such a…what?"

"Nothing." I hastily changed tactics. "Please, Jason. I'll sleep so much better if I can just let her know that I'm alive."

"She knows you're alive. I told her…before the phones crapped out."

Closing my eyes, I took a deep, calming breath. "I *am*

exhausted. But…I'll rest better if *I* tell her I'm okay. I can't explain it…I just need to do this. It'll only take a few minutes, I promise, and then I'll behave like a nice, cooperative little patient."

"Fine," he said and broke our magnetic stare. "You have ten minutes. Then you're resting, even if I have to hold you down."

I smiled at him, reveling in my victory. I wasn't going to let Jason order me around like one of his soldiers.

"Thanks, Jason. And, um, thanks for coming here. I probably wouldn't have made it if…you know." Examining his appearance, I noted the clean fatigues and missing coat. Hesitantly, I added, "And I'm sorry about getting you all dirty earlier." I looked away, embarrassment coloring everything above my shoulders.

Jason reached across the table and placed his hand under my chin, turning my face toward him. He held my eyes and murmured, "It doesn't matter."

Date: December 11, 9:30 PM
From: Danielle O'Connor
To: Zoe Cartwright
Subject: To My Savior

I'm alive. Cam isn't. Jason's here. You probably saved my life by sending him to me. I'm feeling better, but I need to rest for about a year. I'll fill you in later. I can't even express how much of a difference it makes to have your brother here. Thanks, Zo.

Date: December 13, 6:00AM
From: Danielle O'Connor
To: Zoe Cartwright
Subject: Your brother's really bossy

Zo,

I'm still alive. Sorry it's taken me a few days to write. I slept for the past day and a half, literally. I just woke up an hour ago and had to barter with Jason over access to my computer. My computer!

Anyway, your brother brought 12 other people with him from his base, but I've only met Chris so far. I guess the base was on lockdown when they left, so they had to grab some vehicles and go. They managed to take two Humvees.

Jason said we're leaving tomorrow morning. We'll be heading down the coast to Bodega Bay to check on your dad and Grams (and some other people). But, because we'll be stopping along the way to check on those other people, it'll take us a little while to get to BB. I'm not sure what the trip will be like. Is there gas? Do we use money? How many people are dead? How many are alive? Is it dangerous? I haven't had a chance to ask Jason or Chris any of this; either I've been asleep or they've been busy.

After BB, we're heading toward that base in Colorado. There are a few more stops we have to make along the way, so I don't know how long it'll take to get there either. But, I know I will see you there, Zo. I'll send you a message with more details before we leave, assuming the internet still works. Our phones are useless, both landlines and cells, so don't even bother trying to reach us that way. We can't even Skype...the servers must be down or something.

So, I'm not doing so hot with the Cam thing. The dreams...crap, Zo. Every time I fall asleep, Cam is there. And he's always some grotesque version of dead. I'm getting to the point where I don't even want to close my eyes. I miss you like crazy and wish I could sob in your arms every time I wake from the nightmares. Soon.

Be safe,
Dani

6

ZOE

We spoke in hushed tones as we packed food for our trip. Sarah was asleep in the adjacent room, and we didn't want to wake her. Dave's arrival had brought a sense of relief to the house. I hadn't seen him for nearly six months—since our break up—but his presence was unexpectedly reassuring.

From my conversation with Jason a couple days earlier, I knew we needed to head west if I ever wanted to see my brother or Dani again. Knowing they were still alive was enough to re-establish the hope I'd felt so despondent without. Dave was with me, and we had a plan. Everything seemed to be working out—except Sarah was still sick, and I tried not to think about what would happen if she got any worse.

Searching through the cupboards, I thought about the strangeness of it all. *It's like I can feel her pain and fear all of a sudden.*

"Zoe?" I started and looked at Dave. My eyes refocused as I took in Dave's concerned expression; it was easy enough to read with his loose curls hiding beneath his backward cap. His hand brushed my shoulder gently, and I instantly felt a rush of unease.

"Did you hear me?" he asked.

My mind was a muddled mix of emotions—I didn't understand

what I was suddenly feeling or why. Dave's eyes were tired and shadowed, and I felt overwhelmed under his touch.

He smiled and brushed a strand of hair from my face. "I asked if you wanted me to pack the stash of chocolate I found in the pantry. I'm assuming so, unless you're no longer a chocolate fiend and I didn't get the memo." He flashed a cocky, lopsided grin.

"Oh," I breathed raggedly, "yeah, of course. Thanks." The moment he removed his hand from my skin, I felt lighter.

Bewildered, I exhaled and continued packing. I focused on the good news—Dani was alive and with Jason, and Dave was driving Sarah and me to the base in Colorado. I'd see my best friend and brother in a few days…and hopefully my dad, too.

"Zoe?" I jumped when Dave's hand touched the small of my back. *Why is he touching me so much?* I wanted to scream. His fingers lingered on the thin cotton of my t-shirt, and a sudden sense of apprehension nagged the back of my mind. Uncertainty washed over me, though I had no idea where it had come from.

"Did you hear anything I said?"

I stared at him, unsure of the feelings fluttering around inside me.

"Zoe?" Dave's brow was furrowed; his confident air dissipating.

"S-sorry," I stammered, glancing down at my shaking hands. *Am I getting sick again?*

Dave squeezed my shoulder tightly. "What's wrong?" Fear and anxiety pulsed through me, dizzying and disorienting.

Sammy, Dave's chocolate Lab, licked my hand, the contact shaking me from my confusion. I petted him absentmindedly as I tried to wade through the intense feelings.

No. I refuse to be sick. "I'm just tired. What were you saying?"

"Are you sure you're feeling okay?"

"I'm fine. Like I said, just tired." Annoyed at his persistence, I stepped away and eyed him warily. "How about you? Are *you* feeling okay?"

He rubbed his face and sighed in exhaustion. "Yeah, I'm feeling better. I was pretty sick there for a while."

I watched his lethargic movements as he pulled cans of chili from the cupboard. "You should get some rest, Dave. I can finish packing up."

He looked over at me and smirked. "Are you sure?"

"Only if you don't snore," I amended playfully.

Dave wandered over to the couch, and I wondered if I'd ever seen him without Sammy, who was prancing after him. He heaved his body down and took a deep breath. "This feels so good," he sighed.

Laughing, I took the blanket from the back of the couch and spread it over him. Although his forwardness often rubbed me the wrong way, I *had* missed his quirky charm. My hand grazed his arm, and I felt an unexpected wave of desire swell inside me. I froze.

Dave caught my hand and peered up through his dark, blinking lashes. "Want to join me? I'll make room…" His husky voice and coaxing gaze warned me of his intentions.

Smiling, I pulled my hand out of his grasp and finished tucking the blanket around him.

"Maybe in a bit." *Definitely not a good idea.*

Date: December 13, 11:25 AM
From: Zoe Cartwright
To: Danielle O'Connor
Subject: Headed for Colorado

Hey D,

I'm so glad you're alive and that Jason's with you. Thank God you're okay.

Dave's here—he showed up a few days ago with his dog, Sammy. I feel better having him here because things are starting to get crazy around Salem...like really scary. We've heard two gunshots in the last 24 hours, and last night we watched a group of looters running through the street and lighting things on fire. Obviously there are survivors, but most of them are just crazy. Other than Dave's Louisville Slugger and my Maglite, we have no weapons, so I'm ready to get the hell out of here. I'm wishing Jason would've taught me a thing or two so I'd have some idea how to defend myself, but when all else fails, go for the groin, right? Let's hope no one gets close enough to have to worry about that.

Dave heard a radio broadcast about a colony in Colorado. They have food and supplies and are encouraging survivors to head that way. I wonder if it's the same place we're going? Anyway, Peterson is a few days' worth of driving away, so we'll have to stop once or twice to rest along the way, but we'll be there as soon as we can.

Will you make sure Jason keeps me posted on Dad when you get home? I want to know what you find, no matter how bad it is. Miss you!

Hasta la vista,
Zoe

7

DANI

I gripped the doorknob and, not knowing what to expect inside the bedroom, felt my palm slicken with sweat. Questions circled in my mind like crazed vultures. *Will it smell like Cam? Will it smell like death? Will it smell like rotting meat? Has he been decomposing over the past five days, melting into our bed? What will he look like?*

Turning my wrist, I let the door creak open. I instantly focused on the bed—the empty bed. I stood in the doorway for a few minutes, staring dumbly as my mind reconciled the placid, blank scene with the horrors I'd imagined. *Where is he?*

"Get it together, Dani," I mumbled. I was in the damn room for two reasons: to pack and to say goodbye. Cam might not have been there to do the latter, but I could still gather some things together.

I forced myself into motion, gliding around the room to collect certain indispensable belongings: clothes, cell phone, journal, small photo album. I tossed the priceless items on the exposed mattress, and when I added Zoe's recent birthday present —a beautifully sketched depiction of a man in a chef's coat kissing the hand of a seated, curly-haired woman—I nearly collapsed into tears. She had perfectly captured the first time Cam and I had met. The only thing preventing a torrential emotional flood was the violent anger simmering in my blood. *Where the hell is Cam?*

Obviously Jason had moved Cam's body, and he'd done it without telling me...without letting me say goodbye. Fury boiled within me as I snatched a duffel bag out of the closet. *Dammit, Jason!* I shoved everything into the bag, clothes and mementos alike, and hastily zipped it shut. *You had no right!*

With a grunt, I dragged the deformed bag into the hallway, slamming the bedroom door behind me. Seething, I stalked around the rest of the two-bedroom apartment in search of Jason. There weren't many places to look. I'd barely seen him since the day he arrived, so I wasn't surprised to find him absent.

Jack whined and scratched at the front door, capturing my attention. *Where's Jason? Next door?*

In a flash, I passed through the doorway, sprinted down the hall, and burst into the nearest neighboring apartment. Four men, each decked in tan and gray-green camouflage fatigues, rose from their seats at an oblong table and pointed guns in my direction.

I barely noticed and hardly cared. "Jason," I hissed. "Where's Jason?" Jack augmented the question with a menacing growl.

All but one gun was lowered; the remaining aimed at Jack by a youthful, brown-haired man. "Should've killed the mangy fuck when he went after Cece," he proclaimed, clicking the safety back in place.

The only one of the men I'd previously met, Ky, nodded toward the bedrooms down the hallway, and one of the others bellowed, "JASON!"

Seconds later, the farthest bedroom door banged open, expelling an irritated, shirtless Jason. He pulled a gray t-shirt over his head, and sounding completely annoyed, said, "I thought I told you dumbshits to leave us...ah...alone." His voice softened when he noticed me. "Dani? What's wrong?"

Behind him, a small, voluptuous woman emerged from the

same doorway. A smirk danced across her exotic face as she sauntered toward me, her dark, disheveled hair swaying with each step.

"You must be Dani. I'm Cecilia, but everyone calls me Cece." Her warm tone competed with the icy chill in her eyes. "Jason and I were just—"

"A pleasure," I interrupted and brushed past her. Had I been a cat, my tail would've been lashing.

As I neared Jason, he stiffly stood in place, his expression blank.

Stopping within arm's reach, I asked—my words thick with venom—"Where's Cam?"

Jason answered without hesitation. "We moved his body out. While you were getting cleaned up." He watched me cautiously, like I was an injured animal. But I wasn't hurt; I was pissed.

My mind snapped back to our conversation three days earlier, to my confusion at his abrupt change of subject. *This is what he was going to tell me—that he'd disposed of Cam's body without my permission...*

"You should've asked. You should've told me," I said through gritted teeth and swung my arm without thinking.

Jason's eyes closed as my hand smacked against his clenched jaw. When they reopened, his eyes glowed with fierce determination. "You shouldn't have to remember him like that. If we'd left him in there for three more days..."

He's right, dammit! I thought, recalling the horrifying images I'd imagined. But I was still furious. *He should've asked!* I tried to ignore the small, bitter part of me that knew my rage should've been directed inward. *I should have been with Cam when he died. He asked me to stay with him.*

The world around us seemed to fade out of existence as Jason and I stared at each other. His aquamarine eyes pulled me in, their fierce intensity refusing to release me. That he had the audacity to stand before me with those stunning eyes—set in that achingly handsome face—only fueled my anger. My pulse sped, breath coming faster, and I knew we were building to something unforgivable.

I breathed in and opened my mouth. "You—"

"Dani?" Chris asked, penetrating the haze of my fury. Her arm wrapped protectively around my narrow shoulders. "Let's get you some breakfast before we leave, hmm?" She turned me away from Jason, breaking our eye contact along with the building tension, and guided me back toward the front door.

With each step, my anger dissipated and reason returned. As Chris walked me through the apartment's entrance, I looked back at Jason, my chin trembling and eyes pleading for forgiveness.

He closed his eyes and bowed his head.

The door swung shut.

Date: December 14, 8:30 AM
From: Danielle O'Connor
To: Zoe Cartwright
Subject: The Plan

Zo,

I'm just about to leave my apartment, possibly forever. I wonder if leaving this place will help heal the gaping wound in my heart. Or will I forget bits and pieces of Cam, little by little, until I only have the barest memory? I just hope something changes. This feeling is unbearable.

We're not actually setting out on our grand (note the sarcasm) journey into the changed (shitty) world yet. We still have to gather a ton of supplies. The group has cleaned out a bunch of the packaged and canned foods from the apartments in my building, but there are other things we'll need.

There's another big problem—all of the gas stations are out of fuel. One team spent the entire day yesterday in a "borrowed" car checking gas stations all over Seattle. They were all dry. It's like people hung on long enough to use up all the fuel before they keeled over. Dicks. We have some fuel cans which we're filling with gas siphoned from nearby cars, but we can only carry so much. Is the fuel situation the same over there?

In a moment of sheer genius I convinced Jason it would be worth it to stock up on camping supplies. I mean, if we get stranded in the middle of nowhere, that stuff will be super useful. So, we're spending the morning at that huge REI in downtown Seattle—the one you dragged me to last summer. That's where we're going when we leave in...crap...five minutes.

I'm so freaking glad that Dave is with you and that you're leaving Salem; I don't like the sound of all the crazy people in your neighborhood. Maybe you guys should get some guns or something? Maybe not...might be more dangerous with them? Dunno...your call.

Please, please, please update me as often as you can. I'll do the same. Okay, I have to go...your brother is staring at me. Oh, and he says...hey.

Ciao,
Dani

Unsurprisingly, REI's doors had been locked. Surprisingly, none of the glass panes had been broken. I figured Survivors were either moaning in their beds or still in the "let's steal from grocery stores and shopping malls" stage of the Apocalypse. Recreational equipment must not have registered as a high priority. *People are idiots,* I thought caustically, but then I smiled. *One woman's forsaken water filter is another's salvation!*

"Everyone needs to pair up," Jason directed from the slightly raised platform in the entryway. When nobody moved he barked, "Now!"

Chris sidled up to me, and I watched Cece prowl across the polished cement. Her eyes were locked on Jason. He didn't notice her approach, focused as he was on making sure everyone found a partner. When I felt his attention linger on me, I ignored him, instead studying the small, tanned beauty.

Reaching Jason, Cece beckoned, and he leaned down to let her whisper in his ear. His lips parted at her words, and his eyes narrowed with what looked like anticipation. I figured she must have suggested something particularly scandalous.

When his eyes slid to mine, catching me staring, I hastily scanned the rest of the store, pretending to assess its offerings. From the heat in my cheeks, I knew I had blushed bright red.

After confirming that everyone had paired off, Jason continued, "Alright, here's the plan. Each of you needs to collect everything you'd need if you were on your own. Except for Dani, you've all had survival training—if you don't know what you need, you're a fucking idiot. Reconvene here in one hour, and do *not* leave your partner alone." As an afterthought he added, "Keep your weapons ready. We don't know who else might be here."

As he finished, my mind replayed his whispered exchange with the skank. *What did she say to him? Let's do it in a fitting room? Or the bathroom? Or maybe behind the checkout counter? Jason obviously hasn't changed,* I thought bitterly.

The disgusting possibilities swirled through my head as Chris and I found large hiking packs, sleeping bags, and tents. The thoughts receded as we filled our new packs with miniscule stoves and gas cans, water filters, matches, lighters, handheld GPS equipment, knives, and whatever else Chris deemed necessary for survival. When we couldn't squeeze anything else into the bags' bulging pockets, we dropped them off in the entryway.

Grabbing a couple of large, waterproof sacks, we headed to the clothing and shoe section. *Now this is more like it!*

We'd stuffed both huge bags to the brim and were heading back to the entrance when a nearby rack of key chains fell over.

Laughing, Chris teased, "Wow…walk much?" We watched, waiting for one of our companions to pop up looking amused or embarrassed. But nothing happened.

Chris drew her handgun from her thigh holster and slipped me a black-bladed combat knife.

I raised my eyebrows in a silent question. *What the hell am I supposed to do with this?*

Ignoring my expression, Chris held her index finger up to her lips and motioned for me to follow. A rustle and jingle led us to the man tangled in the fallen merchandise. He was small and stinky, wearing a forest-green t-shirt with the store's logo.

"Don't hurt me. I'm not here. Don't hurt me. I'm not here," he repeated over and over. I half expected him to start scuttling around, hissing about his *Precious*.

"Are you okay?" I asked, slipping in front of Chris to crouch down near the terrified man. I was careful to keep the wicked-looking knife hidden behind my back, worried it would scare him further. He was so pathetic, yanking every compassionate string in my body.

He stopped talking.

Encouraged, I reassured him, "We won't hurt you." But when I reached out to help untangle his ankle, he flinched.

He scooted himself and the clanking rack back, and resumed his earlier mantra. "Don't hurt me. I'm not here. Don't hurt me. I'm not here…"

Chris hoisted me up by my arm and pulled me away from the clearly unstable man. "We can't do anything for him," she told me gently.

"But—"

"No, hon, I'm sorry. Something's broken in him that can't be fixed."

Ashamed at how quickly I agreed, I followed her back to the store's entrance, dragging my sack of clothes and shoes behind me.

Date: December 14, 9:00 PM
From: Danielle O'Connor
To: Zoe Cartwright
Subject: Longview, WA

Zo,

So, I can't remember if I told you this already, but we're stopping several places along the way to BB. I don't know why we can't just drop people off and continue on home. This is ridiculous. I need to get down there to check on Grams and your dad. Oh, don't worry; I've argued plenty with Jason about this. I didn't win.

For everyone in the group, we're devoting one full day to searching their chosen stop for survivors. Jason told me this was non-negotiable. He can be such an ass.

Anyway, we're currently in Longview, WA, which is only a few hours south of Seattle. We've traveled really far, huh? Yeah, I totally just rolled my eyes. We're here for Joey, BTW. He's one of those people who would make a perfect thief or assassin because he is just so unremarkable. Anyway, he's hoping to find I-don't-know-who here. We're spending all of tomorrow searching.

Our chosen Longview "home" is a gigantic riverfront house that looks more suited to a stormy ocean bluff in New England than a West Coast river. Internet and power are a few of its prized offerings. Also, the house is large enough that only a few people (there are 14 of us) have to share rooms, like me and Chris. The master bedroom, however, remains unoccupied. A couple of the guys found the house's previous occupants in their king-sized bed, bloated and oozing. I guess it was pretty gross (like spontaneous vomit gross). If I hadn't been sleeping in a building full of dead people for the past week, I'd be bothered by the idea of sharing a roof with the deceased Mr. and Mrs. Whoever. But I'm not. I'm just tired.

Surprisingly, we haven't seen that many living people. I guess Chris was right when she told me pretty much everyone was dead. But, I suppose the other survivors could be hiding. You know what's weird? I think I've been so lost in my grief over Cam that I haven't really paid attention to the fact that the world pretty much ended. It's like an unending nightmare. I keep waiting to wake up.

Alright, Zo, I promised Chris she could use my comp before bed. Let me know where you are as soon as you can. I worry about you all the time. So does Jason, even if he won't say it out loud.

Ciao,
Dani

8

ZOE

The air hummed with apprehension. From inside the truck, Sarah and I watched Dave's third attempt to refuel. I crossed my fingers. *Please work.*

Nothing seemed to be happening.

The seconds felt like minutes until, finally, Dave knocked on the driver's side window and gave us a thumbs up. Relieved, I smiled.

Opening the door, I felt the brisk air sting my face. I pulled my hood up over my ears and zipped my jacket as far as it would go. Looking around apprehensively, I made my way toward the convenience store in hopes of finding a bathroom. The vacant world around me was eerily silent. All I could hear was the creaking of a giant wooden billboard being assaulted by the wind.

How long has it been since anyone was here? Through the dark windows I saw a bathroom sign that looked promising, but I couldn't bring myself to enter. *I wonder if it's safe...*

As I stood outside of the store, I noticed a newspaper box still filled with papers. I leaned closer. The headline read, BILLIONS DEAD, and the paper was dated December 9, right before everything had started to shut down.

I inserted a quarter and snatched out a paper. Scanning its contents, my mouth grew dry and my body stiffened.

...the H1N1/12 pandemic...
...looting and riotous outbreaks everywhere...
...end of civilization as we know it...
...survivors losing their minds...
...governments can't control...
...the Apocalypse...

The newspaper slipped from between my fingers. Frozen in place, I was suffocated by the reality of our situation.

This isn't going away.

The fucking world ended.

Thinking of the strange feelings I'd been experiencing, I once again questioned my own sanity. My thoughts were too loud to silence. My heart thudded, and I couldn't swallow the lump in my throat. Looking out into the abandoned world around me, I realized how alone we really were.

I bent down to reclaim the paper and turned on my heel to head back toward the truck, completely awestruck as the words I'd read replayed in my mind. Each was a reminder that the only world I'd ever known had ended.

Dave and Sarah watched me closely as I quietly climbed back into the truck. "You okay?" Sarah asked.

Without saying a word, I reached back and let the newspaper fall from my grasp and into her lap. The paper crinkled in her hands as she picked it up, and she gasped. As she read the article aloud to Dave, I stared out the window and tried to tune her out. Snow was falling again.

"We better get back on the road," I interrupted.

Dave eyed me and cleared his throat before starting the truck. The engine rumbled in the winter wasteland, and an uneasiness settled in my stomach as the gas station's orange and blue 76 sign disappeared in the side mirror. *How long before we find another working gas station?* I closed my eyes, willing the troublesome thought away.

I settled myself in the front seat and glanced at Sammy and Sarah who were curled up in the back. I was comforted by the thought that I wasn't the only person left in the crazy world.

Unexpectedly, Dave's soft hand settled over mine, encasing it in a protective shell. "Are you sure you're okay?"

A rush of affection filled my senses, and my skin grew warm. I managed a smile and focused my eyes on the snow-covered buildings that zipped by the window, trying to ignore the unwelcome sensations. "I'm just glad I'm not alone," I said. "Why do you ask?"

"You always bite the inside of your cheek when you're worried." He flashed me a conceited smile. "You forget how well I know you."

My relationship with Dave was complicated. I was glad he was there; I'd missed being around him since our breakup. His smile calmed my nerves, and when we talked it was with an ease I'd never felt with any other man. Dave was comfortable. But the way he'd been looking at me was problematic; he seemed to forget that we were better as friends than lovers.

Dave's fingers tightened around mine, and a jumble of images —people and places—flashed through my mind. Before I could discern exactly what I was seeing, Dave slammed on the brakes, and the truck skidded to a halt.

Pulse hammering, I frantically glanced around, following his line of sight. Something ghosted toward us, unhurried, through the lace curtain of snow beyond the window.

"It's a person!" Sarah's hand flew to her mouth.

I could barely make out the hunched-over form. With each step the outline grew closer. "It's a woman," I whispered.

The lady was gesturing emphatically and seemed to be

mumbling to herself. Her hair was ratty and greasy, and she looked like she hadn't bathed in weeks.

"What the hell?" Dave muttered. He hesitated before moving to take off his seatbelt.

"Are you crazy?" I snapped, whipping my head in his direction. I reached out to him, clutching the sleeve of his green down jacket.

We looked back to the woman. "She's unwell," I observed. "We can't risk it."

I immediately sensed relief flooding the truck's cab. The sound of the automatic door locks latching echoed in our sudden silence.

"We can't just leave her out there," Sarah said, a shrill panic ringing in her voice.

"We don't have a choice," I retorted, my tone too harsh. I looked back at Sarah, whose wide, brown eyes hid behind her hanging curls. "Do you want to jeopardize our lives for hers? She's obviously crazy. What if she tried to hurt us?" I asked, surprised at how well I had mimicked my brother's impatient tone. Sarah still looked desperate to help the woman.

I softened my voice, trying to ease her worry. "Look at her, Sarah." We peered back out at the woman as she shuffled through the mounds of snow heaped along the side of the road. Her body was frail, and her face was gaunt. She wore no jacket or shoes, seemingly unfazed by the freezing weather.

"It's so sad," Sarah said, resolved to the woman's fate.

We remained quiet as the stranger disappeared from view. In only a moment, fresh snow blanketed the ground, covering any trace of her ever having been there.

Date: December 14, 11:25 PM
From: Zoe Cartwright
To: Danielle O'Connor
Subject: Attention K-Mart Shoppers

Hey D,

It's strange trying to describe to you what's going on right now. If you would've told me yesterday I'd be sleeping in a giant K-Mart, I would've laughed and said something like "why couldn't it be a Target?" But, alas...here we are.

We perused the store for a bit before calling it a night. We stocked up on things we needed—art supplies and warm clothes for me in particular. Drawing is the only thing that's sort of keeping me sane. Also, we took two solar generators from the Home Depot next door...those should come in handy if the power starts failing, and I grabbed a shitload of batteries and candles too. You never know, right? We got tons of other supplies, but I won't bore you with the details.

It hasn't been all fun and shopping today though. We had some issues finding fuel, resulting in our behind scheduleness (yes, I made up a word). We hope to make it to Dave's family's place in Ohio by tomorrow night, but the gas situation worries me.

On top of that, I've been feeling strange around Dave lately. I'm not sure why or what to do about it either. It's like sometimes I can feel random, unwanted emotions when I'm around him. It's making me feel schizophrenic, but I'm sure it's nothing. I'm probably just tired, right?

Speaking of tired, I should get some rest. I want to make sure we leave first thing in the morning. Night night, D.

Hasta la vista,
Zoe

9

DANI

Date: December 15, 8:00 AM
From: Danielle O'Connor
To: Zoe Cartwright
Subject: Argh…

Zo,

Wow. So I was one of the few people to think of bringing a laptop. Unbelievable. We've developed a rotation…just to be fair, you know? Whatever. It just means I have to make this short…

I'm perma-partners with Jason on days we're searching for surviving family and friends. That's a new development as of this morning. It'll be interesting. Oh...and that was a great idea about the solar generators. I'm going to tell Jason we need to snag some too.

That's pretty weird about the feelings you're having. Maybe you're just realizing that you looove Dave, and it's unexpected. What do you think? I'm sure you're not schizo…but I'll love you even if you are!

D

Please, please, PLEASE let Zo make it to Colorado safely. And PLEASE don't let her be crazy! I squeezed my eyes shut as I begged every possible universal power to watch over my best friend. *I can't do this without her.* I was on the verge of tears.

"Ready to go?" Jason asked from the doorway.

Startled, I leapt from my perch on the edge of the bed only to slip on the hardwood floor and nearly fall on my butt. I glared at the intruder who leaned casually against the doorframe. "Crap, Jason!" I snapped, turning to shove my feet into fur-lined winter boots. "Can't you make a noise or something?"

Hustling around the room to gather my coat and gloves, I wondered how long he'd been watching me. *Did he see my chin tremble?*

"Ready," I said and heard Jack jump down from the bed and trot to my side.

After a moment of hesitation, Jason nodded and straightened from his relaxed pose. He led the way out of the house and paused in the expansive driveway, letting the gentle drizzle of rain dampen us. Gesturing to a silver sedan, he said, "Hop in."

"I thought we were walking…but I guess this makes more sense. Is it theirs?" I asked with a nod toward the house.

A sarcastic laugh escaped from his throat. "Does it matter?"

Does anything? I wondered and shrugged.

On the short drive to downtown Longview, I took the opportunity to examine Jason from the passenger seat. He was different, harder and more closed off than the man I remembered. I'd been surprised when he announced that I would be his partner on search days, especially because I had the distinct impression that he was avoiding me.

"You know," I said lightly, trying to break the ice, "since you found me, this is the first time I've seen you out of your clothes." Realizing what I'd just said, I blushed and stammered, "I mean, your Army clothes…obviously you're not naked…I mean…" I groaned inwardly, reminding myself that I was no longer the teenage girl with a heartbreaking crush on her best friend's older brother. That version of me was long gone.

Jason's throaty chuckle was like lighter fluid on my burning cheeks. With a minimal half-smile and a barely-there dimple, he said, "It's a little cold for that. And wet." He parked the car in front of a long series of storefronts and stared ahead. "But then again, there's really only one good reason to strip down in a car, and that would more than make up for the cold. Don't you think, Red?" After assigning me a new nickname, he exited the car.

Stunned, I gaped at the now empty driver's seat. Very vivid, *very* inappropriate images flashed through my mind. I was sure my whole body was blushing.

Suddenly, my mind screamed, *What about Cam?*

It took me a few moments to calm myself. When I finally exited the car, I tried my best to dismiss the meaningless flirtation. Jason flirted like other men breathed, easily and without thought. It meant nothing.

We spent the next seven hours searching the old brick apartment buildings and stores in the once-adorable downtown area for signs of life. We found few living people—all too insane or afraid to communicate. That, combined with the plethora of dead bodies, made for an unsettling day. With the clinging scent of rotting flesh following me, I wondered if I'd ever be able to enjoy meat again.

"Can we check that place for dog stuff?" I asked, pointing to a little pet shop in an antiquated two-story building across the street.

Jason shrugged. His ever-watchful gaze looked everywhere at once as we crossed the empty street side-by-side.

Once in the store, I followed our recently established routine and kept watch near the shattered glass doorway while Jason searched the building for potential dangers. He had just stepped through the only other doorway in the shop—a squeaky swinging door that led to the store's back area—when four men rounded the block outside. They weren't as dirty as the few other living people we'd seen, but they looked a hell of a lot meaner.

I ducked into the shadows and whispered desperately toward the back door, "Jason."

Nothing.

I tried again, a little louder, "Jason!"

Still nothing.

The scruffy survivors stalked in a direct path toward my hide-out, and I stifled a curse. "C'mon Jack," I said softly, but my dog was nowhere in sight.

Just as I turned to rush toward the back of the store in search of Jason, Jack backed through the swinging door—he was dragging a very annoyed Jason.

"What the hell, Dani? Can't you keep him under control?"

Jack's chest rumbled, his mouth still full of Jason's sleeve.

I stepped toward them and tried to explain, "Jason, there's—"

"Well, well, well…what do we have here?" a gravelly voice interrupted from behind me. A chorus of deep, taunting laughs enhanced its menacing effect.

I froze mid-step, terrified. Based on the sound of the man's voice, I estimated I was halfway between the strangers and Jason. I stared into Jason's furious eyes, feeling like a horde of monsters would seize me from behind if I even dared to breathe.

"Come here, Dani." Jason's voice was calm and soothing—completely incompatible with his aimed pistol and threatening stance. At first, I thought his weapon was pointed at me, but I quickly realized it was fixed on the man behind me.

Did I just hear a footstep? Is he moving closer?

"Come on, Dani. Just come here." Strain marbled Jason's calm tone, nearly fracturing it.

They must be closer. Crap! But fear seemed to have cemented my feet to the speckled linoleum floor.

Jack padded to me and, snarling ferociously at the intruders, leaned against the back of my frozen legs; I had to either step or fall. After the first stride, there was no stopping me until I was safely stowed behind both Jason and Jack.

"There's no need for that, son. We just want to have a little fun with the girl." Irritation clouded the menace in the stranger's voice, making him sound, of all things, a little whiny. His cronies shuffled and puffed up, looking like they were spoiling for a brawl.

Reaching around Jason into his unzipped coat, I pulled a handgun from his shoulder holster. I couldn't help but notice the extreme tension in his body; each muscle was coiled like a viper preparing to strike. He was ready to take them all on...but there were four of *them* and only one Jason.

I stepped up beside Jason and raised the gun, though we both knew it would prove useless if the confrontation actually erupted into physical violence. I didn't even know how to turn the safety off. Hell, I didn't know where to *find* the safety.

But our aggressors didn't know that.

Ominously, Jason warned, "Get the hell out of here. If I see you again, you're dead." As a chilly afterthought he added, "If you'd touched her, you'd already be dead. Leave. *Now*."

They did.

I didn't lower the gun until the men were long gone. I just... couldn't. Jason had to pry it from my shaking hands.

I was still standing in the same spot, my arms hanging stiffly, when he spoke. "That was smart thinking, Red. I don't think they'd have walked away like that if you hadn't pulled the hot little badass card."

Did he just call me hot? It worked as well as a slap, pulling me out of my frozen mind.

Hints of concern tightened Jason's eyes as he hunched down to my eye level. "You okay?"

Listening to Jack sniff the nearby items in the store, I nodded and whispered, "No."

Jason laughed. "Good answer. So how about that dog stuff? Find what you need. I'll keep watch."

I nodded again and wandered off in the direction of Jack's sniffing and tail-thumping. I found him with his head stuck in a bucket half-full of two-foot-long, stretched and dried bull penises. *That's my dog*, I thought.

Date: December 15, 7:20 PM
From: Danielle O'Connor
To: Zoe Cartwright
Subject: An interesting day...

Zo,

Today wasn't quite what I thought it would be. We found lots of dead people in their homes, mostly in beds and bathrooms. They were also in some of the shops and in a bunch of the abandoned cars. And they definitely didn't all die from the flu. I saw some that were obvious suicides. Holy crap, can I just say that dead people are GROSS. It sounds stupid and, I don't know, flippant...but they are! It's hard to think that they were alive like us a few weeks ago. It's frightening to think about what the world might be like in another week. Or a month. Or a year.

And the living, they're almost worse than the dead. Every person we found was crazy or violent. Or both. Jason and I started calling them "Crazies". Seemed fitting.

So, I need to vent about something. You know how I'm search partners with Jason? Well, there's this one Air Force chick (everyone else is Army Special Forces, aka...badass), who was super pissed when Jason announced the search partners. Something's going on between them. It's not surprising—she (Cece) looks like a perfect, curvy little Inca princess. Well, she would if she didn't have "I'm a perma-bitch" stamped on her face all the time. Whatever. The point is, I'm now on her shit list. Awesome.

Want to hear something scary? Jason has decided I need to learn how to use a gun. This has DISASTER written all over it. He's waiting for me right now. I'll let you know how it goes when I write to you tomorrow.

Ciao,
Dani

10

ZOE

The graveyard of motionless, snow-capped cars made driving along the highway eerie. *Where were they going? Home? The hospital? Did they know they were dying?* The air was heavy with silence. We all knew many of the vehicles scattered along the road weren't abandoned—they were tombs for their unfortunate inhabitants.

"We're almost there. It's only another twenty miles or so, I think." Dave smiled back at us through the rearview mirror, patting his chocolate lab on the head with his spare hand. I watched him playfully tug on the dog's ears; Sammy's tail thumped excitedly.

Thinking of my own situation, I grew apprehensive. The sporadic, unwanted emotions I'd been feeling around him had intensified, becoming incessant and overwhelming. I'd been trying to keep my distance.

Why Dave? I wasn't sure why his presence seemed to affect me so much, but the foreign feelings seemed to fit his mood far better than my own.

Are these his *feelings?* The thought was absurd.

Does he know he's doing this? I wished I could ask him without sounding completely crazy.

"Zoe, are you okay? You seem…fidgety." Sarah was looking at me with narrowed, very watchful eyes. She seemed to do that often, and I couldn't help but wonder what she was thinking.

"Sure, I just wish we were there already. I'm starting to feel claustrophobic," I said nonchalantly as I reached for the map in the seat pocket in front of her.

Shrugging, Sarah started to open her book but sneezed all over my arm in the process.

Irritated, I looked at her. "Really, Sarah?"

"I'm sorry." She sniffled and wiped my sleeve with hers.

Grossed out and annoyed, I pulled away from her, but she grabbed my wrist anyway. "I hardly think—" But before I could finish my sentence, I felt a surge of embarrassment warm my body, bringing a flush to my cheeks.

"Nice one, Sarah," she chided herself, but I barely heard her; I was lost in my own thoughts.

It's not just Dave. I suddenly felt nauseated. *It's me.*

Date: December 16, 3:30 PM
From: Zoe Cartwright
To: Danielle O'Connor
Subject: Here at last!

Hey D,

It sounds like there's a lot happening over there. I'm sorry you've had to see all those disgusting, horrible things. I hope being with Jason makes you feel safe enough to get some rest. You've been through a lot this past week. I've been pretty lucky so far, in terms of disgusting, horrible things. There's so much snow on the ground that it's hard to see much of anything. As much as I hate this weather, I'm grateful I've been spared seeing what's underneath.

So that Air Force chick you mentioned sounds like a real gem. I guess personality isn't much of a priority for Jason. Surprise. I know it's probably hard, but try to ignore the bitchiness. It means nothing, I'm sure.

We finally arrived at Dave's cabin today, thankfully. It's actually quite homey. It reminds me of summer camp back in the day. It's nothing fancy, just an old summer fishing spot his family used when they wanted to get out of the city. It's too stormy outside to see much other than the bare, frozen trees and the snow blanketing the ground. But inside the cabin is cozy.

Hopefully we'll be able to rest and recuperate before heading out again. I'm assuming we'll leave tomorrow, but we haven't really talked about it yet. I'm not looking forward to the drive to Sarah's house. I think the close quarters worsen those feelings I've been experiencing. I felt them again today, but with Sarah this time. I have no idea what's going on. I'm wondering if I should say something to Sarah and Dave or if I should keep it to myself. I wouldn't even know where to start. What a mess.

With the exception of the former occupants, it sounds like you're staying in a fancy vacation home...I'm a little jealous. It's snowing here...everywhere...still. It's always snowing, and you know I hate being cold. It doesn't help my mood much. I could really use some Dani time right about now...maybe a few mixed drinks on the beach too :) Why is time suddenly going by so slowly? I'll let you know when we take off or when we even have a plan. Be safe!

Hasta,
Zoe

Standing in the cabin's cramped bathroom, I looked in the mirror as I brushed my teeth and studied the heavily shadowed eyes that stared back at me. *I look like…shit.*

"Zoe!" Sarah screamed from the living room, and fear swept over me.

Spitting the contents of my mouth into the sink, I threw open the bathroom door. My heart pounded against my chest. "What is it!?" I rushed to her.

"Dave's out th—" but before Sarah could finish, I heard Dave's cries for help.

I grabbed the shotgun leaning against the wall and flung the front door open. I could barely hear Dave shouting through the angry howl of the wind. Running out into the frigid night, I headed in his direction.

"Lock the door!" I yelled back to Sarah. My voice was muffled by the blizzard. The cold hit me like razor blades, cutting through my clothes and into my skin with every move. "Dave! Where are you?" I squinted to see through the dense snowfall.

"Sammy!" Dave's voice broke through the violent storm.

My muscles fatigued and my lungs burned as I struggled through the powdery snow, trying not to let it slow me down. I heard Dave's voice right before stumbling upon him. I was shocked to see the form of a large animal pacing nearby. Unsure what to do, I shot the gun into the darkness. Its recoil knocked me back, and I lost my balance.

Squinting, I refocused my eyes just in time to see the creature running away and Dave crawling toward Sammy's unmoving body.

"Dave!" I ran to his side as he tried to move. He was wounded; blood darkened the snow-covered ground beneath his body, and his legs dragged limply behind him.

“Sammy!” Dave was crying and struggling to get to his dog. Helping him up was impossible. He hit my hands away, fighting against my efforts.

“Dave, you have to get inside,” I shouted. My body was achy and numb.

“Sammy!” he cried as he continued to fight against me.

I snapped. I slapped him across the face, desperate for him to focus, and yelled with all the lung power my freezing body could afford. “Dammit, Dave! I’ve got to get you inside. I’ll come back for Sammy!”

He looked at me in horror.

“I need you to help me. Try to stand up!” I could barely feel my legs as I pulled his body toward mine.

He stared back with wide eyes. I could feel his anguish coursing through me.

“I’ll come back for him, I promise.”

Date: December 17, 4:00 AM
From: Zoe Cartwright
To: Danielle O’Connor
Subject: (No Subject)

D,

There’s so much to tell you, but I don’t have much time. Dave and Sammy were attacked by a mountain lion last night. Sammy saved Dave’s life but didn’t survive himself. Dave’s got gashes all over his legs, and he’s lost a lot of blood. I’m taking care of him the best I can, but he won’t let me do much. He’s drinking enough Jose Cuervo that I don’t think he needs any pain meds at this point; though he may never stop bleeding.

I wish you were here. You'd know what to say to him and what to do.

Zoe

11

DANI

"Wow. Nice find, Cece," John said as he looked around the posh hotel lobby. On such a boyish face his wide-eyed expression lent him a look of cherubic innocence. It was deceptive—the twenty-one-year-old was about as innocent as Jason, but unlike Jason, John made sure everyone knew he was a devil in disguise.

Cece simpered and hopped onto the lobby's ultra-modern, granite front desk. Contemporary decor appeared to be the hotel's motif of choice, along with black and white everything.

Crossing her legs and lounging back suggestively, Cece said, "Oh my God, I know, right? This is where my prom was. Isn't this place just sinful?" Her way-too-smoldering gaze lingered on Jason before sliding over to John in the center of the lobby. John seized the unspoken invitation and sidled up to her.

Seriously, how obvious does she need to be? She might as well start stripping on the desk.

Shocked, I watched Jason walk toward the front desk…toward Cece. *He's falling for it?* Jealousy, white hot rage, guilt, and self-loathing flared within me. I'd been experiencing that specific tangle of emotions for several days, always around Jason. I wanted him, though I knew I shouldn't, and I hated Cece for having him. I also hated myself for desiring another man so soon after Cam's death, even if he was the guy I'd pined for since I was a little girl.

Beside me, Chris snorted. I caught a faintly whispered, "fool," but didn't know if it was in reference to Cece, John, or Jason. Maybe it was for all three.

Fierce triumph filled Cece's face as Jason neared her perch. The expression remained for about two seconds until Jason did an about-face to address the rest of us. Sulking, Cece hopped down and joined the edge of the group. I couldn't hide my faint smirk.

"This place is huge. We need to set up base somewhere we can stay close together and easily defend ourselves, like the top-floor suites. Ky"—Jason directed his voice at the half-Japanese man —"go see if the elevators work."

"Yes, Sir." Ky looked to be around my age and followed the slightly older man's orders easily. "They work," he called and jogged back.

"Great. When we get to the suites, just drop your shit off. We'll search the place for food and anything else that might be useful. Keep an eye out for other people, and be ready." The warning was unnecessary; like Jason and me, many of the others had run into hostile Crazies in Longview.

"Ky, you're with me on this floor. Chris and Dani, pair up, you're on this floor too. The rest of you—stick with your usual partners and divide the remaining floors between you."

Cece glared smoldering daggers at Chris, Ky, and me, but I barely noticed. *I'm supposed to be partners with Jason, not with Chris,* I thought as rejection joined the tangle of emotions. My thoughts flickered back and forth between *he doesn't want me* and *I shouldn't want him.*

Belatedly, I realized I was assigned the only floor with two teams. *Because I'm a worthless partner.*

Everyone else could take care of themselves with their special I-can-kill-someone-a-million-different-ways-with-mypinkie military training. I, on the other hand, could talk to any Italian, Russian, Gaelic, or Spanish-speaking people we happened upon. Somehow, I didn't think my background in foreign languages would be a huge help traversing the devastated United States.

Irritated, I huffed into the elevator, huffed while it sped upward, and huffed as I dropped my pack and duffel bag on the floor of the largest suite's living room. At that point I had to stop huffing or risk hyperventilation.

Jack, who had been eagerly sniffing the sofa cushions—happily inhaling whatever had been left behind by other people's butts—followed as I wandered back to the elevators to wait for Chris.

I have a gun, I thought. *I can even use it now...sort of.* It was holstered snugly under my coat, unfamiliar and heavy, making me feel lopsided.

With crossed arms, I glared at my blurry reflection in the brushed-metal door and wished there was something I could do, something I could contribute. And desperately, I wished that my inappropriate feelings for Jason would go away and that Cam's voice would stop haunting me. "*But I thought you loved me?*"

"Shall we?" Chris asked behind me; Jason and Ky were just approaching as I faced the blonde woman.

"Why not?" I grumbled.

The guys exchanged guarded glances while we all waited for the elevator, but Chris just stared ahead, her expression bland.

An electronic 'ding' announced the arrival of the elevator.

On the nine-floor ride down to the lobby, I stood in the elevator's center and stared at the crack between the doors. Behind me there was an intake of breath, immediately followed by a thump and a whispered, "Ow!" from Jason.

"Shut up," Chris hissed.

"Why? I was just going to ask—" Jason's words were cut off by another thump, louder this time. If he'd been about to ask what was bothering me, I was glad that Chris had silenced him, however painful her methods may have been.

"I know. Shut up," Chris told him.

With another 'ding', the elevator signaled the imminent door-opening, and I remained in the center, completely oblivious to my idiocy. I had experienced their super-coordinated elevator-exiting protocol on the ride up, had even participated by pancaking my body against the side wall in anticipation of an ambush. It made sense—there was no way to know what the doors would reveal when they opened. But, distracted by my mental flogging, I stood in the dead-center of the elevator and waited.

A moment before the doors slid open, Jason yanked me behind him and held me against the wall. Around me, all my companions pressed themselves against the elevator's metallic walls with weapons at the ready. When the lobby was revealed and nobody attacked, they all relaxed.

I'm such an idiot. Disgusted with my stupidity, I skittered away from Jason and grumbled, "Come on, Chris, let's go search for things. I can at least do that without screwing up." I marched out of the elevator with Jack growling at my side. Lately, he seemed to have developed the inexplicable ability to match his mood to my own. *Good boy.*

After several dozen paces, I slowed and looked around at the deserted hotel—I needed a plan. The lobby, delightfully absent of dead people, was scattered with abandoned luggage racks that easily could've doubled as pieces of postmodern art. I grabbed one, casting it as a large shopping cart, and wandered into the open-plan lounge. The bar seemed like a great place to start.

At the sound of another cart smoothly rolling closer, I quickly ducked behind the sleek black bar. It had to be Chris. She would make me talk now that we were away from the guys. Though I knew hiding wouldn't stop the determined woman, I couldn't bring myself to stand.

The muffled scrape of chair legs on hardwood and the creak of leather told me she was sitting on one of the nearby bar stools. "What's wrong, Dani?"

"Nothing. I'm fine," I lied weakly.

"Right. Try again, this time with the truth," Chris suggested.

Standing, I took a deep breath and answered, "Well…I'm not really sure." As I spoke, I made my way around the bar to sit on the stool beside hers.

"It's like everything's been building up to this feeling of…of… I don't know. Helplessness. Or maybe uselessness. And now Jason doesn't want to be my partner…not that I mind being with you." The relentless avalanche of words flowed out as I rubbed Jack's ears; he'd wedged himself between our bar stools.

"I can't do anything. Nothing useful to surviving this…" I paused and gestured around wildly. "I can't defend myself. I just end up being a distraction. And this…" I pulled the gun from inside my coat. "What good is this if someone's close to me? And what if I can't even use it, if I'm too afraid? I'm not surprised he doesn't want me as his partner anymore. Once was enough. Cam should've been the one to survive; he could've at least cooked for everyone. Hell, when I have food duty, I might accidentally poison everyone."

With placating amusement, Chris said, "I'm sure you're not that bad."

"No," I said adamantly. "I am. And what's so frustrating is that you and Jason work so hard to keep me safe, nursing me back to health, protecting me…I mean, Jason faced off with a group crazy men! And why? I don't contribute anything, and I…I'm a bad person. I have these feelings, these thoughts I *really* shouldn't be having. I really did love Cam, I swear it, but…" By the time I trailed off, my gestures had become as despondent as my tone, my hands finally settling on the bar.

"Dani, listen to me." Chris grasped my wrist firmly and captured my gaze. "You are *not* useless. You have great ideas. You thought of stocking up on the backpacking equipment—getting all that stuff could end up saving our lives. And those feelings you're having are perfectly normal. Cam would want you to move on, to be happy. Things happen at a different pace in times like these. It doesn't make you a bad person. And, well, you do…I don't know…*something* to Jason. Something good."

I scoffed.

"You do," Chris urged. "You make him seem more human and less like…I don't know…like someone who believes in his own divinity. I chose to follow him off-base because I knew he was a good man and a good leader, but I'd never seen him really laugh or get very angry, or God, *cry* until we found you. He's just different —better—when you're around."

I searched Chris's clear blue eyes and found only truth, but I couldn't believe it. "It's nothing like that," I dismissed, needing to diminish the effect her words were having on me. "I just remind him of his past. Besides, he's always avoiding me…always going off with *Cece*."

Chris snorted. "Yeah…but that's just so he can get his rocks off."

I put on a wry grin, masking the sudden, wrenching pain. My unwanted jealousy was really starting to get on my nerves. Standing, I rounded the bar again, searching in earnest. A jar of maraschino cherries and several blue cheese-stuffed olives were my first finds. A couple bottles of Dom Perignon from the wine fridge were my second.

"He'll be done with her soon enough," Chris said, lingering on the nauseating topic. "Since I've known him he's gone through dozens like her, none meaning more than the last."

I felt like a piece of my heart had been sliced off, seared, and chewed up. *Dozens*. I busied myself searching the cabinets.

Chris quickly joined me behind the bar and was selecting various bottles of high-end alcohol. "For morale," she justified.

Being the busybody mother hen that she was, Chris had found a way to secretly tell Jason about my desperate need to be able to defend myself. He'd thought giving me a gun and showing me how to use it would be enough. He'd been wrong. As a result, several of us were having an impromptu evening training session in the penthouse suite's living room. With the trendy burgundy, black, and gold furniture shoved up against the walls of windows, there was plenty of room for grappling. *I* was learning the basics of self-defense—specifically, how to get out of an attacker's grasp. I was playing my usual role as the victim. And the attacker? Jason, *of course.*

"Oomph," I grunted, thrusting my backside into Jason's unyielding thigh and pulling at the arm he had locked around my shoulders. *I am not enjoying this,* I told my misbehaving nerve endings.

Jason's only response was a deep chuckle.

Wedging closer against him, I heaved again and was surprised when his balance shifted. I had been trying to loosen his hold on me. Instead, I'd placed the majority of his weight against my back. Ungracefully, we collapsed face-first onto the geometrically-patterned carpet. Jason lay slightly askew atop me, well over six feet of heavy muscle shaking against the back of my body.

"What are you…are you laughing? At me?" I squealed in outrage. I squirmed and wiggled until, at the behest of my pointy elbows, he let up just enough for me to flip over. But he didn't move off me—he was laughing too hard.

"Get off me you big turd!"

Jason raised himself on thickly corded arms just long enough to meet my eyes. "Big turd? Did you really just call me that?" He collapsed again, pinning me helplessly to the ground, and buried his face in my shoulder.

My heartbeat grew increasingly erratic, my breathing ragged. *I should* not *love this.* Giddiness and guilt warred in my chest. I wanted to wrap my legs around him. I needed to get away.

"I'm glad you're finding me so amusing," I breathed. I'd been aiming for a more authoritative tone, but with his hard body flush against mine, a whisper was the best I could do. "That's what I'm here for. Ha ha...that Dani, such a *hoot*!" With the last word, I gave one huge, wiggly thrust in the hopes of creating enough room to scoot out from beneath him.

Jason's convulsive laughter vanished, and I wondered if I'd hit a tender man-part. As far as I knew that resulted in more of a moaning, groaning, pretending-to-die display. But, I figured it was possible.

Practically jumping off me, Jason called, "Johnson!" Seconds later, Chris was standing next to him and staring down at me.

"Did you see?" I asked her as I stood. "Is this even worth it? I mean, I don't want to waste anyone's time."

"Ha!" Chris barked, "Who wouldn't crumble under this beast?" She rolled her eyes in Jason's direction. "Nah, just blame him, hon. You're so small...it was pretty much a given you'd end up on the floor."

"Anyway, Johnson...I want you to help train her since you're *slightly* smaller than me." Jason sounded dead serious, but the corner of his mouth threatened to quirk up in a smile.

"*Slightly* smaller! You're such a dick." With a huge grin at me, Chris said, "When I'm done with you, hon, you'll be able to take him down any time you want."

"Yeah!" I boasted, poking Jason's abs through his t-shirt and bouncing from foot to foot. "I'm gonna take you down...eventually."

Wearing a cocky smirk, Jason watched me with glittering eyes. "We'll see, Red. We'll see..."

Some of the others watched the exchange, grinning and chuckling. Cece, sitting in the far corner, wasn't one of them.

Date: December 17, 9:00 AM
From: Danielle O'Connor
To: Zoe Cartwright
Subject: RIP Sammy

Zo,

So much for writing to you yesterday...we searched and worked and trained for so long in our Portland "home" that I fell asleep before my allotted time at the computer.

Dammit! I feel so helpless being so far away from you! I'm really sorry about Sammy. I hope Dave recovers. Did you have all the first aid supplies and whatnot you needed? Did you have to stitch him up? I suppose you could always pour booze over his wounds, but that might sting a bit.

I know this'll seem like small potatoes to you right now, but I forgot to tell you that Joey found some of his people. Back in Longview, I mean. They were holed up in one of the last houses he checked. He decided to stay with them. I'm happy for him...and it gives me hope for what awaits us in Bodega Bay.

Today I'm not searching Portland with the rest of the group. Instead, I'm on watch and food duty with Thomas ("It's Thomas, not Tom!"). Thomas takes himself very seriously. He's not awesome enough to be a Tom anyway, not like your dad. From what I can tell, he's the same rank as Jason, and it rankles him a bit that your brother has assumed leadership of our group. I'm sure you're wondering why I'm not out searching with Jason, my supposed partner...I'm getting to it.

Portland is Cece's stop. Holy effing cow, she drives me insane.

She's 19 and barely out of basic training. She's a horrid, sloppy flirt with every guy, especially your brother. And they all pay her a lot of attention. Oh, and she hates me.

Anyway, we have an odd number now, so there has to be a three-person group. Cece finagled her way into one that includes Jason. The thing is, he was going to stay here at the hotel, but Cece whined about how much safer she'd feel with him nearby. I'm sure his stupid puffed-up ego wouldn't let him refuse. And worse, I feel less safe without him nearby. Crap! I'm just as bad as Cece! Ugh!

Okay, I should get to my unavoidably disastrous food duties. Thomas keeps throwing scornful glances my way.

Stay safe and warm, Zo. Sorry about the snow. My thoughts are with you, Dave, and Sarah.

Ciao,
Dani

12

ZOE

I stared out into the blackness beyond the windowpane. The storm hadn't let up; the wind whipped through the trees, making them moan and creak. I shivered as a chill crept up my spine. *What are we going to do now*?

I wondered how long we'd have to stay in the cabin and if Dave's legs would heal properly. I wanted to get to Colorado, but I knew Dave was in no shape to discuss plans for leaving. He'd been drunk since the incident with Sammy and the mountain lion, fading in and out of consciousness and waking only for another drink before passing out again.

Sarah had been lost in her own world of sadness since Sammy died in her arms. We'd wrapped him in a blanket—it had seemed like the right thing to do—before laying his lifeless body outside on the icy porch.

"Zoe," Dave interrupted my morose thoughts. He cleared his throat, his voice hoarse from lack of use. "You're cold." I could feel his eyes on me.

I looked back at him just as he brought his trusty friend, Mr. Jose Cuervo, up to his lips and took a gulp.

"I'm fine," I lied, walking over to his bed and removing a blanket to wrap around my shivering body. "Why don't I get you something else to put in your stomach? Sarah made potato soup."

Dave looked away and set the bottle down on the nightstand. "I'm not hungry," he said thickly.

He needs a distraction. "Jose might be your friend tonight, but he'll be your enemy tomorrow," I warned with a grin, rearranging his comforter around him.

"He's worth it." A tiny smirk pulled at the corners of his mouth.

Relieved by his Dave-like response, I smiled back, and before I realized what I was doing, I ran my fingers through his short brown curls. *At least he's okay.*

In the dim lamplight, I saw a spark of something illuminate his eyes. He struggled to move his injured legs, making room for me in the bed. His eyes fixed on me as he patted the mattress beside him. "You're cold and tired. I don't care what you say. Come on."

Conceding that his words were true, I smiled sheepishly and climbed in bed beside him.

I couldn't bring myself to deny him in his current state, and I didn't really want to. My body craved warmth, erasing any concern I had that we would find ourselves in a compromising situation. Taking a deep breath, I let myself relax on the soft mattress. I hadn't realized how exhausted I was until my head sank further into the pillow.

Before I knew what was happening, I felt Dave's arousal zap through me like an electric jolt. Ignoring the fatigue and pain shooting through his lower body, he shifted and was suddenly on top of me. His hands grasped my arms with a surprising desperation. His lips were urgent and rough on mine, his breath smelled antiseptic and sour, and his skin was clammy from drunkenness.

Without warning, my mind was invaded by thoughts and feelings that weren't my own. A succession of images flickered in my mind. It took only a moment to realize they were memories of me. But, they weren't *my* memories.

My silhouette standing in front of the cabin window just moments before. My breasts accentuated by my slight waist.

My dark hair cascading over my blue-green eyes. Me looking up at him.

My naked body in his bed. My black hair trailing behind me on white sheets.

My body undulating beneath his. His fingers lingering on the tattoo on my right hip.

Dave's grip on me tightened, and his tongue explored my mouth as if he'd never tasted it before—sampling and probing. It wasn't sensual or intimate like it had once been, but instead it was desperate and hungry.

My body quivering as his lips trailed down my stomach.

The memories were suffocating. Dave's urgency frightened me, and the images of myself were too much to bear. His desire confused my own feelings of discomfort and unease.

I panicked and struggled to push him off me. "I need air," I gasped.

"God, I want you, Zo." His voice was guttural, and I could feel how badly he yearned for me. He knotted his hands in my hair. Tugging too hard, he jerked my head back and caused my body to arch into his. Misinterpreting my reaction, he slid his hands down to the waistband of my sweats.

"Dave, stop it. I can't breathe!" Pushing with all my might, I tried to shove his body off me.

He stilled, hovering. His shaking arms straddled my torso while our chests heaved in unison.

I attempted to catch my breath as I peered up at him, unsure what to say as my mind replayed the images I'd seen. They looped like a broken record. I put my hand over my eyes and licked my stinging lips. My heart pounded like a drum, reverberating through my entire being. *What the hell was that?*

Knowing I'd somehow witnessed his private thoughts, I tried to overlook my stewing mortification and disgust. But I couldn't ignore how dirty and objectified I felt. Uneasiness settled inside me like vines tangling in my stomach.

Dave's eyes narrowed and then widened as he registered the revulsion on my face. Rolling onto his back, he looked up at the ceiling. He was embarrassed. I could feel him simmering in it, thick and sticky like his breath. "Sorry, I thought you still had feelings for me or something crazy like that," he said bitterly.

"Dave, it's just that I—" *I can read your mind!* "It's complicated," I muttered. Running my hands through my hair, I hoped to pull the tension away from the sudden headache pounding in my skull.

"I get it," he grumbled, reaching to grab the booze from the nightstand. I could tell his ego was as wounded as his legs.

"I just wasn't expecting that, okay?" My voice rose slightly as I tried to control my impatience. "I'm not well." I'd surprised myself with the admission, but Dave sulked and ignored me while he took another swig.

"I should get some rest," he said between drinks. "You should probably go check on Sarah or something." And just like that, Dave was gone. He'd completely shut me out.

Trying not to lash out at him, I reminded myself that he was brokenhearted by the loss of his best friend, was in a lot of physical pain, was sexually frustrated, *and* was drunk. I took a deep breath to gather my few remaining bits of patience.

"Go away, Zoe," he ordered.

At his words, all my sympathy instantly vanished. "Fine, *asshole*!" With a rush of anger, I threw the covers off me, grabbed my blanket, and stalked out of the room. I made sure to slam the door behind me. *So much for not lashing out...*

Date: December 18, 2:00 AM
From: Zoe Cartwright
To: Danielle O'Connor
Subject: Dave's an asshole and I'm losing my mind

Hey D,

I know it's late (or early), but I can't sleep. Too much shit's happened in the last 24 hours, and it's polluting my mind. With Dave's injuries and the whole situation with Sammy, I haven't gotten any sleep. But oh wait, there's more...

Tonight was really unnerving. I'm not even sure how to describe it. You know how I've been having those strange sensations? Well, I know this will sound really crazy, but it just got worse. I thought maybe I was losing my mind, but now I know I am. Either way, it's screwing everything up.

Dave came on to me—like full on tongue-down-my-throat,

rocking-hip action—and it didn't turn out well. He was drunk, which didn't help, but I also saw these jumbled images of myself flash in my mind. In some, I was lying naked in bed beneath him. Why were they in my mind?

I know this sounds impossible (trust me), but I think they were his memories of us, from when we were together. I felt completely overwhelmed and violated, so I pushed him away. Needless to say, his ego is totally wounded. He won't even talk to me.

Just thinking about seeing myself that way makes me sick to my stomach. I feel objectified. I want to rip him a new one and tell him to stop thinking about me like that. But what do I say, "I saw your memories and I don't appreciate them, so stop it"? I knew Dave still had feelings for me…I've been sensing them since he showed up at my door last week, but I guess it's just shocking to actually see how real his feelings are.

Now, he's being such an asshole that I'm not sure what to do. Keeping my distance is probably the best thing, but I feel like I need to fix this. I also need his truck, and for that, I need him. I know it's selfish of me, but my main concern is getting to Colorado. I feel like I should tell him why I pushed him away, but I don't want him to have another reason to shut me out. He's in such a bad space. I'm not sure what his reaction would be if I told him I could feel what he's feeling and see what he's remembering. This is way outside of my shit-I-can-handle comfort zone.

Thanks for the update on your travels. It sounds like that Cece girl is more of a super skank than I thought. Sorry you have to deal with her. Hopefully Jason will get tired of her soon. He generally has low tolerance for stupid people.

I'm surprised and a little upset with Jason's strategic planning during your trip. He's taking his sweet-ass time getting to Bodega Bay. Why isn't he making Dad a priority? Did he give you a good reason? If it were me, I would've been there already. I understand he wants to help everyone find their families, but why can't he break people off into teams?

Anyway, I should probably go. It's really late, and I need to decide what I'm going to do about Dave. I worry about you. I hope you're doing okay. You'd let me know if you weren't, right?

Hasta,
Zoe

The sun barely shone in the gray sky. The air was bitter cold and burned my lungs as I stood under the frozen trees. The storm clouds lingered, but the snow had ceased falling and the wind had died down earlier in the morning. I was grateful for the reprieve.

It was the first time the snow had stopped since we'd arrived at the cabin. I took the opportunity to escape Dave and the close quarters I'd been trapped within.

The snow crunched beneath my feet as I made my way around the back of the house and toward the barn. I'd noticed the structure when we arrived a few days earlier.

I spotted an old shed next to the barn and approached it. Its metal door barely hung on its crooked hinges. With glove-padded fingers, I pulled the creaking door open, exposing the shed's inhabitants; a leaf blower, a rake, and a hedge trimmer looked lonely hanging on the rusted metal wall. Something bright and red situated in the corner beside a lawn mower caught my attention: a gas can.

I picked up the can, listening as its liquid contents sloshed around inside. It was half-full of the precious fluid we so desperately relied upon. A triumphant smile spread across my face—a small victory, but a victory nonetheless.

Holding the can away from my body, I left the shed and walked toward the barn. I was trying to keep the dirty container as far away from my white jacket as possible. *It's brand new*, I rationalized, realizing my silliness.

As I neared the barn's red doors, I noticed icicles hanging from the corners of the roof. I set the gas can down and took a deep breath before entering.

Although it was dark inside, I could make out a go-cart tucked away in the back, a chainsaw hanging on the wall, and a small snowplow parked in the corner. Assuming there would be much more snowfall before we left, I knew the plow might come in handy. Unfortunately, all the fuel tanks were empty, so I walked back out into the cold December afternoon.

A crow cawed above me as I closed the barn door. I spotted the black, iridescent bird on a nearby tree branch. Its head cocked to the right and then to the left as it examined me through its binocular vision.

A chill raced through me, and for once it wasn't from the frigid air. I thought of the mountain lion attack and wondered what had provoked it. I tried to recall any other animals I'd seen acting strangely. Other than Sammy and the big cat, the lone bird was the first animal I'd noticed since arriving at the cabin. My imagination ran away from me, and I began to feel uneasy standing outside alone. I suddenly felt miles away from the safety of the cabin. Staring up at the bird, I wondered if it had been changed by the Virus too.

Just as I decided the thought was probably ridiculous, I laughed, and the bird leapt from the flimsy branch and flew away. Its caw disturbed the still, crisp afternoon air.

Following the bird's departure, my gaze fell upon a tire swing hanging from another barren tree branch. The seemingly insignificant sight broke something inside me. My heart seemed to seize as memories I'd kept buried for days came flooding to the surface of my mind, unhinging my composed façade.

My father stood beside me. His eyes seemed lifeless, but he smiled down at me as he pushed me on my brother's old tire swing,

"Is he mad that I'm on here?" I cried as Dad pushed me gently, back and forth.

"No, he's not mad. He hasn't used it in years, and besides, he can share."

"Then why is he being so mean to me? He's always so mean!" I held on to the inside of the tire more tightly.

"It's not you, sweetie. Don't cry. He isn't having a very good day, that's all."

"He never has a good day."

I felt something warm on my cheek, but couldn't break my train of thought…

"Another scrape, sweetie?" Dad's scruff had grayed, but his eyes were the same dull, muted blue.

"I fell," I whined and pointed to my scraped knee.

He smiled at me and brushed my hair out of my damp face. "Don't cry; it's not that bad."

"It's ugly," I countered.

He kissed my knobby knee and whispered the words I would never forget. "Every scar is a memory, Zoe, and a reminder of how strong you are, that's all. Besides, this one'll go away. I promise."

"But what if it doesn't?"

"If it doesn't? Then, it'll just be a reminder that you'll get hurt, but you'll get better too. Scars remind us we can live life without

fear because no matter what happens, we'll heal. We'll get better."
Dad's eyes watered as he stood and walked away.

While I wished to see my father again, I feared I never would.

Dad stood in the corner of the tattoo parlor, ignoring the scene taking place before him.

"Are you sure you don't wanna watch, Dad?" I teased.

"Definitely not. I can't control what you do to your body now that you're an adult, but that doesn't mean I have to watch it." He didn't look up from the magazine he was pretending to read.

I glanced over at Dani and smiled. "This is so awesome!" We giggled and whined as we got our matching tattoos. Dad only participated out of guilt for forgetting my eighteenth birthday, as he had other birthdays. I took less offense as the years passed, knowing he was a royal mess when it came to Mom, whose birthday was the day before mine.

The memories disintegrated into anger, sorrow, fear, and loneliness that gripped my heart and tugged on it as though they were trying to remove it from my chest completely. I dropped to my knees in the snow and gasped for air as my heart fractured. The tears I'd been fighting for days broke free, searing down my cold cheeks. I was exhausted and alone, left with no other option than to face the harsh reality that my dad was likely gone.

Would he ever again utter words of wisdom to me or shake his head disapprovingly? Would he ever again touch my face, stroke my hair, or tell me how beautiful I was and how much I reminded him of the mother I'd never really known? Would I ever again feel the strength of his arms around me or hear his deep voice rumbling when he scolded me or told me to stop being so dramatic?

If I ever loved a man or had children, would they ever know the person who had raised me, had loved me in his own way, and had done everything he could to take care of me on his own? Would my dad ever see the woman I would become?

I feared I would never see my father again, and the thought shattered my heart into a thousand pieces.

My world shrank, becoming small and empty as my fears seemed more and more like reality. I wished Jason were with me to tell me it would be okay, but even he wouldn't know what to say. He never did.

December 18, 1:00 PM
From: Zoe Cartwright
To: Danielle O'Connor
Subject: Checking in...

Hey D,

We heard the man on the radio again today. He sounded very serious, but I guess with recent news, I'd sound like that too.

He said that at least 87% of Americans are dead, and that the rate is still climbing. How does he know this, and how exactly are we alive again? I mean, I know they say it's because most of us have already had the H1N1 Virus, but seriously, what are the odds? And what about the rest of the world? He said 845 people are alive and well at the Colony, and more are arriving every day. All sane people are welcome.

Dave still isn't really talking to me, but I'm hoping to leave within the next couple of days. I figure we can head to Sarah's house in St. Louis as long as we have enough fuel. I hope we don't run into any "Crazies" as you called them, and I hope you're finding a lot of survivors (sane ones).

I'd better go. Dave keeps hollering that there are strange noises coming from outside, but I don't hear anything. Now that I'm wearing the pants around here, I guess I get to go check it out. Yay.

Zoe

13

DANI

Cam's tacky fingers tangled in my hair, forcing me closer to him. Usually I would've found the experience enjoyable, but his extreme and evident deadness combined with his uncommon aggression marred the interaction. A lot.

"No Cam!" I screamed and beat against his decaying chest. "You're dead! Cam! Please..." He pulled me closer, threatening to assault me with his melting lips, and I screamed. It was the same blood-curdling scream I'd voiced in my nightmares every night since his death.

Abruptly, Cam was gone. In fact, all of my surroundings had changed. I was now immersed in a vast, misty grayness. A tall man's silhouette was visible a dozen feet away, the only distinct thing in the all-encompassing gray fog.

"Who are you?" I asked. I'd never before been a lucid dreamer, but I seemed to be developing a knack for it.

The mysterious guy startled me by answering, "I'm sorry. I don't think you're ready yet." He sounded so sincere.

Drenched in cold sweat, I started awake. I sat up, my heart beating rapidly. I could feel Jack's head resting on my ankle and could see the faint glint from his eyes in the darkness.

Chris, tangled in the sheets next to me, groaned with frustration. "D'you have another one?" she croaked.

"Yeah," I said hoarsely. "Sorry. It's just so real. Why is this happening? Why is he always…why do I keep…why…" I trailed off into heaving, silent sobs.

Jack whined and scooted further up the bed until he was cuddled next to my hip.

Chris's hand began the increasingly familiar, slow backrub. "Hush now, hon. Hush," she soothed, her voice and touch noticeably easing my turmoil. Sometimes, especially when she was comforting me, her Midwestern upbringing truly shone. I was certain she contained some sort of emotion-drawing, mind-cleansing magic.

Eventually sleep reclaimed me.

The following morning, after consecutive nights of poor sleep, I was feeling restless and ornery. We'd finally arrived at our destination—a winery—and the estate's huge, white Victorian farmhouse loomed ahead. I hopped out of the Humvee, grateful the lengthy drive from Longview to some Podunk Oregon town was over, and looking around, I stretched my legs. Along with the dense woods surrounding the manicured grounds, the house oozed the potential for ghosts and creepiness…or Crazies.

It's not like I've been sleeping well anyway, I thought, glaring at the beautifully maintained building.

"So, isn't this place great?" John eagerly asked Cece. He'd suggested we stay at the winery, claiming it was "the coolest place in Gold Hill."

I rolled my eyes as I stretched, sickened by John's desire for Cece. In fact, anyone's desire for the petite but impossibly curvy woman made me want to vomit. Repeatedly.

Studying John, I wondered if I was judging him too harshly. It was entirely possible that he sincerely cared for Cece and wanted to comfort her—her search group had found her sister's body in Portland the previous afternoon. Kasey obviously hadn't died of the Virus—according to Jason, she'd been inhumanly sliced up. Strangely, seeing her sister's mutilated corpse hadn't seemed to affect Cece; she was still throwing herself at Jason, John, and anyone else with a penis. I had tried to express my condolences, but I'd been worse than shut down; I'd been ignored.

Jason exited the same vehicle as Cece and ordered a security search. Ky, along with Hunter and Dalton, two of the Army Rangers, immediately headed for the house with weapons at the ready.

Instantly and irrationally peeved, I closed the distance to Jason. "If there are people in there, you know they now have no option other than being hostile," I stated quietly. I hesitated, uncomfortable going against Jason's judgment, then continued, "I mean, they might be regular people like us, not Crazies or violent on their own, but with our guns in their faces…"

He stared back with eyes that could have been carved from an iceberg.

"Come on, Jason! You can't believe everyone is trying to kill us—we can't just go around threatening to hurt every person we come across." Running my fingers through my slightly tangled curls, I glared up at him.

"I won't let you make us into *them*, into those crazy people," I hissed, standing on tiptoes to get closer to his stony expression. "I won't let you hurt good people who're just trying to survive."

At first Jason's only response was a slight flare of his nostrils. A tiny twitch at the corner of his mouth followed a moment later.

"And what will you do to me, Red, if I don't change my evil ways?"

I poked his annoyingly firm chest as I stuttered for an adequate threat. "I'll…I'll…"

His arrogant almost-smile spurred me on. "I'll spit in your food, but only sometimes, so you won't know! And…I'll put my dirty socks in your bed!" I toed his boot with my own to make the threat sink in.

With utter seriousness he said, "That's disgusting…although—"

His response was cut short by the approach of the recently dispatched scouting trio.

Jason leaned down and whispered near my ear, "If those socks are still on your feet…" He held my gaze as he stepped back a few paces. "I'll keep your *suggestion* in mind."

I looked down to hide my suddenly burning face. *Damn him!*

"All clear," Ky reported. He looked like he was trying really hard to not focus on Jason and me—a difficult task considering he was talking *to* Jason.

After shooting me one last frustrated look, Jason addressed the whole group. "Alright, listen up. Grab your shit, and find a roommate and a room. You have until tomorrow morning to yourselves. Just stay within sight and sound of the house."

I held back, waiting for the clustered bodies to clear away from the trunk before grabbing my pack and duffel bag. Chris waited slightly off to the side with her things.

"Roomies?" I asked her once I'd retrieved my bags.

She snorted, "As if I'd sentence anyone else to your pointy elbows!"

Offended, I rubbed my left elbow with my free hand. It wasn't *that* pointy. "At least I don't tear the blankets away from you—you practically mummify yourself every night!"

"I do not!" Chris exclaimed. She pointed to Cece, who was

hurrying toward the red, barn-shaped winery. "Maybe you'd rather room with her?"

We shared a speculative look, watched Cece stalk away, and exploded in uncontrollable laughter. The idea was just too ridiculous.

Wiping happy tears from my eyes, I repositioned my bags and elbowed Chris gently. "C'mon, let's grab a room before all the good ones are taken." Calling Jack to join us, we hustled into the house.

Fifteen minutes later, I was exploring the winery with my dog. Huge steel tanks, presumably filled with liquid happiness, occupied the cavernous space. I passed them by, hoping to find where the bottled wines were stored so I could bring an armful of them up to share with Chris. And maybe Jason. If he was nice.

Jack scurried around the nearby alcoves, sniffing everything his nose could reach. All *I* could smell was wine and oak.

Entering a smaller, darker room, I heard a muffled noise—a scuffle of shoes, a rustle of clothing.

I paused in the open doorway, but Jack didn't. He stalked into a room that reminded me of a library, but instead of shelves filled with books, there were towering rows of oak barrels on metal racks. As Jack stalked down the main aisle, silent as a wolf, he abruptly halted, and his ears perked up. He was staring into one of the dark recesses on the right. Too curious to resist, I quietly followed his path, stopping beside him to peer into the shadows. I'd found the cause of the noise.

Cece was there…and Jason. Barely ten feet away, he stood with his back against the wall, his face tilted up slightly. His expression, with closed eyes and parted lips, turned my insides molten. In front of him, Cece's mouth was latched onto his neck like she was an oversized leech, and she was murmuring and moaning. Her arm was working methodically, and I didn't need to be any closer to know which of Jason's appendages she grasped in her hand.

I squelched my churning emotions, an extremely uncomfortable mixture of arousal and disgust, but couldn't tear myself from the scene. Like watching a car crash, I stood by, stared, and felt despicable.

To my unmitigated horror, a deep, menacing rumble began in Jack's chest.

Like lightning, Jason's eyes were open and boring intensely into mine. He inhaled sharply and seized Cece's arm with one hand, the back of her neck with the other, immobilizing her.

Seeing his eyes open and focused on me, I froze for the briefest of moments. Then I fled. I sprinted back out the way I'd come in, not stopping until I was in my shared bedroom. Panting, I leaned against the door.

"I really…need…some wine…like…right now," I told a startled Chris between breaths.

She shrugged. "Sounds good to me." She set aside the laptop and hustled from the room. Minutes later, she returned with four different bottles of wine and two enormous glasses.

"Well, hon, what'll it be?" she asked, displaying her spoils like she was hawking fake designer bags on a street corner.

"Is there a red? A really big, really fat red?"

Once I had a generously filled wine glass, I proceeded to describe the whole sickening encounter in the winery. If I held back my inappropriate, voyeuristic response, well, some things are just too embarrassing to admit out loud.

Date: December 18, 3:00 PM
From: Danielle O'Connor
To: Zoe Cartwright
Subject: Eyeball vomit

Zo,

Pervy Dave is lucky that Jason wasn't sitting near me reading your email over my shoulder. He's been known to try, the nosy slime ball! But Dave stopped, right? He didn't try to force you or anything, did he? I'm learning how to fight, so I could kick his ass for you if he did.

Holy crap! You're like a member of the X-men! You see people's memories? Seriously Zo, you're like a goddess. It's kind of awesome...except for the part where Dave is such a pervert and has creepy sexual memories playing through his head. But they are his memories. I mean, I have lusty imaginings I wouldn't want anyone else to see either.

But now Dave is being a baby? He's just pissed at you for denying him. I think you should do two things: 1) hide or throw away all of the booze (I'd vote for hiding it) and 2) tell him about your amazing new talent. Maybe knowing what really happened will make him act like less of an uber-douche dickhead. If he really cares about you, which you seem to know because of your super-power, then he shouldn't react too badly, right?

Besides, the longer you wait to tell him, the worse of a betrayal he'll feel. He'll think back, Zo, and based on your reactions, he'll know that you were seeing into his innermost thoughts and feelings. I really think that if you ever want him to know, you should tell him (and probably Sarah) as soon as possible.

So, we're over halfway to Bodega Bay! Yay! We're actually in Gold Hill, a one-gas-station town in Oregon. Unfortunately, we're staying here for three nights and two whole search days because it's the hometown of John AND Hunter. Apparently they've been friends for, like, ever. At least we have a neat place to stay...a winery!

I have a feeling that tonight is going to be pretty wild, especially since we've barely been here for an hour and most of us are already nursing open wine bottles (notice my use of "us"). I'm currently working on my second large glass of Merlot and feeling quite happy about it.

To answer your question about Jason's strategy, he really does have a good reason for the slow pace. I guess he made an agreement with everyone who came along, thinking numbers would bring safety. He doesn't want to split us up. He says we'd all be too vulnerable then, especially at night. At least that's his reasoning.

On a totally different subject, I keep dreaming of Cam. Maybe nightmaring is a better word. He's always dead, and he's always rotting, but he's still talking to me. Still touching me. It's HORRIBLE. He forces me to kiss him and asks why I don't want to be with him, why I left him. But last night it was weird...there was another man. He was tall, but that was all I could see because he was sort of hidden. The thing is, when he showed up, Cam disappeared. Crazy, huh?

Oh, um...gotta go. I'll continue later if I can...

Dani

I inched down the creaky stairs. Twice, the sound of shattering glass gave me pause during the descent. Jack's taut body leaned against my leg, and he whined softly with each step. Three voices grew discernible from the room at the bottom of the stairs—Jason, Hunter, and Cece.

"She needs to leave…she's a *hazard.* This is *our* group, and *she's* not one of us," Cece stated heatedly.

Hunter reasoned, "C'mon, Cece, you can't really blame her for—"

"Of course I can!" she interrupted, her outburst slurred. "Can't you see it? She ruined *everything*! A day earlier and Kasey'd still be alive! *Dani*," my name was spat out like a curse, "made us wait. *She* made us too late! *She* killed my sister!"

Jason's even voice came next. "Cece, calm the fuck down. You chose—"

"Jason," I interrupted, exiting the stairwell with my dog.

Jason held my gaze with unexpected emotion: worry and guilt. It took minimal consideration to understand that he hadn't wanted me to overhear the exchange. He'd have kept the incident from me completely if he'd had his way. I wished he'd stop sheltering me like the little girl he'd once known. She was long gone.

"If you have a problem with me, talk to me," I told Cece, who looked smug…not to mention a little unsteady on her feet.

"Talk to *you*? Fine," Cece seethed. "*You* are the reason my sister was murdered. If we'd gotten to Portland a day sooner, she'd still be alive. With *me*. But you killed her because you're *weak*. You couldn't get over your stupid dead *boyfriend*, so we all had to stay and wait for poor little *you* to get better. WELL GUESS WHAT?! YOUR STUPID FUCKING WEAKNESS KILLED MY SISTER! YOU KILLED HER, AND I'D GIVE ANYTHING FOR YOU TO BE DEAD INSTEAD!"

Stunned, I let my fiery Irish side kick in and forfeited control of my mouth. "At least *I* mourned my dead. You really looked like the grieving sister while you had your hand down Jason's pants out in the winery! I might be weak, but at least I'm not a slut. Your sister dies, and all you can think about is the next guy you're gonna bang. You *disgust* me."

Cece took several steps closer and hissed, "bitch," right before she slapped me across the face. Hard.

I covered my stinging cheek with one hand as Jason maneuvered between us, attempting to block the irate woman from reaching me again. I worked my jaw slowly, surprised by how badly it hurt.

"Back the fuck off!" Jason growled at Cece, his voice slicing through the tense atmosphere like a blade.

She backed up and continued her tirade. "You know what? Everyone else'll blame you too. Know why? Because it's *your fault.* All the murders and suicides...we could've saved them if we'd been quicker, if we hadn't waited for *you.* You should just leave!"

I stepped out from Jason's protective barrier. "I'm sure you're used to getting whatever you want," I told Cece. *Like Jason,* I thought and glanced angrily at the man trying to protect me. "You think I'll just bow out and let you walk all over me. Well you can go to hell. I'm sure you're expected."

Straight-backed and only a little hurried, I ascended the stairs to my room. Once I was alone, shielded by the closed door, I began to cry.

Date: December 18, 4:30 PM
From: Danielle O'Connor
To: Zoe Cartwright
Subject: Am I a Murderer?

Zo,

Sorry I had to end that last email so abruptly. There was an incident downstairs. Cece was raging about how I needed to leave the group because I caused the death of her sister. You see, everyone had to stay in Seattle longer than planned. Because of me...because it took me a few days to recuperate...and Cece's sister was murdered only a day or two before we found her. Jason said it was brutal, almost impossible to look at. If they hadn't waited around for me to regain my strength, Cece might've made it to her sister in time to prevent the murder.

So now I sit here, writing to you and watching Jack's worried doggy face as he whimpers at me. Oddly, I feel like he's telling me, "bite, attack, kill," not, "I feel sad." Now why would I think that?

I feel like crap. I'm going to finish this bottle of wine and then try to fall asleep. Hopefully I won't dream for once.

Dani

14

ZOE

Still shaking from the cold, I wrapped the army-green wool blanket more tightly around me. As I watched our new military acquaintances settle in for the evening, I leaned against the arm of the shabby, apple-red loveseat and soaked up heat from the fire. It felt like a weight had been lifted off my shoulders—a weight I hadn't realized I'd been carrying. We were no longer alone.

Since their arrival, the group of three had transformed our kitchen into a makeshift command post. They hustled around like bees readying the hive for a queen, rattling off commands and acronyms I didn't understand. They seemed capable and in control, a façade I struggled to maintain.

"The signal's too spotty—I can't hold a connection," Biggs announced as he searched for a specific radio frequency. He shifted from one computer screen to another fluidly, like he was performing a dance he'd practiced a thousand times. I envied him; he had a sense of purpose, a duty to uphold, and he did so without hesitation. They all did.

"Hopefully it's just the storm. We'll have to wait until it passes. Keep it on this channel. If someone tries to communicate from Fort

Knox again, I want to know about it," Lieutenant Sanchez said, her voice calm and collected. She was busy jotting down notes, sketching on maps, and strategizing for their departure in only a day's time.

Biggs's fingers pecked at a keyboard efficiently. "I'll check the satellite again. Maybe the storm will pass sooner than we thought."

"Here," a pleasant, confident voice said, pulling me from my thoughts. I looked up to see Harper's outreached hand, offering me a cup of tea. He smelled of rubbing alcohol and mint.

"Thanks." I nodded at him gratefully and accepted the steaming cup with numb hands. The hot ceramic stung my frozen fingers, but the smell of chamomile tea conjured thoughts of Grams, making my discomfort bearable.

"Are you warming up?" Harper's smile was kind and sincere as he stood across from me and sipped from his own mug. Shaking his head, he sat down on the edge of the couch opposite mine. "I still can't believe you heard us outside."

"I didn't hear you. Dave did, miraculously," I scoffed, thinking of Dave's drunken state. I sipped the scalding liquid. It burned when it touched my lips, but I welcomed the heat as it warmed my body from the inside out.

"I was surprised to see you outside with so little on." Harper's eyes surveyed my now blanket-covered body. "We thought you were crazy at first." He winked and leaned back, relaxing for the first time since their arrival.

My heart skipped a beat as I considered the strange sensations I'd been experiencing. *If you only knew…*

"Yeah, well, I guess I wasn't thinking clearly. But I'm getting warm now, finally." I closed my eyes, appreciating the heat that licked up the side of my face from the fire. The chill in my bones was smothered for the time being, only to be replaced with exhaustion.

Sarah loudly repositioned herself on the couch as she realized Harper was sitting beside her.

"You're a fast reader," Harper observed, looking at a stack of books on the coffee table. A smirk formed on his face as he read the titles…one love story after another.

"Yeah." She smiled, but didn't look away from her novel.

"Thanks for the great dinner by the way. I can't remember the last time I had ravioli." Harper was trying to strike up a conversation with Sarah, but she continued reading with a dismissive nod.

"It's her sixth book this week," I explained. "She gets sucked in. It's like she suddenly has a passion for reading or something." I looked at my friend, who was nestled against the arm of the couch. "What are you reading this time?"

"Science-Fiction. Apocalyptic, ironically," she clarified absent-mindedly. Her eyes focused on the end of a sentence, and then she turned the page.

"So you're a book lover." Harper seemed interested, as if he'd found some common ground. I wondered if he was attracted to her. It wouldn't be surprising—her brown eyes were glittering in the glow from the fire, and her curly hair was a perfect tangle of seductive femininity.

"Book lover?" she practically snorted. "Not until recently. In fact, I don't think I've ever read this much in my life."

"Well, a lot's happened in the last few weeks. We all cope with things in different ways. Maybe your way is reading—escaping to a world different from your own. Although apocalyptic stories seem to defeat the purpose." Harper smirked, looking over at me.

"And how is it you all find yourselves here, in our seemingly abandoned neck of the woods?" I asked. We were seven miles from town and at least a mile from any neighboring properties.

With a sigh, Harper took a sip of coffee and thought for a moment. "We've been trying to stay away from heavily populated areas. It's safer that way…," he trailed off. He stared into the flickering flames until something clanging in the kitchen brought him out of his daydream. Glancing at me, he asked, "What about you, Zoe? How are you doing with all this?"

"Oh, you mean between the end of the world, people I care about dying, Crazies, animal attacks, Sammy dying, and my missing family?" I was being dramatic, my tone borderline hysterical. I shrugged. "Oh, I don't know; I haven't had much time to think about it," I joked bitterly, curling deeper into my spot on the couch.

"You and Dave haven't been getting along very well," Sarah chimed in from the corner of the couch.

She chooses now to say something? And what's that have to do with anything anyways?

"What's going on with you two?" Her eyebrows rose in curiosity.

I wanted to reach over and wring her neck for providing Harper the opportunity to ask me unwelcome questions, but I instinctively knew she'd meant no harm. "It's complicated. But I think it's safe to say he's realizing we're better as…friends." *If that's even what we are.*

My eyes darted to my captive audience, hoping they'd be satisfied with such a vague explanation. Sarah seemed unconcerned with my answer, but Harper's grin had grown wide and knowing.

"Sounds like a lot's been going on lately," Harper observed. "Maybe you could use a distraction."

His eyes fixed upon me like a predator's on delectable prey. *Is he referring to friendship or sex? He couldn't possibly mean sex…*

Harper was hot, but it was ridiculous to think he'd proposition me in front of other people. Rationality vanished as my eyes inspected every inch of him, starting with his golden-brown skin and muscular build—he definitely intrigued me. Harper was friendly and fun, a change I welcomed. Unlike Sanchez and Biggs, whose noses were buried deep in their work, he was personable, taking the time to get to know us. His amiable persona made it easy to forget he was military trained and could probably kill someone with his bare hands. *Not all military men are rough around the edges like Jason,* I reminded myself.

"A distraction?" I asked, needing clarification before I lost myself in thought.

"Yeah, a distraction." His dark eyebrows danced over his green eyes. There was no misinterpreting his meaning. *Sex. Definitely sex.*

Biggs snorted as he sat at the kitchen table behind Sarah, shaking his head. "You'll have to excuse Harper. He isn't always as smooth as he thinks he is."

"I'm not trying to be smooth. I'm being honest, realistic, human…take your pick," Harper retorted. "I put myself out there with no expectations, no false pretenses. If she's interested, fun times ahead, and if not, that's fine too. Life's too short to pussyfoot around."

Shocked by the confirmation that I *had* just been solicited in front of the others, I looked back into the inquiring eyes of my new, very forward friend. I cleared my throat, seriously considering his pitch and trying to find the right words to respond. "Well, your um…*offer* is very flattering. I'll keep it in mind."

Harper studied me for a moment, assessing my hesitation. "You do that." Winking again, he finished off the contents of his mug and stood. "I think you and I will get along just fine, Baby Girl."

With a thud, Biggs dropped his backpack onto the ground beside me, and Sarah's bright eyes glanced up at him. Eager to refocus everyone's attention, I quickly asked, "What about you, Biggs? Do you like reading as much as Sarah here?"

Indifferent to my smart ass tone, he said thoughtfully, "I do, actually. But, I don't get to read as much as I'd like, unfortunately. Since this—" he searched for the word.

"Ending," Sarah chimed in again.

"What?" Biggs looked at her curiously.

"The Ending. This is the ending of the world as we know it. I mean, it's literal I guess, but it makes sense."

"Yeah, I guess it does. Well, since this 'Ending' I haven't had any free time to read."

I gestured to the stack of novels on the table. "I'm sure you can borrow one of Sarah's books," I suggested. "She won't mind."

Harper returned with his mug refilled. Again studying the titles on the spines, he chuckled. "Yeah man, there are some romances in there. You could probably learn a thing or two." He looked from Sarah to Biggs and shook his head when he noticed his friend gazing intently at the brown-haired beauty.

"Sure you can. I'm not sure what you like to read, but they aren't *all* romances." Sarah's eyes flicked indignantly to Harper before returning to Biggs. "You're welcome to borrow any of them," she offered. As Biggs bent over to look through the pile, I sat back contentedly and watched.

There was a sense of hope and excitement coursing through the room as a silent conversation passed between the soldier and my friend. It was a nice diversion.

"Anyway," Harper said, reclaiming his spot on the couch beside Sarah. "I took a look at Dave's legs. He's doing really well, Zoe. I think you did a great job dressing his wounds." He sighed, leaning forward to rest his elbows on his knees.

I set down my tea. The palms of my hands were sweaty from the warm mug. "I couldn't have done it without Sarah's help. That girl has a way with gauze that I'll never have."

"Don't let her fool you. I barely did anything. I throw up at the sight of blood," Sarah added, quickly looking back up to Biggs with wide, horrified eyes. "I mean, not really *throw up*, but..."

"Well either way, you should be proud of yourselves. You probably saved his legs." Harper leaned back and took a deep breath. Under his playboy exterior, he was a medic first, an exhausted one.

"How's he doing anyway? I mean, other than his legs." I felt foolish not asking Dave myself, but I knew it was pointless—he wouldn't forgive me for a while. *He's always been egocentric,* I reminded myself. I knew I'd have to tell him what was happening to me soon if I wanted to salvage whatever remained of our friendship.

"He's better now that I got the alcohol away from him. He's sleeping it off. So, we'll see how he's *really* doing tomorrow." Rubbing his hand over his short, dark hair, Harper stifled a yawn.

I glanced around the room and realized Sanchez and Biggs were finally digging into plates piled with ravioli. Examining their tired expressions, I asked, "When was the last time any of you got some rest?"

Shoving a fork full of pasta into his mouth, Biggs muttered, "It's been a while."

Setting her book down, Sarah's attention was on Biggs again. "How long were you out there before you saw the smoke from our chimney?"

"About a day or so," Biggs answered. "We've been trying to stay out of the towns. The last time we ventured into one we lost members of our team." With his words, a black cloud seemed to settle over the room.

"We haven't seen any uninfected for two days," Sanchez explained from the table.

"Uninfected? You mean 'Crazies'?" I asked.

"Crazies, sick…anyone not normal," Sanchez clarified sharply. "We knew this might be our only chance to regroup." Frowning, she continued, "It's hard to know what to expect, so we aren't taking any unnecessary chances." Looking at her plate, she grumbled, "Not anymore."

Abruptly, Sanchez stood and carried her empty dish to the sink to submerge it in water; she took her time before joining Harper, Sarah, and me by the fire. "Up until a couple days ago, there were nine of us. We lost our commanding officer to a group of looters."

"There were just so many of them," Biggs interjected, still seated at the kitchen table.

"I don't know if they were infected," Sanchez continued, "but they were definitely insane. They ambushed us and tried to steal everything we had. We were able to fight them off long enough to regroup." Peering up into Harper's solemn eyes, she sighed. "It's hard to know what to expect. Everything's different now."

Sanchez looked back at me. "We thought we'd killed them all, but then another wave of them showed up. Our CO and two others were killed, and we lost two soldiers to the Virus before that. There hasn't been a lot of time for resting," she said flatly.

"As you can imagine, there aren't many warm places to stop in an area like this. We hoped the occupants of this cabin were dead, no offense. We weren't sure what we'd find inside when we saw the blood on the porch," she admitted. "Is that a body wrapped up out there?"

Sarah's high, defensive tone startled me. "It's Sammy. The weather's been too bad. We haven't been able to bury him."

"Sammy was Dave's dog," I explained.

"It's not like *we're* crazy or anything." Sarah looked over at Biggs, who was just finishing up his dinner.

His blue eyes were sympathetic as he nodded in understanding.

"We know that now," Sanchez whispered.

A deafening silence filled the room. The memory of fallen friends and lost loved ones colored everyone's faces—dark circles, worry lines, and creased foreheads created a painting of grief. The sorrow-laden air was overwhelming. The others' raging turmoil swelled inside me, fighting for control. Tears crept into my eyes, but I forced them to retreat.

While everyone's thoughts lingered in the past, something pricked my senses, and I suddenly felt self-conscious. I looked over to see Sanchez's eyes transfixed on me. Their intensity was disconcerting, and she wouldn't look away. *She couldn't possibly know there's something wrong with me*, I tried to rationalize, but I wasn't sure of anything anymore.

Refocusing on the crackling fire, I cleared my throat to speak. "Well, I'm glad you're all here." *Except for Sanchez, maybe.* "We weren't sure what to do next."

Sarah nodded, absentmindedly stroking the scratches on the back of her wrist that she'd received while trying to save Sammy.

I suppressed a smile and chose my next words carefully. "Sarah, you keep touching the scrapes on your arm. Are they bothering you? I thought I saw blood…" Feigning concern, I looked at her barely marred skin. *Sell it*, I coached myself, knowing that if I could get Biggs's attention, he'd take the bait.

"I'm fine, Zoe." Sarah's eyes were wide with confusion, and her ears were red with embarrassment. "It's just a small scratch." But before she could say another word, Biggs appeared behind her.

Victory! I smiled proudly and leaned back to observe the fruits of my labor.

"Can I take a look?" Biggs pointed to her right arm.

Cranking her head to the left, Sarah ended up with her face mere inches from his olive-colored belt. She looked up at him. "Oh, sure, but it's nothing, really."

Happy my scheme was working perfectly, I watched Sarah's gaze lock with the blond soldier's. The attraction between them was obvious. I could practically feel the butterflies in their stomachs, elated and flighty, as they stared at each other.

Sarah's curls bounced as she stood and followed Biggs over to the bag of medical supplies. *She reminds me of Dani.* But, unlike Sarah, Dani would've jumped at the chance to flirt with a handsome man in uniform. Still, Sarah's curls, recoiling up and down as she walked, mimicked the way Dani's fiery red locks always jostled and drew the boys' attention.

I heard a throat clear. Harper was watching me intently, one eyebrow arched. Smiling guiltily, I shrugged. "I couldn't help it. Thank God for you and your medical supplies. Perhaps she won't lose her arm after all."

"We wouldn't want that." Harper grinned and stood to stretch. "I guess I should check on our patient."

As he walked away, I felt Sanchez's eyes on me again. "Is

something wrong?" I lashed out anxiously, not sure I wanted to know the answer. I slowly turned toward her.

Standing, Sanchez shook her head. "You remind me of someone," she said as she walked away.

"*You look so much like him*," I heard and hoped I'd only imagined the woman's voice in my head.

Date: December 18, 9:00 PM
From: Zoe Cartwright
To: Danielle O'Connor
Subject: Houseguests

Hey D,

Sorry you're having such horrible nightmares. I can't imagine seeing Cam in that state. I suppose this is how your mind is dealing with everything, but it still seems a bit morbid, especially for you. Are the dreams getting any better?

As for Cece, everything about her screams "BITCH." I can't believe she's blaming everything that happened with her family on you. It's not like you have any control over other people's actions. She's the one who has a fascination with Jason. So, just remind yourself that she made the choice to stay behind with him. Don't let her take her anger out on you. None of that is your fault, D. Someone needs to slap her around a little bit.

I'm sorry your day's been so shitty. Too bad we can't finish that bottle of wine together—a nice fire, a blanket, Jack curled up at our feet...sigh. The truth is, I'm in a weird spot too, so I could really use a drink. Dave and I still aren't speaking to each other, so I haven't had a chance to tell him about my...well, superpowers. I'm planning on telling him, but so much has happened with our new houseguests showing up unexpectedly that there hasn't really been time.

Yes, I said houseguests. They're a military outfit from the East Coast. I think they're Army Rangers. They're under the leadership of a tight-lipped woman named Lieutenant Carmen Sanchez. She looks like a Latina pinup girl more than anything, but she's really serious and seems pretty badass. There are two other soldiers with her. Sergeant Dustin Harper is a medic. He's an island boy—super fit and hot, and he knows it. I think I'm gonna like having him around. I also feel much better knowing that Dave's legs aren't going to fall off. Then there's Sergeant Riley Biggs. He's the tech guy and also seems nice. He's youngish and has a baby face and very pretty blue eyes.

Our new friends couldn't have come at a better time. There are no working phones, the snowstorms haven't really let up, and Dave and I obviously aren't communicating well. With their skills and knowledge, we can finally get out of here. Thank God for generators, Internet, fire, and sporadic radio signals. I'm sure there's plenty more to be thankful for, but you get the idea.

Please be strong, D, and don't let Cece get under your skin. She'll come to her senses. If she doesn't, you better kick her ass. I'll write more tomorrow. I'm gonna put my tunes on and try to get some sleep. Hopefully your wine kicks in soon. Have sweet dreams, and give Jack a squeeze for me, or a pat...whatever he prefers.

Hasta,
Zoe

15

DANI

Cam kissed me excitedly.

I couldn't wait to be with him again. I trailed my fingers through his hair, over his shoulders, down his chest—I was not to be denied. Still locked to his lips, I began removing his t-shirt. Some of his skin followed.

I screamed.

Grasping my shoulders, he rasped, "I tried, D! I really tried to hold it together!" His arms tightened around me like a vice, squeezing the air out of my lungs. "Won't I ever be enough for you? Why'd you leave me, D? You're tearing me apart!" For emphasis, he ripped a fist-sized chunk of flesh from his chest.

"No, no, NOOOO!" I cried out in horror.

His weeping, decaying figure withered before me.

"You're dead, Cam! You left me! This isn't my fault! I wish...I wish so much that you were still here. But you're not...you died!" I turned abruptly and ran—straight into a tall, blond, mysterious man. When I glanced behind me, Cam was gone.

The mystery guy, who I somehow knew was the hidden man from the previous night's dream, raised his hands to my face. His thumbs grazed my cheeks and wiped away my desperate tears. His light skin and chin-length blond hair made him seem almost angelic, though the effect was offset by his roguish five o'clock shadow.

The rest of his fingers moved from my face until his gentle hands tangled in my hair. Compared to Cam's melting grasp, his touch was comforting...his touch was alive.

Before I knew what was happening, he was kissing me. The soft pressure of his lips against mine. The tightening of his hand behind my neck. The whisper of tangled breath.

Hesitantly, he pulled away. "Hmmm...I think you're ready," he told me with a triumphant smile. "Oh, I'm definitely going to—"

Abruptly, I woke to Jack's low growl. When I opened my eyes, I realized he was standing over me—guarding me. My heart pounded, and I tried to control my sudden need to pant. *Someone must be behind me...*

As Jack's warning sounds grew louder and more menacing, I slowly turned over. I kept my breathing even and opened my eyes the smallest possible amount, trying to maintain the impression that I was simply moving in my sleep.

Jack crouched closer over me, his growl vibrating against my torso and long strings of saliva falling from his retracted lips.

In the darkness a few feet away, a shadowy form coalesced into someone recognizable: Cece.

What the hell? Where's Chris?

Slowly, the unwelcome woman inched forward. Completely focused on staying clear of my dog, Cece was utterly unaware of my wakeful state.

Confused and afraid, I remained still in the heavy darkness.

Cece neared until she was only a foot away, and the tension in Jack's body increased, making the bed quiver. Wildly, I thought, *Why is she in here? Is she going to hurt me? A plan...I need a freaking plan!*

Before I could think of something, of anything, Cece's concealed hand came into view, and my eyes burst open. Moonlight glinted dully off a combat knife clutched in her grasp, and time seemed to stand still…

Jack's body coiled like a spring.

Cece raised the knife.

My breath caught, and I thought, *I'm going to die.*

…and then it was like the world pressed PLAY. Simultaneously, Jack lunged for Cece's knife hand, and I lashed out. My nails caught the flesh on the right side of her face, gouging a trail from eyebrow to jaw. Using the momentary advantage, I scrambled backward across the bed and fell off the opposite side. I was perfectly happy to huddle on the hardwood floor, peeking over the edge of the mattress.

Still on the bed with Cece's wrist in his mouth, Jack shook his head, and the knife clattered to the floor. I couldn't believe Cece wasn't screaming, considering the massive German Shepherd with his fangs sunk into her flesh. Instead, she started to cry.

Taking momentary pity on the woman, I commanded, "Drop it, Jack." It felt exceptionally odd telling my dog to drop a person's wrist.

He obeyed, though he retained his aggressive stance.

"Come here, Jack," I said weakly. I had to repeat the command twice before he would listen.

Finally, with the bed between my attacker and me, and with my dog by my side, I cautiously stood.

Minutes passed before Cece was able to do anything but weep. Looking through me, she mumbled, "I just wanted to see…to know…why he would…why you're…" Her pitiful attempt at an explanation faltered as her eyes focused on me.

Her expression soured, turning ripe with hatred. "You're done, *murdering bitch*. And you'll never have him!" she hissed. Pivoting unstably, she stalked out of the room.

The whole confrontation had been so quick and quiet that it

almost felt like it had been a second nightmare. Except, Cece's knife was still on the floor where she'd dropped it, the only evidence of what had just transpired...besides her wounds.

What'd she say? I'll never have Jason? I could've told her that. I sat heavily on the end of the bed after shutting the door. Unexpected laughter bubbled out of my mouth, and I could feel myself teetering on the edge of hysteria. The whole situation was unbelievably ridiculous. *Just my luck—the psycho wants to kill me, not because of her sister, but because she wants to keep me away from Jason.*

A deep, angry resentment simmered in my veins, and my laughter turned bitter. I'd been enamored of Jason, my best friend's older brother, pretty much since the first second I'd laid eyes on him as a little girl. But he'd never shown the least bit of genuine interest in me. Sure he'd flirted, stringing me along affectionately, but we both knew there was nothing behind it. *How dare he?! It's his fault Cece has it in for me!*

As my laughter died down, my thoughts turned morose. *Cam would be so pissed if I got killed because of Jason...*

Unconsciously, I wrapped my right hand around my opposite wrist. My thumb pressed into the familiar Celtic knot tattooed there, immediately evoking thoughts of Zoe. Clear reason washed over me; thinking of Zoe usually had that effect on me.

What should I do, Zo?

You get your little butt over to Jason's room and tell him what happened, that's what you do! Now! I decided that listening to my best friend, imaginary or not, was probably the wisest plan.

Tiptoeing slowly down the hallway, I wondered what I'd find in Jason's room. Would Cece already be there, weaving lies into a tangled web? Would they be locked in a passionate, nauseating embrace?

I reached the door and knocked quietly. Chris's voice, talking and laughing, was audible through the wood. "Do you think she's come back to try again?"

Jason scoffed loudly. "I doubt it—I couldn't've been any damn clearer."

The door opened, and I just stood in the hallway, staring at Chris. My lips parted in an attempt to form words, but all I could do was take jerky breaths. For some reason, seeing Chris's earnest blue eyes brought me close to tears.

"Dani?" Her jovial tone instantly melted into motherly concern. "What's wrong?" She hustled me into the room, shutting the door quietly behind her. "You must be freezing! Why aren't you wearing something warmer?"

Jason, sitting at the small table across the room, straightened. He seemed to be studying every inch of me. His eyes scanned up and down my body, never resting on one part for too long.

Numbly, I examined my state of attire. I had on my skimpiest set of post-apocalyptic sleepwear: tiny purple cotton shorts and a pale green tank top. The sudden realization that I was standing in front of Jason, barely covered, transformed the touch of his eyes. They singed trails of fire along my skin.

Before I could die of embarrassment, Chris wrapped a fuzzy, caramel-brown blanket around my shoulders. She sat with me on the foot of the full-size bed while Jack settled at our feet.

"Thank you," I said, surprised by the calm in my voice. *It's Zo*, I realized, *giving me strength.*

Still grasping my tattooed wrist, I recounted my recent confrontation with Cece. As soon as I finished talking, Chris rose and began pacing. Jason, however, remained seated at the small table, keeping his eyes locked on mine. After several long deep breaths, he opened his mouth to speak.

And the door burst open.

John and Hunter marched into the room with Cece trailing close behind. She hung back in the doorway, watching me like a cat with a cornered mouse. Slowly, the corners of her mouth twisted into a self-satisfied smirk.

Hunter, however, being entirely focused on Jason, hadn't

noticed me perched on the bed. "Sir, I know Cece was pretty cruel earlier, but that's no reason for Dani to attack her…with her dog! I mean, look at what they…," he said, trailing off when he finally noticed me.

"We had good reason," I said in chorus with a growl from Jack. Cece flinched at the sound of my dog's low rumble, making me smile inside.

"Puh-lease," Cece whined, her voice dripping with self-pity. A huge fake tear rolled down her cheek, and she winced when it crossed the angry red scratches that had been gouged by my nails. "She *attacked* me! So did her stupid mutt! Look!" She motioned to her face with her swollen, bleeding wrist, drawing attention to both of her injuries.

I rolled my eyes at the ridiculous show and embraced the cold anger crackling within me. "I defended myself, you psycho! Maybe if you hadn't been in my room *with a knife*, I never would have scratched your pretty face."

Hunter looked confused, but disbelief clouded John's expression.

Cece took a bold step into the room, and Jason exploded from his chair. In four furious strides he was in front of her, appearing larger and more dangerous than I'd ever seen him. "You are never to go near Dani again. I'm watching you. If you touch her, you're gone." I wasn't sure if 'gone' meant expelled from the group or implied a more permanent solution.

Cece cried genuinely and reached out to touch Jason's hand. "But Jase, I—"

"GET OUT!" he roared.

She did.

In the ringing silence, John surprised everyone by saying, "You can watch Cece all you want, but I'll be watching that one." His finger pointed straight to my heart. He walked out of the room, pausing in the doorway to gloat. "I hope you enjoy looking at what you can't have anymore. Cece's with me now. She *chose* me." And then he was gone.

Hunter took a single step toward the exit to follow his friend but didn't complete the action. He turned to meet Jason's eyes and then mine. "I…I'm sorry," he apologized weakly. "She lied. Said you attacked her for no reason. I don't know you very well, but I do know her—I should've known better. I assumed the worst of you, and I'm sorry. I…I hope someday you can forgive me." He hurried out of the room.

Shutting the door, Chris said conversationally, "Well, I thought that might actually end in a fight. Can you imagine? Our merry little band of travelers would completely collapse…there'd be blood…probably some of us would die…"

Ignoring her, Jason squatted down in front of me. "Why don't you lay down in here and try to get some sleep? It's just after midnight, and Chris and I still have some work to do, so…," *… we'll be here…we'll look out for you,* hung unsaid.

In the background, Chris continued talking to herself. "…At least four of the men've had their eyes on Cece…I wonder how many she'll have believing her by morning…could be difficult though…divide us further…"

"Really? I mean, um…okay," I said, accepting Jason's offer with relief. I really didn't want to be alone.

As Jason and Chris resettled at the little table in the far corner, I curled up on top of the bed's quilt, dangling my hand over the edge to rub Jack's scruff.

An hour later I was still awake, silent tears sliding across my face. I'd been crying long enough for my pillow to grow noticeably damp. *What would I do if our roles were reversed? What if Cece had caused a delay that kept me from getting to Zoe in time? What if Zoe had been murdered?*

I'd blame her. I knew it for truth the second I thought it. Guilt seemed to wrap around me, heavy and constrictive. *It's my fault.*

I tried to remain quiet, but the tears grew more insistent, demanding the participation of my whole body.

A chair creaked in the opposite corner of the room. "No," I heard Jason murmur. "I got it. Let's call it a night."

There was the scratch of chair legs on the floor, a dozen muffled steps, and the groan of the mattress depressing behind me. Remotely, I registered the sound of the door and figured Chris had left the room.

Softly, Jason touched my arm. "You okay?"

I could feel his heat radiating near my back. With only the thin blanket as cover, I was cold. It had taken the suggestion of Jason's warmth for me to notice.

I shook my head and managed to croak, "It's my fault Kasey's dead," before silent, convulsive sobs overtook me completely.

"It's *not* your fault," Jason whispered fiercely. "Cece should blame herself. She could've gone straight to Portland, but she *chose* to follow me. I'd decided to go after you hours before we left, and she knew it…and *dammit*, Dani, I'd make the same decision every time if it meant you'd survive."

I cried harder.

In a heartbeat, Jason's arms were around me, his body curled behind mine. I could feel his breath rustling my mussed curls as he promised, "She won't touch you again. I won't let her."

Finally, warmth! I thought ecstatically as he held me tightly against him. Once again, I felt like I was in the protective embrace of a warrior—vengeful and fearsome. Slowly, my sobs died down, and I fell asleep.

When I woke, the pale light of the December morning poured through lacy curtains, illuminating a white-washed dresser and rickety oak table on the opposite side of the room. I was nestled against Jason's relaxed body—my head rested on his chest and my arm draped haphazardly across his middle. His heart beat loudly beneath my ear, far too rapidly for someone still sleeping. One of his arms was hooked around my back, allowing his hand to grasp my waist. The other moved gently as he twirled one of my stray crimson curls. At some point during the chilly night he had covered us both with an antique patchwork quilt.

Oh. My. God. I'm cuddling with Jason! Umm...uh... My thoughts faded to incoherency as I pretended I was one of the women Jason truly desired, not just one he comforted out of pity.

I hesitantly looked up at him, and as soon as our eyes met, the tranquil expression slid off his face. *He didn't know I was awake,* I noted, disappointed. *He was probably imagining I was someone else, too.*

"Are you feeling better?" he asked softly. The handsome face gazing at me could have been carved from marble for all of the emotion it showed.

I nodded.

Seconds later, Jason extracted himself from our tangled position, and I was suddenly cold and alone on the bed. "Well, um," he said gruffly, "we should get ready." He disappeared out the bedroom door, letting Chris slide in.

"I see you're up," she said, and the day began.

Date: December 19, 8:00 AM
From: Danielle O'Connor
To: Zoe Cartwright
Subject: Drama, drama, and more drama!

Hi Zo,

So, wow...you've got some visitors. Do you think you'll all stay together? I'm glad you have some more people to interact with. I know you were getting pretty frustrated with Dave. And they're military people so they can do a really good job of keeping you safe. That makes me super happy!

Okay, I've got a lot to tell you, but I don't have much time. I apologize in advance for the potential incoherency of this email.

First, Cece sort of attacked me last night while I was sleeping. She seems to think that, along with killing her sister, I'm out to take Jason away from her. Too bad for her, he's already gone. Not that he's with me...he's just not with her. Ha!

Anyway, John is apparently her boy toy now, and he jumps at her every whim. Since he woke this morning, he's been trying to convince members of our group to blame me for pretty much every death not caused by the virus. He and Cece have managed to sway a few other guys to their way of thinking. She's eerily good at manipulating people...well, guys mostly. Maybe she trades them sexual favors or something?

K, I know you tend to get weirded out when I gush about your brother...which is understandable, but you're the only best friend I've got (lucky you!), so suck it up and listen. Yeah, umm...Jason slept with me. I mean, like sleep slept. I was crying, he comforted me, and then we just fell asleep. Really, NOTHING happened. Just cuddling, I promise. Though my stomach does get kind of fluttery when I think about it. But that's bad, right? I mean, so soon after Cam? Besides, wanting Jason means almost certain misery—he's like a Venus Flytrap for women. You can stop gagging now...

Also man-related, there's a mysterious guy who keeps showing up in my horrible Cam dreams...and he sort of kissed me before I woke up last night. I didn't mean for it to happen. Oh my God, why am I even talking about this—he's not real!

My thoughts are too chaotic…I need you to tell me what the hell is going on in my head. How could I possibly dream of kissing some strange man when Cam has barely been gone for 10 days? How could I even consider being excited about cuddling with another guy? What the hell is wrong with me? I loved Cam! I know I did—I still do! Agghhhh! I miss you and need your amazing insight. Like, a lot.

Ciao,
Dani

16

ZOE

Date: December 19, 11:00 AM
From: Zoe Cartwright
To: Danielle O'Connor
Subject: I'm telling Dave tonight and Cece is a BITCH

Hey D,

First of all, I really want to beat the shit out of Cece. Just thinking about her makes me want to punch something. Got a picture and some darts? It could be therapeutic...I'm just saying.

Oh, and under NO circumstances should you be held responsible for anyone's death, D. No matter what Cece or any of her tools say. I'm so frustrated that you're even in this situation. Nothing that's happened in this goddamn apocalypse is your fault! Trust me.

As for helping you interpret your chaotic feelings, I'm not sure what I can do. I know you loved Cam, so I can't even imagine how difficult it is for you to be away from him. I'm sure the fact that he never liked Jason makes all of this even harder. But, I also know you've always had feelings for Jason. It doesn't surprise me that you're battling feelings for him now. You're only human, D. I say just go with the flow. Just be careful. I know that probably isn't very helpful. And kissing this MG (mystery guy)? Well, you gotta get action somewhere (kidding). I wouldn't worry too much about it. It is just a dream.

Unlike the soap opera you're starring in, there's nothing too crazy going on over here. Sarah and Biggs are batting eyes at each other, and Sanchez and Harper are hard at work mapping out a route to Fort Knox. Apparently, we're headed to Kentucky, and yes, I said "we." We've decided to stick together, and I'm really happy about it. Anyway, Sanchez thinks there are more military personnel there and that it would be a good idea to team up with them.

On the Dave front...he's still ignoring me. The bitchy side of me wants to say "screw you, get over yourself," but I need to patch things up with him. If I don't, I know I'll regret it later. It's not like I have a plethora of friends and can afford to burn bridges. I've decided I'm going to talk to him today. I just have to wait for the right time, whenever that might be. I'm not really looking forward to it...at all. I'll keep you posted. Wish me luck! This could turn out really good or REALLY bad.

Remember to keep Jack with you at all times, and stay away from Cece. SHE'S THE DEVIL!

Hasta,

Zoe

After taking my third shot in an hour, I could feel liquid courage seeping its way into my body. As Harper dealt a fifth hand of poker to Sarah and me, I tried not to think about how Dave would react when I told him the truth about what was wrong with me. I wasn't sure if I wanted the others to know about my strange ability, and I wondered if he would tell them.

What if they banish me from the group? I was probably over-thinking everything, but I couldn't help it. Booze tended to jump start my dramatic tendencies.

I'd planned on confronting Dave right after I woke, but the

potential repercussions had frightened me into silence. Not sure what to do, I'd turned to one of the bottles of Tequila we'd hidden from Dave. I'd needed to settle my nerves, knowing the talk would happen sooner rather than later.

Part of me pondered the probability that he would be disgusted or think I was a liar. But another part of me—the enlightened, drunk Zoe—was sure he'd gather me into his arms and tell me we'd figure out what was happening together. I wanted him to tell me everything would be okay.

Tossing the playing cards onto the coffee table in victory, I pulled my right leg into my chest and rested my chin on my knee. My insides were warm and coated with temporary liberation.

"You win again, my raven-haired friend." Harper winked at me and excused himself to grab another drink.

As I worked up the nerve to talk to Dave, I recalled the many times he'd come to my rescue. Not just in my weakest moments, but by being my friend and confidant in Dani's absence. Dave had picked me up and taken care of me after my wisdom teeth had been removed. He'd given me tickets to the Smithsonian after my first exhibit opening, and he'd taken me to the National Arboretum to see the redwoods; I'd always missed them, being away from home.

Although cocky and self-centered, Dave was a good guy, and remembering his kindness gave me the fortitude to tell him everything. *Right now*, I rallied.

He'd limped his way outside moments before, and if I didn't act fast, I would miss my opportunity to be alone with him. Standing from my warm perch by the fire, I stumbled slightly before catching myself on the arm of the sofa. Harper's arm found its way around my shoulders, holding me upright. Wide-eyed, I looked up at him, wondering what his strong hands might feel like on the small of my back.

I shook my head.

"You okay, Baby Girl?" His eyes darkened as we both considered our proximity. *Baby Girl, again?* I tried to be annoyed, but I was lost in his asking eyes.

I'm drunk. I smiled and straightened myself. "Yeah, I just stood up too fast. Thanks."

Inching backward to remove myself from his enticing hold, I continued toward the front door. I could still feel the heat of Harper's gaze as I walked away, but he said nothing.

"Where're you going?" Sanchez inquired as she stepped out from the hallway. Her hair was down, and she wore a tank top and sweatpants. I was surprised by how normal she looked without the formality of her uniform.

I nodded toward the front door. "Dave's outside. I thought I'd check on him."

"Dave isn't using his cane…maybe you should," she said dryly and walked away. *Was that a joke?* I couldn't believe it.

Readying myself for the blistering cold, I approached the front door. I stuffed my too-long hair into the neck of my pullover, pulled up my hood, and added a black scarf for good measure. Grabbing ear muffs and a blanket, I opened the door.

The cold air was icy against my face, but the alcohol that flowed through my body still warmed my insides. The night was dark and quiet. If it were a clear night back home, Dani would've come over to watch for shooting stars and make wishes about boys. But that seemed like a lifetime ago.

Trying to stay on course, I scanned the shadows for Dave. He was right where I'd expected him to be, sitting in an old rocking chair at the far side of the porch and brooding. As I moved to sit in the chair beside him, his eyes remained fixed on the blackness that swallowed the landscape around us.

I shuddered as the cold snuck into my warm cocoon of clothing. "It's freezing. What're you doing out here?"

"Getting some air," was all he said.

We sat in silence for a moment. I craned my neck to look out beyond the porch awning at the twinkling stars.

"I'm sorry about the other night, Dave. I didn't mean to—"

"I don't want to talk about it," he said sharply.

"Well you have to," I snapped back. "You're barely speaking to me. I think you've said three words to me all day, and only because you had to."

I watched him, expecting a denial or an explanation, but no words came.

"Look, you're upset with me, and I understand why. I just need you to know what's going on with me." Everything after that came out in a rush. I knew it was going to sound insane to him regardless of my delivery, so I let the words flow before I chickened out.

"Something's happening to me. I know you're going to think I'm crazy—that's why I haven't told you until now. But you need to know why I pushed you away." I paused for a response, but he pretended to ignore me, so I continued, "I've been feeling weird lately. I get these strange feelings when I'm around people. It's like a rush of sensations and images, but they're not mine. It's so unbelievable I don't even know how to explain it. I don't want it to happen, but I can't help it. I can't control it at all." Uneasiness gnawed at me, but I tried to calm myself.

Hearing my own words, I wasn't surprised to see I'd gained his full attention. He was staring at me, his hazel eyes like black holes in the darkness.

Finally, I thought. "When I touch you, I *see* things. They're memories, I guess, in your mind. And I can *feel* what you're feeling. When we were in the bedroom the other night, I saw myself in your mind, and…it was just too much."

In the shadows, Dave looked like a statue, expressionless and completely devoid of life. Gone were the cocky grin and charming glint in his eyes.

"Are you going to say something?" I snapped. *You make me want to scream!*

Just as I was about to, he said, "Are you telling me you can read minds? That you've read *my* mind?" His voice was thick with disbelief, and he laughed at me. "All this time I was dating a psychic," he joked.

"Don't be an ass, Dave. It's more of a feeling, and it just started happening. I can't predict the future or anything."

The relief of finally telling someone made me want to cry tears of joy, but the fact that it was Dave and that he was being a dick made me regret my decision. I was fearful of what might happen next. In the palpable silence, I could hear my heartbeat quicken with dread.

Oh my God. Dani was wrong. I shouldn't have told him. This isn't what I expected. I don't know what I expected. I should've told Sarah. He's going to tell everyone. They'll leave me here!

"Dave?" I leaned toward him cautiously, realizing drinking in preparation hadn't been the best idea. The alcohol made me feel out of control and paranoid. *Stop it, Zoe. You'll be fine. Just lie and say you're drunk and don't know what came over you.* Somewhat satisfied with the idea, I took a deep breath and said, "Never mind. I'm drunk. Don't mind me. You were right; I really just don't have any feelings—"

Before I could finish, the front door creaked open, and Biggs stepped out. "Hey, where's the police station? We want to check it for working vehicles and gas." I caught his attention as I brushed a loose strand of hair from my face, and Biggs straightened. "Sorry, Zoe…I didn't realize you were…out here."

"I'll show you on the map," Dave offered and stood.

"Dave—" I reached for his arm, but he shrugged me off as he hobbled into the house.

For the first time, I wished I *could* see his thoughts. And kick his ass. *What happens next?*

Date: December 19, 10:45 PM

From: Zoe Cartwright

To: Danielle O'Connor

Subject: I told Dave

Hey D,

So my plan to tell Dave backfired. About 30 minutes ago, I told him why I was acting strange and that I didn't know what was wrong with me or what to do. He didn't say much and then just walked away. What if he tells everyone? Worst-case scenario: he thinks I'm losing my mind and tells Sanchez. If they think I'm one of the Crazies, they'll leave me behind. Maybe I AM, and they SHOULD leave me behind. I don't feel sick, but I also have no plausible explanation for what's happening to me. Is it because I was sick for a while? But if that's the case, if it's because of the virus, it wouldn't just be me, would it? Other people would be experiencing the same thing too.

So far, it doesn't seem like Dave's told anyone. I hope he doesn't, but honestly, he's a wild card at this point. He won't even look at me. Harper, on the other hand, knows something's wrong. He keeps watching me and asking me if I'm okay. I want to tell him everything. I feel like I can trust him, but I felt that way about Dave too. Now look at the situation I'm in.

BTW, we should be in Fort Knox by nightfall tomorrow. I'll write to you when I can. Wish me luck. I think I'm going to need it. Take care, my friend.

Hasta la vista,

Zoe

17

DANI

"I think he wants to talk to you about something," Chris told me quietly, nodding in Jason's direction. He walked several paces ahead of us on the cracked sidewalk.

I watched his confident movements and shook my head. "So why doesn't he just do it?" I asked, thinking back on the dozens of times throughout the day that Jason had met my eyes, only to stride away.

Chris pursed her lips and took a deep breath. "I don't know. He's acting like a little girl."

Maybe he likes me, I thought as butterflies whirled erratically in my stomach. *Maybe he wants to set things straight, to tell me he's not interested.* The butterflies turned sickly and died.

Seriously, how old am I? Jason wasn't the only one acting like a little girl.

Lost in thought, I peered around the small-town street we'd been exploring all afternoon. In reality, there hadn't been much to explore, and what there *had* been was pretty run-down. The shops had offered little, but the building we currently approached held promise—it was a library, and it stood out in its modernity. *Maybe we can find some books on something useful, like foraging or repairing power plants or building time machines...*

Jason reached the glass door first and held it open for Chris and me.

"Such a gentleman," Chris exclaimed as she entered the building. "Who would've thought?" Within seconds she had her assault rifle drawn and set out on a sweep of the aisles and alcoves.

My entrance, however, was halted by Jason's firm grip on my arm. Looking down, I was inappropriately excited to see his gloved hand wrapped around my sleeve. My heart gave an enthusiastic thump, which I tried to ignore.

"Jason, what—"

"Can we talk?" He looked down at me intently, his clenched jaw making the already sharp angles of his face more severe. I briefly wondered what it would be like to have an irate Jason staring me down as he'd done to Cece the previous night. I hoped to never find out.

Beside me, Jack barked, and I turned my attention to him. "It's okay, Sweet Boy. Go with Chris."

He whined but trotted off obediently. *He might be the smartest dog ever.*

Jason led me inside and locked the door behind us. He didn't let go of my arm until he'd dragged me through the open entryway, beyond several aisles of reference books, and into a secluded nook created by two towering bookshelves and a sky-blue wall.

"Well?" I asked, pressing my back against the wall while he paced. Three steps away. Stop. Turn. Three steps back.

Pausing while facing me, Jason stared at the wall a few inches to the left of my head. "It's my fault, what happened last night," he said quietly.

I shrugged my shoulders in an attempt at nonchalance. "Oh? I didn't know anyone was to blame. We're both adults—a little cuddling's no big deal." *It's not like I've been thinking about it all day or anything*, I thought sarcastically.

Jason's eyebrows lowered, and his eyes suddenly locked on mine. "What? That was—" After a moment of tense silence, he shook the scowl off his face. "That's not what I'm talking about. I meant what happened with Cece." His pacing resumed.

That was...what? Amazing? A really big mistake? As I watched him, the now familiar tangle of emotions—self-loathing, guilt, and desire—nauseated me.

Taking a deep breath, Jason faced me again. His eyes bored into mine, imploring. "Before she went to your room, she stopped by mine. She thought we could just keep...that things would stay the same. After everything she said to you. After she *hit* you." His eyes squeezed shut and his mouth pinched at the corners.

When he finally opened his eyes again, they gleamed. "I could kill that bitch for what she did."

My breath caught. "I...I don't understand," I said and stepped away from the wall. "What's that have to do with what she did to me last night?" I stopped a foot away from Jason, his size making me feel smaller than usual.

He squeezed his hands into fists at his sides and gritted his teeth. "When she came to my room, I turned her away...said I was done with her, that she disgusted me. I'm pretty sure the next thing she did was sneak into your room."

"Jason, it's—"

"I can't believe I was so fucking stupid. She could've *killed* you." He reached his gloved hand out but let it drop before he touched me.

"Jason. It's okay." In one step, I closed the distance between us and wrapped my arms around his neck. He was so unbelievably solid. "I'm okay," I said against his thick jacket.

He returned the embrace fiercely, lifting me until I was on tiptoes. With his chin resting on my head, I could feel him swallow, could feel him clear his throat. I pulled back enough to meet his eyes and inhaled to speak, but he beat me to it.

"Well," Jason said hastily, releasing me and taking a step back, "we should look around. See what trouble Johnson's gotten into." He strode out of the alcove with me following a few steps behind.

Um, okay...

Looking over his shoulder at me, Jason wore his familiar, knowing half-grin, hiding whatever shreds of real emotion he'd let escape. "You know, Red, she probably thinks we've been playing naughty librarian in a hidden corner. Too bad you don't wear glasses..."

I stalked after him, berating myself for enjoying the images his words conjured. He was so damn frustrating. Whenever he let a hint of vulnerability show, he would try to fluster me with suggestive comments, attempting to make me forget. But forgetting was impossible.

Shortly after our return to the winery, I found myself flat on my back on the cold, damp grass behind the house. I stared up at the slowly darkening steel-gray sky while I recovered my breath. From having it knocked out of me. Again.

Chris's smirking face invaded my view of the thick cloud cover, and she held out her hand. *She could at least have the courtesy to* appear *winded!*

"Ugh...Chris...I think...I'm done," I managed to pant out eventually.

She leaned down and grasped me under the armpits to haul me up. "Hon, you're nowhere near done." She strode several paces away and sat on a white bench bordered by bloomless rose bushes. "Come here. We can take a little break before Jason has a hissy fit." She finished with an eye roll.

I plopped down next to her. "Maybe I'm just not a fighter. What if I never get any better?"

"Then you never get better. But that won't happen." Chris watched the two men grappling thirty yards away. Jason had Ky in a particularly uncomfortable position on the lawn.

"What makes you so sure?"

She caught my eye and grinned conspiratorially. "'Cause I'm training you…and I'm awesome."

I tried to laugh, I really did, but I couldn't stop myself from dwelling on the fact that I barely knew anything about Chris. She definitely *was* awesome, but what else was she? Who had she been before? Why had she left the base?

"Um…I've been thinking," I said, but hesitated.

Chris laughed softly. "You tend to do that. It drives him crazy sometimes, you know."

"I'm sure." I joined her soft laughter. "But why are you here? Okay, wow, I didn't mean that to sound so horrible." I shook my head in frustration.

Angling my knees toward her, I tried again. "Why'd you leave the base with Jason? Why'd any of you leave? When you guys talk about it you make it sound like you had to escape or something. What…I just don't understand…"

Still looking straight ahead, Chris's eyes became distant, and she swallowed. "My boys—twins—got sick. They both passed the last week of November. They were almost five. Would've started kindergarten next fall." She shook her head, her face reminding me of a stone angel in a graveyard.

I clasped her hand and cleared my throat, but my voice was weak when I spoke. "Oh Chris, I'm so sorry. I…I had no idea."

"Why would you? I didn't tell anyone. Jason's the only one who knew anything about my family before…this." She gestured mildly with one hand. "My ex and I'd been divorced for a year. The boys were staying with him when they got sick. They barely lasted two days, and I blamed him. I wanted to beat him to death for killing them, but the Virus killed him a few days later."

I squeezed her hand, horrified by what she'd been through.

"Children aren't supposed to die before their parents. That's what everyone says. But dammit, I don't think any of this was *supposed* to happen," Chris said desperately.

Of course not, I thought.

"Our base was on lockdown. But this was unlike any lockdown I'd ever seen. Hundreds of soldiers patrolled the perimeter day and night after the first reported flu death." She squinted in thought. "That was in mid-November. I doubt you heard about it…the military kept it quiet. We heard gunshots all the time. Jason told me…" She shook her head. "He said people were getting shot when they tried to leave base. I didn't believe it until I saw it myself—we *don't* go after our own, not like that."

After a long pause she continued, "But the real kicker was that some people *were* allowed to leave—only if they were wearing a special yellow armband on both sleeves of their uniform. Like they were chosen. Like they were ready for this. *None* of it makes sense."

Unable to speak, I swallowed repeatedly. I felt like a vacuum had sucked every drop of moisture from my mouth. Her words implied that the military had known about the Virus…had known about it and had just let it kill everyone. My next thought shocked me like a bucket of icy water. *Holy crap…did they* create *the Virus?*

Chris started up again, "Jason knew what'd happened to my family, knew that I needed to get away from that place. They'd been dead for over a week when he came to me with his plan. So we gathered our little group, *barely* managed to steal some of the yellow armbands…that was really weird actually. The guy guarding 'em was literally about to shoot us until Jason stepped closer to talk him down—it was like the guard got really confused all of a sudden. Anyway, we got the hell out of there a few hours later. It didn't go the way we'd planned, but we got out."

Finally looking at me, Chris said, "And now we're here."

I sat back heavily against the bench. "Um…okay. Wow."

"Well, now I need to blow off some steam," she patted my thigh. "Run through the exercises I taught you. Twice." Chris stood abruptly and marched straight for Jason and Ky.

Her opening strike at Jason was the last thing I noticed before I lost myself to the yoga-like poses. As I replayed her words and considered the possibility that somebody had orchestrated the end of civilization, images of maniacal scientists danced through my head.

"Bend your knees more, but keep your back straight," Ky said behind me.

Startled, I fell on my butt. "What is it with you Green Berets? Did you all take advanced classes in 'how to sneak up on people' or something?" I complained, picking myself up and brushing off my stretchy black pants.

When I rounded on Ky, he held his hands in the air like he was caught in a stick up, but merriment crinkled the corners of his slanted eyes. "Sorry, D."

"D." I smiled sadly and shook my head. "Cam…that's what he called me." I resumed my previous pose, appearing to sit on an invisible chair.

Looking down at the slightly overgrown grass, Ky stuck his hands into his pants pockets and said, "Oh, um…sorry. I won't…"

"Don't worry about it. It's also what Zoe calls me…she's Jason's sister," I clarified. "Hearing you call me that makes me feel a little better…reminds me of before." I lowered myself to the ground for the next position. "You know, being around you guys makes this whole thing easier to deal with. Everybody's lost someone—lots of someones really. We're all going through the same thing. Plus, I think Chris is magical or something. It's like she draws the shitty feelings out and heals me from inside. She makes me feel…okay."

I laughed breathily, *Can he tell I'm serious? He'll think I'm nutso!*

Ky sat down on the bench and watched Chris and Jason spar. I was surprised by how well Chris was holding her own against Jason.

I looked up at Ky. "Sorry, that was probably way more info than you wanted."

"No worries. It's good to hear someone talk about what's going on." He gestured toward the estate house. "These guys aren't big on sharing. The military doesn't exactly draw in the touchy-feely type. So we walk around pretending everything's cool, but really all this repression just turns us into hair-trigger dickheads."

Tell me about it, I thought as I stood to stretch my tired muscles.

Ky continued, "I, uh, I've noticed that about Chris too. We should all be freaking out way more, but something about her…I don't know. It's like she *really* does something. And—" He paused to take a deep breath. "There's something else. Have you noticed anything different? About you, I mean."

About me? Like what? Like Zoe? "Um…no?" I sat down beside him. "Have *you*?"

Ky closed his eyes for so long I thought he might not answer. He raised one eyelid, watching me through the narrow slit. "I get these feelings. It's been happening ever since I recovered. From the Virus, I mean."

When he turned his reticent gaze on me, my heart melted. *He's afraid. Of what?*

"I felt it when Cece went into your room last night. It was like I was watching a horror movie, and the suspenseful music was playing and getting louder and louder. I knew something bad was about to happen. And it also happened this morning in town right before I opened the door to a house. Some psycho bitch was waiting for us inside…with a baseball bat. She nearly smashed in Dalton's head before I shot her. It's like I can tell when bad stuff is going to happen—*before* it happens." He looked away. "I know it sounds insane."

Yeah, I thought, but my heart wasn't in it. This wasn't the first crazy-sounding power I'd heard about. I stared ahead and watched the end of the battle between Chris and Jason. She beckoned for him to start again, but he shook his head and headed our way.

"Crazy or not, I have to warn you," Ky whispered.

Surprised, I turned to face him. "Warn me? About what?"

He leaned in. "Cece. The feeling's building up around her like it's gonna explode. And she hates you…sorry. So I'm thinking the explosion isn't gonna mean anything good for you. Be careful, okay?"

This isn't real, right? He can't know that, can he? But…what if he is *like Zoe? And what about Chris?* My thoughts were frantic. I grasped my left wrist as dread seeped into my body, turning my bones to ice.

Ky straightened and laughed. "Hey man, I saw you get your ass kicked by a girl. Was she too much for you? Is that why you ran away?"

Jason glanced between Ky and me before he responded. "She needed it." His tone was razor sharp.

Ky stood abruptly and backed toward the house. "Right, well… I just remembered…I've got this thing…" He turned and jogged away.

Jason quickly took Ky's spot on the bench. "What was that all about?"

"Nothing," I responded instinctively. *What the hell is up with this bench today?*

"It didn't look like nothing."

I rolled my eyes and heaved a sigh. "He was just telling me something…about *himself*, Jason. It's got nothing to do with you."

"Fine, whatever. Show me what you learned today. Johnson!" he called to Chris, who was doing sit-ups on the lawn. "Get your ass over here."

I groaned, "You can't be serious. I'm too tired!"

He stared at me with all the sympathy of a stone.

"Ready to go again?" Chris asked him when she reached us.

"No," Jason said, not looking away from me. "Spar with this little girl. I want to see if anything's sinking in."

As I stood and walked away from the bench to face off against Chris, I made sure to add a little extra sway to my hips. *Little girl, my ass.*

Date: December 21, 11:55 PM
From: Danielle O'Connor
To: Zoe Cartwright
Subject: You're not alone

Zo,

I'm sorry that it's been a few days since I wrote. Jason and Chris are working me extra hard. It's just 'cause they're worried and want me to be able to protect myself...but now I'm always pooped!

They were both with me yesterday as we searched Gold Hill. I appreciate their support and protection, but it kind of reminds me that half the group hates me right now and that I'm a weakling of a partner. I'm trying my best to believe what you said, but it's hard not to feel responsible for so many deaths, especially when I'm surrounded by people who think the exact opposite.

Today, I was with just Jason. We scouted for gas but found little, only in cars locked in garages. What use will cars be when the fuel's completely gone? At least the garage shopping led us to some other useful supplies. We found a stockpile of MREs—those totally disgusting military meals that stay good for like a million years—and some guns. They were locked up, but that didn't stop Jason. We stocked up on enough weapons for everyone in our group several times over and enough ammo for all of us to get in plenty of target practice. I'm working really hard on learning how to use my little handgun. It's funny...I always hated guns or was at least afraid of them, but now I sleep with one.

To update you on the Cece situation...we're avoiding each other like the plague (ha). I honestly think Jason would kick her to the curb except he's worried about losing the bodies that would go with her (and supplies too). Seriously, a bunch of the guys worship her now...they're like her own personal harem of dutiful slaves. It's creepy.

Anyway, tomorrow we head out again to continue our insanely slow journey to Bodega Bay. I'm pretty sure we only have one more stop until we get there. Will we be too late? I'm trying not to let myself dwell on that thought. I haven't been very successful.

BTW, Dave is a weak asshole. Forget him. I'm really sorry that I encouraged you to tell him about your superpower. I feel kind of responsible. Sad face. Hug.

I know you're totally freaking out about what's happening to you, so I thought this might make you feel better. I think it is happening to other people too...like, it's a mutation caused by the virus or something. See, Chris, she's sort of able to make people feel better. And I don't just mean giving a hug and talking it out. She sits down with someone who's about to have a meltdown, and five minutes later they're fine. She's done it to me a bunch of times. I think it's the reason I'm handling Cam's death so well. Because, really, I'm handling it too well. Like, unnaturally well. Plus, this guy in my group is pretty sure he can feel when bad things are about to happen...in fact, he feels it all the time around Cece. The point is—you are not alone (cue the Michael Jackson song).

So you're going to Fort Knox? That's sort of hilarious. You should take a bar of gold just for fun. Ha! But, wherever you are, stay safe, okay? I miss you.

Ciao,
Dani

18

ZOE

It took us seven excruciating hours to drive to Fort Knox. Luckily Biggs and Harper had found a fuel-filled police cruiser, making our journey less cramped. Unfortunately, any potential silence was interrupted by the sound of the police scanner clicking in and out of range. If it hadn't been for Harper's friendly smile and his seductive, throaty laugh, Dave's sulking probably would've driven me mad.

"Hopefully we'll hear another broadcast today," Harper said as we neared our destination. He looked back at Dave and then up at me, sensing the tension between us. I'd been trying, unsuccessfully, to ignore my memory of the horrible conversation I'd had with Dave two nights earlier. I'd originally offered to ride with Sanchez and the others in Dave's truck, but being around her was equally unnerving, so I'd opted to ride in the same car as my fallen-out friend.

Dave had made himself right at home in the uncomfortable backseat, stretching out his legs and folding his arms behind his head. He was pretending to be unfazed by my presence, and I didn't mind—I really didn't want to have a confrontation in front of Harper. I did, however, allow myself a smile every time Dave repositioned himself on the vinyl seat. There was something satisfying in seeing him behind the metal cage separating us.

Finding fuel had been difficult, but Biggs and Harper's resourcefulness had resulted in just enough gas to transport us to Kentucky. *But what about to Colorado?*

"What makes that base in Colorado so special anyway?" I asked and cleared my throat—my voice was hoarse from disuse. "I mean, I'm surprised the Colony isn't in D.C. or in Virginia by the Pentagon…someplace that makes a little more sense." I looked at Harper. "Any idea?"

He shrugged. "We heard the same broadcast as you."

I tried not to grow hopeful. "Maybe they've created an anti-Virus." *Maybe they can fix whatever's wrong with me.*

"Yeah, maybe." Harper squinted skeptically, but the rest of his expression remained unchanged.

I looked out the window, watching the abandoned town outside of Fort Knox pass by as we wound our way through the deserted streets. I imagined its lonely storefronts crowded with people—eating at the quaint cafes, waiting at the bus stops, and walking in and out of the little shops. Instead, the sidewalks were desolate and littered with garbage. I tried not to think about the rotting corpses and the Crazies that surely haunted the dark corners of the town, instead taking inventory of what supplies the town might have to offer.

I pointed to a large, boxy building behind a taco joint. "There's a hospital over there."

"Good eye," Harper approved. "We'll have to check it out later when we have the whole team…I'm sure there are a few Crazies waiting for us in there."

Dave barked a laugh but said nothing as he pulled a bottle of Tequila out of his pack and brought it to his lips.

I twisted in my seat. "Where'd you get that?" I asked angrily, knowing nothing good would come of him drinking again.

"Don't worry about it." Dave's voice was snippy, and he still hadn't blinked an eye in my direction.

Trying to control my temper, I rolled my eyes and faced forward again.

Harper glanced over at me sympathetically, but I pretended not to notice. "What's going on with you guys anyway?" he asked.

"Nothing. Just a lover's quarrel," Dave joked caustically. "We have a history. Some sort of *connection*, if you will…"

"I've noticed," Harper said, keeping his eyes on the road. "You shouldn't be drinking." He glared into the rearview mirror, and I could feel his disappointment. "Not with all the pain meds I gave you."

Dave scoffed. "*I'm* not the one you should be worried about," he muttered under his breath.

"Dammit Dave! You're such an asshole! Get over yourself, and stop pouting!" I shouted. "It's like we're in fourth grade."

"If you two are finished…" Harper pointed at two imposing tanks flanking the entrance to the base. *Welcome to Fort Knox*, the sign read.

Ignoring Dave, who was humming circus tunes in the back of the squad car, I took in the lifeless scene around me. The landscape was mostly barren except for the woods that crept up behind the towering brick buildings ahead.

Harper hunched over the steering wheel to get a better view through the windshield. "This place is so old. I'm surprised it's still standing."

We followed Dave's truck along the winding roads in search of the location the broadcast had identified as the makeshift command post—the civilian barracks. "They said there were Survivors, but it doesn't look like it," Harper said, putting the car in park.

As we sat in front of a large, gray building, the hair on the back of my neck stood on end. A sudden wave of wretchedness washed over me when I stepped out of the vehicle.

I don't like this place.

Date: December 21, 5:15 PM
From: Zoe Cartwright
To: Danielle O'Connor
Subject: Something's not right...

D,

We have arrived! We're at Fort Knox, and I'm completely creeped out right now. Captain Jones and Second Lieutenant Taylor (they seem particularly attached to their titles) are the officers in charge here. In fact, they appear to be the only military people left. I don't like the way they've been looking at Sarah and me. There's an unquenchable thirst in their eyes. It's really disturbing. Since we arrived, Harper and Sanchez haven't been away from Jones, so I haven't had a chance to tell to them about my bad feeling.

At least I have Harper to talk to amidst this whole fiasco. Sarah's lost to her swooning heart, and Sanchez and I aren't really on friendly terms. Dave is deplorable. Harper though, he seems to have befriended me.

As for my weird powers, I'm definitely comforted to hear that some of your people are experiencing something like I am. It makes me feel a little less...crazy. However, I'm not so comforted by what your friend said about Cece. I reiterate...BE CAREFUL. Please.

Jones is walking toward me. Great...he looks like he wants something. I'll write again soon.

Hasta,
Zoe

19

DANI

"*LEARN.*"

It's him. *Turning in circles, I attempted to peer through the endless, gray mist. It was everywhere, dense and warm. I tried to escape it by running a dozen steps in a random direction, but the mist remained. It was oddly comforting, like soaking in a bubble bath with only candles for light.*

"LEARN."

Where is he? *I looked up, but there was still only mist. Embracing, soothing, caressing—the foggy gray substance surrounded me. It seemed to exist in all physical states at once. It was gaseous, allowing movement and breath. It was liquid, pressing against every inch of my body. It was solid, brushing against my stomach and tickling my neck.*

"LEARN."

Is he doing this? He's not even real! So, am I doing this? *My body grew warm. My pajamas became uncomfortably tight and itchy. Brushing sweaty palms against my cotton shorts, I drew a ragged breath. My fingertips had grazed the bare skin of my thighs, causing a burst of fiery pleasure.* What the hell?

"LEARN."

"Learn what?" I rasped. The fog brushed against my ankles, then my knees, and then my thighs, creating unbearable tingles. I licked my lips and groaned, overwhelmed by the sensation. It was too much. I cleared my throat and screamed, "LEARN WHAT?"

"LEA—"

Suddenly the mist disappeared, and I floated in a sea of soothing, white nothingness.

"Dani, wake up," a man whispered.

In bed, I lurched into a sitting position as I opened my eyes. In the faint dawn light I could see Jason's face, tensed with a hint of concern, inches from my own. He was sitting on the edge of the bed with his hip pressed against the outside of my thigh. His hands gently gripped my bare shoulders. Everywhere he touched me, my skin burned with pleasure. Everywhere else ached for his touch.

"You were moaning," he murmured. "Bad dream?"

Closing my eyes, I took a shuddering breath. I desperately needed to regain control of my body before I did something embarrassing. "Not exactly," I breathed.

When I reopened my eyes, Jason's iris's shone with such intensity they seemed to be composed of burning natural gas. Slowly, like falling feathers, his hands slid from my shoulders to my wrists.

I looked down at the quilt, overwhelmed by the intensity of his gaze. "Please," I whispered, unsure of what I was requesting. My body hummed in anticipation of where he might touch me next. At the same time, a small seed of doubt took root in my chest. *Is he just teasing me?*

"Please what, Red?" he breathed, the words brushing against my neck like a caress. Out of the corner of my eye, I could see one side of his mouth quirk up in amusement. So he *was* just teasing me. He probably thought my infatuation with him was just one big decades-long joke.

"Please stop touching me, Jason," I said, proud of the steadiness of my voice.

His hands closed around my wrists, and his thumbs stroked the sensitive, transparent skin. "Are you sure that's what you want?"

No. You are such an asshole. "Yes," I snapped, ripping my wrists from his grasp. Using my go-to maneuver, I clambered across the empty bed, my escape only slightly hindered by the sheets, and fell off the opposite edge. At least I was running from humiliation rather than a crazy girl with a terrifyingly sharp knife.

"Get over yourself. You're not *that* amazing," I spat. I stomped across the hall to the bathroom and slammed the door.

"I'll meet you on the lawn in fifteen minutes," Jason called through the whitewashed wood. He was laughing. *Dick.*

What the hell kind of dream was that? I wondered grumpily while I glared at my reflection in the mirror. My vibrant curls stuck out in all directions. Evidently it was a French braid day…again. I pondered chopping off the whole frizzy mess, but I figured a short, red afro wasn't really my look.

As I deftly braided my hair, I studied my face. *How long has it been since I wore makeup? Two weeks? More?* The thought was equally shocking and reassuring. I wasn't just girly Dani anymore. I'd become survivor Dani, equipped with sore muscles and a practical fashion sense.

After washing up, I returned to my room to dress and arm myself with my usual shoulder holster and pistol, assured that my nerve endings were back to normal. I tore open a peanut butter and chocolate chip protein bar as I exited the bedroom, tripping over my dog on the way out.

Jack wagged his tail happily while I righted myself. "Good morning, Sweet Boy," I said between bites.

He yawned dramatically and bowed, earning the last nugget of the tasteless bar.

As I lumbered down the stairs, a plan of revenge formed in my mind. I waved at Chris and Ky, apparently the only other people awake at such an ungodly hour, as I neared the front room's largest window. I peeked around the heavy tan and green-striped curtain and spotted Jason standing on the lawn—he was staring off into the woods. Smiling, I led Jack to the back door, and we silently slipped out into the damp morning chill.

Pausing on the back porch, I clicked my tongue, and my dog watched me intently. "Okay Jack," I whispered, kneeling down in front of him. "You're going to go that way." I pointed to the left side of the house, and his eyes followed. "Find Jason. You need to be happy and loud." I scratched his neck with both hands. He licked my cheek in return.

"Go find Jason," I commanded quietly and stood. Jack instantly trotted away, barking every few steps.

Stalking in the opposite direction, I made my way around the house and found Jason watching Jack frolic like a month-old puppy. The grass muffled my steps as I snuck up behind him. I crouched, gliding the last few steps, and held my breath. *Revenge is so sweet!*

I raised my foot and jammed it into the back of Jason's leg, making his knee buckle. Before he could regain his balance, my arm snaked around his shoulders and yanked him to the ground. On his way down, he grasped my wrist and pulled me to the grass with him. I used the added momentum and sat heavily astride his abdomen.

He grunted. "Ow," he said once he'd regained his breath.

Smiling down at him ecstatically, I bounced and proclaimed, "I win!"

"You think?" he asked, raising his eyebrows.

"Ha! I *know*!" I slapped his chest with both hands, hoping for another grunt. It didn't come.

Instead his gloved hands found my thighs and slid up to rest on my jean-covered hips. I was suddenly *very* aware of the fact that I was straddling him. Without warning, his hands tightened, and he flipped me over onto the cold grass. He grabbed my wrists and held them together above my head.

I squirmed, attempting to dislodge his hold on me, but I might as well have been fighting against iron restraints.

"Oh, Red. You'll never beat me," he whispered near my ear.

In all of my wriggling, I'd managed to maneuver my right leg between both of his. I'd expended quite a bit of energy flailing about, but I had just enough left. With a grunt, I brought my leg up against his groin—hard.

Groaning, Jason rolled off me and curled into the fetal position on the lawn.

Jack ceased his enthusiastic prancing and jumping to crouch in front of Jason's face. He sniffed and nuzzled the man until he received some weak pets.

I sat up and reached out to touch Jason's shoulder. "I'm sorry, Jason! But…you told me that's what I'm supposed to do if a guy has me pinned to the ground." He didn't respond.

"Jason, I…Are you mad at me?" I asked weakly.

When Jason finally sat up and faced me, he was smiling, if a little sickly. "No. That was perfect. I wasn't sure you had it in you to really hurt someone, but now I know."

"Oh. Um…thanks?"

Jason stood, brushing off stray bits of grass. I did the same, still breathing heavier than normal from the exertion—and, possibly, from the excitement.

"I'd say you're warmed up," he said. "Let's wake everyone with some target practice."

We walked in silence, and as we neared the makeshift shooting range, I froze in horror. Three of the cardboard targets had been painted, each with a different blood-red word.

SHOOT.

YOURSELF.

DANI.

It was Cece's doing—it had to be. Unbidden, tears welled in

my eyes, and I blinked them away angrily. *I won't let her make me cry!*

"This needs to end," Jason growled, turning back toward the house. He made it three steps before I planted myself in front of him.

"Jason, don't you dare!" He stepped to the side to go around me, and I mirrored the motion.

"Dani. *Move.*" His voice sounded hollow, determined.

"No!" I yelled. In my best impression of my angry Irish grandma, I placed my hands on my hips and demanded, "You're not going after her because of this. Can't you see that's what she wants you to do? She and John and the rest of her idiots are probably waiting for you right now. If you go after them…then what? We all get in a huge fight and end up killing each other? What happens to the rest of us if they take you out? Jason…you…your calm logic…that's the only thing holding us together. Safety in numbers, remember? We need you. *I* need you."

His jaw clenched at my last statement.

"You're staying here, with me, and finishing this damn training session!" I tried my best to loom over him, which was difficult considering Jason was about a foot taller than me. I took a step toward him.

Miraculously, he stepped back.

Pretty sure he would follow, I brushed past him and returned to the shooting range. I hoped he didn't hear my gigantic sigh of relief. *If they kill him because of me, I don't know what I'll do.*

Jason stood by my side for the next hour and coached me until the hateful words were riddled with enough bullet holes that they were no longer legible.

Date: December 22, 9:00 AM
From: Danielle O'Connor
To: Zoe Cartwright

Subject: It's getting old...

Zo,

So, I kind of had a run-in with Cece this morning. Is there such a thing as passive-aggressive bullying (I feel like I'm in elementary school saying "bully")? If so, that's what she's doing. She's such a bitch. Anyway, Jason woke me super early to get in some extra how-to-be-violent training. When we got to our little makeshift shooting range, the words "SHOOT YOURSELF DANI" were written on the targets. Jason was ready to march off and end things then and there, but somehow I managed to rein him in. Who would've thought?

I know you probably disagree with my decision to stop him, but I think they (Cece, John, and company) are trying to get Jason to attack them. Because, you know, that way they'd have a good excuse to "depose" him as group leader...maybe even kill him. I had a good reason, you see? I had to keep him safe. It's hard though—I don't know how much longer I can stand this.

Anyway, we're about to leave for Fort Bragg, where we have another two-day stop—this time for Ky and Holly (Army Ranger chick...the only other one besides Chris). We'll be a three-hour drive from Bodega Bay, but I'll have to wait three more days to get there. This is so frustrating!

By the way, I really don't like the sound of those two new guys you mentioned. Please be careful around them.

Ciao,
Dani

I walked around the driveway, studying my new surroundings. The house sprawled around me, enormous, beige, and boxy, looking more like a modern stucco apartment building than a family home. Dense chunks of forest surrounded the house, breaking up the fields of tall grasses.

I meandered over to Ky, who had grown up in the outrageous place, and asked, "Are you sure about this? I bet we can still go somewhere else."

Smiling, Ky placed his arm over my shoulders and pulled me into a side hug. "Nah. I had to come here eventually, and I'd rather stay at my house than another random place. Sometimes it just feels right to come home. You know what I mean, D?"

"Yeah," I agreed. *I want to go home too.* My desperation to drive the three more hours to Bodega Bay was overwhelming, keeping me on the verge of tears.

Ky tightened his hold on me and whispered, "It's worse here—like the mother of all thunderstorms is building up around her, and I don't know what to expect. All I know is that it's gonna be bad."

Goosebumps pebbled my skin, and a chill seeped into my body.

Before I could respond, Chris appeared on my other side and slipped her arm around my waist, making us a sweet little trio of comfort. "What're you kiddos doing over here?" Seconds after she touched me, my dread simply evaporated.

"Just talking about home," I replied wistfully.

Chris leaned the side of her head against mine. "We'll just have to be each other's home."

Ky laughed softly. "Are you ladies gonna cry? 'Cause if you are, I'll just be on my way," he teased, but he didn't move an inch.

"Ha! As if you'd ever give up the chance to cozy up with us." Chris gave him a friendly slap on the gut.

"I hate to interrupt this…whatever it is," Jason cut in from behind us, "but I need to talk to Dani. Alone."

Ky's arm retracted from my shoulders like he'd been burned,

and he hopped a yard away. "Right. Of course." He ducked his head and hurried off. *Weird.*

Chris's arm tightened around my waist as Jason stepped in front of us. "You too, Johnson. And take Jack," he said.

She let go of me and stepped so close to him that their shoes nearly touched. "If you make her cry, I'll punch you," she threatened.

"Really?" Jason's eyes strayed to my face. "Looks like you've already done a pretty good job of it. Does that mean *I* get to punch *you*?" I hadn't even noticed the wetness streaking down my cheeks.

"Those are happy tears, you ass," Chris snapped before stomping off with my dog. Chris and Jason's friendship was…strange.

"Dani, I know you're probably angry, but—"

I stepped closer to him, and he tensed. "Angry?" I hissed. "You think I'm angry? Try pissed. Try frustrated to the point of needing to scream. Grams, your dad—who knows who else—might need us right now, and we could get there in a few hours. But no, we'll sit here for *three days* while they might be *dying*."

Reaching out, he grabbed my shoulders tightly. "Fuck, Dani, I know! Don't you think it's the same for me? Don't you think it's killing me to be so close and not be able to help them?"

"I don't know!" I practically yelled. My gaze dropped to the flagstone driveway beneath our feet. "How could I possibly know what you're feeling? You never talk about it. For all I know, you don't even care." I met his eyes, pleading. "Please, Jason, just let me go with Chris. We'll find a car and get down there tonight. We won't take any of the group's supplies, and you can stay here with everyone else and honor your agreement."

He swallowed and opened his mouth, but no sound came out. Intently, his eyes searched mine.

"Please, Jason," I begged, my chin trembling.

Suddenly, he pulled me against him in a tight hug and rested his cheek atop my head. "I'm sorry, Dani. I can't let you go. I'm so sorry."

An avalanche of tears poured down my cheeks, accompanied by hiccups and moans. Jason hid me in his arms as my sobs played out, sparing me the shame of breaking down in front of everyone.

Once my tears had dried, he walked me up to the room I was sharing with Chris and settled me on the bed. He sat on the edge, reminding me of the incident that morning—how good his fingers had felt on my skin.

"But my stuff," I mumbled, hoping to keep his mind from the same topic mine had drifted to.

He pointed to a corner of the room where my pack and duffel bag sat. "Chris already brought everything up."

"Oh. Where is she?" I asked. I sounded like a lost little girl.

"I think she's helping with dinner. Dani, I—"

"I know," I interrupted. If he stayed much longer, tried to comfort me some more, I'd start crying again. "Can I just be alone for a little while?"

"Sure," he replied and leaned in to brush a stray curl out of my eyes before standing. "I'll send Jack up."

"Thanks."

When Jason opened the door, we were both surprised to find my dog sitting patiently in the hallway. He trotted in and hopped onto the bed beside me for some much-needed cuddling. As I curled around him, I heard the door shut quietly.

While I lavished attention on Jack, I felt something odd attached to his collar. I lifted my head so I could see it and found a folded piece of paper wrapped around the leather band. Curious, I unwound and unfolded the paper. Feminine, bubbly handwriting covered the page.

Dani-

You have a very important choice to make tonight. You need to leave. If you're still here by sunrise, we'll kill Jason and Chris, and then you and your dog. If you tell them about this note, they'll come after us and we'll defend ourselves. Any spilled blood, like my sister's, will be on your hands. If you and your mutt leave before morning, we'll continue on peacefully. Without you, there won't be any more conflict. Make the right choice. Go.

Jack whined as the note slipped from my grasp. A single train of thought echoed through my mind. *I can't lose him.*

20

ZOE

From my makeshift desk in the mess hall, I could feel Jones's mood—black and bitter—as he strode in. The stark, empty dining room was suddenly charged with an incessant hum, like mosquitoes trapped in a megaphone. I had the sudden urge to flee, but I didn't move.

Meandering over to my table in the corner, Jones smiled and asked, "Zoe, my dear, how're you holding up?" He leaned his back against the wall mere feet from me, crossing his arms and ankles nonchalantly like we were friends catching up on old times. *Creep*.

We were indebted to him for letting us stay on base, so I knew I needed to keep my snide comments to myself as much as possible. I wasn't about to schmooze with him though. "I'm fine, thanks," I replied. "What can I do for you, Captain?"

"What are you working on?" he asked a little too curiously, ignoring my question. He stole a glimpse at my computer screen, but I closed the lid before he could read my email to Dani.

Although I couldn't see his exact thoughts, I could feel his emotions prickling my skin ominously, leaving unwanted goose bumps in their wake. Alarm rang in my mind, but I ignored it—the group was down the hallway if I needed them.

"So tell me a little bit about yourself, Zoe." Jones paused briefly. "What happened to your family? Are they in Massachusetts? Is that where you're from?" Although his questions were harmless enough, his emotions felt malicious. I didn't trust him.

Seeing my wariness, he feigned offense. "Oh come now, my dear. We're practically family now."

My eyes narrowed. Realizing I was displaying my distaste for him too openly, I turned away and began packing up my computer. "I haven't heard from them," was all I said.

"Do you have a history of mental illness in your family?"

I froze. *Why the hell would he ask me if my family is crazy?* My thoughts lingered on the word 'crazy', and a feverish hatred suddenly burned through my body. *Fucking Dave told him. Did he tell anyone else? Harper and Sarah would've talked to me themselves if they knew...*

My first instincts were to deny everything and to claim Dave had misinterpreted my meaning. I'd been drunk and only quasi-coherent; everyone could attest to that. But Jones had approached me alone for a reason, and my instincts told me to keep quiet.

"What are you getting at, Sir?" My tone was more annoyed than I'd anticipated.

Jones smirked sadistically and reached for my hair like an affectionate father. He stopped before touching me, and after hesitating for a moment, lowered his hand. "You have a little spunk in you. Dave said you were different." Pausing, he waited for his words to ignite some sort of response. When my granite expression remained, he continued, "Perhaps you're a little *too* different for Dave. He thinks you might be a...what'd he call it? Oh yes, a *Crazy*." He snorted with laughter. "But, I'm sure you already know that, don't you?" he asked, searching my face for recognition.

"I'm not sure what you mean," I simpered, wondering if batting my eyelashes would be taking it too far. Having this guy as an enemy wasn't making me feel warm and fuzzy.

"Don't be coy, girl," Jones snapped. "Telling me everything will only help you. I guarantee it."

Yeah, right. His presence alone was threatening. I could feel his agitation; he was wound up and ready to burst. He considered himself superior to me and was pissed off that he had to placate me —a lowly woman—to get the answers he sought. I wasn't sure how I knew that exactly, but his emotions were growing stronger by the second. His aggression thrummed through me, and my heartbeat quickened in panic.

"I think you misunderstand me, Captain. Perhaps you can explain what you want from me."

Full of self-satisfaction, he said, "You wonder why I'm not completely freaked out like your friend, Dave. I'll tell you a little secret." He leaned in closer. "You're not *that* special. I've seen others like you. I've *killed* people like you."

I pretended to be indifferent as I finished packing up, but inside, my heart pounded like it was trying to break out of my chest. It took everything I had to appear calm. W*ho the hell is this guy? How many people has he killed? He said he's seen others like me...*

Curiosity overpowered caution, and against my better judgment, I dilly-dallied. I could feel beads of sweat forming in my cleavage. "What 'others' are you referring to? I'm dying to know," I taunted unwisely.

"That doesn't concern you." Jones sat down next to me, gripping my arm firmly to keep me sitting. "What you need to worry about is what your friends will do if they find out you're a *freak*. We got rid of ours." He let his words sink in, then continued with false kindness. "I only want to help you."

Jones's concern was enough to make me vomit, and apparently my disgust was blatantly displayed on my face. He sighed. "Look, let's cut the shit."

"Finally," I grumbled.

Instantly, he was furious; it radiated off of him. "If you want me to keep quiet about your *secret*, you better do the same for me." His tone was harsh, and his words promised that really bad things would happen to me if I disobeyed. "I've got a good thing going on here, and I don't need anyone poking around where they don't belong." He jabbed his index finger against my chest.

For a brief moment I wondered what Jones was hiding, but then an image flashed in my mind; it was of one of the women I'd met when we'd arrived. She was naked in his bed, scared and crying.

Without warning, his calloused hand grabbed the back of my neck roughly, and my body tensed with fear. Low and venomous, he said, "I know girls like you. You always get in the way."

In that moment, I saw his plan to kill me. I saw his combat knife slicing into my side and then into my chest. A gun would be too loud, bringing too much attention too quickly. I didn't know if he was threatening me with the horrific image of my death or if he was merely contemplating how he'd do it, but it didn't matter. I couldn't remain near him a moment longer.

"Get your hands off me!" I demanded, but his fingers constricted. I muffled a shriek as my head snapped back.

Jones's face was inches from mine, and I could smell his rank, sour breath. His eyes bored into mine as he hissed, "You see, girl, I'm a Captain in the United States Army, and I have *zero* tolerance for bullshit. Don't even think about getting close to my girls. Don't cause any problems or ask any questions. I *won't* tolerate it!"

"You're crazy!" I snarled, trying to pull out of his grasp.

"That may be, but I've got my eyes on you. If I see you so much as look at anyone in a way I don't like, I *will* gut you like a pig. You know I will."

I couldn't breathe. The room started to close in around me. *His* anger and *my* fear waged a war in my head until I could neither discern nor push the emotions away. I couldn't ignore them. I thought of Dave's betrayal as my death replayed over and over in my head.

Somehow, I managed to tear myself from Jones's painful hold and flee. I raced outside into the freezing cold of the late afternoon. Through tear-blurred eyes, I could barely see two feet in front of me. I didn't care.

After what seemed like an eternity of aimless running, I finally stopped, my throat raw from inhaling the frigid air. My body was numb with cold, and pain lanced my sides. I had no idea how far I was from my friends.

I doubled over, dry heaving. I wished I could expel all the negative energy balled up inside me, but nothing would or could come out. A tree trunk supported me as I focused on controlling my breathing.

He's insane! He's going to kill me…it's only a matter of time. "I need to find Harper," I said, trying to rally myself, but my voice came out raspy and indistinct.

Looking around, I figured I was in the woods that butted up against the side of the base. The long shadows caused by the setting sun reminded me that winter wouldn't be merciful if I stayed outside much longer. I was improperly dressed for the frigid weather, my long-sleeved shirt and jeans offering little protection from the breeze that crept in through the trees. But I wasn't ready to go back.

Standing up straight and composing myself, I heard Dani's voice in my head. *Come on, Zo! You're smarter than him…and you have an advantage.* I thought of the strange power budding inside me and tried to imagine how I could use it against Jones, but I couldn't come up with anything. I desperately clung to the hope that he was full of shit. But I'd seen his plan…I'd felt his determination like it was my own. If I didn't do something to stop him, he'd *find* a reason to kill me.

Hearing a branch snap behind me, I spun around. Taylor, Jones's lackey, stood only a few feet away, watching me. His breath was visible with every exhale, and in the twilight his smile was demonic. *Shit.*

"This is gonna be *so* much fun," he said, chuckling devilishly. His eyes lingered on my exposed neck and heaving chest, and his hands twitched at his sides. He licked his quivering lips.

As I registered what Taylor wanted, dread washed over me, making me jittery and queasy. "What the fuck's wrong with you people!" I screamed, and my throat seared in pain. I turned away to run, and he sprang at me. Grabbing my arm, he yanked me toward him, and I immediately jerked back.

"Don't touch me, you son of a bitch!" I slapped at his hands. Unrequested, I could feel the excitement coursing through him. Once again, my unwanted ability to feel people's emotions was making it difficult to focus.

Taylor's hold tightened as he laughed and shook his head. "It's funny that you think there's something wrong with *us*."

He wrapped his arms around me, holding me against his chest. His breath scorched the back of my neck as he jerked me to the ground. I struggled against him, but it didn't do any good. My forehead slammed against the hard earth, and my shoulder screamed in pain upon impact. As I felt his tongue sample the delicate skin on my neck, I broke out in a cold sweat. His mouth was slimy and hot, and my body tensed at the thought of what he might do next.

"Get off me, you psycho!" I shrieked. "What do you people want from me?" But I already knew the answer—like with Jones, I could see Taylor's plan as it played out in his mind. He was going to beat me until I couldn't move, undress me one article of clothing at a time, and then he was going to rape me—and probably kill me.

Refusing to accept such a fate, I fought back. Taylor rolled me onto my back, and I jerked my knee up, aiming for his groin, but his body was too close. I attempted to bite him, but his sweaty palm slapped me so hard my jaw popped. I was momentarily stunned.

"Oh come on. I just wanna play with a pretty girl." He wrestled with me, trying to control me; his spittle sprayed the side of my face. In that moment, I knew what cattle felt like in the rodeo—being roped into submission, humiliated and helpless. But I wasn't helpless. He'd have to beat me unconscious before I let him violate me.

Distracted by the sight of my exposed stomach, Taylor loosened his hold on my right arm. I tore it away from him, gouging the side of his face with my nails.

He froze in surprise and pain before slapping my face again. "You stupid bitch!" Anger had replaced his taunting playfulness, and he punched me in the gut. I gasped for air, feeling like my insides had exploded.

"You're gonna get it now," he promised.

Terrified, I started screaming and struggling with every ounce of energy I could muster.

Surprised by my sudden display of might, Taylor studied me with dangerous amusement. "You're a feisty—" He paused, his eyes darting around the darkening woods. "You hear something?"

All I could hear was my muffled cries as I struggled to push him away. "Go to hell!" I screamed and kneed him in the groin, causing him to choke in pain. I elbowed him in the face before scrambling to my feet. As I took my first step to run away, his hand wrapped around my ankle.

"No!" I sobbed as my other ankle twisted and I collapsed to the cold ground again.

That was when I heard it—a dog's snarl and a man's infuriated voice. "Let go of her, Taylor."

My vision was too blurred with tears to see the newcomers, but I continued to struggle. Surprise had loosened Taylor's hold, and I was finally able to scurry away, putting several yards between us. I crouched against the trunk of a tree, trying to salvage what little remained of my shredded composure.

"What the hell are you doing here, Vaughn? I thought you were dead." Taylor shook his head as he stood, momentarily forgetting about me. The stranger nodded to the Husky at his side, and it trotted over to me. I shrank away, unsure what it would do, but the dog only nuzzled my face and hands.

I attempted to wipe the moisture from my eyes so I could see more clearly. The sweat on my hands was like glue, picking up loose leaves and dirt from the cold ground, and the debris scraped my stinging skin; the tender spots on my cheeks were throbbing.

The man—Vaughn—stood in the distance, and although I couldn't see the expression on his face, I could tell he was a solid force to be reckoned with. I detested the thought of anyone seeing me in such a state, but I was immensely grateful he'd shown up. *He just saved my life.*

"You're a piece of shit, Taylor," Vaughn said in an even, scathing tone. He raised his left arm, aiming a pistol at my attacker.

Taylor scoffed, but he looked nervous. With wide eyes and a wavering voice, he spoke. "What are you gonna do with that gun, Jake?" *Jake. Jake Vaughn.* Suddenly, Taylor seemed more sure of himself. "I don't think you have it in ya to kill someone." He took a step forward.

"There's a lot you don't know about me," Jake said as he glanced in my direction. There was recognition in his eyes I didn't understand.

"I should've known we couldn't get rid of you that easily," Taylor spat. "You've been causing problems since you got here." In the blink of an eye, he pulled out his own handgun and trained it on Jake. I screamed in warning.

Before Taylor could pull the trigger, Jake put a bullet in the left side of my tormentor's chest. Taylor fell to the ground, and blood seeped from the bullet hole. I hoped he'd been hit in the heart.

Jake didn't move, studying the dying man crumpled in front of me like he was waiting for him to get up. The dog at my side barked just as I heard new footsteps coming up behind me.

"Well, well. I thought you were dead." Jones's voice was eerily calm as he approached his fallen comrade.

"I've been hearing that a lot lately," Jake said dryly. His eyes veered over to me, assessing my wounds from a distance in the dim light.

My body shook violently as I sat on the ground, clinging to the Husky. Jones's presence erased any relief Taylor's death had brought me.

"What did you do to my man?" The Captain asked as he bent down and felt for Taylor's pulse. He stood up immediately. "You son of a bitch." His voice was eerily calm. "You killed him. Did you kill Bennington too? It's like you're *trying* to piss me off."

"That's what I tend to do when people are trying to kill me," Jake said dryly.

Advancing on Jake, Jones drew out his sidearm. In the seconds of chaos that followed, gunshots cracked as they briefly exchanged fire. I covered my ears and was about to run away when I looked back at Jake.

"Shit," he hissed, crouching on the ground and holding his arm against his abdomen. His face was twisted with pain, his breathing was ragged, and his sleeve was saturated with blood—Jones had shot him in the shoulder.

But Jones was down too. "Fuck!" he shouted, clutching his kneecap. Before Jones could lift his gun to fire at Jake again, the dog lunged. It tore viciously at Jones's arm, then clamped its sharp teeth onto his injured knee. The gun fell from Jones's hand, and I shoved it out of his reach.

"Aaah!" Jones cried out in pain. The Captain's torturous screams harmonized with the dog's angry snarls, composing a gruesome ballad that reverberated through the woods. Leaning against a tree, I covered my ears with my shaking hands. *Please stop,* I begged.

As if by request, the world seemed to slow to a crawling speed.

"Cooper!" Jake yelled, calling the dog off his assault on Jones.

As the Husky trotted over to his approaching owner, Jones remained on the ground, writhing in pain. His clothes were ripped and bloodied from the dog's teeth, but that didn't stop him from rolling over and reaching for Taylor's gun.

Before I could scream another warning, a bullet hit Jones between the eyes, and he collapsed. I easily swallowed the bile rising in my throat as I realized my tormentors were dead. Jake had killed them.

I looked up to find Jake leaning his good shoulder against a tree. As he repositioned his wounded arm, he flinched, his face pinching with pain. I hobbled over to him, my ankle throbbing with each step. When I reached him, I pulled off my long-sleeve shirt, not caring that I was left wearing only a tank top, and pressed the wadded up fabric against his bleeding shoulder.

"Oh my God," I said, visually searching his body for more wounds. "What can I do?"

"Nothing," he said coldly and pushed me and my blood-soaked shirt away. Before we broke contact, I mentally glimpsed a dark-haired woman, bloody in his arms.

Date: December 22, 6:25 PM
From: Zoe Cartwright
To: Danielle O'Connor
Subject: I've had better days...

D,

Have I told you recently that I hate Cece? Well, I do. Who the hell does she think she is? She thinks she can get away with all this bullshit, does she? Well, I think this is a perfect excuse for Jason to get rid of her. Seriously, he has no reason to hold back now. She's obviously a nutcase.

Speaking of crazy bastards...you know how I mentioned Jones wanted something last night? Well, my encounter with him was less than ideal. Our conversation started with an interrogation and ended with me running away. Hindsight is a bitch. I really wish I would've handled the whole thing differently. I won't bother you with the morbid details.

What matters is that they're dead. No, it wasn't me who killed them. A man named Jake Vaughn showed up and helped me. I don't know anything about him other than everyone thought he was dead, and he saved my life. I haven't seen him since. Regardless, I'm really happy Jones and Taylor are dead and NEVER coming back. You can't imagine how horrible they were.

Although those two assholes were crazy, there are some women here who seem okay. I've only briefly met them, but they are nice enough...Clara, Stacey, Tanya, and Summer. I'm pretty sure Summer's unwell, as in sick and mentally shattered—I can feel it when she's around me.

Anyway, now that the psychopaths have been disposed of, everyone is settling into their new rooms in the barracks. I'm currently "rehabilitating" in my new "sleeping quarters" (we're being very official). I have my own room, bed, and even a pleasant view of absolutely nothing. Well, that's a lie, there's a dead dogwood tree outside my window, but that's about it. This base is pretty desolate as far as any scenery goes. But I'm anxious and moody, so now I'm just finding things to complain about. Not a surprise. In all honesty, I feel cooped up and about ready to scream. I haven't been out of my room at all today—Harper's forcing me to rest for a day.

I'm not sure how long we'll stay here, but I'll let you know as soon as I hear anything. I'll check in with you tomorrow.

Zoe

21

DANI

Date: December 22, 11:30 PM
From: Danielle O'Connor
To: Zoe Cartwright
Subject: I'm SO Sorry

Zo,

I wish I had the magical power to teleport to you. That would fix so many of the problems we're both having right now. We could look out for each other, and I really just need to get away from all of the crap going on over here. You see, the whole Cece thing has escalated. A lot. I know you'll be pissed at what I'm about to do. I'm so sorry, Zo.

Earlier this evening, I found a note from the evil bitch. She warned me that I needed to leave the group. She said she (and her harem of idiots) will kill Jason and Chris if I don't leave tonight. I just lost Cam, and though I know it's not the same thing, I can't handle losing Jason too. Or Chris. Or anybody else. Plus there's the chance that all of this drama will calm down if I'm gone, and my friends will still be able to benefit from the "safety in numbers" deal. So, I have to leave.

When you get this, can you send an email to Jason explaining why I left? As soon as I have a chance, I'll try to contact you. If I can't, I'll see you in Colorado. Nothing will keep me from finding you. I love you, Zo.

Dani

"I'm done, Chris. Do you want to use my comp?" I asked after I'd signed out of the incriminating email account.

From her reclined position on the bed, Chris nodded and held her hands out to accept the silver laptop. I quickly handed it over.

Purposely fiddling with my fingers, I said, "I'm going to Jason's room for a bit. There's some stuff I want to talk to him about." I put on a good show, making sure to sound a little breathy and anxious.

"Mmhmm," Chris mumbled with a small smile, her eyes already glued to the glowing screen. "Have a nice time."

I rushed out of the room, Jack at my heels, confident that my performance had worked. As far as Chris was concerned, I should be spending the entire night in Jason's arms. She wouldn't be concerned when I didn't return.

My next stop really was Jason's room but not for either my stated or implied reasons. I tapped quietly on his door, two rooms down from mine. *Make it quick, or this won't work.*

The door opened partially, exposing Jason's expressionless face. Upon seeing me, he cleared the way to the room and motioned for me to enter. He was shirtless, and seeing his muscular torso paralyzed my tongue. I shook my head, finding it difficult to form the words I'd planned to say.

His eyebrows rose in surprise. "You won't come in?"

"No. I just came to say goodnight." *To say goodbye.*

"Oh, I thought…never mind." *You thought what? That I wanted to fight more? That I wanted you to finish what you almost started this morning?*

"I guess all the crying wore me out," I explained. "But…I wanted you to know that I'm not mad at you." *I wanted to tell you I'm leaving, and that I can't stand the idea of being away from you.*

"Oh, good," he said, sounding genuinely relieved. His eyes softened as he looked at me, and I felt an overwhelming urge to do something completely stupid.

Taking a step forward, I stood on tiptoes and brushed my lips against his cheek. His rough stubble felt heavenly against my sensitive skin. "Good night," I whispered mere inches from his ear. My fingertips were pressed lightly against his bare chest. *I can't lose you.* Before Jason had the chance to react, I stepped back and pulled the door shut between us.

Like stalking cats, Jack and I ghosted down the rest of the hallway. Ky's family home was quite large, equipped with two sets of stairs connecting the first and second floors. I headed for the narrow set at the rear of the house, conveniently leading me to the mudroom and backdoor.

Earlier that day—shortly after finding Cece's heinous note—I had gathered all of my essential belongings into my backpack and stowed it in the mudroom closet. With everyone focused on dinner and consuming the excess wine we'd brought from Gold Hill, it had been easy to complete the task unnoticed.

The closet door creaked faintly when I opened it to retrieve my pack. I paused, hoping desperately that nobody had heard. Only the muffled sounds of drunken laughter permeated the door separating the small room from the rest of the house.

I resumed my movements, covering my body with suitable outerwear before quietly hoisting the pack onto my shoulders. Without a backward glance, Jack and I slipped out the door into the unconventional safety of a moonless winter night.

We made our way slowly up a rolling hillside behind the house, me being especially careful not to twist my ankle in a hole or trip over anything. It was a long shot, considering the tall grasses masking the ground. After about twenty minutes, my eyes adjusted to the darkness and my surroundings grew clearer. I finally felt comfortable with my decision to not use a flashlight.

"Can you smell the horses, Jack?" I whispered to my cautious dog. I knew they had to be close; we'd passed a stable and expansive pastures on our way to Ky's house that afternoon.

Halting, Jack raised his glinting black eyes to mine and sniffed the air. I felt like he really *was* searching for the scent of horses.

On a hunch, I whispered, "Where are they? Take me to the horses, Jack."

Jack instantly surged forward and trotted through the tall grass, slowing only when he realized I'd fallen behind. He took a path slightly more to the right than I would have, making me question my decision to use him as a guide.

Suddenly, the faint stench of hay and manure wafted around me, and a long, gray-brown building came into view. *The stable!*

"Good job, Jack!" I whispered. Trusting my dog had been the right decision after all.

Picking up my pace, I headed for the stable. Jack bounded around me with uncontrollable excitement. By the time we reached the door, he'd stopped to pee twice; apparently the excitement had been too much.

Once we were safely inside, I relented on my flashlight ban. There were only a few tiny windows letting in the glow from the stars, and I needed light to find the necessary equipment. Unfortunately, as I began exploring the building's interior, I immediately noticed that an essential element of my getaway plan was missing: horses.

Before I could investigate further, I was interrupted by a loud bang. "Shit!" I yelped, nearly jumping out of my boots. *Is someone here? Did I screw myself by using the damn flashlight?* Still, I didn't have the nerve to extinguish the little light.

BANG! Instead of running away and hiding, I slowly moved toward the far end of the long building, where the sound seemed to originate. *I wish Jason was here.*

BANG! Jack rushed forward, scratching at one of the large sliding corral doors.

BANG! The German Shepherd whined, and his scratching became more enthusiastic, punctuated by brief moments of digging. *He wants me to open it? What the hell is on the other side?*

"Jack? What—"

BANG! My dog barked loudly, over and over again.

"Okay, but if I get mauled, it's your fault," I told him.

He backed away from the door, lying gracefully on the cement floor.

BANG! Grumbling, I held the end of the flashlight in my mouth and grasped the enormous metal door's handle with both hands. With heavy screeches and groans, it slowly slid open, and a huge Paint horse burst through the space. I stumbled back several steps and dropped my flashlight. *Well, that solves the horse problem,* I thought as I bent to retrieve my sole source of light.

The majestic horse ceased its anxious prancing and turned to face me. I couldn't believe that Jack was just lounging on the floor, oblivious to the potential danger posed by the larger animal. As the horse hesitantly approached me, I understood why. Every element of its body language screamed, *Help me; I'll help you.* The sense of mutual need was so strong that I could feel it in my bones; it seemed to echo in my thoughts.

The horse nudged my shoulder with its silken nose and raised its head to study me in the darkness.

"Hello, beautiful," I said, tentatively reaching out my free hand and stroking its neck. In the flashlight's minimal light, I could tell very little about the horse's appearance, only that its coat was composed of light and dark splotches and that its legs were caked in mud. I resolved to get it cleaned up at the first opportunity.

"I have to get away. Will you come with me?" I asked the horse, staring into its unwavering gaze.

Taking an easy step forward, it rested the side of its face against mine. It definitely didn't mind me, and leaving it behind would mean it would die a slow death of starvation. There was only one option—the horse was coming with me.

With a renewed purpose, I searched the storage room near the middle of the stable for the items I needed. Luckily, everything was neatly organized and had been kept in good shape.

After an hour of packing and saddling, my small company of woman, horse, and dog was ready to ride off into the night. I started us slowly, allowing the horse and myself to grow accustomed to each other, but my urgent need to flee soon overwhelmed the steady walk. By the time we reached Highway 1 and were following the coastline, my new companion and faithful dog were cantering at a matched pace along the gravel shoulder.

My consciousness seemed to fade in and out of awareness as the night flew by to the beat of hooves and the chorus of wind. I let the animals take charge, only caring that we stuck to the highway that would eventually lead us home. We took occasional walking breaks and a few brief stops, but for the most part, we moved constantly through the chilly night.

When the sun finally peeked over the hills to the east, I decided it was time to for a well-earned rest. Aside from the exhaustion of all involved, we needed to get off the road in case some of my former group members came after me. Or worse, in case there were Crazies out on a road trip.

My body swayed to the steady, slow rhythm of the horse's movements. We passed a sign declaring, "Manchester, POP. 462," and I knew exactly where to stop for the day. My crazy aunt, Janet O'Connor, owned a ranch less than a mile south of town. *Will she be there? Will she be alive?*

But the health status of my extended family didn't surpass my new group's need for a suitable rest stop. I dismounted and led the final quarter mile to Aunt Janet's property on foot. The poor horse had carried me an unbelievable distance and deserved a cooldown before stopping.

By the time we reached the house, my insides were knotted with anxiety. I'd never been overly fond of my aunt; her animosity toward her younger sister—my deceased mother—had driven a wedge between us. She'd always sneered at the decisions my mother had made—the decisions that had led to my birth and my mother's death.

My mother, Ceara O'Connor, had been a wild child. She ran away with an unknown American boy when she was seventeen, found herself pregnant and alone at eighteen, and died in child-birth at nineteen. Only Grams and her unwavering love had saved me from the intermittent bursts of guilt and depression that plagued my childhood. Aunt Janet, on the other hand, had taken those opportunities to remind me of her opinion of my mother—that she'd been reckless and selfish, and that I was better off without her. I'd never believed my aunt, and had grown to resent her.

Regardless, the idea of finding one of my family members dead was almost more than I could handle. But I had to check, just in case. Leading the horse to the empty pasture, I sucked in deep breaths and steadied my nerves. *If she's dead, she's dead, and there's nothing I can do about it. But if she's alive and needs help... I'll never forgive myself for abandoning her.*

The sweaty horse heaved relieved breaths at the removal of her tack. I hauled everything into the barn, and after neatly arranging it all, set out for the house with my dog. *I really don't want to do this.*

As soon as I opened the back door, the stench from inside waylaid me like a freight train, carrying death and sadness as its cargo. I searched the house's interior quickly and found my aunt in her bathroom, her corpse barely recognizable with its gray mottled tones and misshapen parts. *She must have passed early on,* I thought numbly.

"Let's go, Jack," I said trying not to gag. He followed as I rushed from the house, gasping for the fresh, frigid morning air.

I returned to the barn in a daze, found some oats, and brought them out to reward my new equine companion. *Aunt Janet's dead. What about Grams? No! Stop it!* I needed a distraction.

"What's your name, Pretty Girl?" I asked the horse as she ambled closer, eager for the treat I offered. I thought back on all she'd done for me, providing a means of escape from a desperate situation. Without hesitation she'd taken me away, flying through the night like Pegasus.

"I think I'll call you 'Wings'. What do you think?"

She nudged me with her nose and raised her head to study me with an intensely blue eye. I had the odd impression that she was accepting the name.

"Alright, Wings. Let's get you washed up so we can rest," I said, stroking her graceful brow.

She nudged me again, eagerly this time.

As I washed her, I took note of her beautiful coloring—large, coffee-brown splotches colored parts of her coat and mane, contrasting with the snow-white around them. What I'd thought was mud caking her legs turned out to be dark, crusted blood. Wings, however, showed no signs of injury.

"What happened, Wings?"

She snorted softly and looked away.

Was it that bad? Or am I going crazy and having an imaginary conversation with a horse?

She snorted again, and I eyed her suspiciously.

When she was finally clean, brushed, and happily munching on dewy grasses, I settled myself in the barn. With a sleeping bag, a bed of hay, and a roof over my head, I knew my life could have been much worse at that moment. *Jason and Chris could've been dead. Jack could've been dead. Crap,* I *could've been dead.*

Even though I'd just found my dead aunt's body and even though I was separated indefinitely from the few living people I loved, my mind remained unnaturally calm. The thought that I'd done the right thing by protecting my friends comforted me, and my exhausted body coasted toward sleep. With my dog cuddled next to me, I almost felt content. Almost.

22

ZOE

The steam was like a blanket. It enveloped me in its protective warmth, shielding me from the chilly air that awaited outside the locker room. We'd only had access to cold water at the cabin, and a hot shower was something I hadn't been sure I would ever have the luxury of enjoying again. It was better than I remembered—it was intoxicating. I savored the feeling of the nearly scalding water as it washed over my adulterated skin, lessening the tension that saturated my battered, weak body.

Although my muscles protested nearly every movement, especially my shoulder, something about the physical pain was comforting. It was a declaration that I was a survivor; despite the insanity and danger of the last couple weeks, I was still alive. I may have been wincing in pain, but I was still breathing.

Grudgingly, I shut off the water and reached for my favorite oversized towel—it had been among the few possessions I'd taken from my house in Salem. As I limped toward the locker where I'd stowed my clothes, my wet flip flops squeaked against the cement floor.

The locker room was dimly lit; the single working light bulb leaving the room full of shadows. *Why didn't anyone fix the lights?*

I wondered, only to shake the question from my mind. There was, no doubt, some deplorable reason Jones and Taylor would've left people to wander in almost complete darkness, vulnerable and unaware.

After pulling on a pair of navy blue sweatpants and a white camisole, I reached into the locker for my long-sleeved shirt and hairbrush, only to find I'd forgotten them. *Of course I did.* I'd been scatterbrained all morning.

I looked through the nearby lockers, hoping to find a misplaced sweatshirt or extra towel to wrap around my shoulders for the short trek back to my room. In my search, I caught a glimpse of myself in a small mirror hanging inside one of the lockers. I was instantly thankful for the room's dim lighting.

Dark, wet hair framed my pale, battered face. My once delicate features were grossly altered. Normally, my lips were soft and pink, but now they were raw and split in several places. My eyes were bloodshot and shadowed, and the left side of my face was swollen and stained with deep purple and red bruises. At the sudden memory of Taylor's breath on my neck, I looked away. I was glad the bulbs had burned out; I didn't want to see the extent of how badly he'd hurt me. At least I could cover up the rest of my wounds with clothing.

The heat of the shower was dispersing throughout the room, and I could hear the wind outside, whirling around the building. It seemed to be vacuuming out every last ounce of warmth. I shivered, eager to return to my room and the warmer clothes that awaited me there.

Dipping my head down, I wrapped the towel around my wet hair and secured it with a twist. I gathered up my dirty clothes as quickly as I could before hobbling out of the locker room. As I passed through the heavy metal door, I grabbed the green hand towel I'd hung on the handle, signaling the showers were in use by a woman.

Only six more doors, I noted as I shuffled down the hallway.

Although the barracks were huge, our numbers were few, and we occupied only a portion of the dorm-like building's first floor. The rooms were modest, each containing only a bed, a nightstand, a wardrobe, and a desk—though the number of boxes we'd filled while relocating the previous inhabitants' belongings suggested otherwise.

I had apparently wound my hair too tightly inside the towel—my already aching head was starting to feel like it was going to explode. The pressure was too painful to ignore, so I shifted my things into my left arm and attempted to pull the towel loose with my free hand. Abruptly, I tripped on my own flip flop and lost my balance, my ankle shrieking in pain.

"Motherfu—" Thankfully, I caught myself before I fell onto the cold, unyielding cement floor. I straightened with an irritated grunt and yanked the towel once more. When it gave way, my hair fell over my eyes, blocking my vision.

I took a step forward…and hit something solid and warm. "Shit!" I stumbled back, dropping my dirty clothes and damp towel. Strong hands grasped my upper arms just in time to keep me from crashing into the wall, making my bruised shoulder throb.

"Are you okay?" a deep voice asked, low and tense.

Peering through the tangled, black curtain of my hair, I saw Jake—he was frowning. As soon as our eyes met, he let go of my bare arms.

I was surprised to see him, the man who had saved my life, and words escaped me. I'd wanted to talk to him all day, to thank him for helping me. However, before I could say a word, he strode down the hallway and disappeared around a corner. Only then did I note that he'd used both arms to prevent my clumsiness from adding more bruises to my battered body. *He was shot in the shoulder…I saw it! Maybe it was just a flesh wound?*

I limped the rest of the way to my room, shaken by the encounter. I snatched a purple, long-sleeved shirt from the wardrobe, put it on, and began hobbling back and forth. *Why couldn't I just say "thank you"? It's not that difficult!*

I stopped in front of the small window and peeked through the mini blinds, just as I'd done when I'd awakened. I could see the woods beyond the compound—the pines jutted up into the sky like arrowheads along a steep ridgeline. The window afforded me a safe view of the place that haunted me every time I closed my eyes. Chills pricked my skin as I remembered the horrors that had taken place in those woods the previous night. No matter how many showers I'd taken, I hadn't been able to scrub away the memory of Taylor's filthy fingers sliding along my flesh. I could almost feel his hot breath on my face.

"Ahhh!" I yelled as I spun away from the window, too frustrated to mute my outrage. It was infuriating that I'd put myself in that position. Knowing how close I'd come to being that insatiable pervert's next course made me want to kick my own ass. I wanted a do-over. I wanted to show the bastard that I could hurt him the way he'd hurt me. I wanted to see fear in *his* eyes. But I knew that was impossible. Besides, if I was being honest with myself, I never wanted to revisit that terrifying moment—ever. I'd do whatever it took to make sure I never felt that hopeless or powerless again.

Gathering my wet hair into a ponytail, I thought about Mr. Jake Vaughn. *Why'd he push me away in the woods?* Even in the hallway, he'd fled as fast as he could. *Was he embarrassed that he was wounded? And who was that blood-covered woman?* I couldn't figure out why he'd been avoiding me after saving my life. Not that I expected him to comfort me with words or to wrap his arms around me—although my face felt flush thinking about the latter. I flung the thought away. *I can't believe he even* had *to save my life!* I was pissed at my ineptitude, feeling both disappointment and regret.

I tried not to be offended by Jake's rejection, but my efforts failed, and I clenched my trembling hands.

You know, it takes more muscles to frown than it does to smile,

Dani would have told me. *You really shouldn't do that, Zo…I know you don't want* those *wrinkles.* I couldn't help but smile at the memory of the words she'd said to me so many times.

Dani's imaginary voice added, *Look on the bright side,* reminding me to keep my pessimism in check. I was lucky to be not only alive, but relatively unscathed after my close call with the spawns of Satan.

I'll talk to Jake tomorrow, I told myself. Taking a deep breath, I focused on relaxing the tension that had seeped back into my body. I pictured towering redwood trees, seagulls swooping over the ocean, and a puppy-aged Jack chasing floating seaweed at the edge of the surf. And then I thought of Sammy…and Dave. I saw flashes of red, hating him for the pain he'd caused me. Worse, I hated myself for ever giving him the *opportunity* to be such a douchebag.

"Son of a bitch!" I sat down on the bed, working up to a really good scream, when knuckles rapped on the door.

Sarah bounced in with a stack of clothes. "Hey, stranger. How're you feeling?" She busied herself by placing my clean laundry in the wardrobe.

"Thanks, Mom," I said sarcastically, feeling completely useless.

She faced me, wearing a sympathetic smile. Her eyes were prettier than I remembered—chocolate-brown with long, dark lashes fanning around her eyes. With her elegant angles and bubbly personality, it was no wonder Biggs liked her so much.

Her features twisted as she took in my appearance. "Your swelling's gone down a little, but your bruising's gotten a lot worse."

"Great…" I sighed, making my sides ache, and flung myself back onto the bed. I instantly regretted it.

"You don't look like you've been resting," Sarah said, and I could feel her eyes on me.

"Of course I have. I've been doing absolutely nothing all day."

"Pacing and brooding isn't resting, Zoe. And you really shouldn't be walking around on your ankle. Why don't you sit and sketch or something? It might help clear your mind."

"How do you know I've been pacing?" I asked defensively.

Sarah grinned and picked up my hairbrush off the desk. "Cooper's been watching your shadow under the door all morning." She motioned for me to sit up, pulled my hair out of its elastic band, and began brushing. "You need to *rest*. You've been through a lot and—"

"I can't stand being useless," I complained. "I feel like I should be doing something. I hate being coddled." Her final stroke through my tangled locks jerked my head back. "That isn't helping my mood either. I can brush my own hair," I snipped.

"Then do it, because you look horrible." She relented and tossed the brush onto the bed, ignoring my glare. "I'll leave you alone, but you're just being—"

"Zoe," Sanchez said, finishing Sarah's sentence as she strode into the room.

"Yeah, sure, that's what I was gonna say." Sarah studied me appraisingly. "Not that you will, but let me know if you need anything." Shaking her head, she walked out of the room, shutting the heavy metal door behind her.

Sanchez stared at me, her eyes narrow slits of contempt and judgment. "You don't look like you've been resting."

"Yeah, so I've heard," I muttered, straightening the wool blanket beneath me.

Please leave me alone, I thought, looking around the room for something to focus on—Sanchez still made me feel uncomfortable. I wasn't sure why she was in my room, but I wanted her to leave. Unfortunately, she sat down at the edge of the bed and just kept looking at me.

Finally, she said, "I need to talk to you about something."

I raised my eyes to hers, waiting nervously.

"Dave told us what happened."

Groaning, I dropped my head into my hands. I suddenly felt like a criminal waiting for the jury to decide my fate. "Us? So everyone knows?"

"I'm not completely sure. We haven't had a group discussion about it or anything. I don't know who'd believe it anyway. But it doesn't matter." Her eyes softened, and I thought I sensed sympathy. "You're safe with us, and we won't let anyone else try to harm you, no matter what." I was surprised to hear sincerity and conviction in her voice.

"Of course we won't," Harper chimed in as the door swung open. He winked at me and came over to kiss my forehead. "How're you feeling, Baby Girl?"

Relieved, I glanced up at him and smiled, but the expression faltered as my busted lip pulled apart. At seeing my discomfort, Harper winced and set a tray with water and meds down on the nightstand. "I'll try not to tease you while you're healing. You look too pathetic." My mood lightened; I already felt better in his presence.

"*You're not the only one who's experiencing these…changes.*" I blanched—it was the second time I'd heard Sanchez's voice in my head. When I looked back up at her, searching her expressionless face, I noticed the dark shadows around her eyes. She looked exhausted and disheveled, unlike her usual polished self.

Okay, what the hell's going on!? I screamed at her with my mind, but she didn't answer. Regardless, I couldn't tear my eyes away from her. I felt anxiety pouring out of her, charging my skin like electricity.

"There's something I…," Harper began, but his words were drowned out by whatever was happening between Sanchez and me.

"I think Harper can help us," Sanchez explained. *"I haven't told him about me yet, but he has theories about your unique skill. We can't be the only ones experiencing these changes."*

I knew that a few of Dani's companions were experiencing something similar, but reading about it wasn't as reassuring as witnessing it. I finally had concrete proof that what was happening to me was real—my sanity was no longer in question. I wanted to cry with relief.

Can you hear me? I attempted to ask Sanchez, but again there was no answer.

Oblivious to our mental conversation, Harper watched me expectantly. "Did you hear what I said?" he asked.

Crap. I'd forgotten to listen to him. "Sorry, my head's hurting. I'm having a hard time focusing," I lied as I rubbed my temple for added theatrics. When I looked back up at Sanchez, her face was inscrutable.

"I said 'There's something I need to tell you'," Harper repeated.

I looked from him to Sanchez with dread.

Harper stood by my bed with his arms crossed, and before he even spoke, I knew I wouldn't like what he was about to say. I suddenly wanted to throw myself onto the bed in a temper tantrum and sob because everything seemed so shitty. But I refrained, knowing that such a reaction would be unbecoming of a twenty-six-year-old.

"I'm not going to freak out if that's what you're waiting for, H," I fibbed.

"Good, then you should know we're staying here for a while. It's too dangerous to travel during the winter." He opened a bottle of ibuprofen and handed me three capsules along with a glass of water.

I swallowed them begrudgingly. My throat was still sore from screaming in the woods. As I sipped the water, I wondered how the postponement would alter my plans to meet up with Dani and Jason.

Sanchez finally broke the silence. "We know you're eager to meet up with your friends at Peterson."

Seeking privacy, I stood and walked over to the window.

"We're going to announce it tomorrow during breakfast, when

we're all together. We'll go over our plans with the group and see who's on board," Harper explained.

"I'm adamant about staying," Sanchez told me. "Our group just got a hell of a lot bigger. It's not smart to keep traveling now—especially when we have everything we need right here."

It was sound justification, but I still didn't like it. "You need to do what you need to do."

I heard Harper's heavy footsteps as he approached me. "I'll come get you when it's time to eat. Rest up in the meantime, okay?" He placed his hand on my good shoulder and squeezed lightly. I could feel his concern, and I was comforted to know he cared. *There are worse things than staying here a little longer*, I admitted. When he ordered me to lie down and stop pacing, I groaned but promised I would.

Then they were gone. Once again, I was alone with my thoughts.

23

DANI

When I woke, the warmth of the summer sun was seeping into my skin. A gust of tangy sea air caressed me, cooling my body from the heat. My whereabouts were more than a little disconcerting, considering I'd fallen asleep in a barn…in the dead of winter.

I opened my eyes and found that I was sunbathing on my favorite stretch of beach near my coastal hometown. Looking to my left, I fully expected to find Zoe's curvy, bikini-clad body reclining languorously. We only ever came to this particular spot together, but my best friend was nowhere in sight.

Confused, I sat up and looked around. Everything was exactly as it should've been, from the Pacific Ocean's rhythmically crashing waves to the rocky outcropping erupting from the sand several yards away—everything except the tall man silhouetted in the bright morning sky.

As the man Zoe had dubbed MG walked toward me, I should have been nervous and panicking, ready to run away. But I wasn't. I was annoyed.

"You!" I exclaimed, hopping up from my sandy towel. I stomped toward him, ignoring the excessive sway the sand lent to

my stride. In my little purple and green polka-dot bikini, my strut was positively strip club worthy.

"Me?" His smooth voice was growing familiar from our dreamtime rendezvous. He leered, happily taking in my state of undress.

"Yes, you! What the hell? Repeating 'LEARN' and surrounding me by a bunch of molesty fog…that's so not okay! Especially because I dreamt you up to begin with…which means it was really me doing it to myself…" I was growing increasingly weirded out by my own subconscious.

With raised eyebrows and an unsuccessful attempt at not smiling, MG responded, "Is that how it came through? Interesting. And what exactly do you mean by 'molesty'?"

"You know, your fog was totally feeling me up…everywhere. And making me feel…things. It was very annoying. And you should already know all of this. You're in my head!"

He was most definitely smirking. "Are you saying my 'fog' turned you on?" He took several steps, closing the distance between us.

As soon as he was within arm's reach, I remembered the last time I'd met him face-to-face in a dream, the night Cece had tried to slice me open. "I don't want you to kiss me," I blurted.

MG barked a laugh. "Alright. I'm here to teach you. I suppose I can do that without touching you." He finished with a deep, dramatic sigh.

Suddenly, I was completely frustrated with my stupid brain for continually conjuring the strange man in my dreams. "Seriously?" I yelled. "Why do I keep dreaming of you? I don't even know anyone like you! You chase away my rotting boyfriend, kiss me, and tell me cryptic things. What the hell?! My brain is so demented! Maybe I really am one of the Crazies. Ahhhh…this is so incredibly, pathetically me! I dream you up, Mr. You-Are-Ready. Mr. LEARN. Mr. I'm-Here-To-Teach-You. Stop laughing at me!" I shrieked the last words like a banshee.

"Wow," he said with a chuckle. "You're adorable when you're angry."

Jack appeared beside me, and together we stalked off toward the ocean, seeking comfort from its familiarity. Staring into the endless, ever-changing, blue-gray abyss, I heard the coarse sand compacting under MG's footsteps as he approached. For a while he said nothing, standing close enough that I could feel hints of his breath on my neck.

Beside me, Jack began a low, steady growl.

MG heaved a lengthy sigh. "I'm real, Dani."

"Excuse me?"

"I'm real. Not a creation of your sleeping mind. I live. I breathe. I sleep and have my own dreams."

"Right," I scoffed, turning away from the rolling surf to face him. After staring into his sincere, sky-blue eyes, I laughed and patted his cheek. To prove how not-real he was, I kissed him…or at least I tried to.

With a frustrated grunt, MG gripped my shoulders and held me away from him. "I have to teach you some extremely important things, and I can't do my job if you think I'm some fantasy. Not that I'd mind really…" His mind seemed to wander briefly. "But I have to teach you! So," he started, gritting his teeth and squeezing his eyes shut like he was concentrating on something, "when you wake, it'll be 3:23 in the afternoon where you are, and your dog will be standing beside you, whimpering at nothing."

"What?" I asked, unbelievably confused.

"If I'm right, you'll know I'm real. I couldn't possibly be a creation of your pretty little red head because you don't know those things. You couldn't know those things, not while you're sleeping. I'll see you next time."

"But…," I mumbled to a mouthful of hay. I was awake. I was

peeved. And I was staring into the worried face of my beloved, whimpering dog. *Crap! What time is it?*

I hastily checked the watch I'd scavenged several days earlier. It was 3:23 p.m.—exactly the time MG had predicted. *Double crap! Maybe it's just a coincidence...or maybe he* is *real. That's totally insane!*

Thinking through the situation, I realized it wasn't really *that* crazy—especially considering Zoe's unnatural new talent. So why couldn't a man spend his spare time wandering through people's dreams? *Or...I'm losing my mind.*

Sitting up, I shook my head to clear the mental cobwebs and immediately regretted both actions. "Owww," I groaned. "I think I'm broken."

Every muscle, bone, and inch of connective tissue ached relentlessly. I considered braving Aunt Janet's house-shaped tomb in search of prescription pain killers, but I decided a half-dozen over-the-counter anti-inflammatories would do just as well. Pushing through the pain, I ate and got ready in record time and started hobbling around the barn in search of useful items—like a pad for my unbelievably sore, possibly bruised, butt.

It had been about six years since I'd last ridden a horse, and though I kept myself in okay shape, nothing could prepare the body for horseback riding like, well, horseback riding. The last time I'd ridden, I'd taken Grams, Zoe, Jason, and Tom, their dad, on a farewell trail ride. The Bodega Bay Riders' Ranch, my summer employer, had a tradition of comp-ing a family and friends' joyride for employees as a parting gift. I'd worked there for four consecutive years, so they'd been especially generous in their offerings. The five of us had spent the entire day, with a picnic lunch, riding around the coast and hills surrounding our little town.

Zoe and I had both been shocked when Jason had shown interest in the outing. He'd been home on leave for a few weeks and had overheard us talking about the adventure.

"Can I come along?" he'd asked.

Zoe and I, in the midst of consuming copious amounts of chocolate chip cookie dough, had just stared at him in awe. Jason *never* wanted to spend time with us. Not ever. He'd always preferred hanging out with girls he could have sex with. *Which hasn't really changed...*

"Uhhh," I'd said, sounding completely idiotic.

Zoe, being her amazing self, had exclaimed, "Uh...yeah!" Under the table her feet had jabbed into my shins excitedly—she'd witnessed every moment of my obsession with her older brother and had known I would want him to join us, desperately...even if I'd been momentarily speechless.

And so, we'd all ended up on the trail together in a day of simple joy and relaxation. Jason had been friendlier and flirtier than I'd ever seen him. It was the last time I saw him before I met Cam.

And with that errant thought, my mind tried to unravel into emotional chaos. *Cam is dead...and Callie...and Aunt Janet...*

No! I couldn't let myself lose it. *Not now...not here...* I needed to do something to avoid the dark thoughts. They loomed on my mind's horizon like a mass of enemy troops, their attack inescapable. It wasn't a question of *if*, but *when*.

I filled the afternoon—and my disobediently wandering mind—with saddling Wings and loading up our bags. Appearing to sink into the glittering ocean, the sun set as we left the familiar ranch and plodded onto the shoulder of the deserted highway.

No longer occupied with menial tasks, my brain was free to wander once again. It began slowly, the depression lurking around the edges of my mind. Longing thoughts of the world before the Virus crept in, followed by heartbreaking images of death. Every ounce of my being wallowed in loneliness and despair.

Cam, Callie, Aunt Janet...everyone is dead...everyone except the people I just cut myself off from. What if something happens to the few people I have left?

How long will it take me to get to Zo this way? Was this a huge mistake? Should I have stolen a car? Where would I have found gas? What am I even doing?

I shook my head, trying to dispel the questions unraveling in my mind.

What will I find in Bodega Bay? That Grams is dead? And Zo's dad? Will anyone still be alive?

What if Cece lied? What if she goes after Jason anyway? What if she already did? If he died…was dead, I knew I'd never be the same. The Dani who'd recovered from Cam's death, from the death of the world, would cease to exist. I would become the personification of revenge and vengeance, misery and death.

My next thought stole my breath like a kick to the chest. *Am I in love with Jason?*

The pieces of Cam I carried in my heart began to wail and beat their imaginary fists against the inside of my ribcage. *How could you abandon me like this? How could you love him? I just died! Did you even love me?*

No. No. No! I loved you. I know it. I wanted to spend forever with you. But you died!

I suddenly despised myself. *Maybe I deserve loneliness. If I stay away from everyone, I can't betray, hurt, or abandon them. It'll be as if I never existed. They're better off without me.* With that final thought the attack lessened, reducing to a slow barrage near the surface of my awareness. I lost myself in the rhythm of Wings's canter.

In the faint light of pre-dawn, I spotted a sign through bleary eyes: *WOODSIDE CAMPGROUND, NEXT RIGHT*. It had been another long night, and though I was tempted to push through the final twenty-five miles to Bodega Bay, we needed to stop. I was hurting—badly—and the animals were showing obvious signs of weariness.

"What do you guys think?" I asked my animal companions after dismounting. The horse whinnied and bobbed her head while

Jack rolled onto his back and stuck his feet in the air. He was playing dead. My sarcasm, it seemed, had rubbed off on my dog. *Delightful…*

"Let's get you unsaddled and find something to eat," I told an exhausted Wings. Her stamina was impressive—far better than mine—but even she looked utterly pooped.

As I set up my little orange and white tent for the first time, I was thankful for the slowly rising sun. I wasn't afraid to admit that I needed the instructions to manipulate the fabric and poles into something resembling a shelter.

I couldn't help but think about the people I'd left behind. Jason would be waking soon; he always rose with the sun. He was weird like that. In a few hours, he and the others would begin their second day of searching the city of Fort Bragg. I guiltily wondered if Jason blamed himself for my sudden departure. I'd made it abundantly clear that I wanted to continue on to our hometown, and he'd flat out denied me, but not before he'd let me glimpse the deep emotions hidden beneath his stoic façade.

Not for the first time, I wondered how Jason had reacted when he'd discovered I was gone. *And Chris? Ky?*

With my campsite finally set up, I crawled into the tent and then into the sleeping bag, cringing in pain. I hurt like hell. Loneliness and self-loathing kept me company as I tossed and turned, trying to find a comfortable position. My last, hazy thought was of MG. *Will I see him again?* I wondered before finally falling into a fitful sleep.

Again I woke somewhere entirely different from the place I'd fallen asleep. Much to my surprise, I was standing with a badminton racquet in my right hand. As I looked around, my surroundings coalesced into a jumble of odd elements. A perfectly trimmed grass field extended in all directions, met by a cloudless blue sky at the horizon. A net appeared in front of me, justifying the racket clasped in my hand. Zoe stood on the opposite side of the net, patiently waiting for the game to begin.

Conjuring a birdie, I served. The joy of playing with Zoe, especially doing something we hadn't done since the carefree days of high school, overtook me, and I laughed. I felt two hundred pounds lighter, like I might just float away with happiness.

"IT'S TIME FOR DOUBLES MATCHES," announced a booming, disembodied voice. I half-expected it to continue with, "PAY NO ATTENTION TO THE MAN BEHIND THE CURTAIN!"

Out of nowhere, MG appeared and stepped onto my side of the grassy court while Jason did the same on Zoe's side of the net. We had our partners. I took a moment to study the two new arrivals. MG was around the same height as Jason, making him about six-foot-four, but Jason was thicker, his body more heavily muscled, and where MG was pale and blond, Jason was tan and raven-haired. For the briefest instant, both men's clothing disappeared, giving me a full view of their various attributes. I hastily returned their t-shirts and shorts, blushing furiously.

MG smiled like the Cheshire Cat. "What was that all about?"

With my cheeks still burning, I looked back and forth between the two men and mumbled, "Um…uh…"

"Who's he?" MG asked, his smile turning snide.

"Jason. And that's Zoe," I said, pointing at her with my racquet. "Hi guys."

"Hi D!" Zoe replied.

"Hey Red," Jason purred.

Glaring at Jason, MG ordered, "Shut up, both of you."

"Hey!" I shouted and threw my racquet at him. "Nobody tells my friends to shut up in my dream except me! Especially not you, MG!"

"MG?" he asked, cocking his head to the right and raising a questioning eyebrow.

"Umm…yeah. It's short for 'Mystery Guy'? You haven't exactly told me your name," I grumbled.

Laughing, he nodded. "You barely know me, and you've already given me a nickname. I'm honored." He finished with a mocking bow.

"So you were right—it was 3:23 on the dot," I admitted through gritted teeth. I wanted to get the I-told-you-so moment over as soon as possible.

Relief flashed across MG's face and quickly disappeared. "I know," he said.

I was surprised he hadn't seized the opportunity to gloat. "So…"

"So now I'm going to tell you something extremely important… which you probably won't believe." He paused, and I gestured for him to continue.

He stepped closer, letting me see the truth in his eyes. "You see, people who survived the Virus have been demonstrating remarkable abilities. It seems to be a result of the Virus itself—a spontaneous genetic mutation. Every single person I've…seen…has either experienced this mutation or lost their minds entirely. I'm sure you've noticed all of the completely insane people running around."

I nodded, feeling numb. The Crazies. But I'd also witnessed abilities like he was describing with Chris and Ky. And then, of course, there was Zoe.

"Most of these abilities are too weak or so useless that they're inconsequential. A few of the more powerful and advantageous, however, could be essential to human survival. I, for example, can consciously enter the sleeping minds of others, as you've seen. I'm especially drawn to the dreams of people with a certain type and strength of ability." I was getting the distinct impression that "Ability" was an official term wherever MG was. "I've been drawn to you since you recovered."

I shook my head. "Then your Ability must be broken. I don't have any special powers—no sparks exploding out of my fingertips or objects floating around the room." Even so, I needed to keep him talking, explaining. He knew what was happening to Zoe…and Ky and Chris. I glanced at the imaginary Zoe standing placidly across the net.

"You surprise me, Dani. Most are resistant, even angry at the idea. But you…you must already know someone experiencing the change. You know it's true," he claimed, watching me carefully.

I tore my eyes away from Zoe, desperate not to give away her secret. "What do you think I can do? What's my Ability?" I asked impatiently.

"Hmm…I have several guesses, but I know one thing for sure." He smiled knowingly. "I'm not going to tell you. You won't believe me without seeing it for yourself, so…I have an assignment for you. It should help you pinpoint exactly what you can do."

"And that would be…?"

"When you wake up, experiment. Don't talk to your animals out loud, and see how your day progresses."

"Why?"

"Just do it, okay?" he said, suddenly right in front of me. His hand reached out, and his fingertips brushed down my arm. "What were you thinking about when you caused that brief wardrobe malfunction earlier?"

Staring into his inquisitive, blue-gray eyes, I retreated into my mind.

24

ZOE

I'd been awake for hours. Lately, restful sleep had become foreign to me. Every time I woke, I thought. Every time I thought, I worried. I couldn't stop replaying the attack or worrying about Dani traveling alone. I thought about Jason's panicked response after I'd written to tell him why Dani had left, and I feared he would do something rash. I wanted to ruin Cece as much as he wanted to, but the hostility in his email was hair-raising. I also worried about what was happening to me. I was changing, evolving somehow, and though I knew Harper and Sanchez were there to help me, I was afraid.

After repeatedly counting every knot in the wooden rafters over my bed, I managed to memorize and draw them. When I grew bored with that, I sketched seashells and other things that reminded me of home. In the midst of failing at my third attempt to get the shading just right, I gave up and threw my pencil across the room. I heaved myself off the bed, hastily dressed, and hurried out of the barracks, hoping a breath of fresh air would whisk away the cords of insanity unwinding in my mind.

Being outside was uncomfortable; the morning air bit at the healing scrapes on my face and hands, but the sunshine made it worthwhile. I wasn't the only one out enjoying the early morning rays. Off in the distance, a rabbit hopped around on the barren ground, foraging for breakfast. Little finches jumped from branch to branch on a leafless, withered tree, chirping and playing. I walked softly, trying not to disturb them.

Feeling partially rejuvenated, I let my mind run away from me. Hope took root deep inside...*maybe we'll get an early spring*. But my optimism faded as gray clouds drifted in front of the sun, casting baleful shadows.

I let my feet determine the pace and followed a winding sidewalk through the abandoned base. *Where are all the dead bodies?* I wondered, not for the first time. I shuddered and hoped I wouldn't stumble upon any of them. As I strolled down the path, surrounded by dark, empty buildings, an eerie feeling settled over me, like I was taking a guided tour through the future:

Graffiti art was a popular medium of expression during The Ending. You'll notice, "We're all going to die!" painted on the brick buildings to your right and the rusted doors of the personnel offices to your left. When people started losing their minds and/or dying during the Apocalypse, chaos ensued. In all the uncertainty, people left everything behind. They looted and scavenged, leaving Fort Knox the abandoned footprint of civilization you see here today. What was once home to thousands of cavalry, artillery, and infantry soldiers became home to squatters, freaks, and a new breed of humanity.

Nearing the enormous gym, I shook myself from my demented daydream. Sarah had told me that Biggs and Harper had taken to playing basketball there when they had downtime. Concentrating, I could hear the sound of a ball being dribbled inside.

My curiosity was piqued, and I made my way in to see if my friends were playing an early morning game of HORSE. Pulling my hands from the warm sanctuary of my pockets, I pulled the clunky metal door open and stepped inside. The dribbling continued until the door slammed shut behind me.

Walking further in, I spotted a single person in the vast space, and my smile faded. Jake, breathing heavily, held a basketball against his side with one arm as he waited to see who had disturbed his morning exercise. His face hardened when I stepped into view.

It was the perfect opportunity to thank him, but I was distracted by…him. Perspiration glistened on his jaw, and his black t-shirt clung to his brawny, heaving chest. As he rubbed a hand over his short, damp hair, his sculpted biceps flexed, and I found myself silently hoping he would…

"Did you need something?" he asked abruptly. Yet again, he didn't seem happy to see me.

"I was just..." Frustration eroded the thought I was trying to articulate, but before I could make a second attempt, the door flew open.

"There you are." Harper's amicable voice perked my mood up like a thirsty flower given water. "I went by your room, but you weren't there." He nodded to Jake, then caught my eye and motioned toward the doors. "Let's get some breakfast."

I glanced back at Jake and wondered if I would ever get the chance to thank him for saving my life…or to ask him what his problem was. Our eyes met for only an instant before he looked away, but I thought I saw curiosity in his gaze.

Walking back outside with Harper, I asked, "What's his story?"

"Jake? I'm not sure. Why?"

I shrugged, pretending to be indifferent. "Just wondering."

Harper slid his hands into his pockets. "I don't know. You've known him as long as I have. But, I think it's safe to say he's a pretty private person. He probably isn't sure he can trust us. I'm the same way."

"I really can't see you being reserved given your history of scandalous propositions…in front of everyone," I teased.

He winked. "It all depends, Baby Girl."

Laughing, I shook my head. "You know how demeaning that is, right?"

"What, you don't like your nickname? It just seems right. I like the way it takes you by surprise every time I say it."

"I just can't believe I'm *letting* you call me that." A sudden, frigid gust of wind assaulted us, and we quickened our pace. We continued on toward the mess hall in silence.

When we stepped into the giant dining room, a small group was clustered around a long cafeteria table in the far corner. I could feel their eyes on me as Harper and I crossed the room to the breakfast buffet. *They probably wonder whether I'm crazy or not.*

My concern vanished as my mouth began to water at the sight of bacon, biscuits, and gravy. My appetite had definitely returned.

"OJ?" Harper asked, pouring some into a glass.

"Yes, please." We carried our trays to the table and sat down by Biggs, Sarah, and the other women.

Halfway through our meal, I heard shuffling footsteps and looked up to see Dave and Stacey walking into the mess hall. The scrapes on my face pulled as I scowled at the sight of my former friend—I hadn't seen him since the incident in the woods.

Stacey's brow furrowed sympathetically as she took in my damaged appearance, but she quickly caught herself, forced her mouth into a warm smile, and waved. I quirked my lips slightly, trying not to disturb the progress of their healing, and smiled back.

Dave stopped, looking like his feet were suddenly glued to the ground. His face paled, and I lowered my eyes, focusing on my plate of food. I needed to smother the rage billowing inside me. I needed to hit him. *Just ignore him*, I told myself.

"Alright, everyone," Sanchez said as she marched into the room with rolled up maps and blueprints under her arm. "We've got a lot to cover today, so let's get started." She looked around. "Where's Summer? And Jake?"

"Here." Jake nonchalantly strode into the dining hall, pulling a sweatshirt over his head. Cooper, the Husky, trotted in behind him, his tail wagging and his tongue hanging from his mouth. I watched Jake as he walked to the buffet and started plating his breakfast. The other women were distracted by Cooper, fawning over him and playing with his velvety ears and bushy tail. I, on the other hand, couldn't tear my eyes away from Jake. Again, I was surprised he was moving around so well only a couple of days after being shot.

"*Do you mind?*" Sanchez said in my mind.

Snapping my head to the right, I met her stare. I sheepishly looked back down at my breakfast and picked at it with my fork. I wondered how and why *our* bodies reacted to the Virus so differently. With that thought, I studied the other members of the group, considering the possibility that Sanchez and I weren't experiencing these changes alone. *What aren't they sharing?*

"And Summer?" Sanchez looked over to Tanya, Summer's sister. "Where is she? I haven't seen her since yesterday afternoon."

"She's still not feeling well," Tanya said softly. "She decided to stay in bed a little longer. I'll fill her in on everything." Her eyes were full of worry.

"Let Harper know if she needs anything," Sanchez said and clapped her hands together. "Okay, let's get started."

Sanchez began by informing everyone of the decision to stay in Fort Knox for a few more weeks. "We have an armory to inventory. We need to figure out exactly what to take when we do leave." Glancing at Jake and me, she continued, "Some of you are in need of medical attention, and Harper has access to an entire hospital here. We have shelter and enough food to last us months, if needed. There's no logical reason to leave until the weather gets better and we have a plan of action."

There was dissension from Tanya and Clara, two of the women who'd already been on the base when we'd arrived, which wasn't surprising—they wanted to get as far away from the place as possible. I'd only seen a glimpse of the atrocities Jones and Taylor had inflicted upon them, and could hardly imagine the horrible memories that awaited them around every corner.

"I know things haven't been easy for you the last month or so, but I guarantee you'll be safer with us," Sanchez promised them. "Obviously the Virus has changed things. Life's different now, and more than anything, we need to be prepared for what comes next. My team and I will do everything we can to make sure nothing happens to you, but if we leave, it'll be more difficult. We need to know what we're up against before we move on. The more information we can collect before leaving, the better."

Silence surrounded us as her words hung in the air, threatening to dissolve the illusion of peaceful solitude we'd clung to over the last few days. I felt a twinge of anxiety—a few weeks seemed like a long time to wait, but I understood Sanchez's reasoning. I hoped to never come across anyone like Jones or Taylor again.

"That gives some of us time to learn how to defend ourselves too," I said, partially raising my hand to interject. I made a conscious effort not to lock eyes with Dave.

Harper looked at me and grinned. "If you insist…that'll be fun," he said playfully.

Ignoring him, Sanchez nodded. "I'll get to that in a minute."

Biggs joined her at the head of the table. He unrolled a few of the maps and held them up, pointing out the hospital, the repair garage, and several places where we could find more supplies and clothes on base. Sarah's eyes were appraising, never leaving him as he explained our modes of communication and our emergency plan should there be any sort of infiltration.

"The Internet's been on and off all morning, but it's safe to say it won't last much longer. As for transportation…we're working on it. Jake, since you said you know your way around an engine, we need you to get a few vehicles up and running. I'm not sure how difficult it'll be since it looks like they've all been tampered with." Biggs paused, considering something. "You obviously know how to use a gun, so we'd also like you on the patrol team." His eyes shifted to me. “Zoe, you’re going to be Harper’s medical assistant. You’ll begin training with him in the hospital today.”

“I want a full inventory of the medical supplies we have at our disposal,” Sanchez added before assigning the rest of the duties.

As she started to dismiss us, I interrupted, “What about the self-defense lessons?”

Sanchez’s dark eyebrows arched, and she looked like she was hiding a smile. “Those of you who want to learn how to protect yourselves, which I encourage each of you to do, come see me,” Sanchez told the seven civilians in the room. “Zoe, since you’re so keen on the idea, you can start as soon as you’ve healed a bit more.”

“I think I’m—”

“Harper, come see me later so we can discuss her sessions,” Sanchez said, cutting me off. *Or, you could just ignore me.*

When she left, the rest of us returned to our meal, chewing absentmindedly.

“This sucks,” Sarah said under her breath, and we all shifted our attention to her. She looked around sheepishly. “I mean, this whole learning how to survive…thing. I already miss mani-pedis.”

Laughter broke out around the table. Harper stomped his foot and tried not to choke on his coffee as he swallowed. “I’m gonna miss wet t-shirt contests.”

“Reality TV,” Stacey added, and Tanya agreed.

Biggs smiled. “My mom’s chicken and dumplings.”

“Yeah, definitely Mom’s cooking,” Harper agreed. “She could make a mean meatloaf.”

“What about you, Baby Girl?” Harper asked, taking a sip from his mug. His eyebrows danced as he waited for my response, and I knew he hoped I’d say something inappropriate.

Everyone was focused on me, waiting. There were a lot of things that came to mind: fresh-made saltwater taffy, Bob Ross reruns, pub crawls with Dani… “It’s hard to choose, but definitely firework shows on the Fourth of July.”

"I didn't know you liked them so much," Sarah said, raising her eyebrows in surprise. There was a lot Sarah didn't know about me.

"Ever since we were freshmen in high school, my best friend and I would sit up on my roof, drink wine coolers, and watch the fireworks. We looked forward to it every year." I smiled. "Even after we moved away, we'd always come home for that."

"I know what I'm gonna to miss," Dave said, interrupting my happy recollections. "Red Sox games."

I rolled my eyes. *Surprise.*

"What about you, Jake?" Sarah asked. He was the only one at the table who hadn't said anything.

He glanced at me, then around the table. We all waited in anticipation.

"Hurry it up, people!" Sanchez called from the doorway. "Harper, Biggs, I need to talk to you."

Reminiscing forgotten, we hurried to clean up. I gathered the dishes from the table and made my way into the kitchen to help Stacey.

I had just set the armload down on a stainless steel counter when I heard Dave clear his throat behind me; my body stiffened instantly. I spun and attempted to step around him, spiteful thoughts snarling in my mind, but he reached for my arm. The moment his unwelcome fingers wrapped around my wrist, he recoiled like he'd been burned. His mouth hung open, and his wide eyes glanced back and forth between his hand and my arm.

"Shit, Dave. I'm not contagious!" I blurted. *I can't believe I ever had sex with you!*

"Sorry," he apologized hollowly. He was nervous, frustrated, and filled with regret—his emotions were more palpable than they'd ever been before.

I was tempted to shout obscenities at him, but he was too pathetic. Instead, I sighed and rolled my eyes. Part of me, the stupid, kind part, began to forgive him.

His head was bowed in shame, and he wouldn't meet my eyes as he said, "I'm sorry for what I did." Even though I could feel how truly sorry he was, I waited for him to continue, finding vindictive pleasure in watching him squirm. "I was drunk and pissed off. I wasn't thinking clearly," he said, giving me nothing but lame excuses.

My anger flared, stifling the forgiveness that had begun to take hold in my heart. "You can't fix this with apologies and excuses, Dave," I snapped. "They were going to kill me!"

He breathed heavily, seeming to contemplate what he would say next.

Growing impatient, I spat, "Just leave me alone," and turned to walk away.

"Zo, I fucked up. I've been a mess because of everything that happened with Sammy and us, and…I was taking it out on you. I'm sorry. I just…" His hands clenched and unclenched at his sides as his eyes darted around the industrial kitchen. "I just can't stand the thought of you hating me."

For the first time since the cabin, I really looked at him. The old Dave had vanished—his features were drawn, and the egotistical gleam in his eyes had dulled.

"I don't hate you, Dave. I just don't trust you anymore." I turned back to the dishes stacked on the counter, wishing he'd just go away.

He stepped up beside me. "Do you want me to help you with those?"

My palm raised automatically. "We aren't friends anymore, so let's not pretend we are, okay?" Irritated, I escaped the confines of the kitchen, making my way outside and heading toward the hospital. Finding Harper and starting my medical training would be the best way to keep my mind off Dave.

Having fled from the barracks without a jacket, I pulled my sleeves over my hands and folded my arms in an effort to insulate against the cold. It was about noon, and the sun was peeking through ominous, ever-changing clouds as they sped across the sky.

Clear skies seemed like a distant memory, just like my life before the Virus. I had to concentrate hard to remember the way some things smelled, like laundry fresh from the dryer, while others were still easy to recall—Dad's scent of woodchips after working in his shop and Dani's candy-scented perfume.

I found myself wishing I'd done things differently, that I'd embraced life more. *I used to be a fun person.* Dani and I would laugh so hard our faces hurt and we nearly peed our pants. *When was the last time I really laughed?* I thought of Harper and appreciated our flirtatious friendship all the more. *I used to be adventurous, too.* I searched for the elusive Big Foot, went white water rafting, and whittled wood with my dad.

But the last five years were a blur of work and horrible dates. *When did I change?* Between graduating from high school and leaving for the East Coast, I'd managed to lose myself. Had I known life was as changeable as the clouds looming above, would I have taken a different path? Fortunately, I'd reached the hospital —I didn't have to think about it anymore.

As I entered the boxy building for the first time, I took in the bleach-white walls, textured ceiling tiles, and chaotically arranged chairs. Fake plants occupied the corners of the ER waiting room, looking too lively and out of place. I was glad there was daylight so I could see where I was going—unlike the barracks, the hospital wasn't being powered by generators.

The soles of my shoes squeaked as gray and blue carpet gave way to polished vinyl floors. Generic watercolor paintings hung on the walls—a variety of flowers and leaves. I tried to imagine swarms of people rushing in and out of the emergency room doors, barking orders at one another, and hustling from one patient to the next. It disturbed me to think that the facility would never again be filled with so much energy and purpose.

"It's about time," Harper teased from the end of a hall. He was wearing a knee-length lab coat.

"Yeah, I hit a detour called 'Dave'," I told him as he ushered me into a wide-open space filled with a nurses' station in the center, a half-dozen curtained treatment bays along the far wall, and a glass-walled medicine room immediately to my left.

"Here, put this on." Harper gave me a lab coat of my own. "I've already started sorting through the meds, jotting down what we have." He handed me the clipboard he'd been using, pointing out a couple of hard-to-pronounce terms. "These are the vaccines and compounds we need to find, if we can. Let's finish taking inventory today, and we'll see what else we can scrounge up tomorrow. Make sense?"

I nodded.

"Thanks, Baby Girl."

I headed into the medicine room and started sorting through the boxes and vials in the cabinets, compiling a list of everything we had.

Morphine Sulfate Inj. – 5.5mg/mL vials – 7 boxes
Morphine Sulfate Tablets – 15 mg – 100 count/bottle – 5 bottles

"Hey Doc," Jake said, his rumbling voice startling me.

I whirled around to find him standing in the middle of the emergency room. His intense, brown eyes were locked on me, like he was trying to will me away with his mind. As I stared back, I wished I knew what he was thinking. I waded through my emotions, hoping to recognize foreign feelings—Jake's feelings—but my new sensory receptors seemed to turn on and off as they pleased. Currently, they were off, providing no insight into the mysterious Jake.

Suddenly, I realized I'd been looking at him for too long. I turned back to the open cabinet, surprised by the mixture of emotions and excited energy I was feeling. I didn't want to give either Jake or Harper the opportunity to watch my fair skin grow rosy with embarrassment. Wiping my sweaty palms on my jacket, I refocused on my task.

"So you're finally going to let me take a look at those stitches?" Harper asked Jake, his voice growing louder as he made his way over to me. He set a tray full of shiny, scissor-esque contraptions on the counter near me and asked, "Can you find some extra sutures and add them to the tray, Baby Girl?" He winked and turned back to Jake.

"Doctor's orders," Jake said, sounding unconcerned. *If I'd just been shot, I'd be a little more than indifferent about it.*

Abruptly, Cooper bounded into the room, nails clicking on the floor and tongue hanging out. I abandoned my clipboard to pet him, and he leaned against my legs, wagging his tail enthusiastically. *You saved my life too,* I realized, bending down to rub his belly.

"Zoe, would you bring me that tray, please?" Harper asked from the nearest treatment bay. He sounded distracted. "Alright, let's take a look."

As I brought the assortment of pointy tools over, Harper motioned toward the examination table, and Jake settled on the crinkly paper covering it. Cooper followed suit, situating himself on the floor directly below his master.

Looking back up from the dog, I started to set the tray down on top of a waist-high medical cart. "Just hold it for sec, would you, Baby Girl?" Harper walked over to the sink. In his most inquisitive doctor voice he asked Jake, "How have you been feeling?" while washing his hands.

"Alright."

Taking a clean roll of gauze from a drawer, Harper returned to his patient. "I've got a feeling the wound's fine, but playing basketball wasn't a great idea. I'm concerned you've pulled some of the stitches out." Harper frowned as he put on a pair of surgical gloves and said, "Take your shirt off."

"I'm sure it's fine—it doesn't hurt," Jake grunted, pulling off his long-sleeved shirt effortlessly and exposing the most toned, masculine body I'd ever seen in person.

There was no way Harper didn't hear my sharp intake of breath. *Really?* I felt unbearably uncomfortable.

Harper cleared his throat and continued, "You're probably right." He was eyeing me like he'd caught me raiding the cookie jar. "But it doesn't hurt to check," he added.

Before he could begin examining Jake's shoulder, the door swung open. "Harper, Summer needs you!" Clara said from the doorway. Her straight, blonde hair was tangled, and her eyes were wide with panic. "Something's *really* wrong with her. She's getting worse, and Tanya doesn't know what to do..." Clara's voice tapered off when her eyes settled on Jake.

Although only his back was visible to her, Clara didn't seem able to peel her eyes away. *Did she forget about Summer already?* She looked as dumbfounded as I felt, but her heated stare told me there was something more between her and Jake. My fingers tightened around the edges of the tray before I set it down and returned to inventorying.

I remembered the look on Jake's face the night he'd pushed me away and the scowl I'd received every time I'd encountered him since then. *Are they together?* Frustrating jealousy flared-up inside me.

"I'll see what I can do," Harper said. "Zoe, check Jake's wounds while I'm gone."

My heart started pounding. "But—" I was still unsure if my *thing* was public knowledge, and I had no idea if Jake knew. The possibility of seeing his memories and feeling his emotions was enticing, but it felt wrong—like an enormous, unforgivable invasion of privacy.

Harper grabbed his medical bag before coming over to me. He placed an encouraging hand on my shoulder. "You did a great job with Dave's injuries. I'm sure you'll be fine. Just make sure all his wounds are clean and the stitches are still tight. I'll come back when I can." Registering the concern in my eyes, he repeated, "You'll be fine." And with that, Harper left.

As I locked eyes with Jake, my self-consciousness resurfaced; it was both disarming and unwanted.

Jake raised an eyebrow expectantly, seeming to say, "shall we proceed?" When I didn't respond, he looked away.

It's the perfect opportunity to thank him, I reminded myself, but his impatience and dismissiveness made me hesitate.

Jake resituated himself on the table, making his chest and arm muscles flex, and my blood suddenly felt like lava coursing through my veins. Although unexpected, the sensation was thrilling and my body tingled with excitement. Afraid of touching his skin, especially in my excited state, I made sure to grab a pair of disposable gloves from the box beside the sink after I washed my hands.

Cooper whimpered as I approached the duo, his eyes pleading for more attention. Jake bent down and lovingly stroked the dog's head before sitting back up to watch me impassively.

As I began unwrapping his arm, I could feel his eyes on me. I could almost hear the questions forming on the tip of his tongue, but he didn't speak. His eyes—earnest and aware of something I could neither sense nor see—betrayed his expressionless face, but only for a moment. With one blink, his revealing stare disappeared.

Knowing I wouldn't get a better chance, I took a deep, steadying breath, and said, "I haven't had a chance to thank you… for saving my life, I mean." It was excruciatingly difficult trying to thank a man who could barely stand to be around me.

"No need to thank me," he said curtly, looking through me.

The ridiculousness of his answer triggered my defenses. "Why not? I know what would've happened if you hadn't—"

"But, I did. So can we just drop it, please?" His rushed, quiet tone was all I needed to get the point. Whatever the reason, he didn't want to talk about that night in the woods.

"Yeah, sure, whatever," I said coolly as I picked up one of the stainless steel utensils and used it to pull the matted gauze from Jake's wound—it came off more easily than I'd expected. "What happened between you and Bennington?" I asked. Jake's conversations with Jones and Taylor kept replaying in my head.

Jake met my eyes. "He thought he could kill me, but he was wrong." He watched me closely, waiting for my reaction, but I just shook my head at his vagueness. I wanted to think of something clever to spit back at him, but my annoyance vanished as I cleaned the crusted blood from his skin and took my first good look at his wound.

I must have frozen, because Jake looked at me oddly. "What's wrong?" he asked, the baritone of his voice startling me.

"Um…" I didn't want to sound more foolish than I already felt, but something clearly wasn't right. "You needed stitches?"

He crooked his neck to see the wound. "Yeah, what's wrong with it?"

I took a step back, completely astonished. "Absolutely nothing."

The look on Jake's face wasn't one of curiosity or concern—instead, he seemed unaffected by my words.

"It's almost entirely healed," I told him, hoping he'd provide some insight into his apparent lack of surprise. "It's barely been three days."

"I guess I'm a fast healer," he offered casually, looking around the room.

"But I saw the blood. You were in so much pain you could barely move." I replayed the gunfight in my head, remembering how his features had twisted in agony. *He's hiding something.*

I studied him carefully. "You don't seem surprised. Has this happened before?"

He smirked. "This is my first time being shot."

"That's not what I meant. Do you always heal this fast?"

He looked into my eyes but said nothing. His silence was all I needed to confirm my suspicion that he was more than he seemed to be.

Checking the unscathed flesh where his wound should have been, I tried another tactic. “Why do you keep pushing me away?” Frustration had enabled me to blurt out the question that had been nagging at me.

Jake stared at me, his eyes narrowing and his thumbs tapping the padded table.

“Jake,” Sanchez said, hurrying through the swinging emergency room doors with a grin. “We found some more fuel in one of the warehouses, but we’re having a hard time getting to it. Can you help?” Looking around the emergency room, she asked, “Where’s Harper?”

“Checking on Summer. She’s not doing well,” I told her.

Sanchez considered the information for a moment, but her eyes soon brightened with enthusiasm. “Come on,” she said to Jake before heading back down the hall.

Jake glanced at me, reaching for his shirt. “We done here?”

“Hold on, I need to take out the stitches,” I said as I leaned closer.

“Just leave them,” he snapped.

“Well at least let me put some gauze over them until Harper can take them out,” I said, frustrated. “They’ll catch on your shirt and tear out. It’ll take, like, five seconds.”

Jake blocked my hand, and even through the thin gloves, the heat of his touch electrified my skin. “I’m fine,” he responded flatly.

The morning light shining through the high windows washed over Jake’s face only inches from mine, and for the first time, I stared into his eyes. His irises weren’t simply brown like I’d thought, but they were amber with pale golden flakes around the pupil and were ringed with ebony. They held secrets. Suddenly, his emotions invaded my mind. He yearned for something, and his anger and apprehension roared through me. I saw the girl again.

She was looking up at him with nearly violet eyes, and her tears were mixing with blood as they streamed down her cheeks. She took a final, uneven breath.

Like he could tell I'd seen too much, Jake pulled his hand away and yanked his shirt on.

"Thanks, but I'm fine," he repeated roughly before retreating down the hall. Cooper trailed only slightly behind him.

25

DANI

I hadn't thought it was possible, but I was even more sore when I woke from my daylight slumber. I emerged from the tent in the late afternoon, my joints creaking like I was the tin man in need of oil. And my muscles, *oh my muscles*...they seemed to have calcified and merged with my bones.

Just one more night, I reminded myself. My plan to travel during the dark hours each day had proven ingenious so far; I'd been able to avoid my abandoned group—if they were even looking for me—and Crazies alike.

As I puttered around the campsite, my head throbbed with an emotional hangover from the previous day's overwhelming doses of loneliness and despair. I felt numb, mentally sluggish, and a little sick. Not that it mattered—I had things to do.

To appease my dream stalker, I refrained from speaking aloud to my animal companions. I almost broke the rule when it was time to leave.

Where's Jack? He was just here.

In the fading light, I searched the periphery of the campground, crunching pine cones and needles loudly as I moved from site to site. What little heat the December sun had provided during the day was dissipating quickly, and eerie shadows were being cast between the towering redwoods. I desperately wanted to get moving before the chill settled deeper into my body and stole what little mobility I had left.

Just as I opened my mouth to quietly call for him, Jack trotted out of some nearby bushes with a wagging tail. He barked merrily.

I glared at him. *And where have you been?*

He lay down before me, rolling over to offer his neck in submission.

Awareness dawned on me like the rays of the rising sun. It was so simple—so obvious. I *had* been experiencing the symptoms of one of MG's "Abilities" over the past few weeks, I'd just assigned the effects to the wrong being: *it's not that Jack's the smartest dog in the world…it's that I'm in his head.*

Without moving a muscle, I stared at the groveling dog and projected the thought, "*Stand up, Jack.*"

He stood, watching me expectantly.

"Go over to Wings."

Jack immediately pranced over to the horse a dozen paces away.

"Both of you, come here."

Like well-rehearsed actors, Jack and Wings closed the distance between us until we stood in a cluster at the center of the campground.

I can talk to animals…in their minds. Holy crap! Thoughts raced around my head, making me dizzy, and I dropped to my knees on the cold ground. I just sat there, looking at nothing.

Jack sniffed my face and whined. "*Mother? Okay? Hurt?*"

I stared at him in shock, knowing with certainty that the deep, rough voice in my head had come from my dog. *It's not just one-way. How'd I miss this?*

The cynical part of me whispered silently, *Because I wanted to. Because I was afraid. Because I didn't want to be a Crazy.* Belatedly, I thought, *This is the coolest thing ever!*

"No, Sweet Boy," I said both out loud and in Jack's mind. "I'm fine. You're such a good boy." I scratched his neck for a few more seconds before standing and turning my attention to Wings. "I suppose you don't really need this, do you?" I asked, tugging gently on her bridle. If we could talk in each other's minds, I figured we could manage traveling without Wings having several chunks of metal jammed into her mouth.

"No. Remove please." Her voice was as rich and sweet as vanilla custard.

Neither Jack nor Wings actually spoke in words. Rather, it was like I could instinctively decipher the meaning of their projected thoughts, and my brain seemed to translate them into something recognizable. It was the same as listening to someone speak a foreign language for the first time and just *knowing* what they were saying. I wasn't sure how it worked, or why…only that it did.

Obliging Wings, I freed her of the tangle of leather and metal and tossed the entire contraption into some nearby ferns. It took me longer than usual because my hands were shaking with adrenaline. Feeling suddenly awkward about forcing her to carry me, I pointed to her back and asked, "May I?"

She consented with a snort.

As we made our way out of the campground, questions bounced around my mind like ping pong balls. *Am I delusional? Is this real? How can it be?* I let Wings and Jack navigate the highway while I tried to do the same with my thoughts.

A few hours after midnight, we passed the scattered houses on the outskirts of town. Finally, after ten days of painfully slow travel—first by car with the others, then by horse on my own—I had arrived in Bodega Bay. I was home.

During the long hours of the night, I'd managed to wrestle with uncertainty, eventually accepting reality. My Ability was real. I could talk to animals, and they could talk to me. I had also come up with a plan—there were a few places I needed to visit first, but I knew exactly where we would hunker down.

Riding through the abandoned streets of my neighborhood, I felt like a stranger in my own town. It was as though my home had transformed into an Old West ghost town. I half expected to hear rusty signs squeaking and to see a tumbleweed bouncing across the worn pavement. As far as I could tell, I was completely alone. *Maybe this was a bad idea.*

Where once they had been familiar and welcoming, the grassy hills to the west now seemed foreboding—anything could've been hiding behind their gentle slopes. Even the waves crashing against the jagged rocks sounded malevolent, like they were purposely masking any audible warnings of danger.

Apprehension built inside me as we closed in on Grams's house. I hadn't seen a single living person since leaving Fort Bragg, but I was desperately hoping to find one in there.

Dismounting in the driveway, I asked Wings to stay hidden in the nearby trees. I'd expected to feel relief when I finally approached my childhood home. Instead, the steel-gray color of the siding had gone from soothing to dreary, and the various nooks and crannies surrounding the sprawling split-level house provided numerous hiding places for potential threats. My knees trembled as I slowly ascended the front steps.

Jack followed me, his tail drooping.

What if she's like Aunt Janet? I thought, standing on the porch and staring at the familiar, coral-white front door. Or *what if she's a Crazy?*

"If Grams is here, we have to find her," I told Jack. He sat down obediently and waited for me to open the door.

Fear caused my hand to shake as I grasped the doorknob and

thought, *Please be locked.* The handle caught when I twisted it, like it was trying to deny me entrance, but then the latch clicked, and the door slowly swung open. Jack pushed into the house in front of me while I stood on the welcome mat and held my breath. Taming my wild emotions, I exhaled and gingerly breathed in through my nose.

There was only the smell of home—a combination of cinnamon, chamomile, wax, and pine that filled the house year-round from Grams's compulsive cleaning and candle-making habits. It was the most glorious thing I'd ever smelled, and not for nostalgia's sake. Grams *wasn't* rotting in her own home; there was still hope.

"Grams!" I called out, stepping tentatively into the dark house and shutting the door. I flipped the entryway light switch, but nothing happened. "Are you here? Grams?" I roamed around the familiar cluster of rooms, hallways, and stairs, only tripping over an out-of-place ottoman and a pair of galoshes in the inky darkness. "Grams?"

I opened her downstairs bedroom door, hoping to find her asleep in her bed, but my hope proved useless. *She's not here.* I sat heavily on the end of her quilt-covered mattress. "Where are you, Grams?" I whispered into the darkness.

Feeling myself coming unhinged, I reined in my emotions and hurried out of the room. Jack joined me as I reached the front door, and together we went back outside. *I'll find her*, I promised myself and headed down the street toward Zoe's house.

An hour later, I'd finished searching the equally deserted home —like Grams, Zoe's dad was ominously absent. Defeated and disheartened, I guided Jack and Wings across town to the ranch where I'd worked during high school. Not a street light glowed along my path. Not a ray of light shone through a window. *Is anyone even alive?*

Even though it was still dark when we arrived at Bodega Bay Riders' Ranch, the surroundings instantly comforted me. It was the only familiar place I could come up with that Jason might not think to check…*if he even searches for me at all.*

As I dismounted and sent Wings out to pasture, I couldn't help but dwell on Jason—the man I had to avoid in order to protect. He, along with the rest of the group, would be arriving in Bodega Bay in the morning. He would be in the same abandoned town as me, and I didn't know if I had the strength to resist going to him.

To keep him alive, I can.

26

ZOE

I'd been up all night in the hospital, doing everything I could to help Harper make Summer's final hours as pain-free as possible. She rambled incoherently, and her vomiting and convulsions had increased. By nightfall her body was bloated and shivering, and she was delusional. Harper couldn't let her suffer any longer.

"Tanya," he said grimly. "Her kidneys and liver aren't functioning…it's only a matter of time."

Tanya sat beside Summer's hospital bed, clutching her sister's hand. Her puffy eyes stayed locked on her sister's trembling body as she slowly shook her head in defeat. Though Summer's waning skin color and weakening body were obvious, Tanya refused to let her go. *Summer's all she has left.* I wished I could do something, anything, to help the sobbing woman. I imagined myself in a similar situation with Dani, and something in my chest clenched.

Unable to watch the miserable scene any longer, I excused myself and left the room. As I walked away, I heard Harper say, "I'm sorry, but there's nothing we can do for her now. I know this is difficult, but we have no choice—we need to sedate her. She's suffering, and I can't allow it to go on."

Tanya's only audible response was to cry harder. I was grateful Tanya had Clara to comfort her. They'd been through hell over the last few weeks, but at least they had each other. I tried not to imagine something terrible happening to my brother or Dani, the only two people *I* had left in the world.

After giving Summer enough Morphine to put her in a deep, painless sleep, Harper joined me at the emergency room's central nurses' station. I was cleaning up the disarray left behind by the tornado of Summer's decline. Not wanting to disturb the women in the nearby trauma room, Harper spoke softly. "It's arsenic poisoning. I'm almost certain."

My head shot up in disbelief, and I stared at him. "Arsenic?"

"It's the only thing that makes sense, and as soon as I finish the bloodwork, I'll know for sure."

"But how? Accidentally?" *She wouldn't have done it to herself, would she?* I thought about the images I'd seen in Jones's mind of the naked woman crying. *Was she handling things so badly that she'd want to end her own life?*

"Not likely. *Someone* had to have done this to her," Harper said adamantly.

I immediately knew who. "Jones," I whispered.

Harper studied me, his eyes narrowed. "That's my guess."

"He said things, and I saw—" I hesitated. "I know what he was capable of. It was either him or Taylor."

Harper exhaled heavily. "Do I even want to know?"

Holding his eyes, I shook my head. "I think you should pull them all aside—Stacey, Tanya, and Clara, I mean—and see if they want to talk about what happened to them here. I'm sure I saw only a sliver of the monstrous things Jones did." My mind rewound to the woods, to the feeling of Taylor's foul hands assaulting my trembling body, but I shoved the memory away.

Having been a horrible chemistry student, I was pleased with myself when I recalled some facts about the poisonous compound. "Isn't arsenic in cigarettes and rat poison? Maybe she just..."

Entertained by my naiveté, Harper gave me a small smile. "True, it's a lot of places. But what we come in contact with on a daily basis is either organic or in such small quantities that it doesn't hurt us. What Summer's been subjected to is inorganic, which makes it extremely dangerous." He paused for a moment, thinking. "Arsenic's been used in chemical warfare throughout history…it's possible there's some here on base." He ran splayed fingers through his short, dark hair, exhausted and defeated. I could feel guilt weighing him down, clouding his rationality.

I reached out and gently squeezed his shoulder. "Don't blame yourself, H. There's nothing you could've done. You said so yourself." My attempt at a reassuring touch was ineffective—regret was pouring out of him. "You need to get some rest," I told him.

"I should've picked up on the symptoms sooner." Suddenly, Harper's guilt-ridden eyes brightened. "I think I saw arsenic in the armory yesterday."

Hearing soft footsteps, Harper and I turned to see Clara standing in the doorway to the trauma room. Her eyes were bloodshot, and her face was swollen and blotchy. After an uncomfortable silence, she breathed, "Summer's gone."

Harper hurried into the room to check Summer's pulse. She *was* gone.

As everyone said their final goodbyes, relief filled the air, mixing with the suffocating sadness. I left the hospital, suddenly drowning in morbid thoughts of Dani and what horrible things might have happened to her. I hadn't heard from her since she'd gone off on her own, and I knew Jones and Taylor weren't the only sickos stalking around out there. But thinking of Dani triggered my protective instincts, and they quickly overpowered my grim thoughts. *I should make sure Tanya's okay.*

After finding everything necessary for tea in the kitchen and dampening a washcloth with warm water, I headed to Tanya's room. I felt like a stranger as I tapped on her door, wondering if I'd be intruding. When I heard her timid voice call for me to come in, I entered. Tanya and Stacey were sitting on the bed, staring at me with drawn faces. Their grief was thick and palpable; I could feel the intensity of their emotions like they were my own. Sitting in a chair beside the bed, Clara appeared far more composed.

Tanya wiped her red-rimmed eyes and sat up from her curled position on top of the comforter. "Hi," she said raggedly, gathering her unkempt, mousey-brown hair into a ponytail.

Smiling sympathetically, I walked over to the bedside table and set down the tray. "I brought some tea and a wet washcloth…if you want it."

"Thank you," Tanya whispered. She picked up the damp cloth and placed it against her forehead.

"I'll go see what there is to eat," Stacey said as she rose and left the room.

"Is there anything else I can get for you?" I asked Tanya, hoping to make myself somewhat useful on such a depressing day.

"No, I'm fine. Thanks," Tanya said, motioning for me to join her on the bed. "So much has been going on the last few days…I feel like I barely know you."

I appeased her by sitting down. Though I felt uncomfortable being the center of attention, Tanya seemed eager for the distraction. "What would you like to know?"

"I know Sanchez and her team met up with you in Ohio. Is that where you're from?"

It took me a brief moment to recall everything that had happened over the last few weeks. "No. Actually, I'm from California, but I was living in Massachusetts when all…*this* happened," I said, gesturing around the room.

Tanya's face lit up. "Really? I've always wanted to go to California. I grew up in Michigan where I met and married my husband, Steven…the Virus got him early on. He was transferred here right after we married. I've never been anywhere else." Her reminiscent tone became distant. "Summer was visiting me for

Christmas from Texas. That's where she was going to school. She never settled down…said she never wanted to." She looked down at her hands.

"I'm sure she was glad to be here with you. I know I'd be glad to be with my family if I could." I frowned as I thought of my father. *Is he alone? Is he dying? Is he already gone?*

Tanya nodded and shifted, pulling the blankets up around her. After a while, she dozed off. She was small like Dani, and her petite frame almost disappeared under the thickness of the blankets.

In the silence, I examined her room, noting how similar it was to my own. She had a few books strewn on her bedside table and a pile of tissues on the floor close by. Clothes were heaped in the corner, and unlike my quarters, the walls were bare—there was nothing to distract from the sorrow filling the room.

Afraid of waking Tanya, I slowly started to rise but froze when Clara said, "You're very beautiful." Her words were an observation more than a compliment—almost an accusation—and her piercing blue eyes seemed to burrow into my soul.

I hesitated. "Um…thanks."

Suddenly, her expression softened. "Sorry, that sounded less weird in my head." Her smile was demure and innocent. *Maybe she's bipolar…*

"It's a nice compliment. Thank you. I definitely haven't felt very pretty lately." I pointed to my healing face.

"You look much better," she said, her unblinking stare still locked on me.

Tanya tossed fitfully, thankfully interrupting the uncomfortable moment. "Have you known Tanya for long?" I asked.

Clara shook her head and moved to close the mini blinds, shutting out the sun. "Jake and I arrived a week before you did." *Ah, yes. The inescapable Jake.* "I've gotten to know the others well enough since then."

As Clara watched Tanya sleep, I felt the seriousness of her emotions. I could sense her gratitude and suspicion, although I didn't understand what was causing them.

"How long have you known Jake?" I wondered aloud.

Her eyes shot over to me, scrutinizing my face. "A while." Smiling shyly, she added, "We have quite the past, actually."

"Then maybe you can tell me what his deal is."

"His 'deal'?" Her pale eyebrows raised in question.

I threw my hands up. "Why he dislikes me so much."

Clara's nose wrinkled with displeasure, and she looked briefly menacing before moving to fold some loose blankets that had been piled on the floor. "I'm not sure. He's never really explained it to me, and I try not to pry." She looked at me like I was a problem she had to fix. *Warning duly noted.*

"Got it." I had the sudden urge to get as far away from her as possible. "I'm going to check on Harper. Please let me know if Tanya needs anything," I grumbled, leaving Tanya in Clara's care.

I headed down the hall to Harper's room. His door was shut, and I hoped he was getting some rest, so I made my way toward the mess hall instead. At finding Sarah and Biggs locked in an embrace, moaning and groping, I made a quick exit. I did *not* want to watch them making out on a cafeteria table.

I wanted to sketch and needed some fresh air to collect my thoughts. After stopping by my room to pick up my messenger bag of drawing supplies, I burst through the main doors out into the sunshine. The air was chilly, but my hair was pulled back into a ponytail, allowing the sun to kiss my face and the back of my neck, warming my skin. I squinted, basking in the rays. The old me would have grabbed some sunblock to prevent more freckles from dressing my cheeks, but the new me quickly dismissed such trivialities.

As I wandered beyond the yard surrounding the barracks, I stepped off the sidewalk toward a cluster of trees. I spotted a small pond with a few pine trees scattered around it, creating the perfect oasis for me to think.

Except...Jake sat under one of the evergreens, absentmindedly carving something on a stick. I wasn't in the mood to argue with him, but Cooper's head rose at the sound of a twig breaking beneath my shoe.

Jake looked up before I could sneak away. "Is everything okay?"

I brushed away the suggestion of concern, knowing the question had probably been asked out of politeness. "Yeah, just getting some fresh air."

Standing a few yards from him, I debated what to do. My words came out before I could stop them. "What's your problem with me?" I asked, sounding more pathetic than I'd intended. "It'd be nice to know what I did to make you so cold toward me."

Frowning, Jake stood. I'd never seen someone look so frustrated for no apparent reason.

When he said nothing, I continued, "I barely know you, but you're always irritated around me."

"It's not personal," he said, like that was all the explanation I needed. He was just like my stupid brother, detached and in control all the time.

My curiosity melted away, and annoyance solidified in its place. "Right," I said. "So I should just ignore your bad attitude whenever I'm around you? Try not to let it affect me?"

He ignored my sarcasm. "I'm leaving soon, so it won't be a problem," he said, turning away dismissively.

I threw my hands in the air. "Oh, great! Well, as long as you won't be around for long, I *think* I can manage." His calm, collected arrogance was infuriating.

I turned to leave, needing to get away from him before I embarrassed myself with an unflattering outburst. I started to walk away, vowing I would never bother him again, but hesitated. "Do you have any idea what it feels like to know someone saved your life, then wonder if they wished they hadn't?" Keeping my back to him, I continued quietly, "It feels like shit." I hadn't realized the truth in those words until I'd spoken them out loud. "Merry Christmas," I mumbled bitterly, wondering how much worse the coming year would be.

As I walked away, I heard Jake mutter, "Dammit."

27

DANI

"Cam, No!" I screamed as my dead boyfriend's decomposing body lunged at me.

"You abandoned me!" he yelled. Bloody spittle sprayed from his decaying lips. "You said you'd stay with me! Why'd you leave? For him?" He was pointing at a man suddenly standing beside me—Jason.

Cam altered his trajectory, instead attacking Jason, who was utterly unaware of our presence. As Cam pulled him to the ground, he began taking huge bites out of Jason's neck and face. Jason did nothing to defend himself.

"NO!" I leapt at Cam but couldn't grasp any part of his melting skin. I gagged.

He lifted his face and swallowed. "I'll make him part of me—you'll see. Then you'll have to love me again."

I gathered my strength, preparing to attack the man I had loved with all of my heart. Suddenly, I was crouched alone on a featureless, ash-gray floor.

"I'd planned to be here sooner," MG said above me. "Sorry."

"Whatever," I rasped, standing again. "Not your job to look after me in my demented mind. Don't worry about it." Swallowing

roughly, I replayed the image of a rotting Cam consuming Jason's flesh. It was a new twist on the nightmare and almost more than I could take.

MG smirked. "You know...I think I might love you."

"You'll get over it," I told him. "I figured it out, by the way."

He quirked his lips, "You figured—ah...so what can you do?"

Like he didn't already know. I squinted my eyes, feigning deep thought. "Well...I can speak four languages, and I'm really good with computers. And I can solve a mean differential equation."

"Dani—"

I swatted his arm and strutted away. "Calm down, MG. I'm kidding! It's the animals."

"Which means...?"

Still facing away, I said, "It means I can talk to them. And they can talk to me. Well, not out loud—in their minds."

He looked amazed. "Both ways? I haven't seen that yet. What about people? Can you do them too?"

With a hand on my hip, I turned. "Did you really just ask me that?"

He smiled wickedly. "You know what I mean."

"Yeah. And I have no idea. I haven't exactly been surrounded by people lately."

"But I thought there were others with you?"

"Why would you think that? Are you spying on me?" I stalked toward him.

He rolled his eyes. "Calm down, Beastmaster. I could feel their sleeping minds near yours. Kind of an amazing Ability," he said, pointing to himself.

"Right..."

MG, without warning, was instantly gone. Around me, a familiar expanse of beach replaced the ashen surroundings. Feeling a warm breeze on my bare skin, I realized I was once again in my bikini and was looking out at the vast expanse of the Pacific Ocean. The rhythmic movement of the water was hypnotic.

At least, it had been before a certain unrequested dream visitor rose out of the swells and slowly made his way toward the beach.

"You've got to be kidding," I muttered. Wearing only swim trunks, MG glistened as water streamed down his upper body in rivulets. His pale, toned abdomen and shoulders drew my attention —no matter how hard I tried to ignore them.

MG drank in my reaction, stopping several feet away.

I blushed intensely and narrowed my eyes. "Seriously? This is just too ridiculous!"

He chuckled, the noise making me bristle even more.

"Who are you anyway?" I snapped.

"I'm the only person who can help you learn to use your special little skill," he responded. "Now, tell me why you're suddenly alone."

For some reason, I wanted to tell him why I'd left—I just wanted to tell someone...anyone. I needed another human to listen, to understand, and to say I'd done the right thing.

As I sat down on the warm sand and hugged my knees to my chest, MG crouched next to me. The words tumbled around in my head chaotically until I opened my mouth and they spilled out. I couldn't have stopped them if I'd wanted to. By the time I finished speaking, MG knew everything about the situation with Cece and my departure from Fort Bragg. He even knew a little bit about my unrequited feelings for Jason.

At the conclusion of my story he asked, "So Jason—was he the one in the other dream? The guy who called you 'Red'?"

"Yeah," I whispered, wondering if it had been a mistake to include any details about my feelings for another man. MG was right—I did need him to help me understand my Ability, and I couldn't risk driving him off with inopportune jealousy.

MG shook his head. "He'd better appreciate what you've done for him." Combined with the glint of admiration in his eyes, his words implied approval. He thought I'd done the right thing.

"Thank you."

"So…what'll you do now? Stay where you are?"

"I really don't know," I confessed. I wondered why he hadn't invited me to join him wherever he was, considering how much he seemed to like me.

"Whatever you do, you need to learn to control your Ability."

I shrugged. "I don't think it'll be that difficult. Once I realized I wasn't losing my mind, talking to Jack and Wings became pretty easy."

"I'm assuming you're referring to your dog and horse?" I nodded, and he continued, "You can communicate with them, but what about other animals? Do you have to know them? Do they have to be near you? Can you talk to more than one at the same time? And what about people?"

Staring at the ocean's foamy edge, I responded, "I guess I don't know as much as I thought I did."

"Which is why you have me," he said, draping his arm over my shoulders and pulling me closer. I leaned against his warm skin, reveling in the first human touch I'd experienced in days. It wasn't real, but that didn't matter.

"You need to practice." MG told me. "Seek out random animals with your mind, and try to converse with them. Experiment with what you can do…maybe pick one type of animal—preferably a harmless one—and call as many to you as you can."

I nodded slowly. "Okay, I'll work on it. What about the people thing? Can't I try it on you?" I asked, hopeful that he would agree. If I could learn to talk to people in their minds, I might be able to talk to Zoe!

"If, and it's a big 'if,' your Ability works on humans too, I'm probably too far away."

"How far? Where are you?" I pulled away and looked into his pale blue eyes.

Studying me, he ran a hand through his chin-length blond hair—it was curling at the ends as it dried. With a deep breath, he answered, "Like I said, too far."

"Do you know anything about the Colony?"

"Yeah, some."

"Do you know if it's safe?"

He frowned slightly. "I'm really not sure."

"That's where my group is headed, eventually," I explained wistfully.

After a long hesitation, MG asked, "Will you follow them?"

I thought about his question for a while. "I don't know."

He seemed to consider my answer but didn't respond. Instead he said, "I have to go."

"Oh."

"I'm sorry. I'll see you again soon." And with that I was alone.

I woke in the late morning and spent several hours readying a stall for Wings and inventorying my meager belongings. My supply of food was almost expended, with only two packages of freeze-dried meals and a few cups of kibble for Jack. It was time for some scavenging. After checking the ranch's main house—a post and beam building that had been used more as an office than as a home for nearly a decade and therefore held little of use, food-wise—I knew I would have to head into town.

Leaning against the white-washed pasture fence near the stable, I watched the goats and horses graze peacefully. "*Wings*," I called silently.

The graceful Paint trotted to the fence.

"Jack and I will be gone for a few hours. We're going to look for food."

"*Apples?*" she asked eagerly.

I laughed and spoke out loud even though I didn't need to. "I'll look for apples. Will you be okay here alone?"

She snorted. "*Not alone. Many friends.*" She was right—a small herd of friendly horses and goats were munching on grass in the pasture behind her.

Remembering MG's suggestion, I decided it was the perfect time to practice using my Ability…to *experiment*, as he'd said. Hesitantly, I opened my mind, attempting to reach out to all of the horses and goats meandering within the pasture's fences. "*Come to me,*" I projected, and the thought reverberated like a gong.

In a small stampede, every horse and goat began to purposefully move toward me.

"*Mother!*" Jack called with worry. "*Look!*"

"Shit!" I hissed. More than just the ranch animals had heard my call.

Hundreds of small critters, from birds to squirrels to skunks, were scurrying through the grassy fields all around me. They were heading straight for me. As the first few came close enough to touch, I worried they would try to climb up my legs or gnaw on my boots, but my worry proved unnecessary. Those who were close enough sniffed me and rubbed their faces against my legs; the rest babbled eagerly in my head while they chattered and chirped aloud.

Within minutes I was surrounded by a multitude of animals, and in the distance, more were approaching—there were a few llamas, several dozen deer, and a variety of potential predators. At the sight of a large bobcat, I began to panic.

I shooed the animals with my arms and exclaimed, "Go away!"

They continued advancing, amplifying my panic. *What do I do? Oh crap…oh crap…*

It was time for some straw-grasping—I concentrated and remembered how it had felt when I'd called them to me. A myriad of connections snapped into existence between my mind and those of each of the creatures huddling and scurrying around me.

"Leave me, please. I'm *really* sorry for interrupting your day," I said. *There's no way this is going to work.*

Luckily, I was wrong. Hundreds of greetings and farewells flitted through my mind as the small horde of woodland creatures dispersed. I sighed. *Great, I'm an apocalyptic Disney princess. Zoe is going to laugh her ass off.*

Both shaken and relieved, I gathered the one animal I did want as a companion—Jack—and headed toward town with a large, empty backpack. I patted my coat to reassure myself the pistol was still holstered underneath it. *Thank you, Jason*, I mused.

During the mile-long walk, I used the bushes and trees to conceal myself as best I could. My self-defense skills were far from perfect, but my stealth skills were razor-sharp from hundreds of high school nights spent sneaking out with Zoe.

I was just creeping between a ragged thicket of evergreens and a stagnant pond when I saw movement on the nearby road. I quickly slipped behind the thick trunk of one of the pines and peeked around it to watch two men pass. They were repulsively dirty and periodically shoved each other, laughing whenever one of them stumbled. *Are they drunk? Or Crazies?* It didn't matter—either way, they were dangerous.

Once they were out of sight, I slinked to the next cluster of trees. Very cautiously, I made my way to Grams's backyard. Her house seemed like the best place to start my scavenging, especially since I knew where everything was. She'd always been a big believer in stocking up for a rainy day, though I'd always wondered how much rain would justify twenty cases of water and dozens of flats of canned tuna.

Crossing the barren winter garden, moving between redwood planter boxes filled with rows and bunches of herbs, veggies, and dormant berry bushes, I froze. Someone had just passed by the dining room window—their outline showing faintly against the sage-green linen curtains. *Somebody's in my house! Dammit! But... could it be Grams?*

Painfully slowly, I inched back to the planter box at the farthest edge of the property and ducked behind an enormous rosemary bush. Unable to resist, I poked my head above the shrubbery and watched the window. Luckily, my green, cable-knit cap blended in better with the surroundings than my crimson locks.

The shadow reappeared minutes later, but I couldn't identify the figure through the curtain. *Come on. Look outside. Let me see your face.*

Suddenly, the curtain moved to the side, and a familiar, perplexed face looked out into the garden. *Crap! Jason! Crap!*

I huddled closer to the ground, afraid to move…afraid to breathe…afraid to even think.

Seconds later, the back door flung open, and heavy footsteps thudded down the deck stairs. "Dani! Where are you?" Jason called out. At hearing him, I squeezed my eyes shut and my heart skipped several beats.

More footsteps followed, along with Chris's baffled voice. "Jason, what are you doing?"

Jason's voice was rough and insistent, a combination that shredded my heart. "Dani…I thought I heard her. Did you? She told me to look outside."

He heard me. Holy crap…it works on people!

Without my vehement command that he lay down and be quiet, Jack would have launched himself across several empty planter boxes and tackled first Jason, and then Chris. I was tempted to do the same thing. Fighting against my own desperate desires was one of the hardest things I'd ever done. It was a struggle just to keep my thoughts from calling out to my friends.

More voices and footsteps thumped onto the deck. Slowly, I found a sparse spot in my herbaceous shield and watched a nightmare play out.

Cece stood feet away from Jason, pointing at him. "You all heard him! He's hearing voices. He's a crazy freak just like everyone else we find. We can't keep following someone who isn't even sane."

What are you doing in my house, bitch?

With a haughty sneer, Cece turned away to face the handful of men gathered behind her on the deck—her harem. "We need a new leader. Someone who won't make us stay in some little shit-stained town just to look for one whiny little bitch."

What the hell is she doing? She's insane!

Everyone but Chris and Jason nodded in agreement.

Where are the others? Where's Ky? Where's Hunter?

"Good," Cece said smugly. "Now we just need to dispose of you." Turning back to Jason and Chris, she drew her sidearm and trained it on Zoe's brother. Her followers did the same, half aiming at Chris and half at Jason. Both of my friends stood as motionless as statues.

This can't be happening!

"I tried to give you a chance to see things my way. I even got rid of that little—"

"Fuck off you psycho bitch." Jason's hands clenched into tight fists and he snarled, "I never should've touched your skanky ass. I will *kill you* for what you did."

Cece stuck out her lower lip in a mocking pout and tapped the barrel of her gun lightly against her mouth. "You were so unreasonable—taking her side on everything. At least I didn't do anything permanent. Not like what's about to happen to you." She smiled wickedly, again aiming her weapon in his direction. "You really should've been more supportive…more understanding. You had a chance after she left, but you missed it."

"You're fucking insane." Jason stated.

Cece shrugged, dismissing his opinion with that single gesture. In a few steps, she was inches from him. She pressed the muzzle of her weapon into his abdomen and stood on tiptoes to whisper in his ear, pausing to kiss his neck softly. As she spoke, his fists clenched and unclenched. From my vantage point, Jason seemed to be expending a herculean amount of restraint to remain still.

Before she finished talking, her hands still groping him like a lover, Jason made his move. His body blocked my view of his sudden strike, but I could still hear. With a sickening snap, Cece's gun clattered onto the weathered wood. It took Jason less than a second to spin Cece around and maneuver her into a choke hold, clutching the side of her head while she whimpered. Even with several handguns trained on him, Jason had gained the momentary upper hand.

"Lower your weapons, or I'll break more than her wrist," he warned.

Distracted by Jason's deadly grace, I hadn't noticed Chris draw what appeared to be a sawed-off shotgun. She had it aimed at John's chest.

"If you…kill me…they'll kill you," Cece gasped between shallow breaths and pathetic whimpers.

"Worth it," Jason stated coldly, and I knew he wore a sadistic grin.

NO! This can't be happening! The situation was spiraling out of control. There were few remaining options that included my friends' survival. Utter desperation filled me. *Dammit, I can't lose them! I can't lose* him*!*

Of its own accord, a plan formed in my mind. I focused all of my mental energy on Cece. "*Miss me, bitch?*"

Her whimpers suddenly ceased. I hoped it was because she'd heard my voice in her head and not because Jason was following through on his threat. I couldn't let him do it. I refused to watch him die.

Wasting no time, I continued my assault on Cece's mind, "*He'll do it, you know. And then what'll you have? Nothing. You'll be dead. You won't even be avenged. Your little followers won't get a shot off—I'll see to that. Think about it, Cece. If I can talk in your head, what else can I do?*"

Cece sobbed, "No…can't be…it's not possible…" Her words echoed in my mind.

A massive headache was forming in my skull, and my body was beginning to shake from a sudden chill. It was difficult to keep my voice from sounding strained in her head. "*Oh, it is you psycho bitch. I'm in your head...should I stay and play around?"* I attempted to make my tone even colder as I thought, "*Call them off, and get the hell out of here.*"

I couldn't hear her response through the sudden whooshing in my ears. It felt like there was too much blood saturating my brain, making my head throb with an explosive intensity. I tried to see how the scene played out, but my vision was narrowing, dimming. I put all of my effort into watching and listening, but it wasn't enough. Leaden, my eyelids shut, and my head slumped to the ground.

Jack's warm body huddled against me as my world faded out of existence.

28

ZOE

The morning was gloomy. The weather had progressively worsened, and I wasn't excited about training under the looming, possibly rain-filled clouds that churned in the angry sky.

In the warmth of my sleeping quarters I readied myself for a day of flailing and falling. I layered myself in some of the training attire I'd acquired from the one-stop shop on base—the "PX" according to Harper. With the exception of my brown tank top and combat boots, the army-green, long-sleeved shirt, cargo pants, and socks all labeled with FORT KNOX made me look like a walking billboard for the base. My goal: to keep my arms warm, my legs shielded from the scrapes that would come with every scuffle and fall, and to protect my feet from the heel stomping and ankle twisting I would undoubtedly endure. Based on experience, I knew my agility was lacking, but I dressed optimistically. I also knew that the bulkier my clothes were, the more difficultly I'd have bobbing and ducking…and running away.

Hoping to minimize the amount of tearing and knotting my long hair would sustain, I weaved it into a thick braid. With my black tresses pulled away from my face, it was easier to see the faint yellow remnants of the bruise on my cheekbone.

However, taking in my overall appearance, I was pleasantly surprised. I looked pretty badass—*looked* being the operative word. I relished the idea of venting some of my irritation. I was still stewing over what had happened with Jake. His matter-of-fact tone pissed me off, and his inscrutable attitude was getting old. Self-defense lessons would start after breakfast, and unfortunately for Harper, as my trainer and partner, he'd be receiving the brunt of my pent-up aggression.

Walking into the mess hall, I found Harper sitting at a long table with Sarah, Biggs, Clara, and Jake. The last thing I wanted was to sit next to Jake while he exuded the mysteriousness that annoyed me so much.

Outwardly unfazed by his presence, I passed him on my way to the stainless steel tubs filled with mounds of steaming food. With a smile, I filled my plate with hash browns, bacon, and scrambled eggs, and wondered who was to thank for such a glorious meal.

I heard chattering and laughter bubbling up from the tables behind me, and it instantly brightened my mood. The sounds filled the large dining room with vibrancy and comfort.

"Hey Croft, you mind grabbing me some OJ while you're up?" Harper called out.

Assuming he was talking to me, I peered back at him. "Croft?"

"Yeah, you know, Lara Croft—tomb raider, relic hunter…? You look like her today."

"She's hot," Biggs added, and I couldn't help but laugh.

"She's a video game character," Sarah said disapprovingly. "She's not *hot*."

"She kicks ass. That's totally hot," Biggs reiterated.

Jake chuckled. "Yeah, she's pretty hot."

Distracted by Jake's comment, I filled a cup until orange juice spilled over the rim. "Shit," I spat. Wiping my hand on my pants, I headed to the table. Biggs scooted over to make room for me.

"Thanks." Harper nodded and winked as I handed him the sticky cup. His charm and playfulness sometimes made me forget he was a medic. I'd always imagined doctors as old and stuffy. Harper was definitely neither.

I took a sip from my own cup of orange juice and nodded. "Sure thing."

Avoiding Jake's penetrating stare was impossible. He sat directly across from me, his attentive eyes alternating between Harper and me. Guilt poured off of him every time our eyes met, but his closed-off expression remained.

As I slowly ate my breakfast, I lost myself in thought. I couldn't help wondering what Jake had done before the Virus. But even as I told myself I shouldn't care, I knew I did. The simple fact that he *wouldn't* talk to me made me all the more curious.

Jake was tall and strong—someone my dad would've called a "strapping young man". With his military-style clothing and close-cropped hair, he could easily be mistaken for a member of the armed forces. I just couldn't picture him taking orders from anyone. Given his rugged appearance and macho build, he could've been a lumberjack. However, I couldn't picture *that* without the idea of him stripping off his clothes while gyrating to techno music. That made me smile, just a little.

"What are you grinnin' about?" Harper whispered near my ear.

"Nothing," I lied, shoving a fork full of hash browns into my mouth.

"You ready for your lessons today?" He wiggled his thick eyebrows up and down. I laughed, realizing Harper's eyebrows were a character themselves—he wouldn't be the same without them.

I was relieved to see Harper's playful banter had returned. Summer's death had been difficult for him. I could still feel his remorse, just as I'd been feeling everyone else's; it was impossible to ignore.

"I think so. Although…you seem a little *too* excited about it." I smirked. "I'm starting to wonder if I should be nervous." I eyed him carefully, waiting for a muscle twitch or an averted gaze to give him away.

"I'll look out for you." His promise was compromised by a mischievous grin.

"Yeah, I'm sure."

"What, you don't trust me?" he scoffed. "I'm always looking out for the best interest of—"

"Yourself," I interrupted, and he laughed.

I glanced at Clara as she stood. She was watching me intently. When she noticed me looking at her, she flashed a bright smile and glided away. The pale purple of her yoga pants triggered my memory, and nearly violet eyes flashed in my mind. Recalling the look on the mysterious, dying woman's face and the feeling of Jake's misery, I suddenly felt nauseated.

I looked up and found Jake staring at me.

"Are you okay?" he asked. "You look sick."

I had to blink to clear the image from my mind. "Yeah, I'm fine," was all I could think to say.

"Alright, Baby Girl," Harper said as he stood. "Let's go. Time to get to work." He looked over at Jake. "You coming?"

I glanced back and forth between Harper and Jake. "Excuse me?"

Jake studied me with unreadable eyes before walking away in silence.

Frantically, I followed Harper as he marched down the hall. "I thought I was training with *you*, H?"

He shook his head. "No, Jake's your sparring partner." His casualness was maddening. *Great.*

Walking outside, Harper surveyed the ground and bent down to pick up a few branches and sticks…though I didn't know why he needed them. "You don't like Jake, huh?" He examined a few large twigs before approaching me, seeming a little too entertained by my discomfort.

I rolled my eyes. "I'm *trying* to like him, but he's sort of a dick.

He's making it nearly impossible to get to know him…or even talk to him. He won't even let me thank him properly for…you know." I dropped my hands to my sides, realizing I'd been gesturing around wildly.

Harper shrugged which only increased my annoyance. "You don't know Sanchez all that well either. Some people are just more private than others."

Why is he defending him so much? Not wanting to admit it was true, I remained silent.

"Give him a break. Besides, he's leaving as soon as his wounds heal. And to answer your question, I *am* teaching you, but Sanchez brought up a good point—you need to be able to defend yourself against anyone, Zoe." His eyebrows shot up in acknowledgement. "Hey Jake, perfect timing."

I turned to find Jake standing behind me with his arms crossed. I needed to tell Harper that Jake was miraculously already healed. Instead, I was distracted by Jake's inscrutable expression; he looked neither eager nor opposed to being there.

Harper cleared his throat then explained, "I want Zoe to learn how to use things around her as weapons at any given moment. She won't always have a gun or a knife, or…us." He walked over to me, presenting a twig, a stick, and a small branch. "Pick the one you want to start with. We'll switch it up as we go."

I shrugged and grabbed a gnarly, foot-long stick.

After an hour of step-by-step training with Harper, I knew how to effectively knee, kick, elbow, and head-butt my way out of an assailant's hold, in theory anyway. The stick, which was supposed to be functioning as my weapon, ended up causing *me* more bodily harm than Harper. Then, he pulled Jake away from sparring with Sanchez.

"Now, let's see how well you can put everything together," Harper said, grinning. "Show me what you'd do in scenario one, Baby Girl. Jake's bigger than you and five times as strong."

"Oh come on, I'm not *that* pathetic," I retorted.

Harper ignored me and continued, "What are you gonna do if he has his arms wrapped around you from behind?"

It was difficult to stay focused as Jake's observant eyes watched me, waiting, but imagining the pleasure I'd feel at taking out my aggression on him—one scratch, stomp, and jab at a time—was enough to inspire my determination to learn. I stood with my back to him, anxiously waiting for his arms to wrap around me. I desperately hoped my body would have zero response.

Distracted by Cooper barking as he played with Sanchez a few yards away, I spun around. Just as I did, Jake's arms wrapped around me. His scruffy cheek rubbed against mine, tickling my skin. His breath was warm on my neck, and an earthy scent wafted off him, diverting my attention from what I was supposed to be doing. *Wait, what...*the pressure of his solid arms wrapped tightly around me was unexpectedly exciting.

"You're not even trying, Zoe," Harper said, snapping me out of my unwanted, lusty haze.

"Agh!" I finally started to struggle. Jake's hold was unyielding as I wriggled around. After only a few seconds had passed, I was already winded. *This is embarrassing.*

I took a deep breath. *Situation one...a man comes up from behind me. I'm supposed to...* Using my thigh muscles, I leaned forward and immediately sprung backward as hard and fast as I could. With the force of my body movement, I knocked Jake off balance and tried to hit his face with the back of my head.

My efforts were fruitless. He tilted his head to the side, and the back of my head missed his face, nearly giving me whiplash as it ricocheted off the top of his shoulder. "Shit," I hissed, trying to ignore the sharp pain in the back of my neck.

Unsure what to do next, I leaned forward, lifted my legs off the ground, and let my body weight hang limply in his grasp. He stumbled forward, no doubt surprised by my unconventional methods. His head bent down toward me, and I quickly planted my feet back on the ground. As he tried to regain his footing, I head-butted him in the nose.

"Son of a bitch!" he rasped, but his hold tightened—I still couldn't wriggle away. As I continued to struggle, I heard snickering and stopped. Harper and Sanchez were laughing hysterically as they watched us.

"What do you call that? You look like a monkey," Harper said as he continued laughing, and I realized I must have resembled a cat struggling to escape the suffocating arms of its owner.

Jake let go, and I crumpled to the ground with a thud. I was glad to be away from the distracting sensations I felt in his arms, but the sharp pain that shot through my knee upon impact was an unwanted replacement. Catching my breath, I stood up.

"Nice head-butt. It would've been more effective if your hair wasn't padding the contact," Jake told me. Although I knew he was right, I resented his smart-ass tone.

"That was definitely…one way to do it," Harper agreed. "But you didn't get very far, Baby Girl. Try it again; only this time, let's practice using the second scenario." Harper took a step back, clapping his hands in an effort to keep me motivated, and Jake immediately seized me from the front. Winded, I quickly tried to collect myself, but with his arms wrapped around me, his scent assaulted me and derailed my concentration yet again.

As I struggled, my hair stuck to the stubble of his face like Velcro. I must've looked utterly ridiculous with his arms around me and my face buried in his neck.

My curiosity faded as I once again recalled the image of the woman I'd seen in Jake's memories, lying limp and dying in his arms. What part had he played in her death? Unease washed over me at the reminder that Jake was practically a stranger. I reprimanded myself for forgetting that, and common sense kicked in. I was supposed to be kneeing him in the groin. So, that's what I did.

Distracting Jake with a fake head-butt should've worked, but he'd been watching me train and knew the moves Harper had taught me—it was easy for him to avoid my attack. I tried to knee him, but he blocked my attempt with his leg.

He laughed heartily as I struggled in his hold. *He's enjoying this way too much.* Infuriated, I bit his neck with guilty pleasure. Although the element of surprise would've sufficed, I bit him harder than necessary, and he shouted in pain. I kneed him in the groin as hard as I could, and when his grip loosened, I elbowed him in the face. Squirming out of his hold, I began to dance victoriously.

Jake's expression was a mix of anger, pain, and amusement. He winced a couple of times, but my celebration was short-lived—he was in less pain than I'd hoped. Bent over and breathing deeply, he smirked. "Feel better?"

"Actually…yes, I do," I admitted.

Harper sauntered over with his mouth drawn into a proud smile. "Great job, Baby Girl! A little unorthodox, but hey, it worked." He wrapped his arm around my shoulder and pulled me in for a friendly squeeze.

"You said I'd have to think on my feet." I looked back at Jake who was still bent over in fading pain, watching us.

Harper laughed. "Alright, enough play time for today. Let's get to work." He motioned toward the hospital. "Thanks for your help, Jake. See you in there."

I made my way to the hospital with Harper, donned my white jacket, and started preparing the tetanus boosters we'd planned to administer to everyone. I barely had time to pull out my syringes, needles, and vials before Sanchez began sending people in. Dave entered and headed straight to Harper's table in the treatment bay beside mine, thankfully without a glance in my direction. Tanya was next to arrive, and she headed over to me.

"Hey, how're you feeling?" I asked while I wiped her arm with an alcohol swab.

"Okay. Tired, but I guess that's what happens when you don't sleep much."

"You should take a nap after we're finished. You might be sore for a bit, but it'll pass." We talked for a couple minutes after I finished administering the vaccination, and then she excused herself. I smiled as she waved and exited through the swinging doors.

Sarah was my next patient. Dread was painted all over her face; she hated needles and turned green just thinking about getting a shot.

"It's okay—it'll only prick a tiny bit, and then it's over." I tried to reassure her with a promising smile.

"It always hurts. I especially hate when I have to rip the Band-aid off. It always pulls the hairs on my arm and stings."

"Sarah, I promise I'll—Oh, hey Biggs!" As she looked behind her, I stuck the needle in her upper arm.

"Ow, Zoe! That was mean!" Her eyes narrowed, and she stuck out her bottom lip.

Knowing it *was* mean, I mirrored her expression. "Sorry, I was only trying to help." I couldn't help but laugh as I wiped the injection site. "It wasn't that bad, was it? Look, I'll even leave the bandage off for you."

She sighed. "I guess not, but still."

"You're just upset that he wasn't really standing there," I mused. She tried to repress her smile, but I could feel her happiness at the thought of him. *I wish everyone was this easy to read.* "You love him," I said in a sing-song voice.

Sarah hopped down from the table. "Now that would just be silly, wouldn't it," she said dryly.

"And why's that?"

"We've only known each other for a week or so."

"Yeah, well silliness is all we have now, isn't it? Rationality went out the window the moment the world started falling apart. I think it's safe to say you should follow your instincts."

Sarah's face seemed to brighten at my encouragement, and she gave me a quick hug. "Thanks, Zoe." She practically skipped out the door, leaving me with an amused grin as Clara walked in. Although she smiled, my mood immediately soured.

"Hi," she cooed as she sat on the table.

"Hi." *Strange girl.* "You're not afraid of needles too, are you?" I began disinfecting her skin with an alcohol wipe.

She laughed sadistically, sending a rush of chills down my spine.

"I'll take that as a no, then."

Clara didn't flinch or blink an eye as the needle pierced her skin—instead she simply stared at me. At that moment I was both afraid and curious to know what she was thinking. I didn't have to wonder for long.

"What's going on with you and Jake?" she blurted quietly. Her jealousy was apparent.

"Excuse me?" I choked out as she glowered at me.

Suddenly, her lethal gaze melted, and her demure smile returned. "It's just that he and I have a special…friendship, and I want to make sure you're aware of it, that's all."

A switch flipped inside me, and I suddenly didn't care how much Clara unnerved me. "Well if that's the case, then I'm sure you have nothing to worry about." I put on a fake, condescending smile, slapped a bandage on her arm, and called out, "Next!"

Her eyes narrowed in consideration, but right when she opened her mouth to speak, Jake strolled in. I felt the heat of his stare and glanced at him, Clara's eyes following suit. "Jake," she purred. "We were just talking about you."

"Really?" He looked amused. *That's twice in one day.* His eyes swept back over to me.

Clara's face tensed with animosity as she followed his line of sight. I tried not to let my blank expression waver.

"You're over there." I pointed Jake toward Harper's table, and he kept moving.

Obviously dismayed that she couldn't provoke me, Clara folded her arms and stomped away.

29

DANI

I'd finally woken in the small patch of woods behind Grams's house the previous afternoon with only a few hours of daylight left. I hadn't known why I'd blacked out nor where everyone had gone, but I *had* known my continued survival depended on finding more food. Luckily, I'd successfully scavenged some nearby homes and managed to avoid further contact with people—both known and unknown—before returning to the ranch.

With at least a week's worth of food stocked in the ranch house, I was free to focus on settling in. I had to stay somewhere in town, at least until I figured out what had happened to Grams, and the ranch was as good a place as any. Besides, the animals in residence needed someone to take care of them.

Since nobody had died in the house, the air was blissfully gag-free. The ranch house also had functioning plumbing, two fireplaces, and a working gas water heater.

As I cleaned the front room and arranged the rustic furniture in a way that befit my survivor lifestyle—casting a large couch as my bed, a coffee table as my desk, and a bookshelf as my closet—I considered finding a way to contact Zoe…for the thousandth time.

There was no internet, no landline, and no cell signal to rely on. *But...there's always MG...*

My thoughts flashed to the confrontation I'd witnessed between my friends and Cece on Grams's deck. I didn't know how it had ended, but I was pretty sure it wasn't in bloodshed. Unfortunately, one thing was certain—caring for me had almost cost Chris and Jason their lives.

Zoe's better off without me. Everyone is.

By lunchtime, I ran out of things to do in the house. Though there were plenty of chores associated with maintaining the ranch and its dozens of animals, there was an off-site errand that was far more urgent. I needed to figure out what had happened to Grams and to Zoe's dad. I'd made a promise to Zoe.

I rounded up Jack and donned my empty pack to once again sneak through the sparse woods and tall grasses surrounding the town. We made it to Grams's garden without incident and carefully walked the perimeter—nobody was in sight, and there were no fresh human scents for Jack to follow. Jason and Chris were gone. I felt a sharp pang of disappointment in my chest, turning my relief to bitterness.

Feeling strangely empty, I snuck back into my childhood home. Jack and I quickly searched the interior, making absolutely sure the house was vacant. Certain of our solitude, we scoured every room, one-by-one; we found nothing but memories and dust. In the basement we ravaged Grams's fabled food stores, stocking up on canned meats and a variety of homemade dried soups. The house was filled with remnants of the woman who'd raised me, yet Grams herself wasn't there. *Where are you, Grams?*

We finally ended up in the kitchen, the hope of finding any sign of her whereabouts hanging by a thread. As I searched around the room, I spotted a plain white envelope stuck to the fridge. The hand-made magnet holding it up was one of the few presentable items I'd created in the many art classes Zoe had coerced me into taking. It consisted of a thin circle of clay etched with a perfect

Celtic knot representing the love between a mother and daughter, or in our case, a grandmother and granddaughter. It had taken me five weeks and four attempts to get it right, but my efforts had been more than justified by the tears in Grams's eyes when I'd given it to her on her sixty-fifth birthday.

Removing the magnet and envelope from the fridge, I recalled my many failed attempts to replicate Grams's distinctive old-fashioned penmanship. I ran my fingers over the single word written on the front: Dani-girl. My dwindling hope swelled. *She might be alive!*

In a haze of eagerness, I shoved the magnet and envelope into my jacket pocket and rushed back to the ranch. I set the sealed envelope on the coffee table, sneaking glances at it as I scurried back and forth between the kitchen and front room to make tea.

Finally, steaming mug in hand, I snuggled into a blanket on the couch and stared at the beckoning envelope. *What's in it? A letter? When did she write it? Is it good news?*

With shaking fingers, I set down my cup of tea and picked up the envelope. As I opened it, a torn photograph and an antique iron key plunked onto the coffee table's unfinished oak surface. A young Zoe and Jason peered up at me from the faded image, captivating me, but I knew the partial photo couldn't provide the answers I sought. Instead, I focused on the folded letter that was still partially encased in the envelope.

I gingerly pulled it out and immediately recognized the note's flowery stationary. According to the date, it had been written a couple of weeks ago. As I began to read, I both savored and feared each successive word.

December 9, 2012

Dani-girl, my dearest granddaughter,

I hope you know that you have always been more than a grand-

daughter to me. You have been a daughter, and one for which I am eternally grateful. I lost my Ceara, but I gained you. You were worth it.

As you requested, I looked for Zoe's father. I found him. Tom was sitting against a tree on a bluff overlooking the ocean, dead. He had a key on a string and a torn photograph of Zoe and Jason clutched in his hand, both of which are in this envelope. Please give these things to Zoe or Jason if either of them survives...if you survive.

You must know and accept this: I am sick and dying. I'm too old to recover from something killing even the young and healthy. I'm going into the forest for my eternal rest. Don't roll your eyes at me, Dani-girl, it's the only way to guarantee my return to nature with so few people around to take care of the bodies. DO NOT go looking for my body, Dani-girl. I don't want you to remember me that way. I mean it—if you care for me at all, you will leave my body be. I pray that you will one day read this, for then you have survived.

I'll love you always, my Dani-girl,
Grams

With a handful of sentences, my whole world came to a crashing halt.

Grams...she's dead.

She'd stepped in and raised me after my mother died in childbirth, had molded my teenage temper into a tool to be used by a grown woman, and had instilled in me the importance of embracing my heritage by teaching me her native language and traditions. *She's dead. How can she be dead?*

I craved the release of tears, but my body denied me. Numbness saturated me as part of myself seemed to dissolve—Grams was gone. Time passed in my suddenly empty and meaningless world, and I eventually succumbed to the exhausting fog of depression. My eyelids felt swollen with the unfulfilled need to cry. Seeking temporary relief, I closed my eyes and let sleep claim me.

I became aware of the dream only after he arrived, like his presence awakened my conscious mind without disturbing my sleep. Dreams were normal—incomprehensible and forgettable—until MG arrived. He gave them substance and matter. With his involvement, I felt like I was living in two different worlds.

I was huddled on the ground staring at the bodies of Grams and Tom. They looked so perfect, like they might wake up at any moment, but I knew better.

They were gone. Dead.

As my conscious mind merged with my dreaming self, I let out a low, keening moan.

Grams was dead.

Gently, MG crouched in front of me and lifted my face with gentle, graceful fingers. "Dani? What happened?"

Through a barrage of sobs, gasps, and incoherent words, I told him about my discovery...about Grams. I finished with, "Everyone's dead. I shouldn't be surprised."

"Not everyone," he said softly and took me into his arms. "You can always go to Colorado, to the Colony to meet up with your friends. You wouldn't be alone there."

Shaking my head against his shoulder, I whispered, "I don't know. I just don't know. I...I don't think I can handle working on this tonight. You should probably go visit your other people."

He held me close. "They can wait."

30

ZOE

The hospital off-base was desolate—an empty labyrinth completely deserted by its former inhabitants. *Where are all the sick...dead people?* Harper's practiced footsteps were barely audible as he advanced down a linoleum hallway. I couldn't say the same for mine. As we rounded a corner, he scanned the area with his assault rifle, prepared for whatever vile thing we might encounter. Given his usually playful disposition, it was easy to forget he was trained to kill. As we combed through the potentially dangerous building, his training gave me solace.

"Stay close behind me," he whispered, concentrating on the dark corridors ahead.

I shivered. Searching the facility for supplies was a really bad idea; every raised hair on my body confirmed it. "Don't you think we've found enough stuff?" I waited for Harper to answer, but he didn't, so I prattled on, "We can only take so much with us when we leave anyway." I readjusted the canvas duffel bag strap crossing my chest. "Besides, this place is huge. It can't be safe to—"

"We'll argue later," Harper said, dismissing my concerns as he continued down the hall. "Be quiet."

I followed him, my eyes darting around as I tried to focus on anything besides my racing heartbeat. An empty nurses' station was cluttered with medical books and files, and stray papers littered the floor like a rogue whirlwind had swept through the space. Some of the doors lining the hallway were shut, and I couldn't suppress my morbid curiosity. *What's behind them?*

Just as I was wondering when we would reconvene with Jake and Sanchez, the sound of static startled me. "Harper," Sanchez said, interrupting our radio silence. "Get down to the ER. There's something you need to see." Her ominous tone filled me with dread, and I had the sudden urge to run away, screaming.

"That doesn't sound good," Harper said, reaching back to squeeze my hand. *No shit.* "Move fast and keep close."

I hurried behind him as we turned left, right, and then left again before finding a stairway door—an emergency exit. He pushed the heavy door open and walked through, but I hesitated; I didn't want to be immersed in the pitch-blackness. I held the door open with sweaty palms while Harper did a quick sweep of the stairwell. Returning to the door, he looked at me, nodded once, and then motioned for me to follow him. Taking a deep breath, I shadowed him down the stairs.

When Harper reached the first-floor landing, he glanced back at me once more before flinging the metal door open. Again, he scanned the area with his rifle, and I sighed with relief when he found no reason to pull the trigger. Turning to the left, he advanced down the hallway.

"How do you know where to go?" I asked in a quiet rush of words.

He pointed the muzzle of his rifle toward a sign that read "EMERGENCY" and had a long, red arrow pointing in the direction we were moving. *Oh...duh.* Feeling stupid, I shook my head.

The first floor was much like the upper floors, only it was brighter and everything seemed less intimidating. Picture windows lined the walls, letting in daylight and providing a clear view of the parking lot and the roiling storm clouds. I stopped in front of a window, mesmerized by the bone-chilling sight of countless abandoned cars.

While I stared out the window, Harper kept moving. When I turned and found him disappearing around a corner, I ran after him, afraid of being left alone. Rounding the same corner, I slammed into his tensed, motionless body. I staggered back.

Jake and Sanchez were standing beside him, equally still and staring outside through a wall of windows. I followed the direction of their eyes to the courtyard, and my body stiffened in horror. I dropped my bag on the floor.

A mountain of decomposing bodies filled the space. There were hundreds of them, maybe thousands, haphazardly piled on top of each other like an enormous mound of garbage. Before I could look away, I spotted a pair of milky, glazed over eyes. I couldn't stop myself from staring, from memorizing the rest of the face—the gray, decaying skin and the purple, crusty sores clustered around the lips. It was more than I could bear.

"Oh my God," I gasped and turned away, flinging myself at the nearest person—Jake. Unexpectedly, his protective concern blanketed me. Afraid to open my eyes again, I ignored my pride and awkwardness as I buried my face in his jacket.

"Keep your eyes closed," he whispered near my ear, wrapping his free arm around me.

"Looks like some of the fresher ones have bullet wounds, and a lot of them are wearing fatigues," Harper said.

"Who—" Sanchez cleared her throat. "Who stacked them like that?" It was the first time I'd heard fear in her voice.

"We need to get out of here," Harper said.

Suddenly, my mind was flooded with uncontrollable aggression. Images of blood-spattered walls and mangled bodies inundated my thoughts. I shook my head frantically, trying to dispel the scenes from my mind, but compulsive hostility and insatiable anger overwhelmed my control. I couldn't escape.

When I realized the onslaught of images and feelings weren't coming from Jake, I peered up at him, confused. His imploring eyes met mine as a stronger wave engulfed me, and I struggled to keep the emotions and memories separate from my own. The room seemed to swirl around me, and my eyelids became too heavy to keep open. Only partially aware, I felt my body weaken and my knees give out. Jake's arms tightened around me and the sound of gunshots rang throughout the hospital as I lost consciousness.

When I opened my eyes again, a tree was bouncing past me, and I could hear heavy breathing. I blinked, trying to make sense of what I was seeing. It took me a moment to realize *I* was the one bouncing, not the tree—Jake was carrying me while he ran.

"Why are you running?" I asked him weakly. As we distanced ourselves from the hospital, my mind cleared, and I realized something was wrong. "What happened?" I panicked and wrapped my arms around Jake's neck. Straining to look over his shoulder, I saw Sanchez leaning against Harper as she hobbled after us. She was wincing in pain.

"Oh my God." I struggled to get out of Jake's hold. "I'm fine," I said, and he hesitantly set me on the sidewalk. We were in the parking lot behind the hospital, and for some reason, I felt safer knowing there was distance between us and the mountain of dead bodies. I wasn't sure if the breeze really carried the smell of rancid, rotting flesh, or if it was just my imagination.

"Keep moving, Zoe," Harper said as he and Sanchez caught up to us. He pushed me toward Dave's truck.

"Was it Crazies? How many were there?" I asked frantically, flinging open the truck door so Harper could help Sanchez climb inside. She was bleeding from her abdomen. Harper tossed my duffel bag of scavenged medical supplies into the truck bed before he climbed into the backseat after Sanchez, tugged off his long-sleeve shirt, and pressed it against her wound.

"What can I do?" I asked, but they ignored me.

"Get in!" Jake shouted as he jumped into the driver's seat.

I did as he commanded, yanking the passenger side door shut as he sped out of the parking lot. Sanchez's breathing was ragged, and muffled whimpers escaped from her as the truck jostled her around.

I turned in my seat and asked Harper, "How bad is she hurt?"

"I don't think any organs or arteries were hit, but I can't tell for sure. I've gotta get a better look at her." Harper glanced at the back of Jake's head. "Can't we go any faster?"

Jake pressed harder on the gas pedal.

"It had to have been Crazies…how many were there?" I asked Jake, quietly. I didn't want to distract Harper as he helped Sanchez reposition herself in the backseat.

"Five," Jake said, taking a deep breath. "We're lucky nothing worse happened."

I looked back at Sanchez again and hoped she wasn't as bad as she looked. Blood soaked her shirt around the wound and was smeared on Harper's hands and t-shirt.

Jake glanced into the rearview mirror, and his paranoia flooded me.

"How many are still alive?" I asked, worried an army of Crazies would drive up behind us.

"Those five are dead, but who knows if there are more."

I nodded and turned toward the window. Thunder rumbled in the distance, and I figured it wouldn't be long before the clouds burst and poured rain down on us. I rubbed my throbbing head and took another deep breath. Sanchez didn't cry or complain, but her blood-smeared grimace made it obvious she was in bad shape.

"I could use a drink," she rasped. Her comment put a smile on Jake's face—it was the first time I'd seen him smile. The expression seemed strangely natural and welcoming on him.

"I think we can manage that," he said.

I looked back at Sanchez—her head was resting on Harper's shoulder and she was struggling to keep her eyes open.

"You better hurry," I whispered to Jake. "I think she's going into shock."

Harper glanced up to find me watching them and asked, "What the hell happened to you back there?"

I shook my head, trying to recall everything that had happened before I'd fallen to the ground. "I guess I could feel them getting closer. Their emotions sort of blindsided me. They were just too strong…" The horrifying images from the Crazies' minds flashed in my head. "Their minds were…just wrong. They're so far gone." Harper nodded as Jake carefully brought the truck to a stop outside of our hospital.

Harper and Jake unloaded Sanchez, and we rushed into the emergency room. As I hurried toward the first treatment bay behind them, I felt an unexpected comfort at being back on base; it was the closest thing I'd had to a home in weeks.

Sanchez cringed as she was gently set on an examination table. She was taking shallow, quick breaths and was clutching the edges of the table so tightly that her knuckles were turning white.

Harper slipped back into medic mode as he pulled on a pair of surgical gloves. "Zoe, hand me some bandage scissors."

I hurried over to one of the drawers of stainless steel instruments I'd organized for him a few days before and found the scissors. After handing them to him, I hastily collected the supplies Harper would need—sutures, several sizes of surgical needles, iodine, gauze, a local anesthetic, and morphine.

Setting the tray with all of the supplies on a cart beside Harper, I watched him cut off Sanchez's blood-soaked shirt, exposing the bullet wound in her side. The hole itself was smaller than I'd thought, only the size of a dime instead of the gaping wound I'd imagined.

Harper glanced up at me. "Zoe, she'll need clean clothes. Can you go find some?" I nodded, and he added, "Something loose. And bring some for me too."

I nodded again and hurried into the hallway.

Halfway down the corridor, I stopped and wondered what I should tell anyone who happened to see me in my disheveled state. I spun around and ran back toward the emergency room to ask. I slowed just before pushing through the swinging doors and could hear my friends talking in hushed tones.

"If we're staying here indefinitely, we've gotta burn that place down, and soon. We can't risk any of them finding us." Harper's voice sounded strained.

"Jesus, Harper!" Sanchez gasped.

"That was the local…you'll feel better in a few seconds," Harper told her.

I didn't hear Sanchez's reply; I was too focused on the knot in my stomach. *Staying here indefinitely? We aren't leaving?* All rational thought disappeared. I was overwhelmed with the thought of never seeing Dani and Jason again.

Jason won't come here. Or, maybe he would? No…he'll want to stay at the Colony with his team.

Jake's voice broke my chain of frenzied thoughts. "Trust me, it's safer here." *This is his fault?*

Backing away quietly, I turned to leave. I dutifully retrieved clean clothes for both Sanchez and Harper, avoiding everyone but Cooper. The Husky followed slowly behind me as I begrudgingly walked back to the hospital. Before heading into the emergency room, I stopped to steady my nerves. After a few deep breaths, I entered without making any eye contact and handed the clothes to Jake. "I'm going to find Biggs," I lied, offering the first excuse that popped into my head, and hurried out of the room.

As I rushed across the base toward the pond, chaotic thoughts churned in my mind. I looked around at the less than welcoming scenery. Ragged, dormant tree branches reached out like withered witch fingers, beckoning me toward them. The wind picked up, whipping passed me, and I shivered, unsure whether it had been caused by the frigid gust or my outrage.

Were they even planning on telling me? It was clear that if I wanted to go to Colorado, I'd be going on my own.

I thought about my self-defense lessons with Harper and Jake.

Situation one: someone comes at you from behind...

Situation two: someone grabs you from the front...

I had a better understanding of how to defend myself, but I was no expert. I knew the chances of making it on my own were slim—I had minimal instinct and even less survival skill. Amazingly, I wasn't scared of what might happen to me. I was stupidly determined.

As I stood by the pond, brooding, the charcoal-gray sky continued to dim and thunderclouds churned ferociously. The first drop of rain landed on my cheek, quickly followed by others. I welcomed the rain, wanting it to wash away all of my troubles, but I was too cold to stay outdoors any longer. I turned to leave...and jumped. Jake was standing almost directly behind me. I had no idea how I hadn't heard him.

"I thought you went to find Biggs," he said, taking a step closer to me. He seemed unconcerned by the increasing rain.

I really didn't want to talk to him—his mere presence made me combative. "I needed some air," I said icily.

His eyes narrowed. "Are you okay?"

His "concern" was infuriating. "It doesn't really matter, does it?" I snapped, turning my back on him and wandering closer to the water. I didn't want him to see the seething play of emotions on my face.

Hearing his heavy footsteps approach, I blurted, "Why didn't anyone tell me we were staying here *indefinitely*? And when did *you* decide to stay?"

Jake's silence aggravated me even more, and I rounded on him. He was too close, and I had to step back to avoid bumping into him. His eyes were filled with an emotion I had no interest in understanding. I pushed his feelings away and resolved to stop trying to figure him out. Unable to look at him, I started to walk away, but his hand grasped my forearm before I could move out of his reach.

"It's not safe there."

Oh, now he wants to talk, I thought caustically but took the bait. "It's not safe *where*?"

"Colorado."

I sensed his earnestness but was too stubborn to consider his warning. "Well, it's not safe anywhere." I tried to tug my arm from his iron hold, but his hand squeezed tighter.

"You don't understand." Jake's voice was grave, but I barely heard his words. He was apparently oblivious to the water running down his clenched jaw, to the rain-drenched shirt clinging to his torso.

But *I* wasn't. I struggled to prevent my eyes from scanning his sculpted body. My attraction to him was like lighter fluid on my fiery rage. "Of course I don't understand, *Jake*. How could I? You never explain anything, and I'm sick of trying to figure you out!" I shouted.

"I've been there!" His words were like forbidden fruit. I straightened and awaited the explanation I desperately hoped would follow. Finally, he said, "I'm *from* there." The pain in his eyes was obvious. *What happened to him? Why won't he go back?*

"And that has *what* to do with the Colony, exactly?"

Jake's free hand clenched into a fist. "Dammit, Zoe! I'm from Colorado Springs…that's practically on Peterson's doorstep. I left when all this started for a reason."

I staggered back in surprise, and hope surged through me as I considered what he might know. "Have you been to the Colony?"

He shook his head, and my sudden hope evaporated. "No. But trust me, we don't want to go there—*especially* not you."

"Why? What happened?"

Jake hesitated, but then seemed to come to a decision. "My

sister was like you…changed by the Virus. Soldiers came for her near the beginning, and she thought killing herself was better than being taken away by them."

"The woman dying in your arms," I whispered sadly, suddenly feeling the need to comfort him.

For the first time, his silence told me everything I needed to know. He wore grief and regret like an invisible scar—always there to remind him, to punish him.

My voice cracked as I asked, "What were they gonna do to her?"

"I don't know, but they had guns and were ready to use them. They weren't giving Becca a choice…and she refused to go with them the only way she could." As an afterthought, he added softly, "She saw something, and whatever it was…it was worse than killing herself."

Despite the rain dripping down my face and over my lips, my mouth grew dry at the thought of being held against my will…of being experimented on. *Maybe I should reconsider…* I wiped the rain from my eyes as a sudden realization filled me with terror. *Dani and Jason are headed there…and Dani's on her own…*

"I'm really sorry for what happened to your sister, but—"

Jake dropped my arm. "I didn't tell you that to make you sorry. I told you so you could protect yourself. Staying here might be the only way to do that." It was the most emotion I'd ever heard in his voice, and it frightened me.

"I appreciate your concern for my safety, Jake. I really do. And I understand why you think I should stay here, but I can't. I have people waiting for me. I have to go, with or without you guys," I said honestly and walked passed him, heading toward the barracks.

Questions about Jake's past fought to escape my lips, but I held them back. I knew if I lingered to ask, to get to know him better, he might succeed in convincing me to stay.

31

ZOE

After dinner that night, I sat on a couch in the common room, basking in the warmth of the fire. I felt numb. My body was like an icebox—frozen from the inside out—my bones felt brittle, and even in a long-sleeve shirt and sweatpants, I was shivering uncontrollably. Emotionally, I was raw. The Crazies' memories were seared into my mind, and their emotions had felt more severe and unsettling than any I'd ever experienced before. I felt fractured and exposed, and the fire provided much-needed comfort after a day of unwanted surprises.

On the floor at my feet, Cooper snoozed peacefully. He'd taken a sudden interest in me, following me around and staring at me with concerned, watchful eyes.

Focusing on my drawing, I critiqued the likeness of the pond. I was struggling, my hands and mind working disjointedly to convey what I remembered. The drawing was a weak version of the image I saw so vividly in my head—it was drab and boring compared to the life I knew hid in the hibernating landscape.

I hadn't felt like myself for weeks, but I was having a particularly disconcerting evening. My eyelids had grown increasingly heavy over the past hour, but I resisted the urge to turn in for the night. I dreaded the nightmarish images that awaited me whenever my eyes closed. Instead, I'd nested in the corner of the couch, armed with a book, my drawing pad and pencils, and a steaming cup of Chai tea to keep my mind occupied for as long as possible. Unfortunately, thoughts of leaving the group continued to fill my consciousness.

"Hey," Clara's chirping voice jolted me from my restless mind chatter. She flopped down beside me, smirking as my pencil hand jumped across the page. *I didn't want an extra branch there, bitch.*

Clara was one of the last people I wanted to talk to. She creeped me out, especially her bright, vivacious blue eyes—despite their angelic color, they seemed to house the soul of a devil. Her lips were too red, her smile too wide.

Sighing and attempting to smile, I looked over at her, reluctant to give her much attention. "What can I do for you, Clara?"

She situated herself comfortably beside me and analyzed my sketch. "Oh nothing. I just thought I'd come check on you." She looked at me, mimicking the disingenuous smile I'd plastered on my own face. "You've been so quiet since you and the others got back…I just thought I'd see if there was anything I could do to help."

Corralling all the patience I could possibly muster, I turned back to my sketchbook. "I'm peachy, Clara. Thanks for your concern, but I'm really not in the mood to chat tonight." I hoped my sarcastic tone would send her on her way.

"Oh, don't be shy." She batted my arm playfully. "I can tell something's wrong. You've been pouting since you got back from your trip into town. I can tell you're suffering."

I shook my head dismissively. "Well I'm sorry to break it to you, but I'm fine. Don't worry about me." Out of nowhere, Clara's mood shifted, and hostility fogged my senses, even though her feigned concerned expression remained intact.

"Jake told me what happened," she said, sounding sympathetic.

Glancing at her, I wondered if she was full of shit or if Jake really would've told her about our conversation by the pond. *How close are they anyway?* "Oh yeah? And what exactly did he tell you?" Part of me hoped he *did* have a big mouth, just so I'd have one more reason to get as far away from him as possible. But… another part of me felt sick at the idea of Jake talking to Clara about me at all.

At my question, her coy smile faded and her eyes hardened. Apparently that hadn't been the response she'd been looking for. I could feel betrayal and animosity radiating from her as she resituated herself on the couch beside me.

Clearing her throat, she straightened her blouse and avoided meeting my gaze. After a moment, she looked at me with empty eyes. "Oh, don't worry about it," she said. "Your secret's safe with me."

Confused, I shifted on the couch to face her. I could feel myself getting sucked into her conniving trap, but both exasperation and curiosity lead me to ask, "And which secret is that?"

Clara's eyes darted around the room. Her face was flushed, and she seemed extremely anxious. I had to fight the urge to make a wise-ass remark about her seven personalities. My mind reached out to hers, trying to understand her sudden discomfort, and it was an effort to reel it back in.

"Are you okay?" I asked, watching her face redden before my eyes.

"I'm fine!" She shrieked, standing abruptly. "I just hope you know he's with *me*. You're damaged goods, to say the least. I wouldn't get too attached if I were you." For reasons I didn't understand, her scathing words were like claws raking down my flesh.

"Whatever," I snapped. "I'm really not in the mood for mind games right now. Just leave me alone."

"Everything okay?" Sarah asked as she strode up behind the couch, glancing worriedly between us.

"I'm fine!" Clara shrieked again. "Cooper, come!" When

Copper only looked up at her blankly, she huffed and stomped away.

"Wow." Sarah sat down beside me as she watched Clara stalk off. She folded her legs under her, mirroring my position on the couch. Her warmth beside me was comforting—a pleasant relief from Clara's chilly antagonism. "She's really got it out for you, huh?"

"Apparently," I mused. "I'm not really sure what she thinks is going on, but she was clearly a mental patient even before all of this," I joked.

Sarah giggled. "True." She leaned her head on my shoulder and shifted my sketch pad so she could see it better. "Whatcha drawin'?"

"It's *supposed* to be the little pond down the hill by the woods. I've been going there a lot lately." I thought of Jake—he seemed to be a steady fixture there, but I refrained from adding him to the drawing.

"Oh yeah, Riley and I took a walk over there the other night. It's sorta peaceful, isn't it?"

I grinned at the warmth her voice held when she mentioned Biggs's first name.

"Why are you smiling, Zoe?" Sarah blushed and looked away, calling Cooper up onto the couch. He jumped up eagerly, settling in beside Sarah.

"How's it going with you two anyway?" I asked.

"It's good," she said casually.

"Good? That's all you have to say? I saw him come out of your room two mornings in a row!" I whispered, pretending to be shocked.

Sarah only had time to giggle before Harper came in and said, "Everyone in the mess hall. We have to talk." His expression was troubled, and he looked exhausted. I knew they'd planned on setting fire to the other hospital, but I wasn't sure how they'd fared, especially with the rain.

Sarah and I slowly extricated ourselves from the plush couch, both of us comfy in our pajamas. Seeing Harper in his fatigues made me feel guilty for lounging around.

"Come on, people!" he called out as we entered the dining room. Finally, Dave, Tanya, and Stacey strolled in behind us with pool cues in hand, and we all sat down at one of the long, cafeteria-style tables. Harper positioned himself on a neighboring table top, one knee up with his arm resting over it. He rubbed his eyes and sighed.

"Alright, listen up…" He started by telling everyone the condensed version of what had happened in the hospital off-base and reassured us that the situation was being taken care of. Normally Sanchez would've led the meeting, but she was still recovering in her room—she'd been lucky the bullet hadn't hit any vital organs.

"Let this serve as a reminder to everyone—if we face dangers like these here, think about how dangerous it is everywhere else."

I knew it was true, but as he continued speaking, I found myself distracted by the rain pounding against the windowpanes. It was oddly soothing, even though I knew it was only a matter of time before I would be facing the elements alone. The idea didn't bother me as much as I thought it should have. Instead, I wondered if the combination of howling wind and torrential rain was the closest I would ever come to hearing the sound of rhythmic waves washing over the beach again—a sound I'd grown up listening to.

"Zoe, did you hear me?" Harper asked.

I looked away from the windows, surprised to see everyone staring at me expectantly. Even Jake had appeared at some point during Harper's speech. He was leaning against the wall in the back of the mess hall. His clothes were wet, though he didn't seem to care.

I glanced at Harper sheepishly. "Sorry."

"I said, 'We've decided to stay here for a while.'"

"I know, to wait out the winter," I responded, knowing full well he'd meant we were making Fort Knox a more permanent home. I wasn't sure why I was playing dumb, but I found satisfaction in making it difficult for him to break the news to me.

"No, I mean, we aren't even sure we'll leave then. We've decided to stay here…indefinitely."

I just stared at him. Part of me was hurt because he hadn't told me sooner. Foolishly, I'd expected more out of our friendship. But, another part of me didn't feel much at all. "Okay," I said, wanting the conversation to end. The longer he stared at me, the closer I came to breaking down, and I hated crying in front of others.

Harper's eyebrows drew together in confusion.

"Why are you looking at me like that?" I snapped. "You thought I'd be pissed that you didn't tell me sooner? Well it would've been nice if you had."

Harper's confusion melted into exasperation. "Zoe…"

I stood quietly and said, "It's fine, Harper. I know you're looking out for everyone's best interest."

His eyes fixed on me for a few heartbeats before he spoke. "Really?" he asked in disbelief.

"Yeah." Agreeing was all I could do to avoid an argument. "I'm sure they're all okay with staying, especially after what happened out there today." I paused, looking around the room at my uncertain companions before returning my gaze to Harper. "Is there anything else?" I asked weakly.

"No, that's it." He scrutinized my face, trying to read the inner-workings of my mind.

"Stop staring at me like that," I said. I smiled to deflect my prickling tears.

"Tell him the truth," Jake said. The moment I heard his baritone voice, I felt the color drain from my face. *Please don't*, I silently begged. At the sound of him walking up behind me, I turned around and glared at him. I willed him not to say anymore…I didn't want to fight.

"What do you mean?" Harper asked, and I silently cursed Jake.

Meeting Harper's eyes, I tried to keep my composure, but I was too mentally exhausted—on top of everything else, the day's events proved too much for me to handle. "I understand why you want everyone to stay here—"

"But?" he interrupted, his tone sharp and disapproving.

"But, I'm still leaving to find Dani and my brother. I'm sure you understand." Tears blurred my vision, but I feared blinking would only encourage their flow.

"Zoe, you can't—"

"Please don't argue with me," I pleaded. "I really can't do this tonight…I *have* to go."

"No you don't, you can—"

"Yes I do!" I shouted. Acute frustration and loneliness consumed me. "You don't understand!" My tears were unstoppable, pouring down like water over rocky cliffs.

"You've been through a lot today, Baby Girl. Let's talk about this tomorrow." His placating, friendly tone returned as he tried to calm me down.

"I'm not going to change my mind," I sobbed. I was cracking, afraid I would shatter completely.

"You're not going alone," Jake said, the conviction in his voice thick and resolute. Trembling, I looked at him. He was standing at the far end of the table where everyone else sat. They all stared at him, but he didn't seem to notice.

"I won't let you come with me," I told Jake, wiping my eyes. Thinking of how much pain he'd experienced in Colorado, I knew going back was the last thing he wanted to do.

"Jake!" Clara cried, her shrill voice startling me. "You can't leave me! You said you'd take care of me!" She tossed her plastic cup across the room. Everyone looked to her in surprise. Realizing she was suddenly the center of attention, Clara added, "We're all safer here." Desperation dripped from every word. She glanced at me with searing hatred in her eyes.

"She's right," I said. "There's no way you're coming with me."

"Who's going to stop me? *You*?" he asked snidely. "We leave in a week. You better be prepared." He turned and stalked away.

I didn't want Jake's death on my conscious, not to mention his personal misery. Too many emotions bombarded me—my own despair and frustration mixed with the others' worry, confusion, and fear. My body quivered, and I lost all emotional control. When Sarah rushed over to me, I fell against her and cried. The emotions drowned me, but crying felt good.

"Come on, sweetie. Let's get you to bed." At Harper's warm whisper, my heart broke a little more. *Sweetie.* I thought of my father—his seemingly insignificant terms of endearment had told me he loved me even when he couldn't say it outright. *I'll probably never see him again.* Crying harder, I collapsed to my knees on the floor.

Harper crouched down and gathered me into his arms. "It's okay," he said as he stood, holding me close.

I wrapped my arms around his neck and pulled myself closer to him. The heat of his body soothed me, and I felt more comforted than I had in days. "I'm sorry," I apologized through ragged breaths. "I know you have enough to deal with."

"It's okay, Baby Girl. It's been a long day. You just need some rest."

After Harper tucked me into bed, he quietly escaped through the bedroom door. I glimpsed Jake leaning against the hallway wall outside of my room. He anxiously looked in at me just as the door shut.

"It's okay," Sarah said. I'd forgotten she was lying beside me. She wrapped her arms around me consolingly, and I was grateful for her presence. It saddened me to think of leaving her.

I'd always thought I was a relatively strong person, but looking back at the weeks that had passed, I saw how frail and weak I truly was.

I fell asleep to the sound of my choking sobs and Sarah rubbing my back.

The next day, I woke up alone in my bed. I'd slept through the whole night, not even stirring when Sarah left. As humiliated as I should've been after my complete meltdown, I was just grateful for a full night's sleep.

Knowing there was much to do before I left Fort Knox, I readied myself for the day. After throwing on a sweatshirt, I pulled on a pair of jeans, ran a brush through my hair, and headed toward the mess hall. I needed to find Harper—both to thank him and to apologize for commandeering his briefing—but I could take a few minutes to eat breakfast first.

When I walked in, I found Tanya and Clara chatting quietly at one of the dining tables. My confidence wavered as I thought of the gratification my emotional breakdown must've given Clara. But I just smiled and tried to ignore the satisfaction illuminating her face.

"Oh, you're finally awake," Clara said, smirking.

I ignored her and looked around for everyone else. Sadly, the breakfast buffet had already been cleared. *Dammit. What time is it anyway?*

As I stood in the doorway, frowning, Clara sighed impatiently. When I looked at her, she pointed to a foil-covered plate on the counter. "For you," she said and returned to her conversation with Tanya.

Puzzled, I glanced back and forth between her and the dish, uncertain why she would make me a plate of food.

Clara rolled her eyes. "Harper saved you some breakfast. If you don't eat it, I will." She sounded harsh and irritated, no longer making any attempt to mask her dislike for me.

I headed over to the plate and uncovered it. I hadn't eaten

much the night before and was starving, so I carried the small feast of potatoes, gravy, and biscuits to an empty table and sat.

Tanya rose and walked over to my table. “How are you doing?” she asked meekly. She was pale and sickly, and she had dark circles under her eyes, but even in her deteriorating state, her kindness was genuine.

“I’m much better, thanks. How about you?” I hadn’t talked to her much since the night her sister died.

“I’ve been better, but I’m dealing with it the best I can.” She squeezed my shoulder before turning to leave. I felt a strange void inside her, like parts of her had been stolen.

I wasn’t shy as I shoveled the cold food into my mouth, and after inhaling half of it, I realized something wasn’t right. Amidst the savory flavors, I could taste something metallic, and my tongue began to tingle.

Alarmed, I spat out my mouthful of food, but it didn’t help. As I reached for my glass of water to rinse out my mouth, Clara appeared beside me and snatched it away.

“I’m not letting you leave with him,” she said scathingly.

“Get over yourself and give me my fucking water!” I demanded, but there was a high note of fear in my voice. I stood, trying to take the glass from her hand.

As my skin touched hers, I saw her memory of what she’d done—it flashed in my mind like a bolt of lightning, leaving imprints and evil shadows.

She poisoned me. She fucking poisoned me!

“Feeling alright?” Clara asked, batting her eyelashes and smiling innocently.

I hunched over as my stomach gurgled and churned, tangling into knots. Once again I reached for the water, but she yanked it away, dumping it out on the floor beside her.

Her grin lingered. “Sorry, I can’t let you do that.”

My stomach cramps worsened, and I broke out into a cold

sweat—I knew I didn't have much time. I needed to find help. *Tanya has to be close...*

Trying to run for the door, I doubled over in pain and cried out. Fire seemed to be scorching my insides. Bile rose in my throat, and I began salivating profusely, unable to swallow. I spat desperately.

"I really hate you, Zoe. I'm not completely sure why, but I have to admit, this is a very good day for me." Her cheerful voice was like a hammer in my head as I twisted and spasmed on the mess hall floor. The cool cement soothed my hot skin.

My stomach bloated, feeling like it would explode at any moment. I shoved my index finger down my throat, gagging myself until I threw up everything I could. Relief was instantaneous, but it was only momentary. I grew dizzy, and my vision blurred. I tried to scream but only a whimper broke free. I couldn't walk—I could only writhe in excruciating pain. I prayed someone would find me before it was too late.

One last time, I attempted to push myself off the floor, but my arms gave out. My hair was matted to my face, damp with the bile and food that had been inside me only moments before. My intestines cramped so badly that I thought they might rip apart.

Hearing the sound of footsteps in the adjoining hallway, I felt sudden relief that someone was coming to rescue me, but when long seconds passed without any other sounds, I realized it had just been Clara walking away. She had left me there to die, alone.

I thought I heard my father calling for me off in the distance. "Dad," I croaked. I could hear Dani and Jason too, but I couldn't see any of them. *They're not here...I'm dying.*

My fingers and toes itched and burned, and cold tears streamed from my eyes. I was in too much pain to cry out, so I silently gasped for air and hoped each breath wouldn't be my last.

As my body went numb, my slowing heartbeat thudded in my ears. The decreasing pain lessened my fear, and I sighed with relief. I couldn't remember why I'd been so afraid. Slowly, I drifted into unconsciousness.

32

ZOE

I stood among the giant trees, their carmine trunks rough and thick. They towered over me like monstrous blades of grass above a tiny ant. It was peaceful and quiet under their canopy, and white puffs of cottonwood danced in the breeze, blanketing the giants' fallen comrades. Their hulking carcasses rested haphazardly in their forgotten graveyard, strewn about the forest floor to decay unmourned. The moss adorning the trunks was a welcome sight. It had been too long since I'd seen such vivid, vibrant shades of life.

I feared the fantasy would dissolve around me, and it did. Trees were replaced with the worn, over-stuffed furniture and warm fire of Dave's cabin. I saw myself nestled against the arm of the couch, an army-green blanket wrapped around me. Harper leaned down to hand the other version of myself a steaming mug of tea before sitting beside Sarah on the opposite couch, smiling.

The familiar cabin was replaced with unfamiliar surroundings. Brick walls and modern picture windows exposed an expansive, twinkling cityscape. An inky body of water reflected the glowing lights. Soft lighting and smooth jazz filled my senses, and I caught my breath when I spotted Jason and Sanchez—they were sitting together at a table with a group of people. My brother laughed and chatted with Sanchez like they'd been friends forever. She looked beautiful. Her dark blue jeans hugged her hips, and a tight burgundy v-neck sweater emphasized her generous chest. Her lips were rosy, and her cocoa-colored hair was long with loose curls. She was smiling in a way I'd never seen before, as was Jason.

I didn't have much time to watch them before everything around me changed again. I was suddenly walking through a deserted hospital. The wide, bright halls were deathly silent, and my stomach lurched at the rank smell of sickness and decay permeating the air. A petite blonde woman appeared in the hallway. Wearing jeans and a red sweatshirt, she wandered restlessly down the hall. She turned around and a terrifyingly familiar pair of piercing blue eyes stared back at me.

Clara.

Fear and rage made my blood boil, scalding my insides.

"You're taking me with you, right?" she asked with pleading, troubled eyes.

Turning to discover who Clara was talking to, I found Jake standing before me. His forlorn expression was heartbreaking—it was the same look he'd worn when he'd mentioned his sister. He nodded, and they too dissolved from sight.

I woke momentarily, a muted pain thrumming through my body. I tried to recall what had happened to me. I couldn't understand why I felt heavy and numb…why my mind was so garbled. Blinding light burned my eyes when I struggled to open them.

Sanchez and Jake moved hastily above me. Hands on the bare skin of my stomach startled me, pushing and prodding for something.

"Is it like she said it would be?" Sanchez asked softly.

"She wasn't specific," Jake answered.

Foggily, I wondered what they were talking about.

"God…I hope she was right about the other part too," Sanchez said before their voices faded away.

Struggling to remain conscious, I could vaguely see Harper through my veil of dark lashes. I could sense his urgency, a wave of panic washing over me. Immediately, it was dulled by a sleepy fog that was settling in my head.

The metal table was cold against my bare skin, rousing my body out of its dormant state. A faint odor of blood piqued my anxiety, and I felt my body tense. Warm fingers rested on my forehead, exuding calmness.

I felt hands on my arm. It was Biggs; I could feel his steady energy through his gentle touch. His concern put me at ease, and as it did, unconsciousness grabbed hold of me again, pulling me back into darkness.

I was alone again, lying on a hard, cold floor in a blackened room. My body was paralyzed, and I tried to scream, but my mouth was sewn shut.

I heard Clara's gloating words before she appeared above me. "I told you I'd get my way." Her bright blue eyes twinkled with devilish delight, and her mouth curled into a broad smile.

"What's wrong—too dead to speak?" she taunted.

A flood gate opened, and the horrifying reality of my impending death came rushing back to me. My stomach burned, and my mouth watered as I struggled to breathe. Clara stood over me…watching me die.

Like she'd been summoned by my dying brain, Dani appeared beside me. A look of ferocity hardened her pixie-like features. "You didn't get me, and you can't have her!" Dani seethed as she crouched to slice the stitches from my lips with a razor-sharp blade.

"Dani!" I screamed, surging forward. I grabbed my throat; inside, it felt raw. My chest heaved, and my eyes refocused as I tried to make sense of my surroundings. The room was dim and quiet, and I was alone. A single wardrobe stood in front of me, and realistic depictions of seascapes and people decorated the walls—my drawings. I was in my room…at Fort Knox.

"I'm glad to see you're awake," I heard Sanchez say in my head.

Still in a haze of drowsiness, I looked over to see her standing in the doorway. A care-free, fun image of her flashed through my mind. *Sanchez…and Jason.*

"How are you feeling?" she asked quietly as she stepped into my room. I saw something in her eyes I'd never noticed before—a friendly, concerned look that made me feel closer to her. I remembered she'd been shot, but she looked recovered enough.

"You're awake!" Sarah exclaimed, her voice bouncing around in my head as she hurried into the room. She set a glass of water on the desk and ran over to me. "How're you feeling?"

I tried not to whimper as Sarah wrapped me tightly in her arms, but my body ached all over, and a few small sounds leaked out. Noticing my discomfort, Sarah released me, easing me back down with hands on my shoulders. "I'll go get the guys and tell them you're awake. Now we can start!" She abruptly ran out of the room.

I watched her leave, then looked at Sanchez. "Clara—"

"—is locked away. Don't worry about her now. You need to rest," Sanchez said as she moved closer to my bed, resting her hand on my leg to reassure me. She was studying me like a complex equation was written across my face.

"She poisoned me," I recalled aloud. Every word scraped the inside of my throat like a barbed wire, and my head was pounding.

"I know, but we've got her under control, Zoe. You're safe now. We all are." I knew that wasn't exactly true, but I appreciated the sentiment.

Hearing chatter and footsteps in the hall outside of my room, I let out a deep sigh, leaned back against my pillow, and smiled. It was nice to have so many caring people around. However, a rush of emotions and concern flooded my mind, and my throbbing headache worsened.

"There's my girl," Harper said, a forced smile plastered on his face as he walked through the door.

Biggs followed, and Dave, Stacey, and Tanya trailed behind him, one-by-one. Their smiling faces were contagious, and I couldn't help but grin as they all schlepped in to see me. The only person I hadn't seen was Jake, but I brushed my disappointment away.

Dave sat on the end of the bed, his hair curling around the edges of his baseball cap. "How're you feeling?"

"I'm a little confused," I admitted. "How long was I asleep?"

"Three days, but they've been taking good care of you." Dave's smirk was easy and cocky—the way it used to be.

"It's good to see you're awake," Stacey sighed. "Harper said you shouldn't have ma—"

"Stacey," Biggs said, cutting her off.

"But she's—"

"She needs rest." Sanchez's tone was the only directive Dave, Stacey, and Biggs needed before turning to leave with sullen smiles and dragging feet.

As they filed out, I glanced at Harper. Our eyes met briefly before he looked away. His avoidance was making me so anxious I was practically jumping out of my skin.

"Whatever it is, just tell me," I said.

"*Calm down, Zoe. You're fine,*" Sanchez said in my mind again.

"It doesn't seem like it." I stared at Harper, willing him to tell me what was making everyone act so weird.

He eyed me warily, probably wondering what I'd been talking

about when I'd responded to Sanchez. "You shouldn't have survived," he finally confessed.

I shook my head in confusion. "I don't get it. Is it a bad thing that I did?"

He began to pace in the cramped space. "No, Zoe, of course not! It's just that…by the time we finished, you weren't even breathing. Your heart stopped…your kidneys and liver shut down before I…Jake pushed me to keep going and…he was right." Harper was beside himself. He looked at me, mystified. "We did the transfusion, and it worked. Miraculously, it worked," he said in awe, like he was still trying to figure how I'd survived.

"Transfusion? You had to give me a blood transfusion?"

"Yeah, you were so far gone…your body shouldn't have accepted it, whether he has type O or not, but it was the only option we had left."

He? My heartbeat quickened. "Whose blood?" I asked, already assuming it was Jake's.

Harper ignored my question and continued berating himself. "I thought you were too far gone for it to work," Harper repeated. "But…" The sorrow in his eyes was nothing compared to the remorse I knew he felt. "I wasn't going to continue. If I hadn't listened to Jake…"

"But you did. You saved my life, H. If it weren't for *you* and Jake, I *would* be dead." I swallowed painfully. "I can't imagine how to thank you for what you did."

Stopping at my bedside and looking down at me, Harper let a gracious, authentic smile transform his face. He sat on the bed and pulled me into his arms. "You scared the shit out of me, Baby Girl."

I grimaced as Harper's hold tightened around me, but relief at being alive trumped my discomfort.

"I just don't get it," Harper whispered.

"It was Jake's blood," I said, my eyes meeting Sanchez's. They didn't know about Jake's remarkable ability to heal. "You haven't talked to him about any of this?"

Harper loosened his embrace and pulled away. "What do you mean?" Both he and Sanchez were looking at me, bemused.

I shook my head, not feeling completely comfortable with sharing someone else's secret. "You haven't talked to him about this?" I repeated.

"No, I just thought..." Harper looked back at Sanchez who stood at the foot of my bed. "I don't know what I thought."

I watched Sanchez and Harper a while, waiting for them to fit the puzzle pieces together.

"You think it's Jake's blood," Sanchez eventually said. "You think his blood healed you."

I nodded.

Harper watched me closely. "What do you know, Zoe?"

I looked over at Sanchez, who turned away quietly, gazing out the window into the darkness.

"Tell him, whatever it is," Sanchez said. *"It's time to figure this shit out."*

Given the green light, I told Harper everything I knew. I told him about Jake's injuries and how they'd healed too quickly, and that at one point both Taylor and Johnson had thought he was dead. And I told him about Sanchez's voice in my head. I knew that between Jake, Sanchez, and me, we weren't just freaks—we were part of something bigger.

"Where was I during all of this?" Harper asked in disbelief. He glanced back and forth between Sanchez and me.

"Around." I waved a hand in Sanchez's direction. "I don't know why she didn't tell you about her thing, but I never told you about Jake because...well, I don't know. It just didn't feel right. And obviously Jake hasn't been very forthcoming with *any* information, so I wouldn't expect him to tell you." *How's Jake going to react to them knowing?*

"He had to know we'd figure it out," Sanchez said, deep in thought.

"He knew it was the only way to save you." Harper shook his head, seemingly unsurprised. "Is there anyone else you know about? Anything you've seen that might help us understand what others might be capable of…or dealing with?"

I shook my head, completely forgetting about Dani's people, and downed another glass of water, thinking about Jake. The immensity of what he'd done—saved my life *again*—weighed heavily on my mind. I didn't know what the hell to do about it. Thanking him was like extracting teeth from the back of a bear's mouth—intimidating and dangerous. I figured he would play it off like it was nothing more than the right thing to do, infuriating me in the process.

"*Stop worrying, Zoe,*" Sanchez told me as she turned to leave. "*We'll figure all this out together…later.*" My head was pounding, and my eyelids were drooping.

I felt Harper's hand on my forehead and slowly opened my eyes.

He smiled his warm, Harper smile. "Get some rest, Baby Girl." A peaceful calm spread over me, relaxing the tension in my body. My cluttered thoughts dispersed like waves receding from the shore. He was calming me with his own emotions.

I smiled up at him. "How do you do that?" I whispered.

With a faint shrug, he said, "I'm glad it's been working." The warmth of his palm on my forehead soothed me, and I felt sleep pulling me under.

Heavy footfalls broke the silence, and I heard the deep, muted rumble of Jake's voice. "How is she?"

"She's tired, but perfectly fine," Sanchez reassured him.

My eyelids flew open again, though I could barely keep them that way. My body felt light, and sleep tugged persistently at my consciousness. "Jake," I whispered, trying to stop myself from falling asleep mid-word.

Harper lifted his hand from my forehead, his body no longer shielding me from Jake's penetrating gaze. Each of Jake's cautious steps brought the handsome, frustrating, confusing man closer to me.

Too exhausted to overthink things, I could only smile and say, "Thank you."

The furrowed brow shadowing his dark eyes softened. "I'm glad you're okay."

Satisfied that he hadn't completely dismissed my gratitude, I let my eyelids close and fell asleep.

I woke the next afternoon feeling almost completely rejuvenated. Although I was still tired, my body felt strong and healthy. Even more surprising, I was starving. Shuffling into the hallway, I found Cooper curled up outside my door. I called him to come along as I headed for the mess hall.

I ran into Sarah along the way, and after eating an early dinner, she and I took Cooper for a walk. Luckily, the sun was still shining, welcoming me to my second chance at life. As we walked, Sarah kicked the occasional pebble, and I repeatedly threw a stick for Cooper to retrieve. Sarah spewed all the gushy details about her and Biggs after filling me in on what had happened while I was asleep. She giggled and gossiped, explaining in detail what had taken place after Tanya found me unconscious. Her nonchalance made it seem less real, which I strangely appreciated.

"What about Clara? What happened to her?" I asked.

"Jake tore the place apart looking for her. Sanchez had Dave and Biggs put her in a holding cell because she's obviously insane. Not to mention they were worried Jake might kill her...he was *really* angry. Only Harper, Biggs, and Sanchez know where she is

—just in case. I think they're worried about Tanya, to be honest." Sarah's features pinched in confusion. "But she's the one who told them about you and she's sick, so…"

Approaching footsteps interrupted our conversation, and we turned to see Stacey coming up behind us, her shoulder-length, dirty-blonde hair pulled back into a stubby ponytail. She looked at me sympathetically. "How are you feeling?"

"Much better, thanks. Sarah's just filling me in on what I missed while I was…out. How are you?"

"Oh, fine. Well, that's not true, actually. I've been thinking a lot about what happened to you, and I feel horrible about it."

I looked at her, baffled. "Why?"

"It's just that I feel like I should've caught on to all this a lot sooner. I should've said something to you."

"What do you mean?" Sarah piped in.

"It was obvious Clara didn't like you, even though she never went so far as to say she was going to try to physically harm you. I just feel like I should've seen the signs or something."

"Stacey, I appreciate your apology, really, but if we're placing blame, I'm just as guilty," I said, trying to reassure her. "I knew Clara didn't like me, and I would've been able to see it coming if I'd paid closer attention."

"I guess, but I was with her in the gym the whole time you were dying. I feel really shitty about it. I just hope you don't think I had anything to do with it."

Knowing she was sincere, I nudged her shoulder. "Of course I don't. Clara's a psycho. I wouldn't be surprised if she'd escaped from a mental institution or something."

"Well…that *may* be closer to the truth than you think."

"What?" Sarah and I asked in unison.

"Keep in mind that I don't know her much better than you do. She was only here about a week before you all arrived," Stacey disclaimed. "But, she tells Tanya a lot, and I've overheard some conversations that make me think you might be onto something."

"What?" I scoffed. "Like she was really in a mental institution?"

"Maybe. I know Jake found her in a hospital. She told us as much herself. I overheard her telling Tanya she couldn't really relate to losing a sister. She told us she hated her own family…that they might as well've locked her away in a dungeon. She made it *very* clear she'd never forgive them."

"You think they put her in a hospital?" I asked.

Stacey shrugged. "It's possible. She said she hadn't seen them in seven years and that her best friend was someone named Jenson. They were very close until he did something to piss her off, so she said she taught him a lesson. Knowing what she did to you, she probably killed the poor bastard."

"But why would Jake rescue her if she was locked away in a crazy ward? Why was he even *in* a crazy ward?" Sarah wondered.

I thought about the dream I'd had of Jake and Clara when they were in the hospital, and it all started to make sense. "I think she reminds him of his sister," I said. "So he felt like he had to help her."

"His sister? How would you know that?" Sarah asked. "You guys are barely around each other—except for when he's saving your life," Sarah joked. She nudged me and giggled. "Have you two been spending *secret* time together?" I gave her a flat look, and she cleared her throat. "Or not."

"Oh!" Stacey chirped. "I forgot the whole reason for coming out here. Harper wants you back at the barracks."

The sun was setting, and I was getting tired, so I conceded. We made it back to the barracks just as Dave and Biggs were exiting with blankets and steaming mugs.

"There they are," Dave said, smiling at us. "Here." He handed me a cup of hot chocolate and a blanket. "You're gonna need these."

"Um, thanks," I said. "What are we doing?" I asked as they ushered us around the corner of the barracks to an open field between the pond and our building. I wondered why bench seats—presumably from a van—were aligned end-to-end on the dead grass.

Sanchez strode around the corner of an empty building. "It's about time," she said dryly. "The show's about to start."

"The show? But it's dark." My question was ignored, again, leaving me both curious and confused.

The night was chilly, and I was glad to have a blanket to wrap around me as I situated myself on one of the seats.

"I'm so excited!" Sarah squealed as she cuddled up next to me.

"I don't mean to sound like a broken record, but what are we doing?" I asked…again.

"You'll see," was all Sanchez said as she sat down beside Sarah.

"We were going to do this when you woke up last night, but you needed more sleep," Sarah explained.

"Well, sorry to ruin your plans, but no one told me we were having a *show*," I said.

Just then a muffled thump sounded in the distance. A dimly glowing rocket whistled as it soared high above us. With a thunderous boom, it exploded—brilliant red embers burst forth and illuminated the sky. Another bang followed, and I saw a second rocket fly skyward. It blossomed in the darkness, and glittering shades of purple and green rained down, leaving a smoky impression in their wake.

I had tears in my eyes before I could fully understand the implications of the fireworks show. My heart caught as I realized it was for me.

"Isn't this great?" Stacey screeched. "It's just like at home, right?"

"It's beautiful," I said, wiping my eyes. "I can't believe Harper did this."

As the sky flashed red and orange, Stacey's face angled toward me with a look of surprise. "Harper didn't do this."

Looking at her, I waited for confirmation, but somewhere deep inside I knew—it was Jake. His quiet façade was just that. He was an observer; he'd showed me that himself.

As the fireworks continued above us, I struggled to understand the feelings that were swirling inside me. I was confused and surprisingly happy, and I had so many questions. I suddenly felt sick with nervousness.

"Are you alright?" Stacey asked, leaning in as I brushed away another tear.

"I *told* you I liked fireworks," I said, and she and Sarah giggled. We sat, mesmerized, until the final twinkling colors had faded from the sky and the last of the smoke had been carried off by the breeze.

We all started clapping. "Bravo!" Sarah shouted before reaching out to grab my wrist. "Come on, it's freezing. Let's go inside." She let go of me, stood, and wrapped her blanket around her shoulders. I'd been so enthralled by the show that, for once in my life, I hadn't really noticed the cold.

"I'll be in soon," I said, rising. I walked behind the barracks, stumbling through the moonlit night toward the place the fireworks had originated. I had no idea what I was going to do, but I'd never experienced such unexpected kindness. Between the fireworks and Jake saving my life, again, I was unable to form any articulate thoughts.

Finally, I heard Jake's muffled voice and knew he was nearby. My steps became clumsier the closer I drew to him. I wasn't sure he understood the magnitude of what he'd done for me. Wiping away another tear, I rounded a corner just as Harper and Jake exited a warehouse together.

"Hey, Baby Girl," Harper said quietly and continued walking back toward the barracks.

Jake was locking the sliding metal door as I approached him. Time passed agonizingly slowly as I waited for him to face me.

When he finally turned around, a look of surprise filled his eyes. I could feel a mixture of emotions emanating from him.

Without hesitation, I shrugged my blanket to the ground, stood on tiptoes, and threw my arms around him. In the cold of the night, his body was like a furnace, and he smelled faintly of sulfur. "Thank you," I whispered and felt his powerful arms wrap around me.

He held me tightly against his body. "I'm just glad you're okay." The sincerity in his voice made my heart pulse with unexpected delight, and I was filled with a sense of calm. I reveled in the moment we were sharing—one I knew I was lucky to have. Jake had given me the perfect gift.

33

DANI

The days that followed my discovery of Grams's fate passed quickly and unremarkably. I worked around the ranch, getting to know the animals and their needs. After assessing our supply levels, I knew that, before long, I would have to do another scavenging trip, this time to the feed and tack store in Sebastopol. It would be a day-long trip, and I didn't relish the thought of getting back in the saddle so soon. My butt still felt like it had cushioned a fifty-foot fall. I was surprised it didn't resemble a purple and blue watercolor painting.

In the back of my mind, and sometimes in the front, I worried about Jason, Chris, and Ky. I worried that I would never see them again, and that they would hate me if I did. But most of all, I worried that Cece and her minions had somehow overtaken them and that they were dead.

The *nights* following my discovery were another matter entirely, further fracturing the two worlds I inhabited: the fixed world of reality and the fluid world of my dreams. In sleep, MG would join me—always banishing my increasingly horrifying nightmares of Cam. We would then discuss my Ability, increasing my use and understanding of it.

With each passing night, my relationship with the mysterious man blurred. He had gone from stranger to instructor to partner, until eventually we'd become friends. Our discussions grew progressively complex and personal, filled with evaded questions and unexpected reactions.

While I was mucking out a particularly disgusting stable stall, I recalled one especially confusing interaction.

Dumbfounded, MG stared at me from across a round, wrought iron table. At my request for a fully-clothed setting, he'd taken me to a Parisian café for some coffee and pastries. In his swim attire, he was just too distracting—not that I told him that, of course.

"You called how *many to you?" he asked, surprised.*

"Well I didn't exactly count. Hmm...at least a couple hundred? But I didn't mean to. I was aiming for just the animals in the pasture." I shrugged. "I guess my aim was a little off."

"I'll say." He took a healthy gulp of his café au lait, nearly choking on the steaming drink. "And when you dismissed them, they just left?"

I nodded. "For the most part. I had to concentrate, but once I slipped into the right state of mind, it was easy." Smiling, I remembered their soft mental touches. "Most of them said a goodbye of some sort, too. It was sweet...and odd."

Holding up his hand, he said, "Wait. You spoke to them, and they responded? All of them?"

I nodded again, feeling too much like an oversized bobble head.

MG closed his eyes and massaged his temples with his fingers, seeming to focus his thoughts. When he finally spoke, he sounded apprehensive. "And you're certain that woman heard you?"

"Yes, absolutely. And Jason too, even though I didn't really mean to speak in his head." I felt more than a little proud of my rapidly increasing control over my Ability. After I did something

once—like call the horde of woodland creatures—it was easy to repeat. I hadn't had the chance to practice, but I was fairly certain it would be that way with human minds as well.

MG whispered something under his breath that sounded an awful lot like "Fuck" and began methodically mauling his croissant. "Do you think you can do the same things with people?"

"What do you mean?" His darkening mood confused me.

"Can you communicate with hundreds of human minds at the same time? Can they talk back?"

"Probably," I said, raising one shoulder. I knew from his reaction it was the wrong answer.

Sounding completely resigned, he said, "I've come across quite a few people with Abilities similar to yours, but none as powerful. None can hear responses. You have to be careful. You might be one of the most important people left alive, and we can't risk your death." After a deep breath he added, "Dani, you need to go to the Colony. You'll be safer there than you are on your own."

"I'll think about it," I told him.

"Is that where you are?" I grumbled to the nearly clean stall floor. *Would I go to the Colony if MG was there?*

Thinking about going to Colorado to meet MG in person was oddly alluring. In my loneliness, he was the only person I'd really interacted with. He'd earned my trust by comforting me—listening to my struggles and helping me with my exciting new Ability. And above all else, the thought of hurting him with my presence didn't muddle my insides like it did with Jason, Chris, or Zoe. Plus, he was acutely attractive and had made his interest known, which might lead to some pleasant diversions down the road.

For some reason though, the thought of sleeping with anyone besides Cam or Jason made me feel sick. Cam was gone, but Jason wasn't. *Not that it even matters...I might as well be his little sister. He doesn't want me. He never has and never will.*

"Maybe I'll just stay here forever," I told Wings as I passed her stall and headed further into the stable. I'd taken to speaking out loud when mentally communicating with my non-human friends—somehow, it helped me feel less alone.

"*Yes. Good. Stay with family,*" Wings responded, poking her head through her open stall doorway. Of course, she didn't actually say "family," though that was how my mind interpreted it. Instead, it was a jumble of images and feelings revolving around our motley group of animals.

Oddly, her suggestion didn't sound too bad. The heavy work-load around the ranch made the days pass quickly, and the animals offered a certain level of comfortable companionship, especially since we were able to communicate in a rather unconventional fashion. I could become a post-apocalyptic pioneer—living off the land and growing old with nature as my only solace. It would be a hard life but peaceful in its own way.

"Sounds lonely," a male voice said from the far entrance to the stable.

I swung around, pointing the shovel at the intruder. Recog-nizing the man's friendly face, I gasped, "Ky?"

"In the flesh." As he approached, another man entered through the open door. His striking resemblance to Ky—smooth, angular facial features and straight, jet-black hair—barely prepared me for my friend's next words. "That's my brother, Ben."

"Your brother?" Shocked, I dropped my impromptu weapon. It clanged loudly on the cement floor.

Ky stopped a few feet in front of me. "Yep. He found us at our house back in Fort Bragg. He was...surprised, to say the least."

I nodded and then leapt forward, throwing myself into Ky's arms. "I missed you!" I exclaimed, willing myself not to cry. I hadn't known what had happened to Jason and Chris after the whole Cece incident, but if Ky was okay, it was likely that they were as well. "I miss you guys so much!"

Ky wrapped his arms around me. "Me too, D. Me too."

A moment later, I released him and approached his brother. I extended my hand and said, "I'm Dani. It's nice to meet you."

"Likewise," he replied, shaking my hand quickly. His voice, unlike Ky's, was tinged with the faintest Japanese accent. "You've caused quite a fuss. You're…different than I expected."

"Shut up, Ben," Ky told his brother.

Turning my attention back to Ky, I asked, "How'd you find me?"

"Remember what I said about the weird feelings I was having?"

I nodded.

"Well, with Cece, I could feel her anger and hatred building up until she did all that stupid shit. Now it's happening with you, except you're giving off sadness instead of anger. I'm not sure how, but I recognized the sadness as coming from you, and it got stronger the closer I came to you—led me straight to you. And…it feels like you're about to do something really stupid."

"Well I'm not going to kill myself or anything," I said defensively.

Ky looked at his brother, who nodded. *Seriously? Did he really think I was suicidal? And what's with the need for brotherly confirmation?*

"No, but whatever you're thinking of doing, it'll leave you *very* unhappy, even if you don't realize it now. That's why I can feel the negativity—the sadness—pouring off you."

Pondering his assessment, I realized he was right. I'd been considering becoming a hermit, forsaking human contact altogether. Cutting out Zoe and Jason, Chris, and even Ky, would leave me miserable for the rest of my life. I could survive surrounded by only my four-legged friends, but in the end, death would seem like a relief.

But I can't go back. I didn't want to be alone, but I also couldn't stand the possibility that I might endanger my friends again. *Damn rocks and hard places!*

Ky continued, "Come with me and Ben. We'll take you back with us."

Shaking my head, I said, "But Jason and Chris…they almost got killed because of me. I saw—"

"What'd you see?" Ky asked, narrowing his eyes.

Biting my lower lip, I sighed. "I saw Cece go after Jason and Chris at my grandma's house."

After looking at his brother again and receiving another nod, Ky whistled. "So it's true. Jason said he heard you, said he was sure you were out behind the house somewhere."

I brushed his words aside. "You abandoned them! That bitch and her sycophants nearly murdered them and you weren't there!"

Ky held his hands out in front of him and stepped closer. "Dani, you have to understand. Jason made us stay at his place while he and Chris checked your house. Cece and her idiots followed him…they were supposed to be looking for gas. The rest of us…we didn't know what they were doing. We were just following Jason's orders."

"Oh," I said, my anger instantly dissipating.

"You don't have to worry about her going after you or anyone else. She's long gone. So are John and the rest of her flock, and good fucking riddance! I'm pretty sure she's actually controlling them, and not just with her pu—" Ky stopped talking and cleared his throat. "I mean, I think she's like me…but her thing is controlling dumbshits who are stupid enough to touch her." Ky shook his head in annoyance and continued, "The only shitty part about them leaving is that they took the Humvees and everything that was in 'em."

I had suspected as much—that Cece was gone—and felt immense relief. It was short-lived. My stomach knotted as I registered the implications of Cece being able to control other people. *How many can she control? How does she do it? And now she's out there somewhere…*

"Please come back. If you don't, I'm not sure how much longer the rest of us can stand Jason. He was a cold son of a bitch before. Now he's rabid. He's crazy moody, especially when he's drinking. And by moody, I mean completely unreasonable. He's becoming impossible to—"

At his words, fury began coursing through my veins. I tried to contain it, but seeped out anyway. "*And what would you do? Betray him? Abandon him? Attack him? You're just like her!*"

"Holy. Shit." Ky stared at me with wide, wonder-filled eyes. "*No,*" he said tentatively in my mind. "*I'll stand by him. I promise…Is this real?*"

Clenching my jaw, I nodded sharply. Remotely, I registered the confirmation that I *could* hear human responses telepathically.

"What's going on?" Ben asked.

Ky shook his head. "It's impossible."

"Oh, but *your* thing is possible? Don't be such a hypocrite."

"She can…she can…," Ky stammered.

"I can talk in his mind. In anyone's. I guess you could call me a telepath." I finished pointedly.

To my surprise, Ben simply nodded, accepting my claim without argument or exclamation. I studied him. *What can he do? What about Jason? What about all the people Zo's with? Holy crap…what about* all *of the Survivors?!* My friends and I needed to stick together.

"I'll come back," I said definitively.

Ky and Ben just stared at me, and we stood in awkward silence.

"So…I'm surprised Jason didn't come with you."

"He doesn't know we're here," they said in unison.

Interesting. "I *will* come back…tomorrow." Ky looked baffled, so I explained, "I have some issues I need to sort out. Personal things. And, well, I can't do it around Chris…she'll get in my head and try to do it for me. *I* need to do it." I paused, wondering how exactly I would sort out my feelings for Jason by morning.

"Ky, promise me you won't tell Jason where I am." I stared

into his brown eyes, and sensing his reluctance, willed him to give in.

Hesitantly, Ky nodded. "Fine. I won't tell him…today. But, I'm telling him first thing in the morning. You should probably be ready for him to storm up here…"

"Great…," I said unenthusiastically. *An angry Jason…what a great way to start the day.* I took my sudden apprehension out on Ben, who was nodding, again. "Why do you keep nodding?" I demanded, glaring at him.

Wide-eyed, Ben said, "Oh, I…umm…I can tell when people are lying—you're not."

Huh. "That's useful."

He shrugged. "It can be kind of annoying. You'd be surprised how frequently people lie about stupid things."

"I can imagine." Looking outside, I noticed it was dusk. "You guys should get going. You know how the Crazies like to come out and play at night." I stepped forward to give Ben a brief hug. "I'm glad he found you alive." Ky's hug was longer, punctuated by an eager "I'll see you soon".

A timid surge of joy shot through me. Finally, things were looking up.

JANUARY

34

DANI

I'd been sleeping, but I was suddenly awake. I blinked, letting my eyes focus in the darkness. I was staring up at a post and beam ceiling, and it took me a moment to remember where I was —the front room of the ranch house. Grudgingly, I sat and rubbed the sleep from my eyes. The couch was warm beneath me, beckoning me to stretch out and fall back asleep, but there was something nagging the very edge of my memory. I had the vague impression that Jack had been in my dreams, showing me…something. Something important.

Hackles raised, Jack slowly backed through the doorway from the hall, triggering my memory of the dream.

The front door.

The doorknob.

Jiggling…just like I could hear it doing at that moment.

Oh crap! I thought, piecing it all together. Somebody was breaking in, and the only doorway from my makeshift bedroom led to the same hall as the front door. I was in *major* trouble.

I had just enough time to scramble off the couch and crouch by the doorway with Jack next to me before I heard the front door crash open. I panicked as I realized my gun was on the couch on the opposite side of the room—I'd stowed it under my pillow before falling asleep. *Idiot!*

Maybe I can hide. Maybe they'll pass me by. Maybe...

The hallway's hardwood floor creaked under the intruder's footsteps, the sound growing closer with every passing second. I held my breath as Jack moved into the center of the room, snarling ferociously.

"No Jack! What are you doing?"

"Help you," he responded solemnly. *"Run away."*

I didn't have time to protest or even move before the man stomped up the hall and through the doorway. Focused completely on my vicious dog, he didn't notice me flattened against the wall beside the doorframe. As Jack strung him further into the room toward the couch, and unfortunately my gun, I slowly inched closer to the hallway. When I placed my right foot in the doorway, the worn wood floor moaned. Horrified, I froze. I held my breath and looked over my shoulder at the man.

His eyes met mine.

Forgetting Jack, he lunged at me and shoved me back-first into the hallway wall. I hit it with a thud, knocking several picture frames to the floor. Glass shattered around my bare feet, but I'd hit my head so hard that I couldn't stop myself from staggering. A shard sliced into my heel right before the intruder's hurtling body slammed against mine. He smelled of rancid sweat and stale cigarette smoke, and his bloodshot eyes glinted wildly. He was definitely a Crazy.

A second later, Jack attacked him. As he tore at the Crazy with teeth and claws, I attacked with knees and hands. My few self-defense lessons kicked in, possibly saving my life. I rammed a knee into his groin, then smacked his left ear with my open hand. I wasn't sure if I'd actually landed the blows on purpose or if they'd been a random result of my frantic flailing. Regardless, insanity had hindered his physical prowess, and he was unable to block my strikes.

The man stumbled back, tripping over Jack and crashing into the opposite wall.

Without a backward glance, Jack and I fled. We tore down the hallway, out the front door, across the wide gravel driveway, and through the door at one end of the stable. The horses whinnied and stomped as we sped by the first few stalls.

"Be quiet, please! The bad man can't know I'm here!" Instantly, the building fell silent but for the sound of my bare feet slapping on the cement floor.

Just as I sidestepped into the fourth stall on the right, an ominous screech sounded from the door at the far end of the building—the door I never used because of its rusty hinges. I smiled grimly. He didn't know my exact location, but I knew his.

I also knew the next stall down housed almost all of the ranch tools, each a potential weapon. *If I can just get to them...* I studied the darkness, weighing its density, and decided I could probably make it without the Crazy seeing me. *It's now or never.* I breathed in and out once, twice, then held the third breath and slipped out of the stall as quietly as possible. Jack followed me, quiet as a shadow.

The few seconds it took me to reach the next stall seemed to last for days. Shaking with adrenaline, I ducked through the open doorway and searched the barely visible walls for some sort of weapon. Unfortunately, grabbing anything would make too much noise and dissolve my only advantage. Trying not to panic, I squeezed my hands into tight fists and took several deep, steadying breaths.

Quietly, but not quietly enough, the man passed by the empty stalls and unknowingly neared my hiding place.

Desperate, I begged the horses, *"I need a distraction!"* In an explosion of noise, they began kicking the walls and neighing loudly.

I seized the nearest shovel, the same one I'd nearly accosted Ky with, and gripped it tightly in my sweaty hands as I crept closer to the main aisle. Pausing, I told the animals, "*Quiet now.*" Stillness settled in the dark building.

Faintly, I heard the man resume his slow, shuffling pace, unaware of the danger awaiting him—unaware of *me*. As he drew closer, I coiled to strike, my muscles trembling with tension and fear. Besides my shovel, I realized my Ability could also be used as a weapon, repercussions be damned.

"*Stop!*" I shouted in the man's head. His clothing rustled as he froze mid-step and looked around.

"*Damn voices,*" he grumbled and continued creeping along. "*Leave me alone!*"

Crap! He's still coming!

Frantically, I opened my mind and begged anyone or anything, "*Help! Please! I'm being attacked by an insane man. Please help me! Please!*" I felt thousands of minds connect with mine, human and otherwise, draining me of energy almost instantly. Terrified, I broke the connections. *What the hell did I just do?* Adrenaline seemed to be the only thing keeping me standing.

Seconds later, the man moved into sight, all of the horses in the stable thrashed and cried. Other animals scratched and banged on the walls from outside the building. The man looked around, hearing a commotion his eyes couldn't identify in the darkness.

Taking advantage of the momentary distraction, I stepped away from the wall and swung the shovel like a baseball bat. The dull, dirty metal rang out like a church bell when it impacted his skull, causing the handle to vibrate painfully in my grip.

Immediately, he crumpled.

Seconds later, my legs gave out and I followed him to the cold cement floor. Using my Ability on such a massive scale had weakened me, and adrenaline could only last for so long—I could feel my hold on consciousness slipping.

I wasn't sure if the man was dead, but it didn't matter. I was unable to make my muscles listen to my brain's orders to stand up and flee. My head was pounding, and I was shivering, both from cold and from terror.

I curled into the fetal position, letting myself be soothed by Jack's sniffing and whining. I could feel other furry things—some small and some as large as my dog—nuzzling me. They surrounded me with their warmth, cutting through the aching chill that had seeped into my bones, and I slipped comfortably into unconsciousness.

"So…what should we do?" an indistinct female voice asked.

Angrily, a man replied, "I don't fucking know!"

"They're not going to hurt her…at least I don't think they are. Jack wouldn't just stand there if he thought she was in danger," another man said.

"I still think we should shoot 'em. They're obviously dangerous. Look what they did to that guy! They tore him apart!" a shrill voice said.

"Shut up, Holly! You're not helping!" the first speaker ordered. She continued in a softer volume, "I think they're protecting her."

"I agree," said a new voice. "I think we should wait until she wakes up."

"And if she doesn't? What then? We just leave her behind this…this…wall of animals?" the angry man asked.

What the hell is going on? Who are they talking about? Why am I so hot? What's poking me? Wait…where's the Crazy? Did I kill him?

"Look! I think she's moving!" one of the voices claimed.

Me? Are they talking about me?

Suddenly, my eyes popped open, and I gaped in astonishment at what I saw in the darkness around me. I was surrounded by a barrier of pacing creatures, including several coyotes, foxes, bobcats, and a gigantic cougar. And, of course, faithful Jack was among the animals protecting me from the people I'd overheard. I felt like a planet being orbited by a deadly belt of fur, teeth, and claws.

Beyond the fierce predators, a small crowd of familiar people with flashlights watched with a variety of expressions. Ky and Ben were sharing a look of wonder. Holly was scowling at Dalton and Hunter, whose faces were blank. Chris was smiling. But it was Jason who captured my attention. The look in his eyes made him appear slightly more savage than the wild creatures circling me.

I sat up slowly and immediately felt dozens of small, furry bodies wiggle and readjust themselves around me. Instead of panicking, which would've been normal, and frankly, would've made me feel less like a mutant-ninja-animal-whisperer, I smiled at the mass of rabbits, mink, and cats curled up on and around me. Without them, I would have frozen to death, having passed out on the cement floor of an unheated building in the dead of winter. The animals had kept me warm—the wonders of a living blanket.

As Jason took a step closer, my protective guard abruptly stilled, forming a solid, threatening shield intent on one thing—keeping him away from me. Jason paused with one foot forward, his muscles twitching with the need to keep moving.

"Let him pass!" I ordered. A narrow, Jason-sized gap opened between the cougar and a pair of foxes. The three animals separated and sat patiently, looking like stone lions guarding the entryway to a castle.

"No way! Did you guys see that?" Holly blurted.

But everyone ignored her, instead staring in shock at the obedient animals...everyone except Jason. He lurched forward through the makeshift gateway and dislodged a handful of the smaller creatures huddled around me as he crouched at my side. The common cats were the most displeased, hissing and groaning in feline irritation.

"Are you hurt?" he implored, scanning me from head to toe and back again before his eyes met mine. His desperation stole my breath. I wished I had Zoe's Ability so I could understand what he was desperate for.

"I…I don't think so. Jason, I—NO!" I shouted suddenly, snapping my head to the right. Holly had raised her pistol and was aiming it at the cougar, whose muscles were tensed to pounce. Everyone froze, animals included.

"Ow," Ky said, shaking his head. "Was it really necessary to shout so loud *in* our heads too?"

I hunched, leaning away from Jason, away from everyone. "Sorry. I guess I got a little excited…" At least Holly had lowered her gun.

Before the situation spiraled out of control and someone—or something—got hurt, I dismissed my furry defenders. To my surprise, each nuzzled part of my body before leaving, even the cougar. I felt like a piece of land claimed by dozens of property owners. *Delightful…*

After the last undomesticated animal had left the stable, Chris rushed to my side, displacing Jason, who stood and began pacing.

"What the hell just happened?" Holly screeched. "You guys saw that right? That was, like…a *cougar* or something! What if she sicks it on one of us next?"

Jason halted and spun to face her. "Shut the fuck up, Holly," he ordered harshly. "Ky, find the lights in this place," he added before he gathered everyone but Chris around him and began giving hushed, emphatic orders.

Chris and I both squinted when the overhead lights came on, and she continued patting and prodding me everywhere in her search for injuries. She was *very* thorough.

"Hey!" I exclaimed as she pressed against my ribs beneath my breasts. "I like you Chris but not *that* much."

"Calm down, hon. I'm just making sure nothing's broken."

"Well you don't need to feel me up in the process. I'm okay. I promise."

She puckered her mouth, trying not to laugh. "You've got a pretty nasty cut on your heel…how'd that happen?"

I thought for a moment, recalling all that had happened after the Crazy had broken in. Part of me couldn't believe I was still alive. "I stepped on the glass from a broken picture frame…it was when he, um, attacked me in the house," I explained, my voice trembling a little.

Chris gently squeezed my shoulder. "Worst decision he ever made, huh?," she said, but it was her touch more than her words that soothed me. *Damn…I love her Ability.* "Just give me a few minutes to get you patched up, and then I think you and Jason should have a little chat…clear the air…"

I groaned. "Is he mad?" I asked tentatively, watching Jason pace up and down the stable aisle. He reminded me of the cougar who'd watched over me so closely during my loss of consciousness.

Chris barked a laugh and said, "Hon, mad doesn't come close. The email from his sister telling him why you left…that didn't really go over so well…"

"Oh." I looked down at my hands, feeling miserable.

Chris left my side momentarily to retrieve a first aid kit from her pack. I flinched when she cleaned the stinging cut on my heel, but felt lucky that it wasn't deep enough to need stitches. After dropping some antibiotics in my palm and handing me a water bottle, she said, "So, I'm gonna clear everyone outta here…start setting up in the house. Can you and Jason please try *not* to kill each other?"

I gave her a flat look.

"I'll take that as a 'yes'," she said, rising. She walked away without a backward glance.

I sighed, trying—and failing—not to look at the glistening skeleton about a dozen feet away. The Crazy's corpse had been picked clean…mostly. There were still pieces of bloody clothing and globs of hair. I struggled to make my mind reconcile the horrific sight with the man who'd attacked me only hours before. With unexpected pity, I hoped it had been the blow from the shovel that had killed him, not the animals tearing him apart alive. It was too horrible a fate to wish on anyone…*well, except Cece, maybe…*

Picking myself up off the freezing floor, I hurried away from both the ghastly scene and my vengeful thoughts, ignoring the throb in my heel. Unfortunately, I was instead approaching Jason and a confrontation I was nearly as eager to avoid as my attacker's decimated remains.

I fell in step behind Jason as he strode away. "Jason?" I asked meekly. He halted abruptly, and I bumped into his back with an "Oomph!"

While I regained my balance and some modicum of decorum, Jason turned to face me. I took several hasty steps backward. Everything about him was stiff—his clenched fists, his taut neck muscles, and his unusually thin lips. Silently, he stared at me, though it felt more like getting a full-body MRI.

"Jason, I—"

"You *what*?" he exploded, stalking toward me.

I backed up, my pace increasing with his, my sore heel forgotten. Though my mouth opened, no words came out. I was struck dumb by the waves of sheer fury emanating from him. It was how I imagined *I* had looked when I'd confronted him about moving Cam's body, just a hell of a lot smaller.

"You left without a word. You came to my room. You said goodnight. And you *knew* you were leaving," he said coldly, his tone like a thin layer of ice encapsulating an inferno. "Zoe didn't give me your message until the next fucking night. I spent a whole day not knowing what'd happened to you, not knowing if you were dead. And then *my sister* tells me about Cece's goddamn note. *You* didn't tell me!" he yelled, still pushing me back with the force of his anger. "Why the fuck didn't you tell me? I could've helped you."

"You could've died!" I screamed back. "I was trying to protect you!"

"I can protect myself!"

I scoffed. "Sure, like you protected yourself at Grams's house?" As soon as the words were out, I wished I could catch them and stuff them back down my throat.

"How'd you...you *were* there! I *knew* it!" After a brief pause he lowered his voice and added, "You made her leave, didn't you? What'd you do?" Each word was pronounced precisely, making his quietness more ominous than his earlier yelling.

Gulping in the suddenly scarce air, I explained, "I spoke in... her mind. I...threatened her...if she didn't..." Backing into the rusty door, I whispered, "I couldn't let her do it, Jason. I couldn't lose you."

He stopped inches from me, his toes nearly touching mine. "I almost killed her. Multiple times. Fuck Dani, I *should* have! But Chris and Ky might've...If I'd screwed up, Cece and the others would've gone after them, maybe killed them." He turned and walked several steps away, hiding whatever unwanted emotions plagued him.

"Jason, I'm—"

When he faced me, his outward composure had returned. He was, once again, the emotionless statue I'd come to know so well. Quietly, he said, "You should have told me about the note when you first read it. We could have figured it out together."

"I know." It was simple, but true. The realization may have come slowly, but I knew that whatever happened, whatever threat loomed ahead, Jason and I would face it together. The meaning of *together* was still a great unknown. Friends? More? But he needed to know that—to know I believed in him...depended on him... trusted him. "I'm so sorry, Jason. I won't leave you again."

His momentary composure abruptly disintegrated, revealing

frustration and anger, as well as hope and joy. In two purposeful strides he was on me, his hands forcing my shoulders against the door as his lips devoured mine. He was relentless, stroking my tongue with his as soon as our bodies met. It was unlike any kiss I'd ever experienced—devoid of thought or reason, purely based on mutual need. If Jason had continued kissing me forever, I would've gladly obliged. But, of course, he didn't.

Seconds after restraining me, he pulled back and spun away. "FUCK!" he shouted, punching the wooden slats between two empty stalls before striding off.

35

ZOE

"You're not focusing!" Sanchez's voice rang in my head. She was sitting only inches from me on one of the picnic benches in the quad. She'd caught me glaring at the barracks; I'd spent too much time within its walls and was grateful to finally be outside.

"*Really*? Do you have to yell?"

"Well, pay attention," Sanchez said. "Your turn."

I closed my eyes and took a deep breath, trying to remove myself from the present. I tried to block out the beautiful sunset I wanted to watch and the bullfrogs croaking loudly down at the pond. I tried to ignore the fact that I yearned, as usual, for an early spring.

Finally pushing all distractions from my mind, I pictured Sanchez sitting in front of me. I thought of her mind, her face, and the way she tended to glare at me impatiently. But nothing came.

"Let me try something else," I thought out loud.

Erasing the image of Sanchez from my head, I thought of the universe. I thought of blackness and infinity, of all the stars and planets and galaxies, and how insignificant I was in relation to it all.

Again, nothing came.

Taking another approach, I opened my eyes and reached out to touch her. Her impatience was heavy, burdening my senses, so I let go.

"Well, we know touch works without fail," I said in exasperation. *I wish I knew how the hell to control this…thing.*

"And your mind?"

"I'm still working on that one."

Taking a deep breath, I again attempted to reach out to her with my mind. "I have no idea what I'm doing," I muttered. I couldn't help but laugh at the bizarreness of the situation. "I can't believe I'm trying to read your mind."

"Just concentrate—I'm sure you're more in tune with your unique talent than you think."

I focused all my attention on seeking the surges and tingles of energy I felt floating around the periphery of my consciousness. They would come and go as they pleased, meowing and pawing at the back door of my mind like stray cats. I was able to ignore them most of the time, but once I was seeking them out, they'd scurried away.

Trying to concentrate on the unknown was a challenge, but I must've done something right. I felt a tug on my consciousness. Opening myself up to it, I felt a sense of impatience and frustration dancing around me, two emotions I easily identified as Sanchez's. Pulling them closer with my mind, I reached further in.

I saw myself through Sanchez's eyes, sitting in front of her with my legs crossed. I barely recognized myself, and I wasn't sure if it was because I was looking at myself through someone else's eyes or because I'd changed so much. A lot had happened over the past few weeks. I'd lost weight, making my cheekbones more prominent, and I looked weak, even though I felt stronger than I ever had before. Defensively, I sat up straighter.

Losing myself in Sanchez's mind, I watched a montage of

memories parade through my awareness, a tornado of emotions swirling around them.

Sanchez was worried about us. Our group was in the mess hall eating dinner, and she anxiously watched us from afar. Her mind was bombarded by the pressure of being our leader and trying to protect us against the unknown.

Sanchez was looking in a mirror, her face wet from crying. She pushed her emotions away with fierce determination and wiped the tears from her cheeks. Refocusing on her reflection, she made sure she appeared perfectly composed. She sighed before straightening her outfit and walking out her barracks room door.

Sanchez stared down at her fallen squad members—slaughtered and strewn on the snow-covered ground.

Sanchez and Harper were lying in bed together, younger and uncertain, different than I knew them.

Sanchez was driving through the desert, looking out at the barren land around her with a gleeful smile on her face.

Sanchez was peering between her childish fingers as she hid her face. She was cringing as her father's hand came down across her mother's cheek. Her mother was crying and running after him as he drove away.

I'd seen too much, and with a jolt, I pulled myself away from Sanchez's mind. Sitting in front of her, I saw a different woman than I had before—instead of austere and distant, I now saw her as strong, protective, and guarded. She was a true survivor, an independent woman forged from suffering and loss. For the first time, thinking of never seeing her again once I left for Colorado made me feel sad.

"Are you alright?" Her hand brushed my arm. "Zoe, are you okay? You're really pale."

"Yeah, thanks. That was just…" I knew she wouldn't appreciate that I'd seen the memories of her past, felt her deepest fears and emotions. "That was more difficult than I thought."

"What's it like? What did you see?" she asked anxiously.

"It was a rush of images I couldn't really piece together, but at least now I think I know how to access them," I said, giving her half the truth.

She smiled hopefully. "But it worked?"

"Yeah." I nodded as she watched me intently. I wasn't sure what other private memories I would uncover if we continued, so I said, "But it took a lot of energy…I'm sort of zapped. I'm gonna call it a day, okay?"

"Sure," she said, but there was a hint of skepticism in her voice.

To avoid any further questions, I stood abruptly. "Sorry, I'm getting antsy. I need to move around. Must be all that time in bed." I stretched my back dramatically and said the first thing that came to my mind. "I think I'll go for a walk. I'll see you at dinner."

Sanchez nodded, and I strolled away.

Folding my arms, I pretended to be lost in thought as I scuffed my feet along the pathway.

"*We'll talk more later,*" I heard Sanchez say in my head. Without turning, I waved to her and continued toward the barracks. Walking inside, I meandered, unsure of what to do. Dave, Stacey, and Sarah were deep in conversation in the common room, and the others weren't around, so I was on my own.

Realizing that what I'd said to Sanchez was true—I'd done enough sitting around—I snatched my sketchbook and a few pencils from my room and headed back out to capture the final rays of the sunset.

In an attempt to avoid Sanchez, I moved between vacant buildings toward the gym. I hadn't done much exploring, especially not after what we'd found at the hospital off-base. Walking around alone was intimidating, but I welcomed the fresh air. *Maybe I'll find Harper and Biggs in the gym.*

As I continued on, I soaked in the landscape around me. Dead leaves lined the gutters of the well-worn roads, and withered weeds poked through jagged cracks in the sidewalk. I wondered if Fort Knox always looked so desolate. I tried to imagine red and orange leaves on the trees in autumn, and green grass and blooming flowers along the pathways in the spring. But I'd only known it as a barren, abandoned base, and I couldn't picture it as anything else.

Coming around the corner of the small post office, I heard a clanking noise. I froze, unsure if I should continue my exploration. After hearing it again—the distinct sound of metal hitting metal—I decided to investigate. I poked my head around the corner of the building and saw a few old cars parked alongside a repair garage and scattered throughout a small parking lot. In the right stall of the garage, a wheel-less Humvee was suspended on a lift, and a black panel van occupied the stall on the left.

Another bang suggested someone was working inside. Curiously, I wandered closer to the garage, expecting to see Biggs piddling around. Instead, I found Jake bent over the open hood of the van. His long-sleeve thermal shirt pulled tightly over his arms and back while he wrenched. His sleeves were pushed up so they bunched around his elbows, and I couldn't help but notice the muscles in his forearms flexing with each twist of his wrist.

"Hey," I said stupidly, knowing that if he found me watching him and I'd said nothing, it would be even more awkward.

His body jerked and he bumped his head on the van's hood. "Shit!" he barked.

I hid my sudden grin with my sketchbook. "Sorry, I didn't mean to scare you."

He stared at me for a moment—taking me in, ensuring I wasn't a Crazy. Small streaks of grease stained his forehead and left cheek, indicating he'd used a dirty arm to wipe his face.

"What are you doing here?" he asked harshly, but his flushed cheeks and ragged breathing indicated he was just flustered.

"I was taking a walk and heard some noises," I explained as I made my way into the garage.

Surveying the unfamiliar surroundings, I noticed the shop was littered with dirty objects that I knew nothing about. I was sure they were all parts of cars—or tools for fixing broken parts of cars—but the whole mess looked like a bunch of junk to me. Tools with red and black handles were strewn about on work benches, covered in a layer of dust that told me they hadn't been used in a while. The cement floor was stained with grime; I could feel it under my shoes, sticky and gritty. Dirty red rags decorated the large, tiered toolboxes and stools. The shop was a complete mess—exactly the way I expected a repair garage to be…except for the area around Jake.

He had a row of sockets and wrenches lined-up on the floor in front of the van. Descending in size, almost a perfect half inch away from one another, the tools lay waiting to be used. Jake was cranking a wrench, making it click rapidly as his wrist moved in a back and forth motion. A semi-clean red rag hung out of his back pocket, and a folded beanie lay on a stool nearby.

He's a neat freak, I realized. *Probably a perfectionist too.* I nodded to myself. *That explains a lot.* His cool exterior was only a glimpse into his need to remain in control.

As he continued working, I perused the shop. The more I

walked around, the more I realized I liked the unique way the place smelled.

"Why are you smiling?" Jake asked quietly, looking up at me.

"Am I smiling?" My smile widened to a grin. "I guess I've just never been in a garage like this before. I like it." The look on his face changed, a sort of surprise replacing his curiosity. "What's wrong with this one?" I asked, pointing to the van he was working on.

"I thought the battery was dead, but it's…" Registering my confusion, he paused and stood straighter. "I'm replacing the alternator," he said.

"Oh, cool. Nothing you can't handle then?"

"No, not unless I break something else," he joked dryly.

Sidling up to the van, I leaned in. "You like to work on cars?"

"It keeps my mind busy." He turned back to the maze of metal and hoses under the hood.

I nodded and straightened. "I understand. That's why I like drawing."

Jake said nothing and returned to cranking the wrench. No matter how much he played it off, he seemed to know exactly what he was doing. There was no hesitation or fumbling in his movements.

He can fight; he fixes cars; he knows how to put on a fireworks show… "Can I ask you something else?"

Reaching down into the engine, he nodded.

"It's about the fireworks," I said before I could lose my nerve.

Jake withdrew from the engine and straightened, the look on his face reflecting my own feelings of discomfort. Although I was a twenty-six-year-old woman looking at a thirty-something-year-old man, my heart raced like I was a teenager and he was the first boy I'd ever liked. *Liked? I don't know if I'd go that far…he intrigues me…that's all.*

"Why did you do it?" Changing my mind, I amended, "I mean, how?"

He glanced at me, and after a brief pause, shrugged indifferently. "I lit the fuses."

My eyes narrowed in frustration until I noticed something. Although his face was expressionless, there was a glint of amusement in his eyes. He was teasing me.

I might've fallen for his antics a week earlier, when I thought my presence repulsed him, but I'd come to know better. His actions told me more about him than his words ever would. *Two can play this game, Mr. Vaughn.* As I schemed, my pulse quickened.

"Obviously you lit the fuses," I said coolly, inching closer to the van. I wondered what it would take to provoke an honest reaction from him.

I leaned against the van, resting my elbows on the cold metal framing the engine bay. Without fully knowing what came over me, I arched my back, feeling my breasts bulge out the top of my tight v-neck. My pants hugged my ass as I stuck it out noticeably. The motion pulled my shirt up slightly to reveal a hint of my lower back.

Jake's eyes moved over my curves, quickly assessing every inch of me. My mind betrayed me, and I wondered what it would feel like to have his hands on me. He must've wondered something similar because his eyes briefly glazed over with desire. For the first time, I felt strong around him, in control. I grinned in victory, and he narrowed his eyes, looking down to clean the wrench he'd been using.

Letting the moment go, I straightened from my ridiculous pose, waiting for my heartbeat to slow down. "Why do you have to be so vague?" I asked. "I mean, where did you even *get* the fireworks? Or do you know how to make them?"

This time *he* smiled. "No," he said with a chuckle. "I can't *make* fireworks. Harper and I found a stockpile when we were searching for fuel awhile back."

"Oh." The disappointment in my voice surprised me.

Jake must have heard it too, because he gave me a sidelong glance. "You thought I made them?"

I blushed. "No. Yes. I don't know what I thought." *It shouldn't matter.* I shook the distracting thoughts from my head.

Jake set the now spotless wrench aside, and as he wiped the grease from his hands, his questioning eyes met mine.

Feeling awkward, I backed away. The playfulness had suddenly evaporated, and I felt like I was in the way of his work. But I wasn't quite ready to leave. I spotted an old, ratty, leather recliner in the next stall. It had a folded blue tarp draped over its lower half, covered in dust. Reluctant to wander back out into the dying light, I walked over to the chair and peeked under the tarp. It was clean. Knowing I'd found as good of a place as any, I pulled off the tarp and draped it over a nearby lift.

"Do you mind?" I asked, pointing to the chair.

Jake glanced over at me and shook his head. I was glad he didn't ask me why I was hesitant to leave—I didn't know the answer.

I curled up on the chair and opened my sketch pad, trying to ignore the unease in my stomach as Jake repeatedly glanced my way. I quickly began sketching. Although I'd never attempted them before, the shapes came easily. Before long, I had captured the slightly beat-up van on my page. Jake was there too…I hadn't been able to resist capturing his rugged beauty.

I was looking down at the living room of the home I'd grown up in. Muffled sounds came from upstairs. I strained to hear the desperate words being uttered, but my consciousness was jumbled and I couldn't decipher them. I couldn't think. I cringed as the shouting and cursing continued.

My dad and Jason suddenly materialized in the living room, completely unaware of my presence. Like a reclusive spider hidden in the recesses of a wall, I watched what unfolded with trepidation.

My brother was bigger than my dad. Jason's clenched fists and jaw were intimidating, but my dad seemed just as imposing. He was more solemn and threatening than I'd ever noticed before, and he looked older than I remembered. His features were blanketed with an all-too-familiar sorrow; his eyes were filled with loneliness, and their outer corners were wrinkled from a lifetime of worry.

Jason's gestures were forceful as he exchanged harsh words with my dad. His eyes were ablaze with so much anger that I almost missed the sadness crinkling his brow. Like a pair of ear plugs had been removed, I could suddenly hear Jason's venomous words.

"I can't stay here anymore!" he yelled. Both men's chests heaved under their shirts. "She's dead, Dad! I'm not doing this anymore. I don't want this life." I immediately knew who he was talking about...Mom.

My dad pushed his index finger roughly against my brother's chest, and Jason's rage consumed him. Without saying another word, Jason turned and stormed off.

Running his fingers through short hair silvered with age, my dad turned in my direction. Somehow, in my disembodied state, his eyes were able to focus on me, and they widened with shock.

The room from my childhood home abruptly melted away, only to be replaced by another familiar setting: our family car.

No longer incorporeal, I was a little girl sitting in the backseat of our brown and beige Wagoneer. I watched sunlit scenery pass by the window and played with the hem of my dress. Looking down at my lap, I giggled at the sight of my favorite yellow sundress and kicked my small, sandal-clad feet happily. As darkness overwhelmed the sunlight, a sense of dread filled me—something horrible was about to happen.

I smelled a citrusy scent and immediately knew it was my mother in the driver's seat. My eyes prickled with tears. I longed to see her face.

"Mommy?" I asked timidly, wishing she would look at me—wishing I could finally see her face.

She remained silent and ignored me, driving like it was any other day.

I couldn't remember what she looked like. My eyes darted to the rearview mirror where I hoped to catch a glimpse of her feminine features, but the image was blurred, like it was forbidden for me to see.

The foreboding presence of something malevolent hovered around us. The air was thick with a suffocating fear, and I saw my mom's body stiffen as she felt it too. I heard the sound of her hands tightening around the leather covering the steering wheel. Even though I was too small to see around the seat back, I knew my mom's knuckles were white and that her hands were shaking, just as mine were as they gripped the skirt of my yellow dress.

"Mommy," I said again.

"Shhhh," she cooed softly as she looked over her shoulder at me. Where her face should have been, there was nothing but smooth, featureless flesh. "Shhh, it's okay, Zoe," she said again, despite having no lips or mouth to speak from.

Petrified by the empty face in front of me, I tried to close my eyes, but my lids wouldn't shut. I tried to call out for Daddy or Jason, but only faint sobs escaped my lips. The faceless woman reached for me. I tried to pull away from her slow, mechanical movement, but my seat belt was suddenly too tight to move or even breathe. Gasping for air between muffled shrieks of terror, I attempted to yank my wrist away from her cold, bone-white fingers.

"No!" I cried out immediately before my body lurched forward. My neck snapped back, almost broken in half. I could see the front of the station wagon, crunched like an accordion against a dingy

brick wall. Adrenaline made my heart race. I was trapped, covered in blood...I was dying. I couldn't breathe.

The faceless woman sat motionless, pinned against the steering wheel. Her arm was draped over the dashboard, and the fingers that had been on my skin moments before twitched.

My body lurched as I gasped for air. My hands fell to my lap, suddenly paralyzed, and I took my final, searing breath.

Jolting awake in bed, I looked around the room. Moonlight shining through the mini blinds cast striped shadows on the wardrobe and the far wall. I was in Fort Knox, in my room in the barracks. I was safe…and I was alone.

The cotton sheets clung to my sweaty skin. Peeling them from my body, I felt like I was shedding the gloom of my nightmare. My face was clammy, my hair was matted against my cheeks and neck, and my body was shaking. The dream that had haunted me throughout my childhood had returned. Fearing what might come when I closed my eyes again and not knowing what else to do, I climbed out of bed.

I grabbed my sketchpad from the nightstand and made my way toward the door. I opened it, only to trip over Cooper, who was stretched out in the doorway. I stumbled and caught myself against the wall. "Dammit, Coop!" I quietly admonished, but it wasn't his fault that it was dark; we were conserving the fuel we needed to power the generators.

Seeing a faint light flicker down the hallway, I realized someone was in the common room. I headed that way, Cooper moseying languidly behind me. When I saw Jake sitting on the couch, reading by firelight, I paused, but Cooper trotted across the room to him. Hearing the dog's nails clicking on the floor, Jake looked up, and his eyes met mine.

"Hey," I said weakly.

He stood abruptly, looking pensive. "Is everything okay?" His voice was hoarse from a lack of use, and I held back a smile as he cleared his throat.

I nodded. Once again, he had a look on his face that I'd seen numerous times—one of thoughtful concern—but this time I understood it better. "Why do you always think something's wrong when you see me? Am I really that bad?"

His eyes narrowed, and I acknowledged the silliness of my question with a modest smile and a shrug. "Okay, well this time you can't save me; don't worry."

One of Jake's eyebrows arched inquiringly.

"I had a bad dream and couldn't get back to sleep. But it's nothing some drawing won't fix." I held up my sketchpad. "What about you, can't sleep?"

"Something like that."

"You can keep reading. I won't bother you."

He nodded, walking over to the fire. He threw on another log as I situated myself on the couch, wrapped myself in a blanket, and opened my sketchbook to draw. I tried to ignore the awkward silence between us for the second time in a day.

Jake remained by the fire, leaning against the wall. "Was your dream about Clara?"

I shook my head. "No. It was a nightmare I've been having for a while."

"You want to talk about it?" His concern was genuine, but I couldn't imagine explaining it to him. I didn't want to sound even more pathetic and broken than I already did.

Again, I shook my head. "You can sit down," I offered, not wanting him to feel like he had to leave.

Jake looked back at me with a rare grin on his face. "I can?"

Wow, that's two grins in one day. "You know what I mean. I didn't come in here to ruin your chill time."

"My 'chill time'?" he repeated playfully.

Laughing, I rolled my eyes. "Shut up. I'm glad I can entertain you." I thumbed through some of my drawings in search of a blank page.

"Those are really good," he said as he sat down a few inches from me, making the couch feel cozier. "Can I see?"

"Umm…" I hesitated.

"Never mind." He turned away from me.

"No, it's fine," I said hastily. I was so amazed that he was partaking in a conversation with me; I didn't want to mess it up. "Here." I handed him my sketchpad with both reluctance and anticipation. I wondered what he would think…and I tried to remember all that I'd drawn.

"You sure?"

"Yeah, I just have a lot of bad ones in there. It's more of a doodle book than anything." I'd never shared any of my sketchbooks with anyone other than Dani, but for some reason I wanted Jake to see it.

He didn't say a word as he flipped through pages of realistic depictions of some of what I'd seen over the past few weeks. I became lost in thought as I remembered the time and place I'd started each drawing. There were even some sketches I'd completely forgotten about.

Jake lingered on a sketch of a Labrador Retriever. "That's Sammy, Dave's dog who died…and that's the cabin we were staying in when Harper and the crew met up with us." Jake turned a few more pages. "Those are a couple drawings I did on the drive here—they're not very good."

Before I knew it, there were forgotten sketches of Jake—angry ones. His likeness stared up from the page, composed of dark lines and harsh shading that reflected my opinion of him at the time. His drawn eyes were flat, cruel, and judgmental, so different than the pair currently watching me.

"Oh, uh, you can skip those." Blushing, I reached over and started flipping the pages as quickly as I could. "I was clearly having a bad day."

Jake watched me too intently as I searched for something else —anything else—to show him. Finding my drawings of Cooper, I stopped. "You might like these," I said, trying to refocus his attention.

His eyes absorbed the contents of the pages as he flipped through them, but he remained silent, leaving me to wonder what he thought of them. He analyzed the images like there were hidden messages within the lines and shading. Sitting so close to him, I was becoming distracted by our proximity. I leaned away.

The last drawing was of Cooper's face, and just as I was about to speak, Jake's hand moved toward it. He gently ran his fingers over the page like the drawing might come to life. "It's perfect."

"Really?" I whispered, not realizing I'd been holding my breath. "Thanks."

As he reached my most recent drawings, depictions of Harper filled the pages…over and over. The images of him smiling in his white lab coat looked true to life.

"I was practicing," I tried to explain, though I didn't know why I felt the need to say anything at all.

Finally closing my book, Jake handed it back to me and picked up his own. He casually rested his elbows on his knees. "Thanks for sharing." The distance in his voice had returned, instantly annoying me.

"Sure." I pulled myself back into the opposite corner of the couch. "What are you reading?"

He showed me the hardback's dilapidated cover. "The Count of Monte Cristo."

"I've never read it, but the movie was great."

"It's my favorite book…I've read it about twenty times."

I didn't doubt it. With its scuffed cover and worn binding, the book was practically falling apart. "Yeah, the binding needs a little restoration. If you put some sort of cover on it, that'd at least stop the rest of it from crumbling."

His eyebrows rose in question. "I see," he said.

"I know a lot of random stuff when it comes to preserving things. Working in an art gallery was one of my former trades."

"And your other trades?" he asked, sounding genuinely curious.

"Um, let's see…I've never worked on cars, put on a fireworks show, or shot a gun, but I *did* work at an art supply place and was a live model for some of the art classes at the U in Salem."

Jake grinned knowingly.

"My clothes were on," I clarified. "Oh, and I was a bartender for a few years…and I dabbled in making saltwater taffy back home."

"Bartender?" he asked, chuckling. *Even his smile is mysterious.* "That sounds like trouble." *Smiles, laughing, and a little less awkwardness…we're breaking all sorts of records today.*

I relaxed at the sound of his deep, rumbling laugh. "I think that's the first time I've ever heard you laugh," I said, and instantly worried I'd just ruined the progress we'd made.

"Not a lot of things make me laugh, I guess." He leaned back further into the couch.

"Well I'm glad my bartending is entertaining to you," I said, feigning annoyance. "What about you? What are *your* other trades?"

Jake thought for a moment before saying, "Nothing very interesting." He was avoiding my question, but I didn't push him.

I glanced down at my sketchpad, leaving him to return to his book, but I could tell he was distracted. "Do you think we'll ever be…*not* awkward around each other?" I asked, breaking the silence.

My question hung in the air as he continued reading. Finally, he turned the page, and without looking at me, asked, "You mean, like friends?"

"Yeah, I mean…like normal people who can have a normal conversation."

He peered at me. "Funny, I thought that's what we were doing." His tone had hardened.

"Yeah, I guess."

"I don't have a lot of friends," Jake added reluctantly.

I didn't know how to respond, so I leaned back and stared at my empty page. I couldn't concentrate with him sitting beside me. I wondered what he was thinking. I started to doodle on the page, unable to stay focused. I thought about our silent flirtation in the garage, the blood transfusion, and the fireworks. I kept asking myself what it all meant, or if it meant anything at all. I wondered why it was bothering me so much that he wouldn't open up to me—why it preoccupied me to the point of drawing my knot tattoo over and over again.

I sat, stewing in questions, further confused by the sense of unease I felt radiating from Jake despite his calm appearance. The sounds of the fire, book pages turning, and my pencil tracing the length of the textured page were all that filled the passing minutes. Yawning, I guessed an hour or so had passed, and since I had to wake up early, I figured I should get some sleep.

Gathering my things, I stood. "Well, I'm training with Harper tomorrow, so I should call it a night." Folding the blanket and laying it on the back of the couch, I met Jake's narrowed eyes.

"You're still leaving?" he asked, sounding surprised.

"Yes," I said simply, not wanting to start an argument. *And you're* not *coming with me.* "Goodnight."

36

DANI

Careful not to wrinkle the priceless photo sheltered in the safety of my coat pocket, I searched around the ranch for Jason. He wasn't in the house, the stable, or the pasture. After the kiss…*Oh, what a kiss!*…he'd disappeared. I'd enlisted the help of dozens of animals in my search and was keeping the mind connections open in case they tracked him down.

Finally, I heard the faint sound of Jack's howl, and I knew he'd found my quarry. "*Come. Hurry. Strange,*" my dog said as he appeared at the crest of a nearby hill, barking nonstop for emphasis.

"Okay, okay, hold your horses. I'm coming," I grumbled, stalking up the hill. It was cold, and after connecting with so many minds in my call for help the previous night—human and animal minds—I was as exhausted as a person could be without collapsing. Something about using my Ability on *people* seemed to wear me out more than anything I'd ever experienced, and my several hour nap hadn't rejuvenated me completely.

After walking for a few minutes, Jack and I spotted Jason in a sparse copse of cypress trees. He was hacking his way through their trunks, tree by tree. His bare, glistening back bunched and flexed with each swing of the ax. Part of me wanted to just stand and admire him from afar, but I had been looking for him for a reason.

Once I was close enough that I didn't need to shout, I asked, "What are you doing, Jason?"

He paused with the axe raised but didn't face me. "Chopping firewood." *Duh.* He swung again. And again.

"This is kind of far from the house." *Double duh.*

Another pause. "Yep." Another swing.

I rounded the tree he was currently hacking away at, careful to keep clear of the ax's arc and the erratically jettisoned wood chips. Jason avoided looking at me while I studied him. Other than his curt answers, he acted like he was completely alone. He seemed to lose himself in the meditative motion, and I lost myself in watching him. Lift. Swing. Thunk. Lift. Swing. Thunk.

He wore an expression of grim determination as his chest and abdominal muscles rhythmically clenched and released. Clenched and released. It was hypnotizing. And erotic. And annoying.

"How will you get it all back to the ranch?" I asked, watching his focused, granite expression. There was so much beneath his attractive surface. I wondered how many women had bothered to consider who he was on the inside when his outside would more than make up for pretty much any personality flaws. He was complicated and conflicted—he had always been—though he rarely let it show. It took the world ending for me to realize it.

"I'll carry it," he said between swings.

"It'll take a long time…lots of trips," I commented. Apparently I was turning into the Queen of Obvious.

Pause. "Yep." Swing. Thunk. Pause. "That's the point." Lift.

Heaving a huge sigh, I said, "We need to talk." I was growing irritated with his apparent need to ignore me. In my pockets, my hands clenched into fists. I had to remind myself to be careful not to crush the photo.

Pause. "Can't. Busy." Swing. Thunk. Lift.

Stop being such an ass! I thought angrily.

Pause. "But I'm so good at it." Swing. Thunk. Lift.

Crap! I hadn't meant to speak in his head. I definitely needed to get that under control. My mind was overflowing with inappropriate thoughts that I desperately wanted to keep private.

"This is important…and difficult enough without you flinging that thing around!" I snapped.

He said nothing. Swing. Thunk. Lift. Swing. Thunk. Lift.

Around us, dozens of small furry shapes were tentatively wandering closer, making me realize that I'd been maintaining my connection to the animal scouts. I struggled to disconnect from their minds—exhaustion was making my telepathy increasingly difficult to control.

Finally, as I continued to watch Jason take out his pent up aggression on the tree, I lost it. "Dammit, Jason!" I shouted. Tears of frustration swiftly welled and spilled down my cheeks. Silent sobs clenched my gut, making my throat close spastically.

Abruptly, the ceaseless swing, thunk, lift stopped. "Shit," Jason muttered under his breath. He watched me with wide, troubled eyes. "Don't do that…I didn't mean to…I shouldn't have done what I did back there."

"What?" I choked out between sobs. *Did he just say he shouldn't have kissed me?* That made me cry even harder.

He approached me slowly. "With Cam and everything…and my sister…I shouldn't have—"

"Oh shut up!" I shrieked, unwilling to listen to all the reasons kissing me was a mistake. Just knowing he regretted it was unbearable. "This isn't about *that*."

The axe slid from Jason's hand, thumping on the damp ground. "It's not? Then what?" He quickly closed the distance between us and took my face in his hands—they seemed to burn my cold cheeks. "What is it?"

It was so much harder to form the words when he was being gentle, not to mention when he was standing close enough to feel his enticing heat. Like a coward, I closed my eyes. *"I...know what happened to your dad,"* I said in his mind. Determined not to leave him to face his pain alone, I forced my eyes open. "He's dead."

Jason's eyes searched mine, and he swallowed repeatedly. "How do you know?" he asked, his voice hollow and weak.

"Grams left a note for me before she...died," I said, my throat catching on the final word. Unable to speak coherently, I had to finish in his mind. *"She found your dad sitting near the ocean. He was already gone."*

Is it getting harder to talk in his head?

"Oh...I...He...We..." Jason stammered, trying unsuccessfully to voice different thoughts. He abruptly moved away from me, picked up the ax, and threw it with a savage roar. It flew, end over end, and crashed against one of the trees he'd mangled, dropping to the ground with a muffled thud.

I tentatively touched his shoulder, and he faced me, a storm of hatred, rage, and regret churning in his eyes. As he searched my face, the storm dissipated, and his expression softened. A single tear escaped from one of his eyes and slid down the chiseled planes of his face. His palpable anguish threatened to revive my own tears.

He fell to his knees in front of me and wrapped his arms around my hips, pressing the side of his face against my down-padded chest. I ran my fingers through his short, thick black hair. It was a little longer than it had been when he'd found me in my Seattle apartment, but not yet long enough to show the loose curl I knew it held. He was the strongest man I'd ever known; he was my rock. But for a brief period of time, I needed to be his.

"I'd hoped...," he choked out, his arms clenching around me tighter. "I'd thought maybe, just maybe...but it was stupid. Hope," he growled, "is for fools."

I tightened my grasp on the sides of his head and forced him to look up at me. "No, Jason," I whispered. Continuing in his mind, I said, *"Losing hope...*that's *for fools. What do you think happened* *to all those people who survived the Virus and then killed themselves?* They *lost hope.* They're *the fools. But us,"* I paused, basking in the way his eyes drank me in, wondrous and hungry, *"we have wants and desires and people we believe in. We have hope, and when we lose it, we might as well lie down and die."*

Staring up at me, Jason seemed on the verge of saying something. For what felt like minutes he said nothing. Finally, his arms loosened around me, and his hands grasped my hips.

I trembled at the change in his gaze and shivered at the increasing chill in the air. I was suddenly dizzy, unintentionally swaying from side to side, and my head felt like it might explode. *Am I gonna pass out? Not again…not now!*

My vision darkened around the edges, and my knees abruptly gave out. I would've collapsed to the ground if Jason hadn't been holding me up.

"Dani?" he asked. "Dani, what's wrong?"

I tried to keep my eyes open—to breathe deeply—but my brain's commands weren't being received. "My Ability…used too much…"

As my body went completely limp, Jason hooked one arm behind my knees, the other around my shoulders, and stood. Instead of falling to the soggy ground, I was cradled in his protective arms.

"Cold," I whispered against his bare shoulder, acutely aware of the contrast between the frigid air and his scorching skin. "It's dark."

"It's the middle of the day," Jason muttered worriedly as he began walking at a quick clip.

"So cold…tired," I mumbled, my head lolling back over his arm.

"No Dani. Shit! Stay with me," he urged. "I need you to wrap your arms around my neck. Can you do that?"

"I think…maybe…" My tongue felt swollen, my arms leaden. I focused all of my remaining strength on following his directions. I felt the same as I had behind Grams's house and after I'd hit the Crazy with the shovel, except it was a hundred times worse.

"Good," Jason said, hugging me tightly against his blazing body. "Now hold on." He began to run. The jarring motion helped me hang on to consciousness, and in a few minutes, we were crashing through the front door of the ranch house.

Startled by the commotion, Ky asked, "Jason, what's—"

"Her body temp's too low…fill the tub with hot water!" Jason ordered.

Running out of strength, my arms released their hold on Jason, and my head fell back. I blinked and was suddenly lying on the couch I'd been using as a bed, my clothes being gently peeled away. Though I slapped uselessly at the hands undressing me, first my coat, then my jeans, and then my sweater were removed, until I was shivering in only my bra and panties. I was wrapped in layers of blankets like a swaddled infant and scooped up into Jason's strong, comforting arms.

"Is it warm?" Jason shouted ahead as he carried me.

"Yeah, but not full yet," Ky called back.

Jason's voice echoed slightly when he said, "Go. I'll finish." Within seconds he had removed and discarded my cocoon of blankets and partially submerged me in the steaming hot water. It burned, but I savored the feeling, grasping at the chance to be anything but freezing. The situation didn't make sense though—I was in the water, its delicious heat was lapping at my skin, yet I was still enveloped in Jason's iron hold. *He's in the tub with me?*

As the water level rose, Jason slid our bodies further down in the cramped tub, submerging my entire torso. With one arm wrapped around my waist and the other around my shoulders, he kept my face above the water. With my head resting in the hollow between his shoulder and chest, I watched my hands float near the water's surface. My dim vision grew stronger and my breaths came more easily as my core temperature increased.

"Jason," I whispered once the water began to cool.

He tensed. "Yeah?"

"Thanks."

"Sure." He relaxed, letting me melt back into him.

I eyed the two very masculine, bare knees sticking out of the water on either side of me. "Jason?"

"Yeah?"

"Are you…um… wearing anything?"

His chuckle vibrated against my back. "Hmmm…let me think…I believe I left a little something on. Do you want me to fix that, Red?" Though his words were filled with innuendo, he sounded relieved.

"I…I don't…Can I just go to sleep? I'm so tired." I snuggled against him, relishing the feel of his body as my eyelids grew heavier.

"Sleeping in a bathtub…not a great plan," Jason said. "Let's get you out and dried off. Can you stand?"

Peering down at myself, I realized I was wearing only my bra and underwear, and shyness overwhelmed me. "Maybe…will you close your eyes… please?"

"Are you serious?" he laughed. "I just undressed you. And it's not like I've never seen you in a swimsuit."

"Well it's been a while!" I squeaked. "A lot changes in a decade…"

"I've noticed." He paused briefly before informing me, "My eyes are closed."

Carefully, I stood and stepped from the slippery tub. As I did, I turned to watch him, to make sure he didn't peek while I removed my soaked undergarments and dried off. I robed myself in a thick gown of blankets, studying the man whose quick thinking had just saved me from…something.

What the hell was that, anyway? Death by internal freezing? I was quickly understanding that certain uses of my Ability charged a high price—impromptu naps and killer headaches being the going rate—but this had been different, more dangerous.

"Okay…you can open your eyes."

Jason did so and stood smoothly, letting the water stream over the enticing ridges of his body.

I spun away, my heart instantly pounding. "I'm going to go get dressed and lay down," I said in a high-pitched voice.

"Whatever works for you, Red," he teased.

I hurried from the bathroom, slipped into some sweatpants and a t-shirt, and curled up on my makeshift bed. I was out cold before Jason emerged from the bathroom.

"Okay, so stick your foot in the stirrup…no, Ky, the other foot…and then pull yourself up. You're big strong guys; I'm sure you can handle it," I teased.

Jason had already mounted while Ky and his horse were doing a little square dance with his foot stuck in the stirrup.

"Can't you help?" Ky called in my general direction. "Like, make it stand still or something?"

I snorted, unable to hold the laughter in any longer. "Won't help you…you'll just end up doing this again next time. You've got to figure it out."

"Thanks so much, D. You're a huge help."

"I try," I said, quieting my giggles.

Three hours later, we were walking our horses down Bodega Avenue. On our mission to scout and gather supplies pertinent to our impending departure, we'd loaded our bags with medicine and hygiene items, some food, spices, salt, liquor, and dog food. We'd found, but hadn't yet taken, a huge supply of feed and some useful tack at a farm close to our own ranch. We would have to come back for it.

"Oh!" I exclaimed as we passed by a cedar-sided bungalow. "We should stop in there…might be some useful books."

Jason shrugged and dismounted; using as few words as possible had become his new standard around me. It was driving me insane, especially considering that he rarely let me out of his sight. He'd become my silent, ever-present shadow. A big, protective, lethal one.

Ky scrutinized the sprawling, brown home. "Uh, why? What am I missing here?"

"This is Mr. Grayson's house. He is…*was*…a teacher at our high school back in the day. He sort of collected books on everything, and his house functioned as the town's unofficial library. You know…'cause we don't have a real one. He seemed to think he could educate the entire community through the power of books alone," I explained.

"Got it," Ky said.

I was no longer a stranger to breaking and entering, but the whole "let's break into the house of our old teacher so we can steal his books" thing felt odd. Regardless, it ended up being quite the fortuitous stop.

As we were skimming the bookshelves lining the walls from floor to ceiling, searching for anything that might prove useful in our post-civilization world, we heard the crack of a dropped book on the weathered wood floor.

"What the…?" came a man's voice from the front door—it was Mr. Grayson. His hand was still on the doorknob, his mouth was gaping open in shock, and a heavy tome rested at his feet. "What are you…I never thought someone would…books, you know. Wait…Danielle, is that you?" he asked, finally expressing a complete thought.

Pierced by his sharp stare, I was instantly transported back to high school. I rushed to explain, "Yes, Mr. Grayson, it's me, Dani. We, um, didn't think anyone was here or that anyone would mind if we…um…well…"

"Borrowed some books? From my private collection? Assuming I was dead?" Mr. Grayson finished. His expression turned musing as he examined each of us from a distance. "I'd wager," he said, breaking the tense silence, "that your companion is Jason Cartwright. Am I correct?"

"Yes, Sir," Jason affirmed.

Mr. Grayson pondered the situation for another long moment, allowing the silence to expand. I jumped when he finally spoke. "Danielle, if I remember correctly, I would expect to find you here with the younger Cartwright, unless she has succumbed to the—"

"No!" I hastily interrupted. "Zoe's alive. She's just not, well, *here*. Last we heard from her, she was at Fort Knox. With some military people. She's safe though…I think." *I hope.*

He nodded, and his lips quirked into a slight smile. "I see. Well, I don't know this other lad, but I'll assume for the moment that he's fine since he's with you two. I suppose you'd like to know about the past month here in our lovely little coastal paradise." Sarcasm dripped heavily off of the end of his statement. *Good old Mr. Grayson…*

"But I have somewhere I must be in a short amount of time. Will you meet me here tomorrow?" he asked politely.

The three of us exchanged questioning looks and shrugs, finally nodding to each other. *Why not?*

"Wonderful. Does one o'clock in the afternoon work with your schedules?"

I coughed, choking down a laugh. *Schedules. Hilarious.*

Ignoring me, Jason replied, "Yes, Sir. We'll see you then."

As we left, I glanced back at Mr. Grayson and couldn't help but wonder about his pressing engagement. Just the idea that he had somewhere to be was surprisingly foreign…and amusing.

37

ZOE

Waking the next morning was rough. I'd tossed and turned all night, thinking about Jake and the expression on his face when I'd left the common room. I was still exhausted and wasn't even close to ready for a day filled with training and travel planning.

Throwing off the covers, I pried myself from the warmth of the bed and slipped my feet into my brown, fur-lined slippers. I knew I'd need hot water if I was going to carpe diem, so I grabbed the towel hanging over the desk chair and headed out the door.

The frigid air gnawed at my skin as I made my way down the empty hallway. Hearing the clacking of pool balls, I knew Dave was awake and playing his usual early morning game of pool with Stacey. I realized I was probably the last one to get up and dragged my feet lazily along the ground as I entered the empty locker room. The air was still steamy from someone else's shower.

After opening my locker, I sluggishly pulled off my sweatpants. My shirt quickly followed. As the steam dissipated, the brisk air bit at my exposed skin. *I HATE winter.* The cold tortured me as it lingered, seeming to mock my constant discomfort.

Hearing the sound of a plastic bottle hitting the shower floor, I jumped, swiveling around in surprise. I held my crumpled shirt against my exposed chest. The sound of bare feet on tile preceded Jake as he strode around the corner of the line of lockers…completely naked.

Rumpling his hair with a towel, Jake almost ran into me before noticing my own mostly nude body frozen in front of him. He stopped abruptly, his expression shifting in recognition: surprise – confusion – intrigue.

Beads of water glided down his skin, and his arm flexed as his fist clenched the towel hanging at his perfectly trimmed side. My eyes followed the droplets as they trickled down his sculpted abs, gravitating toward his…

Realizing I was gawking at his nakedness, I raised my eyes to his face. He was curiously appraising my own barely covered body. His look was covetous, and he abruptly shifted his towel to cover the evidence of his interest.

"I didn't know anyone else was in here," he said casually. *Why is he just standing there?* He was still naked, and I had to turn away or risk drooling.

"Shit," I mouthed, realizing I was in the most deliciously awkward situation of my life. "I didn't know you were in here either." My boy-short bottoms and tangled mess of waist-length hair were all that covered my backside. One hand quickly moved to cover my face, and I considered putting my shirt back on. *But then I'd have to pull it away from my boobs…*

"I'm pretty sure I put the white towel on the handle," he said. The playfulness in his voice was back, and I could feel heat painting red splotches up my neck and cheeks.

"Yeah, I guess I missed it. I'm not really a morning person." In the locker's small mirror I could see his short hair, wet and spikey, and my body hummed at the thought of running my hands over it. "Are you planning on getting dressed by any chance?" I murmured.

"Am I making you uncomfortable?" I could tell he was smiling.

Facing him, I fought the grin that threatened to expose my delight. "Slightly. I wasn't expecting to see a naked man when I woke up this morning."

"You don't like naked men?" His uncharacteristic joke made me laugh as I tried to focus on only his face.

"Of course I do, I just wasn't prepared"—I pointed at him—"for this!"

He said nothing and chuckled as he strolled toward the door, his firm glutes flexing. I thought I glimpsed a smirk on his freshly shaven face as he turned the corner, wrapping his towel loosely around his waist as he vanished.

Breathe.

Again.

I took numerous deep breaths, gathered my shampoo, conditioner, soap, and razor, and headed for the showers. I was anxious for the hot water to wash away my sudden desire. Seemingly indestructible and with a body fit for battle, Jake reminded me of Achilles, and I wondered what *his* weakness might be. I couldn't help but smile as I recalled his sexy grin.

After my shower, I dressed and braided my hair, put my things away, and headed to the mess hall for breakfast. Of course I found Jake there, sitting at a table with Biggs. *Great, just the three of us,* I thought sarcastically. Suddenly feeling self-conscious, I lost my appetite.

"Feel better?" Jake asked with a barely-there smirk.

"You could say that," I said before I could stop the words from escaping.

A jovial glint danced in his eyes. "Yeah?"

Biggs's head turned back and forth between us until, thankfully, he interrupted. "When you're finished with breakfast, Zoe, we'll start training. Harper can't today, so you're stuck with me. Okay?"

"Yeah, that's great, thanks." I realized I hadn't seen Harper for a few days—not since the fireworks show—and the fact that I hadn't really noticed his absence was surprising…and made me feel horrible. "Is Harper okay?" I asked.

Biggs stopped chewing, like my question required a lot of thought. "Why do you ask?"

"I haven't seen him in a couple of days." I eyed him closely. "Just wondering…," I said, promising myself I would find Harper before training.

The three of us finished eating in silence, and after a while, Jake and I took our trays into the kitchen. As we scraped off our plates, we exchanged stolen glances until we heard Sanchez march in and whisper something to Biggs, who still sat at the table, jotting down notes.

I looked over at Jake curiously. "Do you know what's going on?"

He shook his head.

After a second thought, I asked, "Would you even tell me if you did?"

"I have no idea what's going on," was all he said as we watched the secret exchange.

Biggs looked up at me and smiled weakly. "Sorry Zoe, I have to bail on our training today. I'll catch up with you later," he blurted, hurrying away before I could ask any questions.

"Hmmm…" Abandoning my plate in the sink, I debated whether I should follow after him like an annoying little kid.

"If you're serious about leaving," Jake said, "you need to keep training." He ruminated for a moment, completely unconcerned with what was happening with our other friends. "Do you want my help?" Despite his kindness, he seemed to find little pleasure in his offer.

"Um…" Knowing Jake might convince me to stay, I was hesitant to accept his help. "Sure," I said, accepting anyway—a small part of me simply wanted to be around him.

"I can show you how to fight…and how to use a gun and a knife, but that's about it," he said.

"You *can*?" I teased.

"I know enough to get by." He flashed a mischievous grin, and for a moment I saw the Jake I'd encountered in the locker room.

To begin our workout, we started by jogging to the gym. The day was pleasant and getting warmer as we ran down the sidewalk.

"How do you 'know enough to get by,' exactly?" I asked between breaths, hoping, but not expecting, to catch a glimpse into his past. *Maybe he knows karate?* I doubted it; I couldn't picture a younger version of him being dropped off at a Dojo.

"I got into a lot of trouble growing up," Jake said after a few strides.

"Can you *please* be more specific? I don't mean to pry—I know how you hate that—but as your new trainee, I feel I deserve to know what I'm getting myself into. Are we talking skills and precision or hardcore street-fighting?" I half-joked.

Jake smiled. "I moved around a lot. I was a stupid kid and wasted my time doing a lot of stupid things."

Had he practiced karate as a child or gone target shooting with his dad, my curiosity would've been satisfied, but his dismissive explanation was much more Jake-like, alluding to the untamed side I sometimes saw in his eyes. I fought the temptation to dig deeper, to learn about him through his memories. I thought about how far we'd come the last couple of days, and I didn't want to ruin our developing friendship by knowing too much too fast—plus there was that whole…none-of-your-business vibe.

"So let's just be clear, we're not cage fighting or anything, right?" I asked playfully, trying to keep the conversation light.

"No cage fighting," he said. "Although…that's an entertaining thought." His rough laugh made me giggle.

I stopped jogging. *I just giggled.*

"You okay?" Jake asked as he stopped and stared back at me with a mixture of curiosity and concern.

Reality hit me like a ton of bricks falling one-by-one—each brick an interaction between Jake and me during the short time we'd known each other. As they landed, I recalled every word, every look, every gesture, and my conflicted emotions for him became clearer.

I'm…into him. I like being around him. If the world was normal, I'd want to date him.

The image of his sister dying in his arms flashed in my mind, and I knew I could never have him. *I'm leaving for Colorado. His sister died there. He only wants to come along to protect me because he couldn't protect her. I don't even know how he really feels about me.*

As he anxiously approached me, I grasped for control. "I'm fine, sorry," I told him, waving him away.

"You don't look fine."

"Gee, thanks." I jogged ahead, trying to stay focused on our day of training. "Come on, we've got a lot to do today."

I hated pushing Jake away like that, but I didn't know what else to do. I was too caught off guard by my troublesome feelings for him, and I just wanted to ignore them.

When we reached the gym, we began our session with some kickboxing. Jake started by showing me how to throw a proper punch against a heavy punching bag.

"Harper can show you how to wiggle your way out of an attacker's arms all he wants, but then what? You need to learn how to fight back, otherwise, getting away would be pointless."

As he demonstrated, his triceps flexed with each extension of his arm, taunting me. I wished he'd put his long sleeves back on as much as I wished I could tear off everything he was still wearing.

Why did I have to realize this now? I groaned inwardly.

"Why are you stopping? Keep going," he demanded.

"I hardly see how this is helpful," I whined, getting out of step with the heavy bag. It knocked into me with a thud, and I almost fell over.

"If you can't defend yourself against an inanimate object, how can you expect to protect yourself out there. I won't always be there; you need to learn how to take care of yourself."

I sighed. "You're right. You won't always be there because you're *not* coming with me."

Shaking his head, he hit his bag harder. "Whatever you say," he said, mocking me.

"Why do you have to say it like that? Why can't you just help me and not try to make me feel like shit for wanting to leave? Is it really that difficult?"

"Yeah, it is. I'm surprised Harper's not chaining you to your bed. That's what I'd do."

"Harper's not in charge of me. He's not my dad, not my boyfriend..." Jake's pensive frown told me he'd assumed otherwise. "You thought we were together?" I asked, taken aback.

He just smirked at my words and continued assaulting his heavy bag—left, right, then left again. Between the nicknames and the flirting, I could see why Jake might've thought there was something going on between Harper and me. Beyond that, I was intrigued that he'd given it any thought at all, and happy that the revelation seemed to satisfy him.

"Even *if* Harper and I were together," I said, "he wouldn't get a say." I continued to kick my bag, my building aggression making my strikes more powerful. "Besides, he's got his own shit going on, apparently." I could feel sweat beading on my neck and chest, and fatigue was spreading through my thighs and butt. "Plus, since I have your blood inside me, I think there's a chance I'll be—"

Jake stopped mid-punch, catching his bag as it swung back to him. "Jesus Christ, you can't count on that," he said angrily. "It might've been a one-time thing. I can't believe you're not taking this more seriously."

I rolled my eyes and continued kicking to avoid his scrutiny.

"Turn your foot out, or you'll break your ankle," he ordered and resumed beating the shit out of his own bag.

I stopped kicking and steadied myself to catch my breath. "Would you calm down? I don't want you to come with me," I lied. "So why are you making such a big deal about it?"

Between strikes he said, "Calm down? I didn't save…your life just so…you could leave and…get yourself killed. Sorry if I seem…a little….pissed…about…it."

I took a step toward him. "Why do you care so much anyway?"

Jake stopped abruptly and scoffed. "Isn't it obvious?"

I shook my head. "No, not really. You're about as clear as mud, and you're unpredictable. I have no idea what to think of you."

His chest heaved, and he looked directly into my eyes. His gaze was charged with an electric current I could feel buzzing through me. I swallowed thickly.

Carefully, he said, "I *care* about what happens to you because I *care* about you. I don't want you to get killed."

His sincerity angered me even more. "You don't care about me," I snapped. "Let's be honest, Jake. You just feel like you have to protect me because I remind you of your sister." I couldn't believe what I'd said; I knew it wasn't true.

"You know that's not why," he said through clenched teeth. He stepped closer, and the heat of his body wrapped around me, tempting me to lean into him.

Instead, I timidly took a step backward. "Isn't that why you saved me to begin with?"

Rage filled his eyes as he again closed the distance between us. "Oh, so if I saw you getting raped and you *didn't* remind me of her, you think I would've walked away? Give me a fucking break!" Infuriated, he turned away from me and paced back and forth. "For supposedly being able to read people's minds or whatever, you're really shitty at it."

"I already told you, I try not to. I thought—"

"STOP IT! Tell me what's really going on," he demanded.

I waivered. Everything Jake had said during the last few

minutes was finally sinking in. I desperately wanted to tell him how I felt…that I cared about him too.

Before I could react, the heavy, metal door swung open, and Sanchez stepped inside. "We've got a situation," she said gravely. "Both of you—come with me." She turned and walked out of the gym, oblivious to the argument she'd interrupted and expecting us to follow her.

I glanced at Jake, and the fierce glint in his eyes told me our conversation wasn't over. Both of us were still breathing heavily as we followed Sanchez in silence, hurrying to catch up with her. A gentle breeze cooled my sweaty skin, making me shiver, and I rubbed my arms for warmth. I could see Jake eyeing me from the edge of my vision, willing me to look at him, but I refused. I didn't know what the hell to do; I was ashamed of what I'd said and was afraid of what might happen when our conversation continued.

As we made our way toward the barracks, I spotted Harper. He looked haggard as he eased himself down onto the bench of a picnic table. I ran to him, taking in his appearance, and squatted in front of him. "What's wrong, H?"

Harper smiled and kissed my forehead. "I'm fine, Baby Girl. I'm feeling a lot better, just really tired. I haven't been sleeping very well," he explained as he straightened, portraying the cocky façade he knew I wanted to see. He patted the bench. "Have a seat."

I did and glanced over at Jake, who was standing in front of us. Even he appeared concerned, his eyebrows drawn together and his mouth pressed into a thin line.

Harper's eyes shifted back and forth between us, and he hesitated.

"Whatever it is, just tell us," I pleaded. "Don't beat around the bush. I'll reach in and grab it if I have to," I threatened, realizing my freakish empathy-thing was pointless if I didn't start using it to my advantage.

He winked. "Promise?"

I tilted my head to the side and exhaled in exasperation.

"Calm down. I'll tell you."

The late-morning sun was bright, and Harper squinted into the light before closing his eyes; its rays seemed to rejuvenate him right in front of us.

"I've been seeing things…strange things," he said, watching me to gauge my reaction before glancing at Jake.

"You're like Sanchez, Jake, and me…the Virus changed you too," I clarified.

Harper nodded. "I've been having bad dreams for a while now, but they've gotten worse recently." His eyes didn't leave Jake as he continued, "The night before it happened, I saw Zoe being poisoned."

"Why the hell didn't you say anything?" Jake practically growled.

Harper's eyes narrowed at him, and Jake's fierce expression faltered, melting into shame. "It was too late," Harper said defensively. "When it really *did* happen—when you *were* poisoned—I was…shocked." He looked at me, his eyes filled with regret. "You died in my dream. That's why I practically gave up. I didn't think we could save you." He paused. "But here you are, and not because of me. If Jake hadn't known he could save you…if he hadn't made me do the transfusion…" Harper shook his head, and I could feel his self-disgust.

The look on his face was heartbreaking. I threw my arms around him, squeezing him as tightly as I could. "Jake didn't know for sure, H. You did everything you could. It's okay."

Jake averted his gaze, and Harper scoffed.

Releasing him, I sat up and waited for him to continue.

He rubbed his hands over his face. "And then last night, I dreamt of a fire. I knew it was here on base, but I couldn't tell where. I just know it'll happen. I can *feel* it," he said, shaking his head. "There was death and fear and screaming, but I woke up before I could see anything else."

I studied Sanchez, who'd been standing silently, and then Jake, who'd sat down on the opposite side of the tabletop, his feet on the bench and his elbows resting on his knees. I could feel Jake's fear as he watched Harper intently. I had the distinct impression that there was something they weren't telling me.

When the wind shifted direction, carrying with it the faint scent of smoke, we all straightened in alarm.

"Please tell me Biggs is burning something," I said, but before anyone could respond, one of the common room windows shattered, scattering shards of glass on the ground below. Black smoke billowed out, and flames lapped up the edges of the window frame.

"What the fuck?" Sanchez exclaimed quietly, stealing the words out of my mouth.

Before we could react, more windows burst. The fire spread hungrily, seeming to instantaneously engulf the barracks, the place that had become our home. Greedy flames consumed the walls and windows, and dense smoke filled the sky with a gray haze that blocked out the sun. I was lulled into a horrified trance by the crackling, roaring inferno.

I heard movement behind me and looked over my shoulder to see Sarah, Biggs, and Cooper running toward us. The terrified look on Sarah's face as her eyes found the flames triggered my own fear, and my heart seemed to stop. "Where are the others?" I shrieked.

"Dave and Stacey were playing pool," Sanchez said hollowly.

In an instant, Jake was running toward the barracks…toward the flames…toward the death Harper had seen in his dreams.

Without thinking, I was up and running too. "No!" I heard someone scream as I chased after Jake. It wasn't until the second scream that I realized it was me.

"Someone grab Cooper!" Sanchez ordered, and her arms latched around my chest, ripping me to the ground. I struggled against her, but the more I resisted, the more physical she got, grappling with me on the gravel.

"Get off me!" I cried, but she ignored my demand.

From my uncomfortable vantage point, I watched a surreal scene play out. Cooper's fluffy tail hung low as he sprinted toward the barracks, following Jake. Harper grabbed the Husky and pulled him back, away from the blaze. In vain, I made a final attempt to break free from Sanchez's hold.

"Stop fighting me, Zoe! He'll be fine. He'll live!" she yelled, but I barely heard her.

I saw Jake open the main doors and immediately step to the side, hesitating. A ferocious ball of flames exploded through the doorway, seeming to reach for him. Instantly, I stopped fighting. Sanchez froze behind me, her arms and legs still tight around my body. The moment Jake lunged into the hungry flames, terror flooded my senses, paralyzing me. Although I hoped he would survive, I wasn't ignorant enough to think him immortal.

Dave's in there, too. Tears streamed down my cheeks as I thought of how scared he must be.

Something wet dripped on my shoulder, and I craned my neck to see Sanchez's face, expressionless as tears leaked from her eyes as well. Her grip on me loosened slightly, but I didn't move, feeling her sorrow. She'd mourned the loss of her friends who had died from the Virus. She'd mourned the team members who had fallen victim to the Crazies, and now she was mourning the innocents who were burning to death inside the building after having survived so much.

"I'm getting medical supplies," Harper yelled, running in the direction of the hospital.

Sarah, restraining Cooper by his collar, was sobbing in Biggs's arms. He held her like the universe was ending. His eyes were glassy and all color had drained from his horrorstruck face.

"Isn't there something we can do?" I asked Sanchez, taking a deep breath.

She shook her head. "No," she said helplessly.

I stood and started pacing back and forth, attempting to rein in my hysteria. Jake was probably going to die, and I was so angry at him—at myself—that I screamed.

"He'll live, Zoe," Sanchez said, trying to reassure me again, though I could feel her uncertainty.

After hesitating and looking back and forth at Sanchez and me, Biggs said, "She's gone," so quietly that I barely heard him over the roaring flames.

"What do you mean, Sergeant?" Sanchez asked, her face filled with dread.

"Sarah and I just checked on Clara. She wasn't in there," Biggs explained. "We saw the smoke…" He shook his head. "I should've taken a goddamn radio with me." Biggs looked back at the fire, and his eyes widened with realization. "It spread too quickly…shit, our fuel…" Biggs abruptly ran in the direction of our fuel supply.

Sanchez marched back and forth, completely mystified. "How can she be gone? I'm the only one with the goddamn key!"

Sarah watched Sanchez nervously. "The door to her cell was open," she said. "Somehow, someone let her out."

In the midst of our confusion, Cooper resumed barking and tugging against Sarah's hold, nearly tearing her arm from its socket.

"Don't let him go!" I yelled and pointed at Cooper before I took off running. I knew he'd sensed Jake before seeing him stagger out from behind the burning barracks. With a body flung over his shoulder, Jake barely took three steps around the corner of the building before falling to the ground. My legs carried me toward him faster as adrenaline took control.

Nearing him, I compared his sizzling body to the limp form beside him. Tanya was unconscious with sooty smudges on her face and clothes, while smoke was rising from Jake. His clothes had burned off, and he was covered in a patchwork of raw blisters, melted flesh, and charred, flaking skin.

"Oh my God, Jake!" I screamed. I reminded myself that he was different, that he of all people might be able to survive such severe burns, but his scorched flesh only bolstered my creeping doubts. *The gunshot wound healed,* I reminded myself. *But this is his whole body...*

"Harper! Someone! Help him!" I shouted, but Harper was nowhere in sight.

Falling to my knees, I held my hands over Jake, not knowing what to do. The stench of burnt meat assaulted the back of my nose and clung to my tongue. Trying to bridle the churning of my stomach, I searched in vain for an unmarred part of his body.

"Oh God," I breathed as I turned away. I vomited until there was nothing left in my stomach.

"Harper! Hurry! Please!" I begged, wiping my mouth with the back of my hand. My throat burned, and sweat and tears made my skin clammy.

As I sat on the ground, shaking, I noticed the spiral-bound corner of a singed book peeking out from beneath Tanya's legs—my sketchbook.

My heart felt swollen, and it was difficult to breathe. I thought my heart just might burst open and drown me in misery if I was never able to thank him. *You stupid, stupid man.*

38

DANI

Before the Virus, I'd never really thought about the world ending…at least the world as I knew it. If I had, I probably would've imagined complete anarchy. Well, the world ended, and there definitely were people handling the situation in a more predictable way—raping, murdering, stealing from other survivors—but not on our ranch. Structure and discipline were the backbone of *our* survivor lifestyle.

The morning after we ran into Mr. Grayson, we spent hours setting our schedule for the next several days. We were planning to leave for Colorado in a week, agreeing that horseback would be the most reliable mode of transportation. Mandatory riding lessons were assigned to the morning hours every day; we couldn't afford incompetence or ignorance.

"No! Holly! Pick a direction and stick to it!" I shouted from my perch atop Wings in the arena. Holly was jerking her horse's reins frantically, causing the creature to trot in a haphazard zigzag at her contradictory commands.

I jumped when a hand patted the outside of my thigh. "What—oh, Jason…" I stared at the hand that seemed to be searing its print onto my leg.

"About time to head over to Grayson's," Jason said.

"Now?" I peeked at my watch; it was noon. "Oh. I lost track of time."

"Come on," he said, sliding his hand up to my hip. "Hop down so I can suit you up."

Barely concealing a shiver, I swung my far leg over Wings's rear. I was grateful for the stability of Jason's grasp as I slid to the ground. He'd been watching over me like my own personal secret service since the internal freezing incident.

As soon as my feet touched the ground, he let go and led me into the stable. An array of knives, guns, and holsters were laid out on a workbench. As he helped me secure a thigh sheath over my jeans, I had to remind myself that he was touching me out of necessity, not desire. Regardless, my body trembled.

"Nervous?" Jason asked, glancing up as he tightened the final strap.

"Uh…"

"Don't be. It's just Grayson."

Swallowing roughly, I nodded and shrugged into my usual shoulder holster. I inspected my pistol just like Jason had taught me, checking the chamber, inserting a loaded magazine, chambering a round, and ensuring the safety was on. Even with all the deadly equipment, I looked innocent compared to the lethal badasses that Jason and Ky became. Ever since Dalton and Holly had a nearly fatal encounter with Crazies while hunting, we'd been entering *every* situation—even the most seemingly benign—prepared for combat.

We arrived at Mr. Grayson's house about ten minutes before our scheduled meeting. Briefly scouting the premises for Crazies, we found only soggy grass, dripping trees, shrubs, and a chattering squirrel.

At exactly one o'clock in the afternoon we knocked on the navy-blue front door. We'd left the horses in the backyard, hidden from the road, with instructions to alert me if they spotted any strangers.

"Ky, man, what's going on with you?" Jason asked. "You met the guy yesterday...he's totally harmless."

Ky's hand hovered near the sidearm at his hip, his eyes shifting incessantly. "I don't know. It just feels...something doesn't feel right. There's tension...and worry..." He trailed off, unable to find adequate words to describe whatever ominous sensations he was picking up.

"Right. Well...calm down, okay?" Jason said just before the door opened.

Mr. Grayson stood in the doorway, wearing the same type of wool cardigan he'd always worn in class, along with an unfamiliar expression of frustration. Two men flanked him—one exceptionally chunky, the other quite thin. Chunky held a shotgun, and Thin held a hunting rifle, though both weapons were aimed at the floor.

In one smooth motion, Jason stepped in front of me and drew his pistol, aiming it at Chunky. Ky drew his sidearm a split-second later, his sights on Thin. Of course, Mr. Grayson's thugs responded in kind. It was probably for the best that neither Jason nor Ky had chosen to wield the assault rifles strapped to their backs; Chunky and Thin didn't need further motivation to pull their triggers.

Shocked, I felt fiery anger flood my veins. *How could he set us up?* Immediately after thinking it, I knew the lanky, salt-and-pepper-haired man wouldn't betray us. His obvious frustration was starting to make sense.

"Mr. Grayson," I said calmly from behind Jason. I could feel Jason's tension and was worried any movement would trigger gunfire. "I'm sure this is all just a misunderstanding. We're not here to hurt you, like you're not here to hurt us...*right*?"

After a shaky deep breath, Mr. Grayson unfurrowed his brow. "As always, Danielle, you've seen to the heart of the matter. These fine young gentlemen are here, though unrequested, for my protection." He shot an angry glance at each of them and continued through clenched teeth, "Since I'm in no danger, they can *put away their weapons*." Each clearly enunciated word seemed to be aimed both at his bodyguards as well as at Jason and Ky.

All four armed men hastily lowered their guns, expressing embarrassment with hushed apologies.

"Now that that's over, please come in," Mr. Grayson said, holding his arm out as he stepped away from the doorway. "I have tea and coffee prepared in the kitchen. If you would, just seat yourselves at the table."

An armed standoff followed by tea and coffee...how civilized, I thought, stifling an extremely inappropriate giggle.

Once I was seated at the table with Jason to my right and Ky to my left, I took a moment to examine Mr. Grayson's bodyguards, wondering if they were people I used to know as well. They weren't.

After inquiring, Mr. Grayson served Jason and Ky coffee and made me a cup of tea. He prepared the same for himself and sat in a chair opposite us at the round, walnut table. Apparently satisfied that we wouldn't hurt their charge, the other two men disappeared to some other part of the house.

"It's best if you save your questions until the end of this tale," Mr. Grayson said, his voice sure and resonant like that of an ancient bard. "Otherwise I might leave out something important. Agreed?"

The three of us nodded. I was eager to listen to his rendition of the past month's happenings in our sleepy hometown. Based on Jason's barely discernible expression, he shared my anticipation. Ky, on the other hand, just looked at us, confused. He'd never experienced a riveting history lesson delivered by one of the region's most-loved teachers.

Leaning forward, Mr. Grayson intertwined his leathery fingers and rested his hands on the table. "It was the last week of November when we first noticed people catching the Virus. Our numbers of infected seemed on par with the rest of the West Coast, and we weren't worried. By the end of that week, we'd lost one person—an infant, the first to be infected in Bodega Bay. Sad as it was to lose a life barely started, we still weren't worried. Infants and the elderly are the easiest prey for any flu." He shook his head softly, a small, sad smile deepening the creases around his mouth.

"Entering the first week of December, our town rode on a wave of forced normalcy and departed in a torrent of uncontrolled despair. Most of the young and elderly were dead or dying. From the increasingly sporadic reliable news reports, we gathered that the same had happened everywhere else along the West Coast, if not the whole country. Maybe even the world.

"Eighty percent of the town's population had succumbed to the Virus by mid-December, and news from the outside had essentially stopped. A new town council formed by the end of the third week. The council was composed of nine elected members, including me, and we began creating a plan to help the town's remaining 247 residents survive in this changed world. For a few days, it went well. Everyone was eager to help, willing to fulfill any role they were assigned. We were getting by.

"By the end of the third week, we started noticing a couple of strange developments: first, some people were displaying unusual talents, and second, others were exhibiting a lack of emotional control and various symptoms of insanity. Some abnormal behavior is, of course, acceptable in such extreme situations, but this was far beyond that." He flexed his fingers, creating white splotches on the backs of his hands.

"After the first few people displaying unusual talents were verbally attacked and ostracized by townsfolk—labeled as 'freaks'—everyone started keeping to themselves. Some of the emotionally unstable survivors tried rallying others against the 'freaks,' leading to five violent deaths. Our population was down to 242. After that incident, few people were willing to help with the town's survival planning. Instead they chose to stay in their homes, defending themselves and their remaining family members, and keeping any new talents a secret. They'd only venture out to attend the nightly town meetings." He paused, locking eyes with each of us.

"That all changed on Christmas Eve. The Town Council put together a holiday feast, hoping to create a feeling of community and camaraderie that might help alleviate the recent tensions. Only seventy-four people, a fraction of the remaining townsfolk, showed up. Those present worried about many of their absent friends—people who'd expressed an interest in attending the event. Before eating, we set out in groups to check on the homes of the missing families. What we found was almost too horrible to comprehend.

"Half of the houses were empty, while the others were occupied by the remains of ghastly atrocities. We called it the Christmas Eve Massacre, in remembrance of those who were murdered. You see, it was the occupants of the empty houses who committed the heinous acts, ripping apart thirty-five of the flu Survivors. We don't know why they did it; we only know who they are. We call them the Lost Ones.

"The sane town members, now numbering seventy-four, have relocated to the most defensible position in town—the boats moored at Sand Point Marina. We keep watchmen out at all times and usually travel outside of the defended area only in armed groups. Every person has memorized the names and faces of the 107 remaining Lost Ones. If seen, they are killed if possible and avoided if not.

"Now," Mr. Grayson said, separating his hands and splaying them palm down on the table, "we'd like to invite you and your people to join us at our town meeting tomorrow evening. Due to the many tasks we must attend to during the day, it doesn't begin until half past seven, so I'm afraid you'll be required to travel to and from the marina in the dark. Even so, I sincerely hope you'll attend." He settled back in his chair, folding his hands and resting them on his lap.

Shaken from the spell woven by his hypnotic voice, I was able to feel the cool wetness of tears streaking down my face. I was also able to feel Jason's strong fingers intertwined with mine, our joined hands dangling in the space between our chairs. I met Jason's eyes briefly, and upon seeing the raw horror and sorrow they contained, tightened my grip. An awful thing had happened to *our* town—to *our* people—and there was nothing we could do about it.

"Do you have any questions?" Grayson asked, breaking through the lingering fog of emotion.

At a complete loss for words, I shook my head.

"Thank you, Sir, for telling us this"—Jason paused—"this news. We'll definitely increase our defenses. And yes, some of us will attend your meeting tomorrow night. I'm sure we'll have plenty of questions by then."

Mr. Grayson nodded.

"Now," Jason said, his eyes again meeting mine, "we should be going." He gave my hand one last squeeze and gently placed it on my knee.

I looked from my hand to Jason to Mr. Grayson, and my head finally cleared. "Wait!" I blurted. "Do you think…maybe…could we borrow some of your books? There are still so many things we can learn to have a better chance at survival."

"Oh yes, I forgot. Of course, Danielle. I set aside a handful of books for you based on the ones you pulled and left here yesterday. They're on the table by the door. And please"—he stood and held his hand out toward the rooms full of bookshelves—"take any others you think you could use."

Filled with unexpected relief, I bounced out of my chair, ran around the table, and flung my arms around my former teacher. "It's so good to see you, Mr. G," I said, a hitch in my voice. "I'm glad you're not dead."

Mr. Grayson gently patted my back. "And I, you, Miss. O'Connor."

"Hey there Scrubby D," Ky said as he entered the kitchen.

I was in the middle of an assault on a stack of mismatched ceramic dishes that were slathered with a stubborn layer of baked beans—tasty, but eerily similar to stucco once it dried. Since I was moderately lethal in the cooking department, I usually ended up with dish duty. Honestly, I didn't mind.

"Hey there, Special K," I replied, cringing at my own lameness.

"Special K? Really? I'm cereal? Is that all I am to you?" he teased.

I spared him an eye roll and continued scrubbing.

Ky hopped up to sit on the tiled counter a few feet away. "We need to talk, D."

"About what?" I asked.

"You tell me. You're the one sending out the anxiety vibes."

I ignored him, scrubbing with renewed vigor.

He leaned toward me like he was preparing to tell me a secret. "Holly and Jason are sitting by the fireplace right now. Together," he told me. "They're even whispering…"

What? If he has sex with her I'll kick him in the balls. Repeatedly!

"You do realize you just said that in my head, right?"

"Did not."

"Yep…you said, 'What? If he has sex with her I'll—'"

"Okay! Fine!" I accidentally dropped my latest clean plate back into the dirty water. "So what if I did?" I grumbled, picking the plate back up.

Ky laughed. "So…you can't control your telepathy. You're talking in people's minds when you don't mean to. If certain people hear certain things, then a certain *you* will be very embarrassed. Just saying."

"Oh." I'd known my telepathy was far from under control, but I hadn't known that stray thoughts were leaking out. "Sorry?"

"Come on, D. Let Chris help. She's itching to get her invisible little fingers in your brain. She just won't ask 'cause she's, you know, polite and shit."

"That's creepy."

He shrugged. "You trust her, right?"

"Of course."

"So let her help."

I thought about it. Learning to control my Ability could be invaluable. It could give us a way to contact Zoe, something becoming increasingly important as our departure neared, especially considering that MG had apparently gone AWOL from my dreams. Of course, it could also save me from some horribly embarrassing moments. "Fine."

"You sure? Your anxiety just spiked," he informed me, rubbing his temples with his fingers. "It kind of feels like you're gonna make a run for it."

"I said 'fine,' didn't I?" I snapped. I felt a twinge of guilt for taking my grouchiness out on Ky, especially since my anxiety seemed to be giving him a headache…literally.

"Cool," he said, hopping down from the counter. "I'll tell Chris."

As he left the kitchen, I grabbed a discolored blue bowl and attacked it with the scrub brush. "This'll be *awesome*," I muttered.

Trying to ignore the impending brain torture, I lost myself in the monotony of washing dishes. It was both therapeutic and finger-wrinkling. Eventually, I placed the last dish in the drying rack, drained the dishwater, and washed my hands. When I turned away from the sink, I nearly screamed. Chris was lounging in the chair at the far end of the rectangular, oak kitchen table.

My left hand flew to my chest. "Chris! How long've you been sitting there?"

"Don't know…maybe fifteen minutes," she said, pursing her lips as she studied me. "I'm going to test you. JASON!"

Within seconds, Jason strolled in and leaned his shoulder against the doorframe. "Need something?"

"Yes." Chris pointed to a chair at the opposite end of the table. "Sit. Dani's letting me test her telepathy. Let's see…I think it'll work best if we have you knock on the table each time you hear a full thought from our girl."

Jason's eyes shifted to me, seeming to ask for permission, before he gave a single nod and straightened. He walked across the room and eased his powerful body into the empty chair at the head of the table.

Chris looked at me and explained, "I have a few theories about your…what'd you call it? Oh yeah, your *Ability*. Anyway, I want to test my theories. I'm going to write down a list of sentences and then give the list to you. I want *you* to point to each sentence as you read it so I know which one you're on…and read silently. And don't read ahead. I want you to send *only* the underlined parts to Jason's mind, okay?"

"Got it," I said, moving to sit in the chair nearest Chris.

She took a few minutes to scribble the words in a notebook, underlining select parts as she went, and eventually tore the sheet from the book. She scooted her chair closer to mine and handed me the paper.

"Okay, I'm also going to be paying attention to what's going on in your brain while you're doing this. Go ahead," she told me, her pen poised over a blank notebook page. I felt like the subject of a bizarre psychology experiment as I looked at the sheet of paper.

My name is Dani O'Connor.

Zoe is my best friend, and I miss her.

Puppies are adorable.

Puppies are disgusting and ugly.

This is the end of the world.

Why did so many people have to die?

I promise not to run off again without Jason and Chris, even if a crazy psycho slut bitch is threatening me.

Jason is absolutely gorgeous.

If he sleeps with Holly I might have to kill her.

I love him!

I read the first two lines silently, projecting my thoughts to Jason; he knocked twice. I successfully sent—or refrained from sending—the next three lines, receiving a snort *and* a knock when I told him that puppies were disgusting and ugly.

When I read the sixth line about people dying, images of Cam, dead, filled my thoughts. I felt so much guilt—guilt for surviving when he hadn't, guilt for leaving him to die alone, and guilt for having feelings for Jason. It didn't matter that I'd *always* had feelings for him. After receiving four knocks from Jason, I wondered exactly what my stupid mind had sent to him. I glanced at him just as he rubbed the back of his neck. *Not good...*

I delivered the seventh line according to plan, but the final three were a mortifying mess. I clutched onto the "Jason is absolutely gorgeous" line desperately—against Chris's wishes—but accidentally sent the following line about him sleeping with Holly. When he knocked, making a coughing, choking sound, I wanted to crawl under the table.

With flaming cheeks, I tried not to send the final line—*I love him*—to Jason. I refused to look at him, instead glaring at Chris. She was cracking up. I cursed her for including those final three words.

"Oh my God...too funny..." Still laughing, Chris pointed to the *Jason is absolutely gorgeous* line. "You didn't say that one in his head, even though you were supposed to." She pointed to the *If he sleeps with Holly* line. "But you said that one."

I hoped the universe had a sense of decency and that Jason truly hadn't heard the last sentence.

"What'd she say that made you knock four times in a row?" Chris asked after she'd quieted her laughter.

When Jason didn't respond, I looked at him. He was watching me with a blank expression.

"Well?" Chris prompted.

Jason cleared his throat. "She said," he began, but stopped, leaning across the table and grabbing Chris's notepad and pen. He scrawled several lines quickly, tore out the paper, folded it, and handed it to Chris. "That," he said, his voice rough. Without another glance in my direction, he stood and left the kitchen.

Chris unfolded the paper, read it several times, then crumpled it up in her left hand.

"What's it say?" I asked, frustrated. *Shouldn't I know my own thoughts?*

"You really want to know?"

"Of course I do! It came from *my* head!"

Chris placed the wadded-up paper on the table in front of me. "Fine. But don't make it a bigger deal than it is, okay? I'm sure he doesn't even know who you're talking about; he can be unbelievably dense. Though, everything might just be easier if he knew exactly how much..."

With shaking fingers, I smoothed out the paper and read silently:

Why did Cam have to die? I loved him! I told him I'd stay with him. Why am I feeling like this about someone else?

I studied the thoughts I'd sent to Jason, written in his sharp, slanted handwriting, trying to force them out of his memory and back into my head. His abrupt exit suddenly made perfect sense.

I tore up the paper and grumbled, "Dammit...stupid, crappy brain..."

Chris, who'd started writing furiously in her notebook, paused to peer at me. "Stop that," she scolded. "We learned a bunch of things about your Ability. You can lie—that could be really useful. Your emotions can hijack it, but we already kind of knew that. I wonder what makes it possible for someone to talk back?" She stopped speaking, and furrowed her brow. "Did you hear me say that?" she asked eagerly.

"I didn't hear anything you didn't say out loud," I told her, much to her disappointment. Apparently she'd been attempting to mind-talk.

"Hmmm...well...," she mumbled, making notes. "So it's not that..."

"I'm kind of tired. Do you still need me?" I asked, standing.

She stopped writing and looked up. "What? No. I wonder if...maybe..."

Leaving Chris to her mad scientist mutterings, I slinked from the room. Being a guinea pig was exhausting, and I could feel a mild chill settling into my body. As I tiptoed to the bathroom to wash up for bed, I begged the universe to have mercy on me. *Please don't let me run into Jason!*

For once, the universe obliged.

39

ZOE

Contentment settled over me as unfamiliar, snow-covered mountains appeared in the distance. They lined the horizon, and the green needles of spruces and pines peeked from under winter's blanket.

A young girl's voice carried from within the dense tree line. "Where are you?"

My attention shifted to a treeless hillside, where snow crunched under a young man's footsteps as he trudged uphill. "I'm over here!" he called. "Hurry up!" It was Jake—I could tell by the rumbling timbre of his voice and the tinge of impatience it so often carried. The sun shone down on him, making his damp forehead glisten.

The girl's laughter echoed as she emerged from the trees at the foot of the hill. She looked about eleven years old, with coffee-brown braids framing her round, flushed cheeks. Her eagerness to catch up with Jake was that of a little sister, and I realized I was watching him with Becca.

"You're going too fast," she whined.

"If you wanna know what it is, you gotta work for it," Jake

yelled as she trekked up the hill behind him. I moved closer to him and could see the amusement lighting his eyes.

"What's all this about, anyway?" she asked, huffing as she hurried to catch up with her brother.

"It's just over here. We're almost there." Reaching a clearing at the top of the hill, Jake paused and looked back at Becca.

"Holy moly! That's a steep one," she said, taking dramatically deep breaths as she joined her brother.

With a smile, Jake motioned her to the crest of the hill, and they looked down at the children playing below.

"So this is where they always go," she said solemnly. There was a sadness in her eyes I didn't understand.

"Becca!" A young girl shouted and waved from the bottom of the slope. A tall, blond young man around Jake's age stood behind her, smiling as he nodded at Jake.

Becca's frown was replaced with a broad grin at the sight of her friends. She looked over at her brother and exclaimed, "It's Lizzie and Gabe!"

"Yep," Jake said. "You should go join them."

Her face scrunched in disappointment. "You think Lizzie'll let me use her sled?"

"Why don't you use your own?" he asked with a smirk, but Becca was too distracted by the playing children to notice.

She furrowed her brow. "Helllooo...it's broken. That's why I didn't bring it. You know James and Kristy won't get me a new one."

"What about that one?" Jake asked, pointing to an improvised sled resting against the lone tree to the left of them.

Becca's eyes brightened. "You made *me one?!" she shrieked and ran to it. "Why? I mean, what's it for?" Standing the sled on its side, she studied it excitedly.*

"Your birthday...duh."

"Umm, sorry to break it to you, Jake, but that's still four months away." Becca's eyes focused on part of the sled, and she

gasped. She leaned closer and said, "You used your skateboard... and are those skis?"

"My skateboard was old," he said with a shrug and shoved his hands into his pockets; he seemed to revel in his sister's surprise. "I found the skis. Consider it an early birthday gift."

Becca didn't blink as she inspected every inch of the makeshift sled. "But you love this thing. I can't believe you used it."

"Whatever, don't worry about it," he said. "You've been complaining all winter about not having a sled. Just enjoy it."

Her smile widened, and she ran to him, stood on her tiptoes, and threw her arms around his neck. "Thank you, Jake," she giggled. "You're the best brother...even better than Gabe."

"I should be better than him," he laughed. "I'm blood."

Suddenly, the world turned to night, and I was standing in the shadows of a dark forest. No longer blanketed with snow, the ground was instead covered with a carpet of pine needles. There was the distant sound of a dog barking, and beside me, the crackle of forest debris.

I turned and looked down at the ground. A large body was stirring, struggling to sit up.

I took a step closer. It was Jake again—no longer a teenager—completely stunned as he scanned the area around him, trying to orient himself in the dark, imposing forest. Midnight shadows blackened his eyes as he listened...waiting.

The dog barked again, and with a jolt, Jake tried to stand. He lurched forward onto his hands and cursed in pain. Reaching an arm behind him, his fingers found the hilt of a knife protruding from below his left shoulder blade. He froze in a moment of both confusion and understanding.

"Bennington! You son of a bitch," he rasped.

Twisting his arm further behind him, Jake groaned and wrapped his fingers around the knife's handle. He struggled to pull the blade from between his ribs and roared in pain. After a long, painful moment, he used a tree for leverage and gradually climbed to his feet, letting the combat knife fall from his hand. It landed on the ground with a muffled thud, and his hands clenched at his sides.

Spotting a handgun lying on the ground near his left boot, he struggled to bend down and pick it up. Shoving it in the waistband of his pants, Jake stumbled toward the distant barking.

"Cooper!" he yelled, and his steps faltered.

Almost instantly, the forest disappeared, and a room coalesced in its place. It was illuminated solely by a floor lamp that stood in the corner between a leather couch and an antique secretary desk. Becca, now a grown woman, stood in front of the desk, facing Jake —her nearly violet eyes familiar yet resolved to do something unthinkable.

"Gabe promised they won't hurt you," Jake said, a pleading look in his eyes. "Come on, Becca. We'll figure this out, but we need their help."

Hands behind her back, she shook her head slowly. As she did, the ends of her mussed, dark hair brushed her collarbone.

Uncertainty gnawed at Jake. He didn't trust the military men fanned out behind him, assault rifles at their sides. But he desperately wanted to trust Gabe, his closest friend.

Becca blinked, her lips parted in a slight smile, and she pulled her hands out from behind her nightgown. Her fingers were wrapped around the handle of a long, slim kitchen knife. Without hesitation, she rammed the blade into her stomach, angling it up into her heart. Her legs gave out instantly, and she crumpled to the floor. A mixture of pain and relief twisted her delicate features.

What followed seemed to happen in a single second. Jake fell to the floor beside his sister's writhing body with tears in his eyes. Becca coughed as she tried to speak, blood staining her teeth. I strained to hear her, but her words were inaudible to me.

Spinning around, I looked at the four men standing behind me. Three of them aimed their rifles at Jake, who was still crouched on the floor. Beyond them, Gabe stood in the doorway, his face horror-stricken. He wore fatigues like the other three men, but he wielded no weapon.

Hunched over Becca's now motionless form, Jake was shaking. "Get them out of here!" he yelled. "You knew! You lied to me!"

"I didn't...," Gabe choked out. "She needed help."

Stirring from sleep, I opened my eyes to see the stark walls of one of the trauma rooms surrounding me. I'd unintentionally fallen asleep at Jake's bedside. His burned and bandaged body was lying to my right. Harper stood on the other side of the bed, checking Jake's vitals.

As I sat up, I gently released Jake's bandaged hand from my grasp. I stretched, and Cooper, asleep at my feet, stirred from his slumber.

"How's he doing?" I asked Harper, my voice only a whisper.

He peered at me with tired eyes and rubbed the scruff on his face. Softly, he said, "Hey Baby Girl, I thought you were asleep."

"I was, but he's dreaming. It makes it hard to sleep."

"Slow-wave sleep...that's a good thing," Harper assured me.

"So, he's doing better?" I wondered how it was possible for Jake to heal—any normal person burned so badly wouldn't have survived.

Harper sighed and observed his patient for a moment. "Yes, but it's hard to tell *how* much better. It's only been a handful of hours. I've never really seen burns like these...not to mention had a patient with the potential to heal so quickly." Harper paused, deep in thought. "I'm not sure what to expect."

Glancing down at his clipboard, Harper assessed his notes. "His heart rate is still slower than I'd like, but he's stable and apparently dreaming. I'm just trying to keep him hydrated and as pain-free as possible at this point." Harper looked at Jake. "He's going to have to do the rest."

Jake was having another brief moment of semi-consciousness,

and I could feel his sudden rush of panic and misery. *He's in pain...but at least his pain means he's still alive...*

"Can we give him more morphine?" I asked as Cooper rose and rested his head on my knee, his ears perked forward and his doggy eyebrows raised. I absentmindedly scratched the back of his neck.

Harper looked from me to Jake. "Is his pain getting bad again?"

Nodding, I repositioned myself in the chair beside the bed. I hadn't left Jake's side since Sanchez and Harper bandaged him up. It didn't matter that my clothes were dirty or that my hair was a tangled mess from struggling against Sanchez on the ground. Time seemed to have slowed after the fire, hours feeling like days. "What time is it, H?"

"Late. You should clean up and get some rest—real rest. I'll stay with him," he offered, injecting more morphine into the in-line of Jake's IV.

By the smell of smoke lingering on me, I knew it was time for a shower. "Alright. Are we using the locker room downstairs?"

"Yep. There are scrubs you can put on for now," Harper said, jotting something down on his clipboard. Yawning, he sat in a chair on the other side of the bed.

"Do you wanna grab some coffee or something first?" I asked. "I'll stay with him until you get back."

"Good call." Harper stood, yawning again. "I'll be right back."

I gave him a sympathetic smile as he left. My face felt swollen and dry, and my eyes burned. As I watched Jake's chest rise and fall, I wondered if he could hear us talking. Cautiously, I leaned in so I was closer to his head.

"Jake," I whispered. "I'm really pissed at you. I can't believe you did this...and I can't believe you rescued my stupid sketch-book. What made you think—" I shook my head. "You better not have gone back for it or something ridiculous like that." I struggled to hold onto my irritation, knowing that if I could stay frustrated with him, then I still had hope he would survive. "We can argue about that later," I promised.

Tears blurred my vision. "Tanya didn't make it," I continued quietly. "Dave and Stacey are gone too, but you probably already knew that. We'll have a burial for everyone before we leave, at least that's what Sanchez said. We're leaving as soon as you get a little better. It's not safe here with Clara out there…somewhere," I explained.

Cooper yawned and I glanced down at him. "Coop's watching over us," I said and smiled. "Anyway, after we stock up at the PX again, we're heading west to Sarah's house. We'll be safer there until you're fully recovered."

A giant lump grew in my throat as I thought about what Clara had done. "How could she do this? I just don't understand." At the thought of Dave and our other friends' suffering, I wiped away a tear.

I stood and started pacing to settle my nerves, but questions still tainted my thoughts. "I should've known *something*. I've been practicing. After she poisoned me, I started listening to everything." I was frustrated that all my practice had been for nothing. "I don't understand."

Recalling what Biggs had said about Clara's escape—that her cell had been unlocked—I tried to think of a solution. "Who let her out? Who *would*? None of us would've. Did she somehow force someone to do it?" My mind raced…too many questions, too few answers.

"Take a break, Zoe." Sanchez's voice echoed in my head as I heard her footsteps in the hall. She paused in the doorway, looking comfortable in baggy scrubs, and her wet hair was pulled back into a ponytail.

"Where's Harper," I asked.

"He was falling asleep standing up, so I told him to get some down time." Sanchez walked into the room and took a seat on the other side of the bed. "Go ahead and get cleaned up, I'll watch him."

I looked at Jake once more, told myself I couldn't do anything to make him heal any faster, and made my way downstairs to the locker room. Digging through a stack of clean scrubs, I searched for something that might fit me. Finally settling on a mismatched set—a blue top and green pants—I headed for the showers.

Although the hot water was soothing, I didn't revel in it as I usually would. I was in a daze. *Dave's dead.* I couldn't prevent myself from imagining his final moments. *Did he burn to death? Was it the smoke? Was Stacey with him, or was he alone?* My chest felt heavy at the thought of him dying alone.

We all *could've died today*. Even under the warm water, the realization made me shiver.

My head was still pounding from the earlier barrage of other people's emotions—terror, sorrow, guilt, relief—and from witnessing Jake's dreams. *Embrace it, Zoe. You're alive.* I ran my fingers through my soapy hair. As it fanned down my lower back, I considered whether cutting if off would be more…practical.

After I'd finished showering, braided my hair, and dressed, I headed back upstairs toward one of the empty hospital rooms Sarah had readied for us, only stopping when I heard Biggs's muffled voice coming from behind a metal door. I tiptoed closer to the door and leaned in to listen.

"…to make a choice. We can't do both; we lost too much fuel in the fire," Biggs said.

Harper grumbled something indiscernible. More loudly, he said, "Then we have to go, 'cause we sure as hell can't stay here."

"But how do we move him?" Biggs's voice sounded concerned, and he seemed to have a hard time saying his next words. "Will he even make it?"

"Shit…I have no idea," Harper said.

The sound of someone kicking something startled me.

"He should be fine, assuming he regenerates fast enough. But I haven't seen much of a change yet. I don't know how fast it works or how thoroughly he'll recover."

As I processed their conversation, I wondered how we would get Jake anywhere without hurting him. Because Jones and Taylor had sabotaged all the vehicles we'd found on base, our options were limited—all we had at our disposal was the van Jake had fixed…and Dave's truck. *The police cruiser's too small to be useful.*

"I wish I had better news," Biggs mumbled. "Sanchez thinks we should leave tomorrow at first light."

Not wanting to hear any more, I continued on toward the prepared rooms and didn't stop until I reached a bed. Lying down, my body surrendered to sleep almost instantly.

After a couple hours of restless dreams and another few of prepping to leave, I helped Sarah load our meager belongings into the vehicles. The black van would transport Jake, bandaged and unconscious.

"I'm sort of worried about finding my folks," Sarah admitted as we loaded Harper's medical supplies into the back of the van.

Seeing movement out of the corner of my eye, I jumped. *It's just a bird.* Not knowing Clara's whereabouts was making me paranoid, but I felt safer when I spotted Cooper trotting over to us.

Sarah seemed oblivious to my skittishness and continued, "I mean, I've come to terms with the fact that they're probably dead, but I don't want to *find* them."

I'd pretty much come to the same conclusion about my dad. Sympathetic, I tried to reassure her. "We'll check the house for you, Sarah. You won't have to see anything. I wouldn't want you to remember them that way." *I wouldn't want to remember Dad that way...*

She smiled gratefully. "Did you ever figure out what happened to your dad?" It was like she'd read my mind.

Frowning, I shook my head.

"What about your mom?"

I shrugged. "She died a long time ago. I never really think about her," I lied.

"Oh," was all Sarah said in response. We didn't talk about our parents anymore after that, but I could still feel her apprehension about returning home.

"By the way, thanks for letting us stay at your house. It means a lot to me, especially now...with Jake..."

Lost in thought, Sarah chewed on her lip. Her shame tickled my consciousness. "Zoe, do you ever think about Jordan?"

I shook my head guiltily, but then I reined in my emotions; thinking of the departed was gone was a slippery slope of misery I wasn't willing to slide down. I tucked the last case of medicine into the van, and we walked back into the hospital.

"Really? I haven't either...not that I don't care. I just feel like so much is going on, and I haven't had much time to stop and think about it." She paused. "I feel bad."

I nudged her as we trudged through the emergency room doors. "I think that's normal."

"Maybe it's our mind's way of protecting us," Sarah said wistfully.

"Yeah, probably," I agreed. "Let's see if they need any help moving Jake."

She nodded, and we headed toward the trauma room. When we arrived, Harper and Biggs were still packing up a few things, so we stood beside Jake's bed and waited. My eyes wandered to the charred cover of the sketchbook lying on the bedside table. I still hadn't opened it.

Sarah followed my line of sight. "There's tons of drawing stuff at my house. You're welcome to it," she offered. "My dad used to draw a lot."

I felt an unexpected sense of relief. "Thanks, Sarah. That'd be great."

She watched the sketchbook like it might do a trick. "It's…sort of amazing that he rescued that from the fire."

"I just hope he makes it so I can ask him why," I said, shaking my head.

"He will, Zoe. Biggs told me about his healing thing. What makes the burns any different from the bullet wound?" *Or the knife wound…*

I stared at Jake's gauze-wrapped body. "I guess it's just that, well, it's hard to imagine someone surviving something like this. Don't you think?"

"Of course," she said, "but people are changing. I'm not sure we can count on anything we used to think was normal."

I nodded.

"Besides, I think you know why."

My brow furrowed, and I glanced at her. "Why what?"

"Why he saved your sketchbook." Sarah gave me a knowing smirk. "He *likes* you," she sang.

I couldn't help but smile back at her. "Thank you, Sarah." I hoped she knew how grateful I was for her friendship over the past month. Though her presence used to annoy me, I'd come to rely on it.

Nudging me, she said, "You'd do the same for me."

40

DANI

Closing the lime-green journal I'd been using as a stand-in for writing to Zoe for over a week, I set it on the coffee table, stood, and stretched. I had so much to tell her if—*when*—we finally met up in Colorado: *I'm telepathic, MG is real, there are a bunch of survivors in Bodega Bay...*

I shook my head and felt a slight smile curve my lips. It still awed me that dozens of people from my home town had survived. Seeing and speaking with them at the town meeting last night had been amazing. And what Mr. Grayson told us after the meeting was equally incredible: he would be coming with us. Zoe was going to be so excited when she saw him. Frowning, I thought, *And then I'll burst her bubble by telling her about her dad.* I sighed, dreading that moment even though it was still many weeks away.

Aside from the gentle glow of the fireplace set in the adjacent wall, my cozy, makeshift bedroom was dark, befitting my souring mood. We kept the fires going pretty much all hours of the day; we had a huge stockpile of wood, so there really wasn't a reason not to. Plus, it was cold, and the rain hadn't stopped for two days.

Feeling restless, I snuck down the dark hallway to the kitchen in search of a midnight snack. Two steps into the room, I paused. I'd assumed everyone was asleep. I'd been wrong. Along with the faint orange glow from the great room's fireplace, the murmur of hushed voices was sneaking under the closed door at the far side of the kitchen.

I couldn't help but listen in. My inner snoop needed to eavesdrop on the secret conversation taking place beyond that door. Carefully, I tiptoed closer.

Jason's voice became clear as I approached. "...you. I'm not interested in her like that." *Her? Her, who? Me?*

I wasn't surprised when Chris responded; they almost always spent the late night hours strategizing together. "Well, *she's* definitely interested in *you* like that. You should clear up this little misunderstanding before we end up with another difficult situation. Think about it...we can't risk Dani going off on her own again just because you have women issues." *They* are *talking about me!*

"She said she wouldn't!" Jason snapped. *And I won't! Crap! Shut up thoughts! Crap! Stay in my head!*

"Oh come on, Jason. Don't be so dense. This is exactly the kind of thing that could push her over the edge." After a long pause, Chris added, "We may not be able to find her next time."

Jason's response was too quiet for me to hear.

"You're an arrogant ass, you know," Chris told him.

Ignoring her, Jason said, "I don't have women issues."

Chris snorted softly. "Jason, you've had women issues since the day I met you, and you always will. It's just who you are. Talk to her, soon...while it's still manageable."

"Fine," he said. "I'll do it tomorrow." *Not if I don't let him...*

Having heard enough to make my chest ache, I hurried on silent feet back to my room and crawled under the blankets on the couch. I couldn't believe he'd kissed me—had been nearly naked in a bathtub with me—but wasn't interested. *How could I have been so stupid to think any of that mattered?* He'd been exceptionally distant since I'd rejoined the group, even when he was standing right beside me. *Open your eyes, Dani...he doesn't care.*

Slow, tormenting hours passed before I finally fell into a fitful sleep. For once, my dreams were completely devoid of both rotting Cam *and* my friendly dream invader. Instead my night was filled with nightmares of falling and drowning. I blamed Jason.

When I woke, I felt like a piece of Jack's poo. My poor dog had spent most of the night whimpering softly on the floor beside the couch, staring up at me with worried eyes.

"Hon, you look like shit," Chris told me as I sat beside her in front of the great room's fireplace. Grumpily, I wondered if she was sitting in the same place as she had been when she told Jason to "clear up this little misunderstanding" with me.

"Tell me about it," I grumbled. Zoning out, I watched her stir thick oatmeal in an iron pot on the fire.

During my morning hygiene routine, I'd done everything I could to mask the havoc wreaked by my restless night—my hair was a tangled mess that I'd managed to wrangle into a braid, and dark circles shadowed my eyes. To top it off, I'd run into Jason four times in the forty minutes since I'd left my room. I was pretty sure the encounters were intentional, probably so he could get the "clearing up" over with. Like a real adult, I fled every time I saw him.

His latest attempt to waylay me had come as I'd entered the great room. I'd scurried away and sought shelter next to Chris.

"What was that all about?" Chris asked, motioning in Jason's direction with her elbow. He was leaning against the doorframe, blocking almost the entire doorway as he pretended not to watch me. His arms were crossed, and there was a crease between his eyebrows.

"What?" I asked, aiming for innocence.

Apparently my wide eyes and parted mouth didn't fool Chris. She snorted. "You totally just shunned Jason. Why're you avoiding him?"

Pulling up my knees, I hugged them to my chest. "Maybe I don't want to hear what he has to say."

"Why? You don't want to visit your house?"

"What?" I asked sharply.

"He's going to his dad's place to look through some things and thought you might want to go with him." She frowned. "You know, stop by your grandma's…since we're leaving in a few days and all…"

"But I thought—" I snapped my mouth shut before I could reveal my late-night clandestine activities.

"You thought *what*?"

"Nothing," I said too quickly. My face burned with embarrassment, and part of me wanted to jump into the fire to avoid saying anything else.

"Right. Tell me, or I'll pick you up and carry you over to him myself," Chris threatened.

"Fine," I grumbled. "I sort of…*overheard* you two talking last night."

As she stared at me, I could almost hear the conversation replaying in her mind. She was slowly shaking her head, not understanding what I was getting at.

I pursed my lips. "He said he wasn't interested in me, and you said he needed to 'clear things up' before I get upset and take off again—which won't happen, by the way. He was right about that. At least *he* trusts me."

To my abject mortification, Chris barked a laugh. "I was telling him to clear things up with *Holly*, you ninny. I was worried she'd turn into another Cece, obsessing over him like an idiot." She snorted. "She's already halfway there."

Breathless, I felt like my heart was about to explode. "Oh, I thought…I didn't know she was so into him. I mean, I knew she was into him, just not as much as, um, other people."

Chris watched me with a small smile tugging at her lips. "Other people? Who could you possibly mean?" she asked, batting her eyelashes.

"I don't know," I mumbled. "Just…people."

"Oh!" she said, smacking her palm against her forehead in mock surprise. "You must be referring to the 'other people' I'm talking to right now!"

I blushed furiously and glanced at Jason. He was still leaning against the doorframe, and I was desperately hoping our voices were quiet enough to be drowned out by the crackling of the fire.

"You should talk to him…*alone*," Chris told me.

"Why? What if…I don't know…" Joy and misery mixed into a heavy lump that settled in my stomach. Was it possible that Jason had actually developed feelings akin to mine, that he was interested in me? That he desired me? It was something I'd written off for so long that I had a hard time allowing myself to consider the possibility, even after the kiss. I felt like hyperactive butterflies had taken up residence in my chest.

"Just do it," Chris said, ladling oatmeal into a bowl. She shoved the dish into my hands. "The sugar and stuff's on the table over there. By Jason. Convenient, don't you think?"

I tried to smile my thanks, but I probably looked more like I was about to be sick. With shaking hands, I carried the steaming bowl to the table and set it down. I took a deep breath and faced Jason, who loomed casually a few paces away.

"Dani."

"Jason," I said breathily, voicing his name more like a caress than the curt greeting I'd intended. *God, I'm pathetic…*

"Why've you been…never mind. I'm going to my dad's soon. Do you want to come? We could stop by your house too."

I couldn't believe it; Chris had been right. Part of me had still expected him to crush my heart by telling me my infatuation was hopeless.

"Um...yeah. I'd like that," I said, sounding like I was accepting an offer for dinner and a movie.

He stared at me for a few seconds, face blank, and then said, "When'll you be ready?"

"I just need to eat...and get my weapons...and saddle the horses, so..."

"I can take care of the horses."

My eyebrows raised of their own accord.

"What? I'm a quick learner," he said with a shrug. "Especially when you're my teacher." He turned away from me and walked toward the back door.

What does that even mean? I thought as I watched his retreating form.

"I'll be waiting, Red. Enjoy your breakfast," he said before shutting the door.

I did. As I devoured the brown sugar and raisin-loaded mush, I decided oatmeal was my new favorite food. I ate quickly—mostly because I was eager for the promise of alone time with Jason, but also because I was looking forward to being home again. No matter what happened in my life, Grams's house would always be home.

I scrubbed my bowl clean in the kitchen, stopped by my temporary bedroom to gear up, rounded up Jack, and headed out to the stable...to Jason. I found him in the driveway with Wings and a chestnut Thoroughbred, both saddled for riding. A dense fog spread out as far as I could see. I took my time examining his handiwork while Wings whined incessantly in my head about wearing a bridle.

"Oh, Pretty Girl, I'm taking it off right now," I told the pouting mare as I undid the leather straps.

"Sorry. I forgot she doesn't need one," Jason said as he watched. "Is she...mad?"

I laughed and hoisted myself into the saddle. “Not really. But you owe her an apple—her words, not mine.” Wings began walking lazily down the gravel driveway.

Jason mounted his horse with ease and caught up quickly. “Well, good. I’d hate to have her for an enemy. She seems fierce.”

“He says you’re fierce,” I told the majestic animal beneath me, and her gait gained some prance. “You did a good job,” I told Jason as our horses’ hooves crunched along in the gravel. “I’m impressed.”

Jason chuckled. “Red, don’t you know impressing you is my number one priority?” His words were light and teasing. *Someone’s in a better mood.*

Bringing my hand up to my chest, I gasped melodramatically, “Oh my! If impressing me is number one, what comes in at number two?”

He looked at me askance, his eyes narrowing to mischievous slits. “Wouldn’t you like to know?”

Smiling, I shook my head. The sound of the horses’ hooves changed from crunching to clopping as we reached the paved road.

“Oh, I almost forgot.” I moved Wings closer to Jason’s horse and took the picture out of my pocket, handing it to him. “I’ve been meaning to give you this. I was going to when I told you about your dad, but…well…you know what happened. Grams found it in your dad’s hand. He was also holding this,” I said, fingering the heavy silver chain around my neck. I pulled the attached key out from the collar of my coat; it was warm from my skin.

“Lean closer,” I told him, lifting the chain over my head and holding it out. Jason bowed his head toward me, and I secured the chain around his neck, resisting the urge to brush my fingertips over his smooth skin. “I have no clue what it’s for…”

Examining the old-fashioned iron key, Jason said, “I do.”

We rode on in silence for long minutes—Jason lost in thought as he stared at the key, me lost in wonder as I watched him.

"It opens a box," he finally said.

"A box? What's in it?" Based on his reaction, I figured it must be something important.

With a bitter laugh, he explained, "My dad…he never let us look in it. He always wore this around his neck, but even that wasn't enough security for him. He'd hide the box, changing the location if he suspected we'd found it. By the time I was old enough to unlock it without the key, I'd come to understand that he deserved his privacy and secrets, so I stopped looking. Zoe, on the other hand…"

"What?" I asked, curious.

With a small, genuine smile curving his lips, he shook his head. "I bet she still looked for the damn thing every time she visited. She was obsessed."

I felt like I'd been skewered in the chest with dull rapier. "She never told me about it."

Tucking the key underneath his clothes, Jason laughed softly, but just for a second. "She was probably ashamed. A grown woman…searching through her dad's underwear drawer…"

"Oh…right…"

"What's wrong?"

"Nothing," I lied. *Why wouldn't she tell me about the box?*

Fortunately, unlike Chris, Jason left unsaid words and hurt feelings alone. I was grateful; I didn't want to talk about my simmering emotions. I didn't want to cry in front of Jason again. I'd thought Zoe and I told each other everything, but his revelation made me question that. The willingness to confide our deepest secrets—our darkest fears—was the foundation of our friendship. Yet, she hadn't told me about her obsession with her father's mysterious box. Had I hidden things from her too? *I don't think so…*

"Too late, old man," Jason whispered, breaking me from my mental tailspin. He was studying the back of the picture, reading and rereading the words written by his father. I'd read it so many times that I'd memorized it, though I didn't completely understand the meaning behind Tom's words.

Zoe—Be strong. Your mom and I love you and your brother, never doubt that. And remember, every scar is a memory.

Jason—I didn't listen to the wood—I should have. I'm sorry. I'm so proud of you.

"What?" I asked softly.

Jason began speaking, his words floating ahead of him in the morning fog. "We fought all the time…I'm sure you overheard. He'd wanted me to make certain choices. He forbade me from joining the Army, but I did it anyway. We didn't talk for nearly a year after that."

"I didn't know it was that bad."

His jaw muscles tensed, and he nodded. "But things were getting better. We didn't fight as much when I visited, and we even talked on the phone…just to catch up. But he always sounded disappointed when I talked about my career. He used to say, 'Every piece of wood has a story. If you listen to the wood, the carving will come to life.'"

"So…in this case, you're the wood?"

Jason looked at me sideways, a deliciously crooked grin tilting his lips, and my cheeks heated. "You know what I mean!" I told him, a little shrill.

After a throaty chuckle, he resumed his gaze ahead. As we passed the empty, overgrown lot where Zoe and I had built a girls-only fort, I knew we were almost to his house. Jason seemed to be searching the increasingly dense fog for its outline, or maybe, for his father.

"Yeah…so he finally accepted me. Accepted my choice. And now he's gone."

"I'm sorry, Jason."

"Me too."

His familiar house slowly took shape in the mist, steely-blue and boxy, seeming to beckon us forward. We dismounted in the driveway and fenced the horses in the backyard with Jack.

"Let me know if you hear or see anyone," I told my dog, receiving a bark in acknowledgement.

As we entered the house through the back door, I recalled the thousands of times I'd walked, danced, and ran up and down its halls. My memories were divided into two eras: Jason, and post-Jason. After he'd left for the Army, the walls had always felt a little thinner, the air a little less substantial. And, in not one of my memories of the house was I ever alone with him. Suddenly, the walls felt wild and alive.

I followed Jason as we passed the rooms I was most familiar with—the kitchen, living room, and Zoe's upstairs bedroom. Something about the way Jason moved, the easy set of his shoulders, spoke to the magic of home. He was relaxed in a way I hadn't seen him for years.

"Wherever he hides it, it's always in his room," Jason said. He led me down the second-floor hallway to the furthest bedroom.

I wanted to help Jason search but simply felt too awkward rummaging through my best friend's father's things. "I'm going back to Zo's room…to see if there's anything she'd want me to bring to her."

Jason shot to his feet and purposefully strode out of the room with me close on his heels. He didn't stop until he reached Zoe's bedroom. He entered, took a quick peek around, said, "Go ahead," and then left me alone in the comforting space.

As I soaked up the familiar plum and apple-green décor, I was transported back to my teen years. Practically every other night had been spent giggling with Zoe under the fluffy comforter, gushing about boys and sharing dreams. We'd been so happy…so carefree. *Will we ever feel like that again?*

I wandered across the room to the bulletin board hanging over the desk. It was covered with a hodgepodge of pins, photos, notes, sketches, and tiny trinkets from throughout Zoe's life. She'd been collecting memories on that board since before we became friends in fourth grade, and only her favorites stayed up for long. I was staring at a mini museum of my best friend's life. *My best friend who didn't tell me about the thing she was most obsessed with.*

Reaching out, I unpinned one of the sketches—an exact match of the tattoo on the inside of my wrist. It was the drawing we'd taken to the tattoo parlor where we'd had identical Celtic knots inked on our skin, proclaiming our eternal sisterhood. I had no doubt that Zoe would want it.

I set the sketch on the top of the dresser, exchanging it for a framed photo, and sat on the bed, lost in thought. In the picture, we were perched on the edge of a deck, our backs to the camera. My hand was raised to Zoe's ear, shielding my words as I whispered some *extremely* important secret to her. Considering we were juniors in high school, it was probably about my latest crush or some juicy gossip. I'd always loved the photo, thinking it captured the essence of our friendship so well—always whispering secrets into each other's ears. But at the moment, it seemed to shout that I was the one whispering while Zoe kept her secrets inside. Hidden.

"Found it," Jason said, frowning when I looked up. "Are y—"

"I'm fine," I interrupted, wiping a lone tear from my cheek.

"Okay…I'm heading into my room. Feel free to join me when you're done in here." His eyes lingered on my face for a few seconds before he turned and crossed the hall to his old bedroom.

I wasn't about to miss the once in a lifetime opportunity to explore Jason's personal space, so I pulled my unraveling emotions together, tucked the picture frame and sketch into my backpack, and joined him.

Crossing the threshold into forbidden territory felt like pushing through a force field. Tom Cartwright hadn't redecorated his kids' bedrooms into impersonal guest rooms like empty-nesters tended to do. He'd kept the spaces exactly as they had been, waiting to welcome Zoe and Jason home at any time. In Zoe's case, the drawers and closet had been emptied long ago, leaving behind the shell of the girl who had lived there. With Jason, however, it appeared as though he'd still been occupying the bedroom for the past twelve years.

The walls were nearly bare, with only a few pieces of sports memorabilia pinned to their steel-blue surfaces. A faded, masculine scent clung to the air, making me think of the many nights Jason had spent in the room while I'd been hunkered down with Zoe across the hall. I wondered if he'd been alone…or if my middle school mind hadn't realized he was sneaking girlfriend after girlfriend into his room. Or maybe he'd just climbed down the tree outside of his window and met up with them elsewhere. His epic reputation by the time I'd entered high school—the year after Jason had graduated—suggested that at least one, if not both, was true.

On the wall opposite Jason's bed, a long shelf displayed several dozen wooden figurines and a few framed photos of his dad and sister. While Jason knelt on the floor, digging through a trunk in his closet, I picked up a miniature carved cat, curled in sleep. It was exquisite.

"Did your dad make these?"

"Huh?" Looking over his shoulder, Jason saw what I was holding and frowned. "Ah…some." His head disappeared into the closet again as he clarified, "I actually made most of 'em."

"Hmmm…" I lost myself in examining the little pieces of art. The cat looked so realistic, like it might uncurl its tiny body and arch its back right there on my palm. I was starting to understand what Tom meant about listening to the wood.

"That's the last one I ever made," Jason said quietly.

I jumped, my fingers reflexively closing around the carved cat.

I'd been so entranced by the intricate feline figurine in my hand that I hadn't noticed Jason approach. He was right behind me.

"Sorry," he said. "I thought you heard me." He reached over my shoulder and plucked a simple, slightly disproportionate fish off of the shelf. It was about the size of his thumb. "This was my first."

"They're beautiful. I didn't know your dad taught you to carve," I told him, opening my hand to reveal the sleeping cat.

Jason laughed bitterly and gave a small shake of his head. "He wanted me to follow in his footsteps—take over the family business."

The carvings seemed to unsettle him so much that I felt guilty when I asked, "Can I…I mean, would you mind if I…you know…kept this?" I raised my hand a few inches, showing him the tiny feline.

He shrugged. "Keep it. Keep any of 'em."

Jason returned to the closet as I examined each carving carefully, wishing I could take them all. I settled on the sleeping cat, the lopsided fish, and a remarkably detailed seagull in flight.

Jason finally emerged from his closet with a few items—a rolled-up canvas kit of some kind, an incredibly worn leather journal, and an equally worn, earth-brown leather jacket—and stuffed them into his backpack, along with the pictures from the shelf and a carved bear standing on its hind legs. That one, he said, had been carved by his dad. He also gave me a few old t-shirts to wrap my priceless treasures in; I was worried they would get damaged.

Before we left, we scavenged some peanut butter, crackers, fruit snacks, and an unopened bottle of apple juice from Tom's pantry for lunch. We settled at the kitchen table with our non-perishable feast and ate in companionable silence.

When I rose and carried our empty plates to the sink, Jason asked, "What're you doing?"

"The dishes?"

"Why?"

"Because…huh." I dropped the dirty plates into the sink. "I don't know. It just felt right. Being here makes it seem like things are…normal."

Standing, Jason finished off the apple juice, drinking it straight out of the bottle, and said, "I know what you mean. I keep expecting my dad to walk in and lecture me about responsibility and 'carrying the family torch'." He raised his backpack onto the chair and unzipped it. "It feels normal…except for one thing."

"What's that?" I cocked my head and leaned my lower back against the counter.

"We're here together—just us." He looked at me, his electric blue eyes seeming to really see me for the first time. "The world's not normal. Everything's different. *We're* different."

I nodded, shifting uncomfortably under the weight of his stare.

"Aren't you gonna open it?" I asked, motioning to the intricately carved box he'd just placed on the table. About the size of a cigar box, it was fashioned from cedar and had delicate iron hinges. It had, without a doubt, been crafted by the talented hands of Tom Cartwright.

Jason's eyes shifted to the box, mercifully releasing their relentless hold on me. "Not yet…Zoe'd kill me."

"Oh." *Right… 'cause she's obsessed with it and all…*

"We're done here," he said. He was watching my face closely. "Let's head out."

I nodded, not trusting my voice to hold steady if I spoke. My chin tried to quiver, but I stilled it by clenching my teeth.

Jason quickly wrapped the box in a terrycloth dish towel and loaded it into his pack. Dozens of words were perched on the tip of my tongue, anxiously waiting for my mouth to open so they could fly to Jason's ears. But I clutched onto them desperately, instead settling for companionable silence. As we rode to Grams's house, I basked in the silence, but once we walked through the front door, it turned expectant and tense. It was almost palpable, growing and pulsing in the air around us.

Ignoring the tension, we started in Grams's bedroom, where I searched for keepsakes. Jason sat on the end of her bed, watching me as I wandered around her room. I'd always thought of her possessions as flowery and old-fashioned, nothing I would ever want for myself, but they suddenly held incalculable value to me.

Searching through her vintage, buttercup-yellow jewelry box, I was struck by the realization that I was looking through her favorite necklaces, rings, and earrings, all things she would never wear again. I was surprised to find the long, silver chain with its heavy silver pendant—a medallion the size of a silver dollar imprinted with the hands, heart, and crown of a claddagh ring—that Grams only took off to bathe. It had been a gift from my grandpa on their wedding night. *Did she leave it for me?* With trembling fingers, I picked up the necklace and reverently slipped it over my head, tucking the pendant beneath my shirt. The chain was so long that the cool metal settled low between my breasts.

Before leaving the room, I sprayed a little of Grams's lavender perfume. With horror and wonder, the delicate scent made me feel like she would come striding through the doorway at any moment. Jason sat quietly and watched, letting the silent tension continue to build.

Finally, I led the way upstairs to my childhood bedroom. The closer we came, the more nervous I felt, like I was doing something forbidden. Grams had maintained a strict policy against boys in bedrooms—specifically *my* bedroom. On top of that, Jason had never even been in my house, let alone in my bedroom.

Self-consciousness overwhelmed me as Jason entered the room behind me. Juxtaposed with his undeniable masculinity, the space seemed so much girlier than usual, so innocent when compared to his intense sexuality. I often felt the same way about myself in his presence. Having him in my room—studying my white, vine-embroidered comforter, antique vanity, and menagerie of stuffed animals—felt like letting him open me up to peek inside. I felt exposed. Naked.

With an odd mixture of discomfort and curiosity, Jason stood in the middle of the room. Unlike in Grams's bedroom, he seemed to have a hard time figuring out where to sit. He approached the bed, hesitated, and turned to the vanity chair. He shook his head before making a decision, displacing a large stuffed dog on the window seat. The dog, Ralph, remained in his grasp, resting on his lap.

Again, he watched me but said nothing, letting me look through my belongings undisturbed. It was impossible to ignore his increasingly pensive presence, but I made a show of pretending.

As I perched on the edge of the mattress, searching the drawers of the nightstand only a few feet from Jason, I found the purple diary I'd written in throughout high school. There wasn't a secret written on its pages that Zoe didn't know. But if I read her diary, how much of its cherished contents would end up being news to me? Hot tears slowly snaked down my face, and the silence reached a critical point.

"Dani?" Jason's voice was a soft rumble.

"Hmmm?" I shut the drawer, leaving the diary inside, and turned all of my attention on him. I smiled faintly at the sight of him, such a strong, tough man, holding a stuffed animal.

"What's wrong?"

If I said "Nothing," he would let it go. Or he'd wait until the next time I drowned in silent tears to ask again. But I didn't want him to let it go. I wanted Jason to know me, insecurities and all.

"It's Zoe," I told him.

"And the box?"

I sighed, still arranging my thoughts into a comprehensible pattern. "Yeah, I guess you could say that." I paused, then the words spilled out without thought. "She didn't tell me about it. She's been obsessed with it forever, and she never told me about it. If it's so important to her, how could she not tell me? We're…I thought we were closer than that. I thought we told each other *everything*. Now I just don't know."

Spurred on by my admission, the steady stream of quiet tears flowed more quickly. I wiped them away with both hands.

"Does it change anything?"

I considered his question carefully, thinking about Zoe and everything we'd been through together over the years. "No." My voice was wobbly, but my answer was honest. Zoe was my best friend, and I loved her…even with the stupid secret box.

Jason lifted a single shoulder, not taking his eyes off me. Abruptly, something changed in his face, making the contours more evident. As he studied me, he seemed intensely intimidating. "Why were you avoiding me?"

"What?"

"This morning—why were you running from me?"

"Um, well…I don't think I was actually *running*…it was more of a quick walk. Possibly a slow jog."

Jason's bland expression said, "And…?"

Sighing, I prepared to spill my guts. "I didn't want to hear what I thought you were going to say."

Jason was practically turning to stone before my eyes. Completely monotone, he asked, "And that would be…?"

I giggled unexpectedly, feeling my pulse increase and my hands tremble. The last thing I wanted to say spewed from my mouth before I could stop it. "Did you care about Cece?" Wide-eyed, I slapped both hands over my mouth.

Until I'd blurted the question, I hadn't realized how much his relationship with that psycho bitch had been bothering me. I'd spent a good portion of my life mooning over Jason, so I was pretty practiced at being jealous of any chick he was involved with. It was a familiar, expected feeling. But with Cece it was far more intense…like, at a murderous level.

The question shattered his stony façade, and I watched the shadows of a handful of emotions flash across his face: shock – confusion – embarrassment – fury – worry –surprise – hope – curiosity.

Only the massive amount of time we'd spent together over the past month—where I'd had the opportunity to analyze his every nuance—allowed me to interpret each minute change in his expression.

He shook his head and looked down to study Ralph, the stuffed dog he was still holding. "She was just someone to help pass the time…a means to an end."

To top off my mortification and flaming blush, my mouth opened of its own accord again. "And Holly…is she…?" I covered my entire face with my hands, peeking between my fingers like I was watching a horror movie.

A hint of a dimple appeared on Jason's left cheek as the corner of his mouth turned up slightly. "No. Why do you ask?"

"No reason," I squeaked. With a supreme lack of grace, I scrambled over the bed, away from Jason. I stood in front of the dresser set against the opposite wall and opened the top drawer—what Zoe called my "junk drawer"—to busy myself by searching through its contents.

"Dani?" Jason's voice was hushed, but it still made me jump. I'd been so focused on my fake rummaging that I hadn't noticed him coming up behind me. Again. "You never answered my question. Why were you avoiding me? What did you think I was going to say to you?"

I ceased my pointless searching and grasped the top edge of the open drawer. Defeated, I said, "I overheard your conversation with Chris last night—the one about 'clearing things up.' I thought you were talking about me and…" I paused, closing my eyes and taking a deep, unsteady breath. "I didn't want you to, so I avoided you."

Jason placed his hands either side of mine, trapping me between him and the drawer. "Dani," he said, his voice deep and rough. His breath caressed the back of my neck. "Turn around."

I squeezed my eyes shut and shook my head.

"Turn. Around." Though his words were demanding, his voice held the barest hint of a plea.

After a few seconds of indecision, I removed my hands from their death grip on the drawer and lowered them to my sides. I slowly pivoted until my back pressed against the open drawer, and then I opened my eyes. Standing so close to me, Jason seemed even taller than usual. I forced myself to look up, up, up, and to meet his sapphire eyes. Back and forth, his eyes scoured mine.

"Do you really want to do this?" he whispered.

More than anything. Swallowing consciously, I nodded.

"Are you sure?"

I nodded again, my eyes fixed on his. My heart was beating with such force that I was certain he could hear it.

Only when my backside pressed against the dresser did I realize Jason had slid the drawer shut, forcing me backward. Parts of his jacket and jeans brushed against mine, tickling the hyper-aware skin beneath. I suddenly felt overheated, like I might melt into a puddle right there on my bedroom floor.

He leaned in with deliberate slowness, bringing his burning eyes and slightly parted lips closer to mine. Even though we'd kissed only once, I craved the feel of his lips, the brush of his tongue. His eyes flicked from my mouth to my eyes and back repeatedly. Giving me time. Letting me decide. Making sure I wanted him.

I did.

My heart pounded, and my breaths came quickly, like the air was too thin. *Is this really happening?* Leaning forward, I tilted my face up and brushed my lips softly against Jason's. The barely-there contact still sent a thrilling jolt through my body, charging the length of my nerves and circling back to collide low in my abdomen. The sensation intensified, causing a delicious ache between my thighs.

Jason's eyes darkened to a deep midnight, and he breathed deeply. His hand slid underneath my braid, grasping my neck to pull me closer as his other settled in the curve of my back and held me flush against him. The tip of his tongue slipped out and slowly wet his lips. I watched the movement, entranced.

When his lips again touched mine, I was lost, completely and utterly. My hands slid up over his coat and twined behind his neck, holding him against me. I opened my mouth to him, and our tongues collided. A low purr escaped from my throat, and he answered it with a guttural growl. We kissed as though we were starving; the only thing that could satiate our hunger was more of each other.

I let go of his neck for a single purpose—to unzip and remove his coat, then his holster. They landed on the floor with a soft thump, and seconds later, my own coat and holster joined his. Not once did we break our kiss.

His hands moved over my long-sleeved shirt, seeming to light my nerves on fire. They slid down my back and over my hips, eventually teasing the skin above my belt before slipping lower over my jeans. Abruptly, he gripped the backs of my thighs and lifted me up, encouraging me to wrap my legs around his hips. I did so eagerly.

He carried me to the empty wall beside the dresser, pressing me against it with a grunt. I squeezed my legs and arms around him more tightly, freeing his hands to roam over my body. They seemed to be everywhere—my hips, breasts, neck—almost like he'd sprouted a few extra arms. I moaned at each new sensation, shocking myself with my brazen reactions. I was so incredibly eager for what I hoped would happen next.

Jason had just shifted me from the wall to the bed and was kneeling between my legs, removing my shirt, when Jack's panicked warning invaded my mind. "*Two-legs. Many. Smell wrong. Close. Hurry!*"

"Jason! Stop!" I breathed, clutching his wrists before he could yank my shirt over my head. When he let go, it sat uselessly around my neck like a scarf.

Chest heaving, Jason looked down at me in disbelief. I could see the question form in his eyes—had I changed my mind?

To reassure him, I traded his wrists for his face and pulled him closer for a deep, though brief, kiss. "I'm sorry…we have to leave…now," I said against his cheek. "Jack said people are coming. Crazies."

"You've got to be fucking kidding me!" Jason exclaimed, standing and taking a step back. I instantly missed the feel of him. He raked his eyes over the slender curves of my shirtless body one last time. "Fuck!" he repeated before resituating his clothes and quickly grabbing his holster and coat.

I hastily pulled my shirt back on and rearmed myself as well. Zipping our coats and grabbing our packs, we sped down the stairs and through the kitchen. According to Jack, the Crazies were approaching the front of the house, but he and the horses were still out back. We rushed out the back door, practically leaping into our saddles, and sped off through the sparse woods beyond the garden. As we rode, I used Jack and a handful of volunteer animals to scout both ahead and behind us. The Crazies weren't following us; they were still searching in and around the house.

Our desire for safe surroundings and formidable allies drove us back to the ranch at a gallop. We were all—horses, humans, and dog—panting when we trotted into the stable. Jason jumped out of his saddle and helped me down, having noticed me sway when we slowed at the driveway. During the ride, I'd maintained a mental connection not just with Jack, but with the dozens of other scouting animals as well, and it was exacting its toll.

"Are you okay?" Jason asked, setting me down facing him. His eyes searched every part of me, seeking out an ailment that couldn't be seen.

"I'm fine. Don't worry. I just need a snack…and maybe a nap." I stood on tiptoes and gave him a slow, promising kiss. *To reassure him*, I told myself.

"Can you make it inside on your own?" he asked when we separated.

I nodded.

"Go lay down…I'll take care of everything out here." As I walked away, he added, "And Red?"

I looked at him over my shoulder. "Yeah?"

"This isn't over," he promised.

"*Good.*"

41

DANI

Smiling, I opened my eyes to see the fire's gentle glow on the wall. *Jason must've built it back up while I was asleep.* Quick, heavy footsteps mingled with the soft sound of the crackling wood. *It's him,* I thought excitedly. He knelt near my head and gently pulled the blankets lower. While I waited for his touch, my giddiness was almost impossible to contain.

Suddenly, a rank-smelling hand was over my mouth, and hot, foul breath brushed my ear. "Pretty girl," he said, and he most certainly wasn't Jason. My already increased heart rate spiked. "Wanna have some fun?"

A gunshot cracked from another part of the house, and the man momentarily loosened his grasp on my face. Sensing my only chance, I shifted and bit down on the meaty flesh between his thumb and index finger until blood oozed into my mouth. I gagged on its warmth, on its metallic taste.

Shrieking, the man shoved me away, and I fell off the couch… but not before my fingers closed around the handgun I'd stowed between the cushion and the couch back. I'd finally learned my lesson—guns stay within arm's reach, *always*.

Stumbling, I extricated myself from the blankets and stood, aiming my gun at the repulsive intruder. I spat as much of his blood from my mouth as possible, terrified by what diseases it might be carrying. Almost as alarming was the familiarity of his face—Mr. Monk—he'd been a teacher at my high school, alongside Mr. Grayson. He'd taught PE and had a well-deserved reputation as a pervert, at least among the girls. A large group of his female students had eventually gone to the principal and then to the police, and Mr. Monk had been charged with multiple counts of molestation. Last I'd heard, he was still in prison.

"Bitch!" Mr. Monk howled, clutching his bleeding hand to his chest.

"You have no idea," I growled and fired the pistol. The bullet impacted his shoulder, twisting him to the side. Without hesitation, I pulled the trigger again. The second bullet shot straight through his temple, and he collapsed to the floor, his head hitting the hardwood with a heavy, wet thunk.

Lowering the gun, I spat again, spraying pink saliva in his direction, and hissed, "Asshole!" Anger was all that kept me from crying. Screaming. Puking.

"Dani! Are you okay?" Jason shouted, his voice preceding his arrival. As he ran into the room, I heard more gunshots elsewhere in the house. Jack followed him in, hurrying to my feet and whining pathetically.

As Jason's eyes landed on the crumpled heap on the floor, he froze. Cautiously, he moved closer to the dead man and stared at his hemorrhaging head. "Is that Mr. Monk?"

I wiped my mouth with the back of my wrist. "Yeah. I—I killed him," I said weakly, beginning to shake. Mr. Monk was the second man I'd killed in less than a week, and my psyche was having some not-so-minor issues avoiding the reality of my actions.

I'm a killer.

Jason shifted his intense, blue eyes to my face. "Did he...*touch* you? Did he hurt you?" When I didn't respond, he closed the distance and grabbed me by the shoulders. "Dani!"

Tearing my eyes away from the oozing mound of lumpy, bloody gore that had once been the side of Mr. Monk's head, I whispered, "Not this time." I just wished I could stop shaking, stop remembering.

"What do you—" Jason's mouth fell open. His eyes widened, and he searched my face for answers, his throat convulsing rhythmically. He tried twice to speak before words actually formed. "You were one of them…one of the girls he…?"

I looked away, disgusted and ashamed. "Yeah. But I was a lot luckier than the others. Zo…she found me in his office before he could get his pants down. She knew I had a meeting with him about my grades." I laughed bitterly. "*Grades*. What a joke. I thought I was going to suffocate with his hand over my mouth. I couldn't fight him off. I was too weak…too small. I don't know what she did—I could only see the wall—but one second he was there and I could barely breathe, and the next, Zo was hauling me out of his office while I cried in her arms. Mr. Monk said he'd kill us if we told."

"I didn't know." Jason's voice was tight, restrained.

"Nobody did…except Zo, the other girls, the principal, and the police. It was hard to keep Grams from finding out." I shook my head. "So hard. I didn't want to tell anyone, but Zo made me. She said his threat was empty. She said that if enough girls got together and told the truth about him, he'd go away and never hurt anyone again." I looked at the dead man and smiled. When I spoke, my voice was cold. "Now he's dead."

Jason pressed his fingers against my jaw and gently turned my face back to his. "Why's your mouth bloody? Did he hit you?"

"I bit him." I snatched a water bottle off of the coffee table, took a swig, swished the water around in my mouth, and spat the mouthful into the fire. I did it three times. "I can't get rid of the taste of his blood."

Without hesitation, Jason clamped his hands on the sides of my head and kissed me, hard, giving me something else to focus on. His touch and his taste drove the unhappy memories from my mind. He was the perfect distraction, and I could tell he was desperate to help me forget.

"Fuck!" he growled, breaking contact and taking a step back. "He deserved a slower death. Fucking bastard!"

When I took a step toward Jason, he held out his hand. "We're leaving tonight. As soon as possible. Change into something warmer." His eyes scanned my body, taking in my pajamas—cotton shorts and a tank top. "Something *much* warmer…and get your things together."

"What? We're leaving? But we're not ready! We don't even have a saddle for Mr. Grayson," I said without a breath's pause.

"He can use Dalton's shit. We have to leave. They'll come back with more."

"But Dalton—"

"He's dead," Jason said harshly.

"Oh." I hadn't been close to Dalton, but I could feel tears suddenly welling in my eyes. "Turn around," I said unsteadily and waited until Jason obeyed to swap my pajamas for a bra, sweater, long underwear, and jeans.

"What about everyone else?" I asked, zipping my jeans. *I hope they're okay…*

"They're alive. What do you need to pack?" Jason was walking around the room, picking up the various possessions I'd strewn about. It was remarkable how much I'd settled in since I'd only been staying there for a little over a week.

"It's fine. I can take care of my own stuff. Go get your things together," I told him, setting my hiking pack on the couch.

Jason shook his head and handed me my journal. "I'm not leaving you alone," he told me.

"Jason, I—"

"No!" Very carefully, he repeated, "I'm not leaving you alone."

For a few long seconds we stared at each other, chests rising and falling heavily. It felt like a magnetic force connected our eyes, preventing us from looking away. Finally, I cleared my throat and nodded.

Together, Jason and I packed all of my belongings and then his before heading out to the stable. As the first to arrive, we began saddling eight of the horses for riding and the rest as pack animals. We currently had fifteen horses, including the handful we'd gathered into our herd over the last few days from nearby farms and ranches. We fit the goats with dog collars and leashes, unwilling to leave them behind—the protein from their milk would be an invaluable nutrient once scavenging for food became less reliable. As the others arrived, we added their backpacks to ours on the riderless horses. It was a hurried, late night job that would require a lot of rearranging in the morning, especially considering all of the supplies and equipment we still needed to gather as we traveled.

Once everyone was packed and had mounted their horses, we assembled in a misshapen circle in the driveway. Nudging his mount forward, the same chestnut brown Thoroughbred he'd ridden earlier that day, Jason addressed the group. "We've lost Dalton. He fought until the end, giving us the warning we needed to survive the attack. We all owe him our lives."

Everyone but Holly nodded gravely. She just stared ahead with empty eyes. They'd been close friends, she and Dalton.

"When we have a night to rest, we'll honor his memory." Jason paused, meeting the eyes of each individual. "We're heading east. It'll be hard, but you all know that. Some of us have new, unique skills—Abilities." He looked at Chris, Ky, Ben, and finally, me. "And others may be able to do things we've yet to discover. We have to use every advantage. Ky will lead us, paying attention to the feel of the path ahead, and Dani will be in constant communication with the animals around us. If either of them says stop, you stop. If they say get down, you get the fuck down. Understood?"

Everyone murmured or nodded their assent.

"Alright, we're pairing up for the duration of the journey. Anytime you leave the immediate vicinity of the group, you *will* let your partner know, or better yet, bring them with you." He studied each of us, then said, "Let's go with Hunter and Holly, Ben and Ky, Daniel and Chris, and Dani, you're with me."

It took me a moment to remember that Daniel was Mr. Grayson's first name.

"Any last questions before we head out?" When everyone shook their heads, Jason said, "Today'll be long, so save your strength whenever possible. Ky, lead on."

"You feel different," Ky said, sitting in the chair opposite me. I'd settled in what had been a private dining room, soothed by its rich brown wood, creamy walls, and burgundy carpet. Jason had left me alone in the isolated room to write in my journal while he washed up.

Apparently modeled after a French chateau, the winery was filled with ivory marble floors, rich mahogany furniture, and crystal light fixtures. The main tasting room—a vast chamber with a two-story-high ceiling and ornately carved tables of various sizes —had become our "camp" for the night. Nobody seemed overly interested in privacy after what happened the previous night, instead opting to share one big room.

I eyed Ky. "Um…thanks?"

He grinned. "Anytime. But really…you feel like a bomb that's been diffused. Before, you just felt like a bomb."

"Okay…why are you 'feeling' me exactly?"

Leaning forward, Ky rested his elbows on the table. "Jason's orders. Everyone gets checked out by Chris and me. Making sure nobody's losing it."

"I'm not losing it."

"So you say." Ky cocked his head to the side like he was trying to hear the words of a barely audible song. "Huh…that's interesting."

"What?" Knowing he was listening to what could best be described as my emotional volatility was starting to creep me out.

"Nothing really—it's just that Jason felt similar," he said, letting his eyes refocus on me. They held a mischievous glint.

"Ky…," I warned.

His mouth tensed as he tried not to smile. "It's about time!"

"We are *so* not talking about this!" I scooted my chair backward, planning to flee. My sex life was not about to become a topic of public conversation.

"Do us all a favor and get it over with."

Before I could stand, hands were on my shoulders, holding me firmly in place. "Get *what* over with?" Chris asked from directly behind me, and I groaned.

Ky said nothing; instead, his grin widened.

"Oh, got it…seriously!" Chris agreed. Out of nowhere, she asked, "Have your nightmares stopped?"

Her question threw me off balance, and I'd already been teetering between furious blushes and outrage. "Uh, yeah. A few nights ago."

"Good. There's a bit of a difference here…and here," she said softly. I sensed a ghostly nudge inside my head with each "here". It was the first time I'd actually *felt* her Ability at work, though I knew she'd had a huge part in helping me deal with losing Cam.

"Do you mind!" I yelped. I grasped my head and shook it wildly in a futile attempt to block her meddling.

"Oh, sorry, hon. Didn't know you could feel that." At least she had the decency to sound slightly embarrassed. "Though I wonder what this part does; it's sort of pulsing…hmmm…"

Along with another nudge in my mind, my body instantly

heated and blood collected in several specific areas. "Chris!" I squealed, horrified.

Laughing raucously, she let go of my shoulders. "I thought it might be that. You should probably go find someone to help take care of your new problem."

"That wasn't even a little bit okay!" I huffed, stalking from the room.

I seriously considered ambushing Jason and getting it over with, but even in my unnaturally aroused state, I was just too exhausted. I'd spent the entire fourteen-hour journey mind-hopping from animal to animal, scouting out potential dangers. We'd avoided three small bands of Crazies using the critters' information. At the moment, I just wanted to wash up and fall asleep.

Only Holly and Mr. Grayson, both hunched over a map and talking in hushed tones, were in the enormous tasting room when I walked in. I gathered some clean underwear, socks, sweatpants, and a t-shirt from my pack, along with my toothbrush and toothpaste, and wandered across the marble entryway to the ladies' restroom. I could hear water running in the men's room next door and figured Jason was still in there.

In the bathroom, I took the closest possible thing to a shower using only the sink, hand soap, and about a thousand paper towels. When I was satisfactorily clean and wearing sweats and a t-shirt, I emerged from the bathroom. Jason, lounging against the wall beside the door, reached out to snag my arm.

Pulling me to him, he lowered his lips to mine for a deep, slow kiss. As his fingers journeyed beneath my t-shirt to tease the freshly cleaned skin at my hips, I sighed and broke our kiss, resting my head against his chest. He smelled like soap, and underneath that, like Jason.

He smoothed down my shirt's hem and wrapped his arms around me, making me feel like nothing could hurt me. "You're tired."

I nodded against him. "Understatement of the century."

Jason chuckled. "Come on, I have a surprise for you."

"A surprise?" I asked, eagerly peering up at him. My sudden anticipation fizzled as I looked into his glittering eyes, and just for a moment, saw Zoe staring back at me. They were so different in so many ways, but their irises—a mixture of blue, teal, and green, like shallow water in the tropics—were nearly identical.

"What's wrong?" Jason asked, seeing my grin wither.

"Nothing new—just worrying about Zo. What if she can't get to Colorado? What if we can't find her? What if she's hurt or…or worse?"

Pinching one of my damp curls, Jason held out the vibrant auburn spiral. "I love your hair. Always have. It's bright, like you." Though his words were flattering, I had no idea where he was going with them. "You and my sister—you balance each other out. She's serious and pessimistic. But you…you see the glass half full. Use that. She's strong. She's fine; she has to be. Okay?"

I closed my eyes and nodded, holding back the worried tears threatening to spill down my cheeks. *Zoe's strong. She's okay…she has to be.*

With our fingers intertwined, we headed back into the tasting room, to a corner where tables were arranged oddly on their sides. Combined with the walls, they created an isolated, tent-sized alcove with a narrow opening near one wall.

"Jason!" I exclaimed, laughing. "You built a fort!"

He watched me timidly, possibly a first for him. "I thought we could sleep here…together," he said softly, and all his shyness disappeared. "I don't want to share you, not with anyone. Not in any way." *Oh. Wow.*

It was my turn to play bashful as I took in the two sleeping bags laid out side-by-side within the makeshift walls. "Can they be, you know, joined?" I asked, gazing up at him through my lashes.

A slow smile spread across his face. "They already are."

Looking closer, I could see that the sleeping bags weren't just next to each other, but were zipped together. Narrowing my eyes, I said, "A little presumptuous, don't you think?"

Jason's smile widened into a wicked grin, and he led me by the hand into our little haven. Watching me closely, he slipped into the forest green sleeping bags. I followed, and once we were both lying down, he wrapped his arm around my waist and pulled me closer against him.

"I want you, and I *will* have you," he whispered as his fingers trailed up and down my arm, giving me goose bumps. "Is *that* presumptuous?"

I shook my head, smiling against his faded blue t-shirt.

And I *will have you.* It was my last thought before falling asleep.

42

ZOE

It was practically a miracle that we arrived at Sarah's without a hitch. While the rest of us waited down the road under the skeletal branches of an Elm tree, Sanchez and Harper did a sweep of the house and grounds. Standing beside the van, Biggs and I gawked at the picture-perfect plantation home before us. It was ivory with black shutters, and a porch that wrapped around both the first and second stories. Due to its grandeur, I half expected to see Rhett Butler walk out between the Ionic columns and greet us in the circular drive.

"Holy shit," I breathed, feeling completely inadequate in jeans and a Fort Knox sweatshirt.

"I know, right?" Sarah said as she strolled up behind Biggs and me. Crossing her arms, she stood in the space between us.

"I didn't know there were plantations in Missouri," I said.

"Well...," Sarah said, drawing out the word. "It's not exactly *old*, per se, but it *is* original. Daddy designed it and had it built for my mom for their tenth anniversary."

My eyebrows shot up with surprise. "Wow, that's a...nice gift."

Biggs whistled, and out of the corner of my eye, I saw him

shake his head. "I know you said your parents were well-off, but I didn't realize you meant capital R-I-C-H."

"Same thing." Sarah shrugged, and I could tell she was starting to get self-conscious. "Good for us, right? We probably have everything we need in this place."

Sanchez and Harper finally exited through the front door, giving us a thumbs-up—the house was empty of both Crazies and rotting corpses, and we could proceed inside.

Biggs and Sarah moved Dave's truck up to the house while I followed in the van. As I drove through the gate and up the extended driveway, I had a better view of the grounds. They were sprawling, with hundreds of live oaks spreading over the hills beyond the house. It was obvious that the lawn and flower beds had once been perfectly manicured, but they had been neglected for weeks—the plants were withered, and the grass was overgrown.

After unloading the vehicles, we made our way through the giant, black double doors and into the house. The foyer was bright and expansive, like Jay's house in *The Great Gatsby*. Tiles of ivory marble with gray and black swirls stretched to pristine white walls, where hand-painted, smoke-gray vines twisted ornately above white wainscoting. Long, black runners climbed mahogany staircases that were flanked by intricate, wrought iron banisters—the twin staircases gently wound up opposite walls to meet at a landing directly above the main hall. Pastoral paintings of rolling hills and golden plains hung on the walls leading to the second floor, and there were wilted palms on either side of the bottom steps. I could see a grand piano beside a fireplace in a sitting room to the right, and black leather couches and a wall of old-looking books—all different colors and sizes—in the room to the left. At least four mahogany doors were visible upstairs, presumably leading to bedrooms.

Although the house was practically a piece of art itself, it was the paintings that held my attention. I took a step toward the nearest piece, barely able to contain my excitement. The landscape resembled Thomas Cole's, *The Fountain of Vaucluse*, with its jutting mountain tops and a winding river that raged through a canyon, but something was different—the clouds seemed unfinished, and there was too little shading.

"Oh my God," I whispered, my mouth gaping. *It's an earlier version…it's an* original *Thomas Cole.*

"What's wrong Baby Girl?" Harper asked absently as he carried some of the medical equipment for Jake into the library.

"Nothing," I said, knowing Harper wouldn't share my astonishment. I peeled my eyes away from the painting and approached him, promising myself I would examine *all* of the artwork later. "What can I do to help?"

Harper reassured me he didn't need any help, so wanting to keep my mind off Jake's recovery as much as possible, I busied myself with listless tasks.

After taking inventory of the food in the kitchen and the enormous pantries, I added our reserves to the count. I checked one of the bathrooms for running water and found that the plumbing, like the electricity, wasn't working. I hoped we'd remedy that once Biggs hooked up our generator to the well pump like he planned. I noticed little things, like the thick layer of dust that covered the shelves and furniture, and the stale smell in the air, leading me to believe the place hadn't been inhabited for months. *Where are you, Mr. and Mrs. Thompson?*

As I rummaged through various cupboards and drawers throughout the first floor, I heard Sarah's voice coming from the room with the piano. Following the sound, I called ahead, "Sarah, do you have candles? Where…" I trailed off as I realized she was bickering with Biggs.

"No one's gonna get us," Sarah said in exasperation as they entered the foyer. "The place hasn't been ransacked or anything. Clearly no one knows this house is even here."

"This is a city, Sarah, foothills or not. There *are* Crazies around, I guarantee it. Do you want to take a chance that Clara followed us somehow and will try to kill us in our sleep?" Biggs asked, sounding genuinely concerned.

Sarah blanched. "No need to be so severe, Babe."

"Yeah, well, I'm not assuming *anything* anymore. I'm teaching you how to use a gun too. You see that psycho bitch, you shoot her until you know she's dead," he ordered and walked away.

Sarah caught my eye. "He's losing his mind," she mouthed. I smiled as she walked closer and grabbed my bag. "Come on, I picked out a special room for you," she said. "Since we don't know how long we'll be here, you'll need your own space. Trust me. This house brings out the crazy in people." She looked back at me with an apologetic smile before leading me up the left staircase.

I followed her to one of the doors visible from the bottom floor and stopped short as she looked over her shoulder, her face suddenly aglow with excitement. "This was actually my favorite room growing up," she said, dropping my bag and opening the door to peek inside. She hesitated like she was expecting someone to jump out. Noticing my confusion, she smiled. "I can't stop thinking about Clara now. Sorry." She flung the door open, and I dragged my duffel bag and backpack into the room.

Compared to any bedroom I'd ever lived in, it was humungous and fit for an aristocrat. A huge, four-post bed was backed against the left wall, an antique writing desk was situated in the far right corner, and a plush, camel-colored fainting couch sat in front of drawn, brocade drapes.

"Why do you like this room so much?" I asked. "It's *amazing,* but what about *your* bedroom?"

"Yeah, well, I was grounded a lot, so I got tired of my room." She waved the idea away and grabbed a handful of the drapes. As she yanked them open, I was awed by what she revealed.

"The best view in all of St. Louis…at least *I* think so." She gestured to the giant picture window overlooking what I thought was a pond at first, but from my vantage point, I could see was actually a silvery lake extending between the hills. "My own little paradise growing up," she explained.

"It's beautiful." The sun was sinking into the horizon—a golden sphere seeming to set the withered forest ablaze.

"Yeah, I know. I used to whine all the time about wanting this to be my room, but Mom said she spent too much money decorating mine to give in."

"Decorating?" I pictured pink and purple princess wallpaper and ballerina figurines cluttering her shelves. "Decorating how, exactly?"

Sarah smiled at me and shrieked with glee. "Come see!" she said, running out of the room and down the hall.

"Wow, that's enthusiasm," I muttered. I dashed after her, laughing as I tried to keep up and fearing I'd get lost if I didn't.

Pausing outside a door, Sarah turned to me. Her face was serious, and her finger poked my breastbone. "You have to promise you won't judge me, Zoe. I went through a princess…fairy…phase…thing and my mom never let me live it down."

I tried to control the smile threatening to spread across my face as I promised, "Scout's honor." I was barely able to contain my anticipation.

"Alright," she said and threw open the door, revealing her fairy forest hideaway.

A mural covered the walls—mossy tree trunks reached from floor to ceiling, ferns sprouting at their bases and leafy branches stretching overhead. The canopy bed was pink and white with feathers hanging from the bed posts. Pixie clothes made from feathers, twigs, and flower petals hung between the trees on the walls, and a round mirror framed with metal twigs took residence by the desk. Silk ivy weaved around the doors and windows, and the closet was like another world—a layer of tulle separated it from the living space, and I could only imagine what I might find inside.

"Wow," was all I could think to say.

Sarah turned to me slowly, barely able to contain her building gaiety. "I know!" she squealed. Grabbing my hands, she started jumping up and down, screeching and giggling. I couldn't help but join her.

"Why are we so excited?" I asked breathlessly as we hopped in place.

After a moment, Sarah dragged me over to the bed and pulled me up onto it. "Come on, Zoe, you know you want to," she said.

I rolled my eyes, unsure why I was indulging her, but I couldn't resist. We bounced up and down, squealing like twelve-year-olds. When we finally fell back on the mattress, winded and elated, it felt like we were best friends who'd just been asked to the prom by the cutest boys in school.

Our ridiculousness made me think of Dani, and I wished *she* was with me. She would've praised me for letting go and then chided me for not doing so more frequently. I wondered how she was doing. I wanted to tell her about Jake and Clara, about Dave… but I had no way to contact her; I didn't even have a way to find out if she was still alive.

"Well," Sarah said, sitting up on her knees and straightening her bubblegum pink Fort Knox t-shirt. "I know it's moronic, but thanks for humoring me in a frolic. It's sort of nice to be home, even if it's under such shitty circumstances."

The clearing of a throat startled us, and we both looked at the doorway. Biggs walked in, an exaggerated expression of horror on his face. "Are you expecting me to sleep in this room?" he asked fearfully.

Sarah grinned. "Yep."

"Right. I figured as much." Biggs plastered a counterfeit smile on his face as he looked at me with a "please kill me now" expression. "Harper asked about you, Zoe. I think Jake might be—"

Before Biggs could finish, I was up and out of the room. I ran down the hall and stairs, careful not to stumble down the staircase, and flung myself into the library.

"Is he awake?" I panted, hurrying over to the bed situated in the corner between two walls of books. Jake lay there, still bandaged and motionless.

Harper eyed me curiously, appraising my appearance. "What were you doing?"

"Nothing," I said, smoothing my clothes self-consciously. "Why?"

"Your hair is all crazy and…stuff."

"Oh, whatever, H. Did he wake up?" I looked back at Jake's body. *It doesn't look like he's moved at all.*

"He was moaning a minute ago, but he hasn't moved at all. I upped his morphine dose; I need you to tell me if he needs more."

"Is moaning bad or good?" I asked, walking around the bed. I placed my hand on Jake's bandaged arm, opening my mind to him and waiting for one of his brief moments of semi-consciousness.

"I think it's a good thing, Baby Girl."

Jake's mind roused momentarily. I could feel his confusion and fear, but his panic and misery were almost nonexistent.

"He's okay for now," I reassured Harper. "I think *you* need to take a breather, though. I'll stay with him. It'll make me feel better anyway."

Harper nodded, but before leaving, he winked. "Fix your locks, Croft. I don't want you scaring him back into unconsciousness if he wakes up."

Rolling my eyes, I snatched a throw pillow off the nearest couch and tossed it at Harper just as the door closed behind him. Finding a mirror in the library wasn't difficult—they were everywhere throughout the house, making all the rooms appear larger than they already were. I studied my reflection in the one hanging on the wall behind the couch and snorted. *Horrendous.*

Pulling my hair out of its braid, I combed my fingers through it before gathering it into a ponytail. I could see the muscles on my arms flex as my hands worked and was pleasantly surprised to know my training was paying off. I wasn't a badass by a longshot, but I was different, stronger, better—what I needed to be if I would continue to survive.

I remembered the Zoe who'd worked at the art gallery—the prim and proper, reserved professional who'd sold artwork, curated shows, and struggled as a starving artist. She would shake hands and smile demurely when all she wanted was to tell clients they had horrible taste in art.

And then I remembered the Zoe who'd worked at Earl's. The flirty, cocky, mysterious woman who would bat her eyelashes if it meant she would get a better tip or skimp on putting alcohol in a drink if a customer was being an asshole.

What Zoe am I now? Shaking the inconsequential question from my mind, I searched the shelves of books lining the walls. I studied the bindings, looking for stories that seemed interesting enough to read to Jake.

How They Work: A guide to mechanical engines…Boring.

The Ultimate Man's Survival Guide: Recovering the Lost Art of Manhood…I'll snag that one for later.

Julius Caesar…Too difficult.

Sense and Sensibility…Jake would kill me.

Journey to the Center of the Earth…Hmmm…

That's when I found it—Alexander Dumas's *The Count of Monte Cristo,* broken into two volumes, stood beside its classical companions. Removing the first volume from its resting place among other aged texts, I inspected its worn, navy-blue binding before opening its cover. I gently fingered the brittle, age-stained pages to find the date I was looking for—1846. *Why am I not surprised they have a first edition?*

I pushed an oversized leather armchair to Jake's bedside, settled in, and began reading aloud. The antique pages turned quickly, and the more I read, the more engrossed I became with Edmond's story.

Before I knew it, days had passed, and I'd read the entire book nearly three times. Every time Edmond escaped from Chateau d'If and reclaimed his freedom, I hoped Jake would break free from the mental purgatory his injuries had trapped him within. When he woke, would he tell me my translations of the French names had improved or that my commentary was rubbish? He would probably tell me I was horrible at reading aloud since I didn't change my intonation for the different characters. But I continued reading anyway.

When my voice grew hoarse from overuse, I sketched, trying to capture the sunsets that reached above the lake each day, and when I grew frustrated with drawing, I talked to Jake. I told him how strange it was sleeping in such a large house and that I felt like Scarlet O'Hara in *Gone With the Wind* as I made my grand entrance down the staircase every morning. Except, instead of a hoop-skirted gown, I wore sweats or jeans. I told him that he didn't have to make Cooper sleep outside my door anymore because the dog slept with me every night and followed me everywhere I went anyway.

Some nights, I drank too much and blubbered on about my dreams and my family. I told Jake about Dani and how she was the only person who'd ever cared enough to look out for *me.* I explained that she was more than a friend, more than a sister…that she was part of me. "*That's* why I have to get to her," I told him, desperately wanting him to understand.

As the days passed and I ran out of activities to keep my mind occupied, panic resurfaced. On our fourth day at Sarah's house, Harper decided to check the burns beneath Jake's bandages. "I should've done it sooner, but I didn't want to disturb any healing." He sighed. "There was no bleed-through…I'm hoping that's a good sign."

Mindfully, Sanchez and I helped Harper snip the gauze at Jake's fingers. We started gently peeling it away from his skin, so Harper could clean Jake's wounds.

My eyes became glassy as we freed his perfect thumb from its stained sheath of bandages. I carefully continued uncovering

Jake's entire hand, trying to control my anticipation, and moved up his sculpted arm. I exhaled with relief. It was working; his body was regenerating. He appeared flawless...but he still wasn't awake.

Unable to resist, I slid the backs of my fingers down his forearm to his cupped hand, letting them rest on his palm. Heat flooded my neck and cheeks, and I wasn't sure if I was blushing out of excitement from feeling his skin against mine, or because I was embarrassed about caressing him while he was unconscious... in front of Harper and Sanchez. I looked up to find them both watching me closely.

"Uh, Zoe, let's give Harper some, uh...privacy to work," Sanchez said, escorting me out of the room. She passed me off to Sarah.

Stunned by Jake's recovery, I let Sarah lead me down the hall. I was vaguely aware that we'd left the house and were heading down the path to the lake; all I could think about was Jake.

We walked to the end of the dock and sat down across from one another, each leaning our back against a piling.

"So, this is good, right?" Sarah said, apparently baffled by my quietness. She pulled her hood up over her head and readjusted her bug-like sunglasses.

"Yeah," I agreed, still shocked that Jake's body was healing so well. "He's gonna be okay," I told her, and for the first time, I actually believed it.

"Yep," she said, a smug look on her face. "Shall we celebrate?" With a naughty grin, she pulled something out of her sweatshirt pocket—a black flask with a marijuana leaf etched on it.

Laughter exploded from me. "How can I say no to *that*?"

A toothy grin spread across Sarah's face. "You can't. That's the point." Unscrewing the top, she took a swig of its liquid contents, made a sour face, and passed the flask to me with a wink. "Aged to perfection."

Taking a drink, I cringed as what tasted like rum burned going down, warming my empty stomach. "Where did you get this thing?" I asked, holding up the flask.

Leaning back on the dock, Sarah ignored a heavy breeze and basked in the rays of the sun. She looked like a movie star—elegant, confident, and comfortable. "I bought it when I was in high school…to freak out my mom."

Laughing, we told each other stories about how we terrorized our parents until the flask was empty. When it was too cold to resist the warmth indoors, we headed back into the house, feeling buoyant as the liquor coursed through our veins. We had a few more shots before Sarah disappeared with Biggs in tow.

The night passed in a blur, and when everyone went to bed, I found myself sitting at Jake's bedside. He was sleeping soundly, completely free of bandages. Utterly fascinated, I studied every exposed inch of him.

In the candle's flickering light, stubble barely obscured the clean lines of his jaw. I had to sit on my hands to keep from reaching out and running my fingers over the soft curves of his slightly parted lips. His hair had grown back, short and silky, and occasionally his brown lashes fluttered. The rhythmic rise and fall of his chest was mesmerizing. *He just looks like he's sleeping…*

Eventually, I lost myself in "what-ifs" and "I wonders," and began to doze. I dreamt of seagulls flying above me, screeching through damp sea air. I dreamt of wet sand beneath my feet, molding to the shape of my toes, and the briny smell of the wind as it whipped my hair around my face and stung my eyes.

But my dreams were interrupted by a muffled sound, and my consciousness stirred. A throaty rumble soothed me as I drifted in a state of partial awareness. I felt like I was floating, and a sudden blanket of warmth lulled me back into restful sleep.

The next morning, the click-clack-click of Cooper pacing on the hardwood floor woke me. It took me only a moment to realize I wasn't in the chair, but was instead nestled in a bed. As I took a deep breath, the smell of rubbing alcohol filled my nose.

My hair was splayed over my face, partially blocking my view of the room, and I felt the pressure of a warm body behind me and quiet breathing tickling my ear. My heart fluttered as I realized where I was. Slowly brushing my hair out of my face, I was astonished to find Jake's arm wrapped around me. *How the...*

"*Zoe, what are you doing?*" Sanchez said disapprovingly in my mind. I raised my head to find her standing in the doorway to the foyer, her face a mixture of both horror and skepticism.

Carefully removing the covers, I snuck out of Jake's bed. I tiptoed out of the room, trying not to wake him, and gently closed the door behind me.

"I don't know what happened," I said, shrugging defensively. *Did I climb into his bed?* I hadn't drank *that* much...had I?

"Biggs is making breakfast. Be back down here in ten." Sanchez's voice followed me as I headed up the staircase to brush my teeth and change clothes.

"Yes, Mother," I muttered. I felt like I was seventeen again and had just been grounded for sneaking a boy in through my bedroom window.

As I opened the door, I wished I had time to sneak under the bed's plush down comforter for a quick nap. My mind was still fuzzy from sleep...or maybe from the shots I'd taken with Sarah after we'd returned to the house. Unfortunately, Sanchez's disapproving expression had promised she would retrieve me if I took too long.

After combing out my tangled hair, I brushed my teeth and washed my face, trying to quantify how much I'd drank. Pulling on a clean, purple V-neck and a fresh pair of jeans, I stepped back to appraise myself in the standing, full-length mirror beside the desk.

At least I don't look *hungover.* I shrugged and headed for the door. As I turned the curved, bronze door handle, I heard my name echo in the grand entryway.

"Zoe!" Harper yelled again, and I flung open the door.

"I know, I know, I'm coming. Jesus. You've eaten without me before." I hurried to the nearest stairway. Halfway down the stairs, I froze. Jake, wearing a white t-shirt and plaid pajama pants, stood in the foyer. Everyone else was crowded around him, but he was staring at me.

Sarah gestured back toward the library. "You should sit down, Jake."

"I'd rather stand."

"I need to ask you some questions—make sure you're alright," Harper said.

I could barely hear their demands over my thudding heartbeat. Seeing Jake out of bed, I felt weightless, and the constant worry that had been taunting me all week fizzled away.

"Morning," Jake said, his voice rough. He stood near the doorway to the library with attentive eyes, waiting for a response, but I could only stare at him in astonishment.

After a few rapid heartbeats, I finally whispered, "Morning." My voice was trapped in between excessive excitement and disbelief.

"You were gone when I woke up," he said coolly, but a wry grin followed. It melted every part of me, weakening my knees until I almost fell down the stairs. I barely noticed Sarah and Harper whispering something to the right of Jake, or Sanchez watching us from his left. I couldn't look away from Jake's all-consuming eyes.

"You read Dumas," he added in my silence, and I instantly knew he'd heard everything—what I'd told him about my family and Dani, about Clara, and about how infuriated I was with him for running back into the fire.

Nodding dumbly, I felt my chin quiver and a tear streak down my cheek. Another followed, and before I could stop myself, I was running down the stairs. Running to him. I leapt into his arms, and wrapped my limbs around him, squeezing desperately. I was afraid he would disappear.

"You're awake," was all I could think to say as he held me snugly against him. His chest moved with mine, and I clutched his sleeves in my hands—he was real, and being wrapped in his arms was even more comforting than I'd imagined it would be.

"Thank you," he said quietly, his lips brushing my ear.

"I can't believe you heard me," I choked. "I can't believe you're awake." I suddenly realized I'd launched myself at a man who'd nearly died only days before. I leaned away from him and searched his face. "Am I hurting you?"

He shook his head.

I wiped the tears from my cheeks with one hand. *Of course I'd fall apart in front of him...again.* "I was doing so good," I whimpered.

Jake chuckled and looked deep into my eyes, searching for something. "You were in my dreams."

"Was I blubbering like an idiot?" I asked sarcastically. Suddenly conscious of the scene I was making, I unwrapped my legs and lowered my feet to the cold marble floor.

"Come on, Jake," Harper called from the library. "Let's check your vitals." But Jake said nothing, his gaze holding mine as he backed away, one step at a time.

"Come on, Sleeping Beauty," Harper said, ushering Jake into the room.

Before turning away, Jake smiled at me. "Alright, Doc."

43

DANI

Chris sat on a boulder a few feet away, the weak rays of the fading winter sun turning her blonde hair an ethereal silver-gold as she studied me. Behind her, the surface of an expansive lake reflected the pines and snow-capped mountains surrounding it, looking like Monet's version of the breathtaking alpine scenery. Chris and I were sitting near the lakeshore, several hundred feet from the tents in their dense shield of trees.

"There has to be a way. You can't keep going like this," Chris said.

"I'm fine." I waved her worry away and shifted on my own little boulder—my butt wasn't enjoying the cold stone, especially not after another day spent in the saddle.

She snorted. "Yeah…you're so fine that you almost slid right off your horse."

I shrugged. I'd been maintaining a connection with the animals around us for the past four days, ever since we left Bodega Bay. It was necessary, but it also came at a high price, leaving me completely exhausted…except at night. Once we stopped each evening, I would find several dozen nocturnal animals and ask them to keep an eye out for other "two-legs." Even though I kept the connection with them open while I slept—using my Ability throughout the night—I tended to feel a little better when I woke each morning. I should have been *more* worn out…it just didn't make sense. On the other hand, the unusual dreams about stalking deer through deep woods and soaring over snowy peaks made perfect sense—the animals' thoughts were bleeding into my subconscious and influencing my dreams.

Chris pursed her lips for a minute before speaking. "Maybe it's like a passive and active thing. Like you're trying harder when you're awake. Can't you just turn it down or something, so it's not as tiring?"

"I don't think so…it's more of an on-and-off thing. I'm either connected to a mind, or I'm not."

Frustrated, Chris huffed. "Well you're always connected to Jack, right?"

"Yep."

"But that doesn't wear you out, right?"

I shook my head. "Doesn't seem to."

"So it's also a numbers game. The more minds you're connected to, the more energy you expend."

Nodding, I gave a tight-lipped smile. "And people's minds are harder, like they're trying to kick me out."

"But why are you less tired in the morning? You said you're still doing it at night," Chris said, thinking out loud. We'd already been over it, multiple times. Narrowing her eyes, she asked, "How do you find them? The minds, I mean."

"I don't know…at first it was like casting out a net and seeing what I caught. But the past few days I've sort of been able to see them in my head."

She leaned forward, intent. "Like radar?"

I thought about it briefly, picturing a black screen with sonorous beeps bringing green shapes intermittently to life. "I think…maybe?"

"So right now, can you tell me where the nearest living mammal is, besides me?" Her eyes were bright, excited.

It took only a moment of focus. "Down there," I said, pointing to the ground beneath us. "It's a group of something small. They're hibernating, I think."

"If you do whatever you just did, how long can you just 'observe' without actually connecting?"

"I'm not sure. Want me to try right now?" I asked, and Chris nodded.

Exactly as I'd done with the small, furry family beneath us, I focused on the part of my brain that let me hold conversations in others' minds. It was like removing headphones to hear what somebody was saying. I closed my eyes, blocking out distracting visual stimuli, and a world of living minds blossomed around me.

Every other time I'd entered the "observation" state, I'd been looking so intently for specific individuals that I'd missed the wonder of the collective. It was breathtakingly beautiful, like an orchestra of stars pulsing together in harmony, playing the song of life. I lost myself in their melody. It was balanced and perfect and random and…right. When one throbbing mind extinguished, another appeared elsewhere. Death and life—the natural order of things.

Like the mythical Sirens, each mind hummed, luring me in. I wanted to take the next step, to bridge the chasm separating us. I wanted to connect.

"Dani?" Chris asked softly, pulling me back from the precipice.

"Hmmm?" The sound was wistful. As I opened my eyes I felt rejuvenated, like I'd spent the day at a spa instead of on horseback.

"How'd it feel?"

I smiled. "Great. Gets dark fast here, huh?" It had been late afternoon when I'd closed my eyes, but twilight had fallen.

Without taking her eyes from me, Chris rubbed her hand over her mouth before resting her chin on her fist. Sitting on a rock, with an elbow on her knee, she could easily have been posing for the female version of Rodin's *The Thinker*.

"Your eyes have been closed for almost an hour," she told me slowly, letting the words sink in.

Shocked, I stared at her.

"And you don't feel more tired?" she asked.

I shook my head. I felt awesome—completely alive, like the mental immersion had pumped me full of endorphins.

"Can you tell the difference between people and animals when you're, you know…in observation mode?"

I nodded.

"What's your range?" she asked. At my confused look, she amended her question. "How far can you 'see'?"

"I…," I began but had to clear my throat. "I don't know. I could feel everyone in the camp, but that's not that far."

"Hmmm…," she said, pulling a map out from the pack she'd set down beside her rock. "According to your 'scouts', the last group of people we passed was in that little town about five miles back. Can you try to reach that far?"

I nodded again and reentered the state of concentration. Reaching out, I expanded the diameter of my awareness, each new life increasing the lure of the Siren song. Suddenly, a cluster of armored, human minds appeared, and I gasped.

Gritting my teeth, I said, "I…feel…them."

"Go further," Chris's distant voice instructed. I pushed on.

The further I stretched my awareness, the more clumps of humans appeared. It wasn't tiring exactly, just difficult to resist completing the connections. I was about to pull back—overwhelmed by the millions of living creatures pulsing around me—when I noticed it. It was like the glow of city lights in the dead of night, barely visible over a hillcrest. It drew me in, and again, I pushed on.

As a throng of human minds appeared, the sliver of a gap between my mind and all others threatened to vanish. I was so painfully close to connecting to all of them, thousands of human minds. If I did, I was certain it would permanently fry my brain, but I didn't seem to be strong enough to resist their magnetic pull.

"No…no…too close…too many…," I repeated over and over. I was vaguely aware that I'd begun rocking back and forth on my boulder and had buried my face in my gloved hands.

Suddenly, I was no longer moving, and my mumbling stopped. I could barely think through the need to close that final infinitesimal distance separating my mind from all of the others. Someone was pulling on my wrists, trying to remove my hands from my face.

"Dani, look at me!" Jason's voice was strong, deep, and reassuring. But it also held terror…his was a voice that should never sound terrified.

Barely cracking open my eyelids, I peeked at the man kneeling on the ground before me. His eyes were bright, wild, and his face was ferocious.

He looked away and roared at Chris, "WHAT DID YOU DO TO HER?"

"Not…Chris's…fault," I groaned, reaching up to grasp Jason's wrist. "Too far…too many people…too much…can't stop…"

Jason pulled off my gloves and grasped my hands almost painfully, but his voice was calm when he spoke. "Focus, Dani. Come back to me. You have to fight. You can do this."

The pulsing minds didn't blink out of existence, not like when I'd stopped using my Ability completely, but they suddenly stopped pulling me toward them. It was like I'd flipped a switch that muted their enticing song. I quickly retracted my awareness until it barely extended beyond our camp. I wasn't sure why I hadn't passed out, why I didn't feel the bone-deep exhaustion I'd grown used to, but I certainly didn't mind.

Smiling weakly at Jason, I removed his hands from my shoulders and held them in my lap, ignoring the salty tears on my cheeks. *"Thank you."*

He scooted forward, wedging himself between my knees, and wrapped me in a fierce embrace. "Sometimes you scare the shit out of me," he said, his voice gruff.

"I'm sorry. I don't mean to." If a mind voice could tremble, mine did.

Chris rose and quickly skirted around us, saying, "I'm just going to go do…something…not here…"

"Fuck! I'm not used to this!" Jason exclaimed as he stood and stepped backward, leaving me alone on my rock. The lure of the minds instantly resurfaced at full force.

"Oh!" I exclaimed and leapt up after him. When I seized his hand, the lure faded again. "It's *you*!"

Jason didn't seem to hear me. Unexpectedly, he turned to me, grabbed my face with his hands, and crushed his lips against mine. Rising on tiptoes, I clutched his jacket at his sides and pulled his body closer. I made an involuntary, throaty noise and readied to reel in my awareness completely. *The minds! The lure! Jason!*

"Jason, wait!" I gasped as he started backing me toward our tent. He had taken to setting it up a short distance from the others, so we'd at least have the appearance of privacy. Even so, I was exceptionally grateful the sun had set and our companions couldn't watch us groping each other.

"Jason!" I said sharply once we reached our tent. "Wait! I have to tell you something."

"What?" He unzipped the tent, and then did the same with his coat, shrugging it off and tossing it inside. Our enormous, moss-green tent had two "rooms" and was a few inches taller than me at its apex.

"Something happens when you touch me," I told him.

He held my eyes, unzipping my down jacket and sliding his hands along my shoulders to slip it off. "You have no idea what can happen when I touch you," he said, tossing the coat on top of his in the tent.

As Jason clenched my waist in his hands, pulling my body to

his, I took a deep breath and held on tightly to my thoughts. But his hands were moving under my shirt, sliding up my ribcage. His thumbs traced along the curve of my bra just under my breasts. I shook my head, refocusing. "I mean…something happens to my *telepathy* when you touch me," I told him, and he stilled, his mouth inches from mine.

"What?"

"I gained control when you touched me, then lost some of it when you walked away, and then it came back when I grabbed your hand. It's like you make me stronger."

His face was unreadable, his hands unmoving.

"Jason…I think you have an Ability, too." Not for the first time, I wondered if MG had been right when he'd told me that everyone who survived the Virus would eventually develop a strange new skill…at least, everyone who wasn't a Crazy.

"And that *Ability* is what, exactly?"

Thinking hard, I bit the right side of my lower lip. It was a silly, manufactured habit that had become second nature. I could remember Zoe laughing at me when I'd practiced it on her in seventh grade. Around that time, I'd realized that teenage boys were less interested in smart, nice girls, and instead preferred pretty, flirty girls. So, I'd practiced being flirtatious until I no longer had to think about it. I'd transformed.

Jason's eyes flicked from mine, lower, to the soft, pink flesh pulled between my teeth. His hands tightened around my ribs, and he licked his lips.

"Maybe it's like a megaphone, but it amplifies other people's Abilities instead of their voices?" I tapped my pointer finger gently against my lips—another of those silly habits—before pressing it against his chest. "Or…it could be like a volume dial, turning other people's Abilities up or down. That could be super useful!"

"Sounds boring."

"Not even! What if someone was going to hurt us with their fancy superpower, and they could, I don't know—shoot lasers out of their eyeballs or something—and you could stop them by using your own crazy awesome Ability!?"

He straightened, looking down at me with narrowed eyes. "You think it's possible?"

I smiled. "I think you're already doing it."

When he raised his eyebrows, I explained, "So, there's kind of this guy who can enter people's dreams…and he was entering mine, mostly when I was on my own. He did it a few times in the week before I left, but not when you stayed with me that one night. But anyway, he helped me figure out what I can do; he's actually where the 'Ability' thing came from. And…he hasn't shown up since I rejoined you guys. So I'm thinking—it's you. You must be blocking him somehow."

Stupidly, I'd become lost in my explanation and hadn't noticed Jason's face harden to emotionless stone. *Crap! Idiot!*

His jaw clenched, sharpening his features, and then he spoke. "Some guy's been visiting your dreams? For *weeks*?"

I nodded reluctantly.

"Who is he?" Jason's voice was hot and cold in an uncomfortable mixture that made me want to run away from him.

Instead, I locked my knees, refusing to take a step backward. "I don't know exactly," I told him truthfully. "I call him MG, for Mystery Guy. He's never told me his name."

"What does he do when he visits?"

"Let's see…he was helping me figure out how to use my telepathy. And, he would get rid of my nightmares about Cam, but I don't really have those anymore." Cringing, I added, "And he comforted me the night I found out about Grams."

"Comforted you? How?"

"He held me," I snapped. "That's all." I pushed Jason's hands away and tried to step around him into the tent, but his arm shot out, blocking me.

"I told you, I'm not used to this," he said, looking straight ahead into the moonlit woods. Lightning lit up the night sky as

Jason looked at me, and his eyes glowed like blue fire for a fraction of a second. When darkness returned, I could still feel the heat of his gaze. As thunder rumbled through the mountains, Jason's right arm—the one blocking my path into the tent—flexed and wrapped around me, pulling me into a tight embrace.

My desires overpowered my mind, and I smiled against his sweatshirt. "You can be such an asshole…"

He laughed, deep and rumbling, and rested his chin on top of my head. He began running his fingertips down my back, tracing my spine through my sweater, gently, smoothly, tantalizingly.

"Mmm…that feels good," I purred, squeezing him tighter. "You remember that one winter formal…when you were a senior?"

It was the only dance we'd both attended. I was the only eighth-grader there, invited by a freshman boy who lived down the street from me—Tommy. He was cute but had possessed a decidedly flimsy backbone. When we joined up with his group of friends before the dance, the girls slowly pressured him into ignoring me. By the time we arrived at the dance, oohing and ahhing at the tacky attempts to turn the gym into a fantastical ice kingdom, I might as well have been invisible.

"Yeah, I remember," Jason said. "I didn't like seeing you sitting there alone."

Jason had found me sitting by myself at a table in the corner of the gym, near tears, my dress's layered, purple tulle skirt fluffed out around me. He'd sat in the chair next to me and lifted my chin with a single finger. "What'd he do?" he'd asked.

"Nothing," I'd whimpered. That had been the problem; it was my first high school dance, and my date hadn't talked to me since we'd arrived, let alone danced with me. And I'd always *loved* to dance, not that I was any good at it.

"Want me to kick his ass?" Jason had asked, making me smile a tiny, sad smile while I shook my head. He'd grinned then, heartbreakingly handsome in a charcoal-gray suit with a tie that matched his sapphire eyes perfectly. "Want to dance?"

I'd looked up at him as he'd stood and offered his hand, my lips widening to an elated smile. "Um, yeah…I'd love to," I'd said, feeling like the most beautiful girl in the gymnasium. He'd danced with me for four songs, including a slow dance, before his friends caught on, passing me around like the belle of the ball. One of them, a junior at the time, I actually dated the following year.

"You made me a legend that night, you know," I told Jason, laughing.

"What do you mean?"

"On the first day of school the next year, I showed up, and all the girls either wanted to be my friend or hated me because 'Jason Cartwright totally had a thing for that redhead'," I quoted. "It took me two months to convince everyone I wasn't your secret girlfriend—ridiculous, I know—and then a ton of guys asked me out because they thought I *had been* your secret girlfriend at one point. As if you, Mr. Hot-shit senior, would've dated an eighth-grader."

Jason chuckled. "Did you notice your little shit of a date wasn't nearly as popular the next year?"

"What'd you do?" I wondered, looking up at him with fascinated horror.

Jason smirked wickedly. "I didn't actually do anything to *him*…but my boys and I *did* threaten to kick the shit out of anyone who was nice to him."

"Jason!" I scolded, smacking his chest.

"What? He deserved it," he said, lowering his head to press his lips against mine. It was the perfect way to shut me up. "No more talking," he breathed. His hands slipped between us, and he unfastened the top button of my jeans.

In response, I pulled away from him, stepped into the tent, and slipped off my boots. I removed my sweater, long-sleeve shirt, and tank top in one smooth motion. At the sound of the tent zipper, I turned to see Jason had followed me in, zipped the tent, and was watching me as he removed his boots. My jeans and long underwear came off together, collecting my socks along the way. In the chill of the winter night, I was standing in a dark tent, nearly naked, with a fully clothed man. With *Jason*. Despite the cold, I felt near melting.

"I wish I could see you better," Jason whispered, his rough voice sounding too loud. He disrobed quickly, not even pausing before removing his snug boxer briefs.

Lightning flashed, illuminating him completely for an instant. He was so terrifyingly masculine…so powerful and so beautiful. A low, appreciative sound escaped from my throat.

I'd seen him naked once, though he didn't know it. Near the end of my junior year of high school, Jason had come home on leave after finishing a tour in Afghanistan. I'd been laying in Zoe's bed, my best friend sleeping deeply beside me, and had turned to face the partially open door when he'd walked by. It was early, maybe five in the morning—he probably hadn't expected anyone else to be awake. At least, that was the only excuse I could come up with for why he'd walked from his room to the bathroom, completely nude. Even in the dim morning light, I'd been able to see his incredibly defined physique and his impressive manly attributes. It had actually been the first time I'd ever seen a fully nude man in real life. He'd ruined all other men for me, setting a standard they couldn't meet simply because they weren't him.

I twisted my arms behind me to unclasp my bra and flung it on top of the pile of my other clothes. Or at least I thought I did—I was too busy savoring the sight of the statuesque man before me to care. I didn't have time to slip out of my underwear before Jason reached me.

"Let me," he said, plucking my hands from the top of my panties. He frowned suddenly. "Do we need—"

"I'm on the pill," I told him, cutting him off. I'd been good about taking my little yellow pills and had scavenged a several-year supply, just to be safe. The last thing I wanted to bring into the tortured world was a kid. And then I remembered it was Jason, a man who'd been with who-knew-how-many women. Unwanted pregnancy might not be the only thing I needed to worry about. "Unless, you know…we need to because, um…" *Awkward…*

He shook his head. "I'm good." *I bet you are…*

After a long, lingering kiss, Jason's mouth laid a path over my chin and down my throat. On his way to my purple boy shorts he was diverted by various landmarks, paying special attention to a couple of popular ones and a few less visited, before reaching his destination. He took note of the touches that made me gasp or giggle or clench my fingers in his hair. Each time he looked up at me, I knew that no guy, not even my beloved Cam, had stood a chance against the man immortalizing my body with his mouth.

As Jason knelt and slid my panties down, freeing first one foot, then the other, I shivered.

"Are you cold?" he asked, his voice even rougher than usual.

Under his penetrating stare, I shivered again. "No."

Holding my gaze, Jason slid his hands up my legs, from ankle to thigh, and higher. I gasped; Jason was finally touching me where I'd wanted him to touch for over a decade. When he felt the evidence of my desire for him, he growled. My throaty moans grew more ardent as his fingers gave way to his mouth, to his tongue. Eventually, his firm grasp on my hips was the only thing keeping me upright.

When Jason stood again, I was frustratingly close to the edge and aching to feel him inside me. I needed him more than I needed air to breathe or gravity to hold me to the earth. As I closed my hand around his length—asking, demanding—he inhaled sharply.

He wasted no time in easing me down to the sleeping bags and settling himself between my thighs. My legs shook as he entered me in one smooth motion. He wasn't gentle. His eyes never left mine, darkening to obsidian when I wrapped my legs around his body and urged him on—to hold nothing back.

Hovering above me, he sheltered me from the harsh, decimated world while we joined in one of the few truly beautiful legacies of our broken species. We needed each other, needed to feel connected more than we needed satisfaction, though the end result came regardless.

As he pushed me to ecstasy, I groaned and arched and trembled beneath him. His climax erupted immediately after mine. I savored his every sound and expression as he shuddered within me. Around me. Over me.

"I never thought this would happen," I told him quietly, running my fingernails up and down his smooth back. He nuzzled my neck in response, his breathing ragged.

Later, when we were lying together in the joined sleeping bags, he tightened the arm he'd wrapped around my middle and pulled me closer to his still unclothed body. "Did you think about it often?" he asked, and I could feel his breath against the back of my neck.

I nodded, burying my face in the little half-pillow. "But I think you already knew that," I mumbled, embarrassed.

His deep chuckle confirmed my suspicions—Jason had known I'd wanted him for...pretty much ever. "Will you keep thinking about it?" he asked, kissing my shoulder. His low, rough voice made me want him again, made my body ready for him.

"More than ever," I whispered.

He groaned. "Just knowing that is going to drive me *in-fucking-sane*."

"Good," I breathed. Minutes later, I corralled all of my courage and asked, "Did you ever think about it—about me—before everything happened?"

"Does it matter?"

"No," I said, assuming I had my answer.

Jason touched his lips to the skin beneath my ear and whispered, "I did," before grasping the inside of my thigh and easing back inside me.

44

DANI

"I don't see why you two can't just ride together…like, share a horse. Then he can boost your power the whole time," Holly said, sitting directly across the morning campfire from Jason and me. We were all bundled in our warmest clothes—though the winter had been mild so far, we were camping high in the foothills of the Sierra Nevada, and the current temperature was near freezing.

Jason and I had just finished telling the whole group about the previous night's discovery—that Jason seemed to be able to amplify or nullify other people's Abilities. We definitely didn't tell them any of the night's *other* developments, but I was pretty sure everyone knew—though we'd tried, we hadn't exactly been quiet.

"Yeah, Red," Jason said, grinning wickedly. "I could *boost your power* the whole time."

I elbowed him gently at the lame innuendo, and he chuckled. "We'd be too heavy," I explained to Holly.

"But you're like, totally small," Holly said.

Jason leaned closer and murmured near my ear so only I could hear, "You really are *very* small…I almost couldn't fit my—"

Cutting off his taunting whisper, I blurted, "I may be small, but he's huge." My already blushing cheeks flamed as I realized what I'd just said.

Jason roared in laughter and squeezed my hand while Holly gaped.

"That's not what…" I trailed off with a sigh, wishing I could execute a foot-from-mouth extraction.

"Whenever you're finished," Chris said, settling a wry look on each of us, "I have a suggestion." She looked at me. "Maybe today you could just use your mental 'observation' while we're on the road. If you need to actually use your telepathy, I'm sure Romeo here," she glanced at Jason, "…will be close enough to touch. That work?"

Jason flipped her off, and I nodded in agreement.

Chris added, "Maybe it'd be a good idea for you to not speak out loud at all, to always use your telepathy…it'll be like intensive training for your brain. It'd be nice if we could get you strong enough that you don't even need him." She nodded in Jason's direction.

I shrugged and said, *"sounds good,"* in her head, then turned to Jason. His expression had blanked—a sure sign that he was hiding some strong emotion. Making a wild guess, I said to him alone, *"Don't worry...I'm sure you can give me some other reasons to keep you around..."*

His expression didn't change, but a mischievous glint flashed in his eyes. "I'm sure I can," he said, confusing everyone but me.

Five hours later, we were hugging the mountainside as we rode along snow-covered Highway 50, just south of Lake Tahoe. It was snowing steadily, and we were all hunched over in our saddles, trying to retain as much body heat as possible. All of a sudden, a fairly large cluster of people burst into life in my mind, momentarily destabilizing my control over my Ability. I slowed Wings, which was Jason's signal to stop the rest of the group. He always rode beside me, especially since being in observation mode made me semi-oblivious to my surroundings.

"There's a large group about five miles ahead...they're either on or near the road. And they're stationary," I told him, glad I didn't have to lower the wool scarf wrapped around my face to speak out loud.

Jason relayed the information to the rest of our group and removed one of his gloves before reaching for my hand. He gently pulled one of my own fleece-lined gloves off and intertwined his fingers with mine, asking me to communicate with some of the creatures near the group of strangers.

Surprisingly, Mr. Grayson was the first to comment on the news. "I don't know what you're planning," he said, looking at Jason. "But...I think we should seriously consider staying with these people tonight." When Jason and Chris both looked at him dubiously, he explained, "I doubt the snow will let up any time soon, and it will be far easier to protect ourselves from the elements in an established camp. We can't forget that these are the same mountains that defeated the Donner Party so gruesomely."

After several minutes of discussion, everyone agreed that, for once, approaching other people would be worth the risk. As my companions briefly strategized, I received information from a couple of my scouts. I relayed their intel to Jason and Chris. *"The eagle said the two-legs cover an area about the size of the water next to her nest...not a big help, I know, but the bird seemed proud of the size of her lake. Plenty of fish for her young, or something like that. From what I can tell, I definitely think there's more than a hundred of them, but I'll be able to tell more when we're closer. Oh, and the mountain lions said they smell like good meat, not like the bad meat two-legs they've been coming across. So...I'm guessing they're not Crazies?"*

Jason stared at me, unblinking, his face unreadable. I smiled and gave his hand a squeeze.

"I didn't know mountain lions ate people," Chris said.

Ky moved his horse closer and asked, "Mountain lions? What are you talking about?"

Seeing his confusion, I included Ky in my next thought. *"Sorry Ky. Maybe, maybe not, Chris, but they said they've come across a bunch of dead two-legs—not sick, just wrong. They didn't say anything about eating them, just that they were 'bad meat'."*

"That's creepy," Ky said silently.

I shrugged. *"They're predators...it's what they are. Can you sense anything?"*

He shook his head. *"Too far. Maybe in a couple miles."*

Jason cut in, "Okay, well let's keep moving. We can talk as we ride."

Jason and the others came up with a plan that we would stick to unless Ky sensed impending violence—we would approach the strangers as a group, with Ky and Ben feeding their impressions to me, which I would then share with the rest of our group telepathically. If anyone lied or intended us harm, we'd know. I would pretend to be a deaf mute, requiring Jason to lead me around, and therefore have an excuse to hold his hand, boosting my power the entire time. When touching him, I could maintain constant contact with every member of my group.

It was late afternoon, and we were nearing the large group of strangers when I sensed two of them start to move directly to the left of us—in our direction. *"A couple of them are headed straight for us...I think they know we're here,"* I told Jason as I dismounted, trying not to sink too far into the snow. He followed suit, grabbing for my hand as soon as his boots hit the snow-covered highway.

"Tell everyone. Remind them not to talk to you out loud. Not ever," he told me, and I nodded, doing as he ordered.

The crunch of twigs and crusty snow preceded the pair's

arrival. A man and woman, both exceptionally unremarkable-looking, emerged from between the pines and firs that lined the road. They wore jeans, navy-blue down jackets, and hiking boots.

"Greetings travelers," the man said, quickly followed by the woman's, "We've been expecting you."

"Really?" Jason asked doubtfully.

The man gestured to the abandoned highway. "The Prophet Mary foretold your passage along this road."

"Ben says he's telling the truth," I told my group. *"This Mary chick must be able to do something 'special' too."*

Using a significant amount of false charm, Jason grinned and said, "Well, lucky us! We've been looking for more people. Gets pretty lonely out here. Are there many more of you?"

The man and woman smiled beatifically. "The Prophets asked us to welcome you and to show you around," said the woman, not answering Jason's question.

The man's words followed as soon as she finished speaking. "I'm Mark, and this is Jen."

After introductions were given, I told my group, *"They're giving me the creeps. Anything, Ky?"*

"Nope. In fact," he added, *"they're the most peaceful people I've felt. It's a nice break."*

"Lead on, my new friends," Jason said, motioning toward the woods with his free hand. To me he said, *"Wait until they're a ways ahead, and then put a bridle on your horse."*

"I don't have one."

"I do," he replied, rummaging through one of his saddle bags. He handed me the bundle of leather straps once Jen and Mark turned away. We waited a few minutes for our guides and companions to blend in with the trees before bridling Wings.

"Is there anything you aren't *prepared for?"*

"Us," he answered, holding my gaze as he reclaimed my hand. *"Come on."*

After twenty minutes of weaving the horses and goats through the seemingly endless forest, artificial colors came into sight. They filled every possible clearing between the evergreens. We seemed to have arrived in a city of tents—bright fabric spreading as far as the eye could see. Which, considering we were in a forest, really wasn't *that* far, but the sight was odd enough.

"You may stay here for the night," Jen said, indicating a small clearing near the edge of the mass of tents. "The Prophets will send for you in the morning."

"Explore as you like, but please don't approach the Temple until your morning escort comes for you," Mark added. Abruptly, Mark and Jen turned and waded into the sea of tents. *Empty* tents. *Where the hell are all the people?*

As the pair walked away, we converged in a huddle. There was a lengthy discussion about the potential benefits and dangers of staying the night, and then we voted. Everyone agreed that one night wouldn't be too big of a risk, and it would allow us to mingle and gain some valuable intelligence. That is, if the people who used all those tents ever showed up.

"You're anxious," I told Jason hours later as we huddled together on a fallen log beside our campfire. It was well into the night, and we were alone, having been assigned the task of "guarding our shit." Our friends were making nice with the natives, who had returned to their campsites after sunset in a massive wave of bodies.

Jason tightened the arm he had draped around my shoulders and kissed my temple. *"No...I'm* alert.*"*

"How late do you think everyone'll stay out?" I asked, yawning as I finished the thought. With every passing minute the fire's warmth was lulling me closer to unconsciousness.

"No clue," he replied. *"But I'm guessing late."*

Hoots and joyous screams and raucous laughter had been echoing throughout the forest since the campers had returned from wherever the hell they'd been. I felt like a parent waiting up for her teenagers to return home, wondering if they would miss curfew. I also felt tired, which I emphasized by yawning, again.

"Go to sleep, Red. I'll stay up."

I shook my head against Jason's shoulder. *"I'm staying up with you."*

A quiet chuckle rumbled in his chest. *"We'll see."* About fifteen minutes later, I was nodding off under the cozy safety of Jason's arm.

I woke in our tent, glued against Jason's side. He was already awake, staring blankly at the nylon roof. It was, after all, well after sunrise, though that fact was barely noticeable from the light seeping through the cloudy sky. Jason always rose with the sun.

"Hey! I said I was going to stay up with you!" I complained.

He shrugged. *"And I said 'We'll see.' It's time to get up. We don't know when they're coming to take us to these 'Prophets'."*

"When did everyone get back?" I asked, ignoring the whole "getting up" thing. I kissed his bare chest and gently bit down.

One of Jason's hands slipped under my t-shirt, teasing the sensitive skin below my belly button. *"Careful, Red. If you start this, everyone here'll know you're not really a mute. The noises you make...,"* he said, groaning softly.

"I'm not that..." I trailed off as he slid his fingers lower, over the thin cotton of my underwear. I moaned softly but involuntarily. *"Okay...point taken..."* He didn't stop but instead caused me to make a few more throaty noises. *"Jason!"*

His fingers stilled. *"Sorry."*

"You'd better be!" Even my mind voice sounded frustrated. He'd done a good job of getting me worked up, and I couldn't do anything about it. *"Dammit!"*

Removing his hand from my nether regions, Jason planted a soft kiss on my lips and met my eyes. *"I'll make it up to you tonight. Promise."*

I squeezed my eyelids shut, blocking out my view of the desire burning in his eyes. *"That's* so *not helping."*

Jason laughed softly and kissed my neck. *"Back to your question...not everyone came back last night. At least, not by two o'clock, which is when I carried you in here. Holly kept watch... said she hasn't been sleeping much anyway."*

"Oh, that's...um...very...um...would you stop that!" My breath quickened as Jason continued to pay attention to my neck.

"Nope. Not until you get up."

"Fine," I mentally huffed. I shoved the sleeping bag lower and scooted out, slapping Jason's hands away as he continued to find sensitive bits of flesh to tease. *"You are such an ass!"*

Smirking, Jason propped himself up on an elbow and watched me dig around the tent for the long underwear and jeans he'd stripped off me the previous night. *"We've already established that."*

I snorted and glanced at him over my shoulder.

He slid out from the sleeping bags, looking like an underwear model who'd just finished a photo shoot, and joined me in the search for warm clothes. Eventually we found everything we needed, including thick down jackets, boots, gloves, and wool hats, and we stepped out into the blessedly snow-free morning. Jason glared at the sky, like his menacing scowl alone could frighten away the chance of snow. Everyone except Ky was already sitting around the campfire, looking...nothing. Not hungover. Not laughing. Not talking. They were blank.

"They look weird to you?" I asked Jason as he spat toothpaste

onto a low shrub. He nodded. I continued brushing my teeth beside him, pondering the reason for my friends' odd behavior. Maybe they'd discovered something really disturbing about these people. Or maybe they'd all participated in an orgy and were too horrified to admit it. I didn't know, but I was sure as hell going to find out.

"Where's Ky?" I asked everyone after I'd stowed my toiletries.

"Oh, Ky?" Chris replied. *"I think he's with—"*

"The Prophets are ready for you," Jen, the eerie woman, unknowingly interrupted. "You'll need to leave your dog here," Jen said.

Mark explained, "The Prophet Cole has outlawed dogs from the camp entirely."

"Jack comes," I growled in Jason's head.

"He's a service animal," Jason said, holding up my hand. "You see, she's a deaf mute, and he's her hearing dog. Either we all stay out here, or the dog comes with us. The Prophets are more than welcome to—"

"Mark," the woman said. "The Prophet Cole is reasonable. I'm sure he won't mind."

"Lie," Ben told me, and I shared the information with the rest of my people.

"Does she have a leash for him?" Mark asked while I smiled at him dumbly.

"Make sure he sticks to you like glue," Jason told me. "I've never seen her use one, but I've also never seen him leave her side. It's unnecessary."

"Very well," Mark stated. "Follow us."

While we meandered down a narrow, zigzagging pathway between tents, I asked Chris, *"What's up with you guys. You're all acting sort of zombie-ish."*

"I don't know what you mean," she said. *"Everyone here was really welcoming last night. I've never felt so free...so at peace."*

I didn't say anything more and just looked around at the others. *Free? At peace? Now?* As nice as it sounded, it was one of the most ridiculous things I'd ever heard. I passed my concerns on to Jason. He agreed.

I wasn't sure what I was expecting—maybe not a step pyramid or a colonnaded Greco-Roman temple—but definitely not a yurt. Resting on an outcropping of sand near an expansive lake, the rough, octagonal, log structure had a steady stream of smoke rising from its center. It didn't really have a roof, but instead was more dome-shaped, and was maybe thirty feet in diameter.

"This is the Temple of the Prophets of the New World," Jen proclaimed, holding her arms out wide like the yurt was a magnificent sight to behold.

Mark urged us forward, shooting a surprisingly irritated look at his companion. It was the first show of real emotion I'd seen on anyone besides Jason all morning. "Come. It is not good to keep the Prophets waiting."

As we followed our guides through the structure's arched entrance, we were wrapped in unexpected warmth. A substantial fire burned in the fire pit in the center of the yurt, and three oversized, rough-hewn chairs were arrayed on a small platform beyond it. Their occupants—a man and old woman on either side, and a short, rotund woman in the center—sat in the chairs like they were thrones.

The man, evidently the Prophet Cole, was an attractive, middle-aged gentleman of average height and build. In the previous world, I would've marked him as a lawyer or a corporate businessman. The far woman was so elderly and frail-looking that I couldn't believe she'd survived the Virus.

The middle chair was larger than the other two, as was its occupant. She was obese, or what Grams used to call 'dumpy' out of kindness, and had a splotchy face that was simultaneously round and saggy. Her sheer unattractiveness was at odds with the two gorgeous, shirtless men kneeling on either side of her chair, petting her arms, hands, legs, and whatever else they could reach.

"Oh my God," I said to Jason. *"Is that—"*

"Ky." Jason completed my observation with appropriate disgust. Ky was one of the partially naked men fawning all over the grotesque woman.

"Chris knew...this morning...she was about to tell me where he was...she didn't care." I paused, and my stomach clenched. *"Jason, something's really, really wrong."*

In perfect harmony, the three seated people spoke, "We are the Prophets of the New World. We have foreseen your arrival and desire you to join the followers of the One True Religion. With us, you will find safety, and above all else, peace. We welcome you."

"Rehearse much," I thought sarcastically to all of my companions, hoping the cynicism might break through their fog.

"We would like to stay with you and your people for a few more nights," Jason said, "but then we really should continue on our way."

"A few more nights...are you nuts?" I asked him.

"No. Just wait."

The fat woman eyed Jason appraisingly and smiled. "I am the Prophet Mandy, and these are the Prophets Mary and Cole. You are more than welcome to stay with us for as long as you like. Let us dismiss this talk of leave-taking until you've seen everything we have to offer," she said, her voice turning throaty.

"Why's she talking like she stepped out of a Jane Austen novel? And why's Ky fawning all over her?" I asked the group. Nobody responded.

Watching the two young men caress the repulsive Prophet was making me feel sick, and not only because the display disgusted me—I was pretty sure I knew what was going on.

"How do you all feel about the Prophet Mandy? Anybody feeling warm and fuzzy?" I asked my companions.

"You're kidding, right?" Jason said.

Chris, standing on the other side of Jason, said, *"She doesn't seem too bad. But...I don't know...something seems...off."*

"I think she's amazing," Holly said, and Hunter and Mr. Grayson echoed her thoughts.

Ben's response was the most conflicted, convincing me that my hypothesis was at least semi-accurate. *"She's not entirely truthful, but I want to trust her. She's just so...I don't know. I want to stay with her. I feel at peace around her."*

"Jason!" I said frantically in his head alone. *"She's doing something to everyone. Like what Cece did to some of the guys, controlling their minds or something...except it's working on everyone. I think I'm safe because you're unconsciously shielding yourself from her, and I've been touching you since we arrived, so you must be protecting me too. And Chris is standing closest to you so she's not quite so...enamored. But Holly, Hunter, and Mr. Grayson are practically in love with her! Plus Ky...that's just wrong!"*

"Shit...," Jason said silently.

"Can you use your Ability on them...you know, null them or whatever?" I asked Jason.

"I don't know how to fucking control it!" he snapped. Out loud, he said, "Prophets, do you mind if I speak with my people for a moment? Your kind offer is very persuasive."

The hideous Prophet Mandy inclined her head regally, and Jason gathered the others close to him. He carried on a show of bland conversation, discussing the many benefits of staying with the obviously mind-controlled cult—leaving out the mind-controlled cult part—while I explained the situation in their minds. Once everyone was within a few feet of Jason, the "Mandy fog" started to clear from their heads, and they grew panicked.

"Tell them to keep calm, and stay close to me if they can. I'll try to...I don't know...I have no idea how to use this fucking Ability!" Jason said.

"It's okay. It'll be alright. I'll tell them. We'll figure it out...you and me, okay?" I replied, attempting to calm him down.

"What is your decision, Jason?" Mandy asked with husky familiarity.

"We'll stay indefinitely, of course," he answered, smiling. He was so good at masking his emotions; it was unnerving.

"Very well," she said. "Everyone may leave—except you." She looked at Jason. "And my Pretties, of course." She patted Ky's shoulder as she spoke. To my surprise, the other two Prophets rose to leave with the rest of my companions.

"She's got to be the one controlling everyone," I told Jason, and he silently agreed.

When the yurt was empty of nearly everyone—only Jason, Jack, Ky, the other shirtless man, Mandy, and I remained—the fat woman simpered, "Why is that stringy little thing still here? Send her away."

Jason nearly choked on his words. "Oh…great Prophet…she's harmless, and she's only comfortable when I'm around. Besides, you can say anything around her, and she won't hear a word."

Mandy stood, flinging the hands of her worshipers away, and I watched with avid fascination as her lumps and folds rearranged under her weather-inappropriate chiffon gown. It was emerald green, strapless, and way too tight, and with her hair teased into a poofy up-do, she carried an uncanny resemblance to Ursula.

"I said, send her away. If you refuse, my Pretties will kill her," Mandy threatened, motioning for Ky and the other man to approach us.

From behind them they drew long knives with blades that shimmered like mirrors, reflecting the fire's flames.

"Over my dead fucking body," Jason growled, drawing his sidearm and aiming it at the self-proclaimed Prophet.

At my side, Jack was snarling ferociously, his hackles raised and his lips retracted to show his gleaming canines.

Abandoning my vow of silence, I pleaded, "Jason, wait! What if—"

But Jason didn't have the luxury of waiting. Ky and the other man would be on us in seconds. Without hesitation, Jason pulled the trigger, and slimy chunks and crimson ribbons erupted from the back of Mandy's head, coating her throne and spattering the wall behind her. It took her massive body a few moments to collapse onto the dais, and by the time it had settled, the fog of her control had lifted completely from Ky and the other man.

Ky looked at us, his face frozen in horror, and his knife slipped from his fingers. "Oh God…What am I…Fuck!" I had no idea what he'd been through over the past nine hours, but I could tell by the horrified look on his face that it was bad—like scarred-for-life bad.

More than a few blood-curdling screams sounded from outside the desecrated Temple, and I wondered what atrocities the "followers of the One True Religion" had endured under Mandy's manipulation. *What would Cece have done in Mandy's place?* I shuddered, hoping I never found out.

"Holy shit," Jason muttered.

The second "Pretty" had launched himself onto Mandy's corpse and was ferociously mutilating it with his knife. The three of us just watched him, unwilling to interrupt what we could only assume was well-deserved retribution.

"You're always telling us you want it harder, deeper…is this hard enough?" he cried out as he stabbed again and again, and blood splattered onto his body. "Do you want it deeper, *Mistress*?" It was almost a mercy that the monstrous woman was already dead.

I grew instantly nauseous, both from the verbal confirmation of how Mandy had been wielding her mind control and from the sloppy sound the knife made as it ripped through her seemingly endless layers of flesh. Parts of her body no longer resembled anything human, looking more like ineptly butchered cuts of meat. Finally, when his blade was clinking against bone with every strike, the man dropped his knife and crawled and scooted away from the decimated corpse awkwardly. He was headed straight for me, and I was too stunned to move.

Jason's hands gripped my upper arms painfully as he picked me up and flung me toward Ky. I stumbled into my friend right before the man's gore-covered body collided with Jason's legs instead of mine. Jason staggered backward from an impact that would have sent me sprawling on the floor.

As soon as I'd fallen against Ky's solid torso, he'd caught me in a fierce hug; he seemed to need the comfort as much as I did. The abruptness of being manhandled shocked me out of my horrified trance, and my brain finally processed the slaughter I'd just witnessed.

Slipping out of Ky's desperate hold, I lurched to the yurt's wall and vomited. It was all too much—too much blood and carnage, too much cruelty, and too much messed up behavior. The world had just become too much.

Tears streaked down my face, and as the convulsive heaves ceased, my body trembled. I wiped my mouth, welcoming the white-hot rage that had slowly overpowered my need to vomit. That woman, that vile *thing*, had enslaved innocent people, scarring them, claiming their lives—she deserved worse than she'd received.

When I turned to face the others, I saw Jason helping the bloody, shell-shocked man to his feet. I approached them, voicing my anger. "Jason, these people were enslaved. Not just their bodies, but their minds…she took their will. *Ky's* will. This is goddamn mind-rape." My words were dripping with revulsion. No doubt, my fury at what Mandy had done was fueled by my intense hatred for Cece, the only other mind-controlling bitch I knew.

Reaching Jason's side, I desperately wished for a way to clean out my mouth—it tasted of bile, and my throat burned. I stared up into Jason's eyes to find him looking at me with such despondency that I could no longer hold in my disbelief. "She wasn't even a Crazy. She was just mad with power. God, Jason…she probably wanted to make you one of her toys." The thought of him being used—controlled—spurred me on. "Promise me, if we find any more like her…we stop them."

"We'll do what we can," he said, finding my hand and squeezing it. "We should get the hell out of here…who knows how these people are gonna react now."

Before Ky or I could respond, the man with blood dripping from his fingertips regained his composure enough to speak. "Uh, I don't suppose…would it be okay if I came with you guys?" His voice was surprisingly timid. "I don't have anyone left, and I can't stay here. It's too…there're too many memories."

"I don't know," Jason said hesitantly, likely considering the group's safety. However, the excuse he voiced was, "We don't have any extra horses."

I studied the man more closely, trying to look past the thick coating of crimson covering his body, and realized he was far younger than I'd thought. "How old are you?"

"I turned sixteen last week," he said. *He's just a kid...no wonder he reacted like he did.* An idea formed in my mind.

"How much do you weigh?"

He looked confused, but answered, "One forty, maybe a little more."

"He can ride with me on Wings," I suggested to Jason.

"But you said two people couldn't—"

"No. I said you and I couldn't...you're too big. But Wings can handle this kid and me."

"He'll be touching you…all day," Jason growled.

"I won't touch her," the kid said, sounding frantic. "Why would I touch her? Not that there's something wrong with her, you know? I'd totally touch her…no, I mean…shit!"

"Hush," I told the teenage boy. Under all that blood, he truly was adorable. He'd probably been a heartbreaker at his high school before the world went to hell.

"He's just a kid, Jason," I implored, raising his palm to my lips. *"Besides, if he's riding with me, he can make sure I don't fall*

off. You and Chris both keep telling me about how I'm swaying in the saddle."

After a moment of thought, Jason answered, "Fine, but he's your responsibility. And if he steps one foot wrong, he's out." Despite his harsh warning, something in his eyes told me he was glad I'd given him a reason to say yes.

"I won't step a foot wrong. I swear!" the kid promised.

"Thank you. You're a very good man," I whispered to Jason, wishing I could wash the sour taste from my mouth so I could kiss him. "Um…you don't have any gum, by any chance, do you?"

"Uh, yeah, I think I do." Miraculously, after fishing around in several pockets, Jason pulled out a deliciously minty stick of breath relief wrapped in its pretty foil package.

"Oh my God! You're so amazing!" I moaned after the first few chews.

Jason chuckled but said nothing. Catching the devilish glint in his eyes, I turned rosy.

"What's your name?" I asked the young man as we exited the yurt.

"Carlos."

"Carlos," Jason said. "Go wash that shit off." He motioned toward the lakeshore a few yards away. "And do it quickly." The kid obeyed, even though the lake water had to be painfully cold.

Eventually, we made our way back to our campsite, stopping briefly at Carlos's tent so he could change and gather his things. The scene surrounding us was utterly heart-breaking—some people wailed and moaned on the ground, while others screamed and tore at their hair. Even the other Prophets seemed to have been set free from Mandy's control, and they looked equally as miserable as everyone else. *What did she do to these people? Will they ever be okay again?* Despair, self-hatred, and guilt clouded the impermanent village, and I couldn't help but think, *Zoe would be in hell right now.*

When we reached our companions, Jason introduced Carlos

and said, "From now on, we avoid all groups of people larger than our own until we get to the Colony, understand?" While we'd been at Carlos's tent, I'd filled the others in on everything that had happened inside the Temple, so nobody argued with the need to pack up and leave as quickly as possible.

Everyone nodded, except Holly and Hunter. "I'm staying here," Holly said.

Jason studied her face for a long moment. "Are you sure?"

She nodded. "It's just too hard without Dalton…He was a good friend, and I really need a change. Besides, I think these people could use all the help they can get." She was right; the crowd of strangers seemed lost, completely helpless.

Hunter stepped up beside Holly. "I'm staying too."

"It's your decision," Jason said and nodded toward the horses. "You can keep your horses and a goat each, but the rest of the animals come with us. We've got too much shit to give up a pack horse."

They agreed, we all said tearful goodbyes, and they disappeared among the despairing survivors. It was surprisingly difficult to watch them walk away, considering I hadn't known either of them well. But Holly and Hunter had been there, unrequested but constant companions, for a month. *Will we ever see them again?*

I shook my head, reminding myself it wasn't the time for long, introspective moments. "We should probably get going," I said to nobody in particular.

"I know," Jason said.

"We can still get a pretty good day's ride in."

"I know. Pack it up, guys."

"It'd be nice to have some daylight by the time we make camp today…especially with that promise you made earlier," I said, looking at Jason with wide, innocent eyes. There were several scandalous things I'd been planning to do with him in the light of day. Besides, I needed something to focus on other than the image of Mandy's mutilated body.

"I know, Red," Jason said, his eyes blazing. "Everyone, move your asses!"

"You're riding with me, kid," I told Carlos after everything was loaded back onto the pack animals.

"Kid?" he asked dubiously. "I'm bigger than you!"

"Stick with 'kid' and things'll go easier for you. At least, as long as you're riding with me. Trust me," I said. Out loud I followed with, "Have you ever ridden a horse?"

Carlos nodded. "My abuelo owned a ranch in Texas. We'd visit every summer. He had a bunch of horses."

"Well, hop up then. We need to get going." It was definitely going to be nice to have another person in the group who knew their way around a horse.

It took us a few tries to figure out the best position for two riders, but we settled for Carlos in the saddle with me wedged between the horn and his lap—it only worked because I was petite enough to fit. It wasn't exactly comfortable, but the young man could easily hold me in place if I started to sway. Unfortunately, Jason's jaw clenched every time he looked at us. I was getting the distinct feeling the arrangement wouldn't last for long.

"There are rules," I told Carlos as the horses trudged along the snow-laden highway later that morning. "Well, it's really just one rule. Do whatever I tell you…or Jason," I said and felt his body tense against mine. "Don't worry, it won't be anything crazy. Besides, if you don't like life with us, you can always leave."

"I heard what you said back there…about making the big guy agree to take out anyone like Mandy," Carlos said. "I want in. And…I won't leave you."

"It's your choice," I told him.

"That's why I won't leave you," he said softly, and I nearly crumbled into tears. To have no will, no choice, was abominable. I clung to the hope that the Colony would prevent us, including the young man sitting behind me, from ever falling into such a twisted trap again.

That evening, after we'd put in another full day on horseback and had set up camp, the sun ruined my indecent plans by setting —not that it stopped Jason. At the first opportunity, he dragged me into our tent and practically tore off my clothes.

"I don't care if I have to walk. You're not riding in that kid's lap again," he stated, removing our final pieces of clothing.

"Fine." I lured him down to the sleeping bags, pushed him onto his back, and straddled his hips. "I'd rather ride in your lap anyway," I whispered, sheathing him inside me and savoring his satisfied groan. I spent the rest of the evening showing him just how much I really meant those words.

FEBRUARY

45

ZOE

"Wake up!" Sarah hissed near my ear. It felt like I'd barely closed my eyes when she tore the blankets off me. "Wake up!"

"Whaaaat?" I whined, peeling my eyes open. The remnants of another restless night made my head feel like an overgrown jungle of thorny thoughts. Ever since Jake told us that Clara had held some sort of power over Tanya, I hadn't been able to shake a feeling of dread. When Clara wasn't in my dreams, my dying mother was. It had been days since I'd had any restful sleep.

"I need your full attention—every single drop of it. Come on." Hurrying to the drapes, Sarah pulled them open, and the light of dawn stung my eyes.

"The sun is barely up," I groaned, but my complaint fell on deaf ears. "What's so important," I huffed. "And why so early?" I stretched and wiggled in bed, trying to shake off the fog of bad dreams and to loosen my achy muscles—training had resumed and was kicking my ass.

"Listen to me closely, Zoe. I need the brutal honesty you've always been so good at giving...to *other* people."

My eyebrows pulled together as I considered her words. "I'm going to assume there was some flattery in there somewhere."

Sarah waved my words aside and began pacing.

Groaning again, I sat up. The thought of leaving the pillow-top mattress made me even grumpier. "Do I look as bad as I feel?"

"Yes, probably," Sarah answered as she appraised my appearance.

I folded my arms and leaned back against the pillows, annoyed. "That was a rhetorical question, Sarah. Now, get on with it. What's going on?" She was anxious, still pacing back and forth. Her hair bounced in its ponytail with each troubled step. "What?"

Pausing, Sarah looked at me through pleading, tired eyes. "I think I'm…I think I'm pregnant."

"What!" I screeched before I could stop myself. Sarah having a child seemed like a cruel joke, but I could feel her turmoil and immediately felt horrible for thinking that. Seeing the pathetic look in her eyes, I made an effort to regain my composure. "I mean, are you sure?"

Shaking her head, Sarah resumed her preoccupied stride. "Not completely, but I missed my period. It was supposed to come over a week ago. I'm starting to assume the worst."

"What are you gonna do?" Astonishment softened my voice.

She hurried over to the bed. "That's what I need your brutal honesty for, Zoe. I'm freaking out." Her chest was rising and falling like she'd just run up a dozen flights of stairs, and I could hear hysteria creeping into her voice. "I need you to tell me what to do."

"You don't know for sure that you're pregnant," I reminded her.

"Again, I'm starting to assume the worst." She walked toward the window, popping each of her knuckles as she stared outside.

Realizing the implication of her words—that being pregnant would be a worst-case scenario—I asked, "I know it's not ideal, given the circumstances, but would you *never* want a baby with Biggs?"

"Do I seem like mother material to you? Because I'm pretty sure I'd make a terrible one. Not to mention, this isn't the best time to be procreating." Curling a tendril of her hair around her finger, she resumed her pacing by walking to the door and then back again.

"Don't you…you know…use protection? I mean, how did this happen? No, don't answer that." I squeezed my eyes shut and shook my head, trying to dispel the images I'd conjured.

"I was on the pill for a while, but I ran out. We were being careful, but there were a couple of times when we got a little… forgetful, I guess you could say." Her eyes were fearful. "This is huge, Zoe! What if he doesn't want a kid?"

Resting the back of my head against the top of the mahogany headboard, I thought of Biggs and knew he'd be a great father. He had enough patience and compassion for the both of them. I smiled, trying to placate Sarah. "Don't jump to conclusions, okay? First, let's talk to Harper and see if you're right. You might just be late. *Then* we'll worry about Biggs and what to do, okay?"

Sarah nodded and seated herself on the edge of the bed, biting her fingernails nervously. "I've been feeling sort of sick lately," she confessed while I got dressed. "I thought it was because of stress…maybe with Clara and the whole Jake thing, but my gut's telling me that's just wishful thinking."

"Well, there's only one way to find out. I'll go get Harper, and you can tell him what you told me. He'll know what to do." I headed toward the door.

"But what if he tells Riley?"

I stopped in my tracks. "*You* should tell him. You're right, Sarah, this is huge. Biggs needs to know."

"I *will* tell him. I'm just scared. I've never been in this position before. What if the thought of me being pregnant is revolting to him?" she whined.

Placing my hands firmly on Sarah's shoulders, I looked into her eyes and very carefully said, "Whatever happens, just remember that Biggs loves you. He'll be supportive. He would want to know that you're this upset." I straightened. "Who knows, he might even be able to make you feel better about the whole thing." I flashed a supportive smile and crossed the room to the door. "I'll be right back…try to think of fairies and princesses while I'm gone," I said, trying to lighten the mood before I scuttled out of the room.

"That's not funny!" she called through the door.

I searched the first floor, listening for muffled voices that would give away my companions' whereabouts. As I was heading into the library, I heard the steady footsteps of someone hurrying up behind me. Unwanted, Biggs's lust for Sarah and images of her tussled hair and naked body infiltrated my mind. *Eww…Crap!*

"Hey Zoe," Biggs called out as he ran up to me. "Have you seen Sarah?"

I smiled as convincingly as I could, trying to force the images of them having sex from my mind. *Friggin' stallion.* "She's in my room. Girl talk stuff," I said nonchalantly, fleeing into the library before he could get any more information out of me. "We'll be done soon."

He followed me, and I wondered why he was suddenly feeling sympathetic. *Strange.* When I faced him, he shook his head and said, "I'm sorry, Zoe. Harper told me about your whole…prophecy thing. I mean, I *knew* about it before, but I guess I just didn't know all the details. You doing okay?"

I was instantly confused, knowing *I* didn't possess any sort of prophetic ability, but I nodded anyway.

"That's gotta be weird to think about," he said.

Oblivious to what he was talking about, I fished for a satisfying explanation. "Yeah…" I nodded again. "What are your thoughts about the whole thing?" Biggs was always so chatty—I hoped that, if I kept him talking long enough, I could get some answers.

"Honestly, I'm not surprised by much anymore. But man, I can't imagine how it feels to know someone *predicted* your death." He placed a supportive hand on my shoulder and slowly shook his head. "I'm just glad I'm not in Jake's shoes. I don't know how I'd handle knowing I was predestined to cause someone's death. It's all pretty crazy, right?" He paused, waiting for me to agree.

"Yeah, it's…weird," I said hollowly, trying not to let his words overwhelm me. A few seconds passed as I grasped for some kind of understanding. My confusion turned to shock, and finally betrayal took root in the pit of my stomach as Biggs's words sank deeper. *A prophecy that I would die because of Jake? And no one said anything to me?* Every nerve in my body bristled with unease as Jake's confusing behavior toward me started to make sense.

Biggs's eyes widened, and I could feel his acute discomfort. "But you made it through, yay…" His fist pump was weak, and he forced a timid smile before his face dropped. "You didn't know about any of that, did you?" He ran his fingers through his short, blond hair, clearly distressed. "Shit."

"Nope," I said slowly, my voice low with disbelief and anger.

"Okay…so…I'm gonna go now. Will you send Sarah down when you ladies are done chatting, please?"

"Sure," I said flatly, and Biggs hurried away. Turning on my heel, I marched toward the dining room, hoping to find Harper.

The fact that Harper and Jake hadn't told me such a huge secret —*about me*—pissed me off. After everything I'd been through with Jake, he hadn't uttered a word, and Harper, who I'd thought was my friend, had been just as secretive. *How the hell did I not sense this?*

Harper and Sanchez were debating whether we should stay or leave as I stomped through the swinging kitchen door and into the dining room. I tried to remember that Sarah needed my help and that I had to focus on *her* situation, not mine, but when Harper smiled warmly at me, anger heated my cheeks, and I glared at him.

Sanchez turned in her seat to face me. "Yes, Zoe?"

I ignored her. Refusing to look at either of them, I stared at the crystal chandelier hanging above the oversized mahogany table. "Harper, Sarah needs you upstairs…in my room." When they said nothing, I added, "It's sort of important," hastily turned, and walked away.

Hoping I wouldn't run into anyone else before reaching the sanctuary of my room, I hurried toward the entryway. Unfortunately, as I got to the foyer, Jake and Cooper strolled in through the front door. I ignored the warmth in Jake's eyes as I hurried up the left staircase and disappeared into my room. I slammed the door behind me.

"You okay?" When I heard Sarah's trembling voice, I was instantly grateful it wasn't me sitting on the bed, crying about pregnancy and babies. She fiddled with the hem of the sheets, and her eyes were red-rimmed and puffy.

Forcing a smile, I answered, "Yeah, fine. Harper's on his way. We'll get this figured out, don't worry. Everything'll be okay, you'll see." I sat down on the bed beside her, wringing my hands with unease.

A light knock on the door startled me, and Harper popped his head in. "Can I come in?"

His nice-guy charm was suddenly irritating. "Of course you can. I asked you to come up here, didn't I?"

His relaxed facial features hardened at my curt tone. "Whoa, who spit in your porridge this morning?" he asked incredulously as he strolled into the room.

"We'll talk later," I said with false cheer and stood. "You need to focus on Sarah right now." I walked to the window, hoping to find a distraction floating on the choppy waters of the lake below. I listened as Sarah explained her situation and as Harper encouraged her to believe that everything would be alright, no matter the outcome. Eventually, I tuned them out entirely.

I thought of better, simpler times, when the most difficult decisions I had to make were which shifts I wanted to take at Earl's or which art pieces I wanted to showcase at the gallery. I *wanted* to worry about what to wear to work and not have to deal with freakish Abilities or Crazies or prophetic secrets.

A despairing whine snapped me out of my daydreams, and I turned to face the bed. Sarah had received a positive result from a urine test, and her eyes were again filled with tears. She threw herself back onto the bed, moaning and cursing about the unfairness of it all.

Not knowing what to say, Harper and I stood awkwardly beside the bed. "Good thing I had what we needed," he said under his breath.

"Are you sure?" Sarah asked, oblivious to his comment. "I mean, should we run the test again?"

He sighed. "We've done it three times, Sarah. I'm 99 percent sure you're pregnant. You need to tell Biggs."

Before Sarah could argue, a voice from near the doorway startled us. "Did I hear my name?" Biggs peeked around the door, his eyes falling upon his distraught girlfriend, who immediately sprang to her feet. "What's wrong, Babe?" He saw her teary, swollen eyes, and hurrying over to her, wrapped his arms around her. Sarah shook in his hold, divulging the news between staggered breaths.

"But that's great news!" he shouted and looked around the room. "Did you hear that? We're having a baby!"

"It's still the very early stages," Harper cautioned him from the attached bathroom as he washed his hands.

But Biggs didn't seem to hear Harper, or he didn't care. Instead, he lifted Sarah up and swung her around like she'd just accepted his marriage proposal—only, her face was blotchy and distressed, while his was filled with immense joy.

"You *want* to have a baby?" Sarah asked in between his laughing and hooting.

"Of course I do…don't you?" When Sarah didn't say anything, Biggs's enthusiasm deflated. I could feel his joy drain from him as he looked into her frightened eyes.

"I'm not sure how to be a mom," she said truthfully, watching his face for another heartbreaking reaction. "And, I can't say we're living in a baby-safe environment. We don't even know where we're going from one week to the next." Her lip quivered. "We're like…bums."

I stifled a laugh before it could escape my throat.

Biggs's eyes continued to watch Sarah closely—so did mine—as she deliberated aloud. "What if something happens during the pregnancy or birth or after? There're no hospitals, no medicine…"

He gently pulled her toward him, and she shuffled into his arms once more. Resting his chin on the top of her wild hair, he sighed. "Things may never get better, Babe, but I know that I don't want to stop living after we've survived so much." His eyes were suddenly alive again and his tone elated. "I could teach the baby everything about survival…at least everything that I know. We have Zoe and Harper and everyone to help us. We won't be alone…" He searched her eyes for some sort of acceptance. "Sarah?"

As she brushed away a stray tear, her face widened with an unexpected smile. "It sounds kinda nice when you say it like that."

Biggs gathered her up into his arms and carried her out of the room. "I'm gon-na be-a dad-dy! I'm gon-na be-a dad-dy!" His chant echoed throughout the cavernous house, and Sarah's giggles faded as they disappeared down the hall.

Distracted by the excitement, I hadn't noticed Harper coming up beside me until I saw him out of the corner of my eye.

"Now," he said and paused. "What's wrong? Are *you* pregnant too?"

I rolled my eyes. "You have to have sex to get pregnant," I snapped, turning to face him.

"Hey, I offered," he teased, but I ignored him. "Well, then, what's wrong with you?"

I gave him a withering stare. "What do you think?"

He shrugged, clearly annoyed.

"Damn it, Harper. Why am *I* the last to know about this prophecy thing between you and Jake? What the hell's going on?"

Harper's look of frustration disappeared, and his eyes clouded with guilt. He sighed and sat down on the edge of the bed. "Sorry."

"Don't I get any explanation? Biggs mentioned something about Jake being involved in my death like it's common knowledge. Apparently you've all known about it for a while, and all I get is 'Sorry'? How long did you guys know I was *supposed to die*?" I paced, trying to ignore the regretful look on his face.

"First of all, we didn't tell you because we didn't know if it was true. Jake sure as hell didn't…at least, not until he actually saw you for the first time. And even then he wasn't sure if he should believe it. This is all so surreal; you know that as well as anyone. We didn't know what to do. This is new for all of us, Zoe." He finally took a breath. "I'm sorry you feel—"

"Betrayed? Frustrated? Pissed?" I seethed.

"Yeah, but this has been hard on all of us too. We didn't know what to do," he repeated. "There's no manual."

"No shit," I spat. I couldn't decide what was bothering me the most—that I hadn't known what was going on or that I felt betrayed.

Suddenly, fear bubbled up, replacing the anger that had laced my words only moments before. "I could've tried to protect myself, H."

When Harper threw his arms up in exasperation, I walked toward the stairs. I suddenly felt claustrophobic and needed to get out of the room.

"We didn't know it was Clara, Zoe." I could hear his footsteps on the landing behind me, and I paused at the top of the stairs. "We didn't know if it would really happen. Jake was only told that you'd die and he'd be the cause, but how were we supposed to know if that was true? It's not much to go off of so why tell you? So you can stew in fear for who knows how long?"

Groaning, I sat down on the top step. Too many questions

floated in my head, so I grabbed the most tangible one. "Who told him this…prophecy?"

I looked back at Harper when he didn't answer. He shoved his hands into his pockets. "Why don't you talk to *him* about it? He knows the details," he said quietly.

Just then, Jake stepped into the entryway and looked up at us. Based on his somber expression, I could tell he'd overheard our conversation—but I wasn't ready to talk to him about it.

"I want to be alone," I said quietly, standing. I passed Harper and went back into my bedroom, closing the door behind me.

"We all decided to not tell you," Harper called through the door. "It wasn't just Jake's decision." Eventually, I heard him pad down the stairs, exchanging muffled words with Jake. I tried to ignore them and sat on the bed.

My mind was a bottomless pit of questions. In an effort to avoid them, I thought about Sarah and her baby. I worried about her—while Sarah had been born into wealth and luxury, her child would be born into more primitive circumstances—no prenatal care, no epidurals, no pediatricians. We were still learning about how to survive in our new life—about the Abilities and about the Crazies. *How can she possibly take care of a kid?* There were too many uncertainties, and I certainly wasn't convinced she'd make the best post-apocalyptic mother.

"Well, I'd be pissed too!" Sarah shouted, her voice jarring me from my musings. She flung open my bedroom door; apparently privacy was a foreign concept to her. "There you are! Is everything okay? Riley told me what happened. It's so creepy," she said and sat down beside me. She rested her hand on my shoulder in an attempt to comfort me.

I didn't want to talk about my situation, so I smiled reassuringly. "I'm fine. I'm just glad you're doing okay." I gestured to her tummy.

"The more I think about it, the happier I get, especially around Riley. There's a lot that needs to be worked out, but we have a while, right?" Her smile spread from ear to ear as she beckoned me to follow her downstairs. "I told Riley I wanted to wait for you before we started," she said, but stopped and stood at the foot of the stairs. Turning to me, she began squealing and dancing in place, unable to control her excitement.

"Was that the Running Man?" I laughed as she pulled me into a hug before scampering through the foyer.

"It's so strange—I mean, a lot of things are strange—but how much has changed in the last two hours is *really* weird," she said as we paraded down a long hallway toward the kitchen. "I was so scared before. But Riley's so happy that I can't be upset or worried, no matter how hard I try. You should see him, Zoe. You think *I'm* crazy, but he hasn't stopped celebrating since I told him. How can I be pessimistic about this whole thing when he's so ecstatic?"

As I continued following her, I couldn't imagine having a baby at such a troubling time, but I smiled anyway. "You can't."

She tugged me along, and we practically fell through the doorway into the lavish kitchen. To my surprise, about fifteen different bottles of liquor were lined up atop the green granite-topped island in the center of the room.

"Holy…Where'd you get all the booze?" I asked.

"My dad has an extensive liquor cabinet. It's about as big as a wine cellar—normal people's wine cellars, I mean. Anyway, I took out what I thought you could use. There's more in there if this isn't enough."

"I think this is plenty…but what do I need this for, exactly? I'm not planning on needing my stomach pumped at ten in the morning."

"I've volunteered you to be the bartender during today's festivities. Duh!"

I was instantly confused. "Newsflash, Sarah. Drinking is generally frowned upon in your current condition."

She swatted my arm. "Yeah, well, *I'm* not drinking, at least not alcohol, but that doesn't mean no one else can. Besides, I know you can make me a fancy, nonalcoholic drink that will make me feel special, and I can pretend I'm partaking with you. Consider this a baby shower…Jake recovery celebration…thing. And we can't celebrate without drinks; it's absurd." She dismissed the thought with a wave and gestured to the array of bottles before me like the Vanna White of distillates.

I laughed, looking at the impressive collection. Deciding I could definitely use a drink—or three—I canvassed the assorted bottles, determining what type of potion I should concoct first.

Tequila…hangover city.

Rum…tempting.

Vodka…I could definitely get creative.

Knowing Sarah liked berries, I settled on vodka crans to start, using carbonated water to liven up her drink a bit, and contemplated what our next libation might be.

Although I was still irked by my recent discovery, I was determined to play nice with everyone for Sarah's sake. I wanted to enjoy a few drinks with my friends, even if my oblivion would only last for the day.

Jake and Cooper showed up moments after I made the first round of drinks, and gratefully, Biggs and Harper enlisted Jake's help with something outside, so there was no awkwardness or opportunity to talk.

After a toast to the proud parents-to-be, we started prepping for an early, very large lunch—baked beans, venison freshly killed by Jake and Cooper, pasta salad with a balsamic vinaigrette, canned corn, and skillet cornbread. As we laughed and dirtied the kitchen, my mind periodically wandered to Jake, and I found myself pouring stronger drinks with each new round.

Eventually, we all made our way out onto the back porch. Harper and Jake manned the grill, babysitting their drinks while I downed mine, hoping my variations of lemon drops and cosmos would keep my spirits up. Although the cocktails were a little girlie for my taste, I drank them happily, knowing Sarah was giddy over their virgin counterparts.

We continued celebrating into the late afternoon. Sarah basked in the attention she received from Biggs, but no matter how much she played the happy mother-to-be around him, I knew she was still wary when he wasn't there.

Biggs, on the other hand, was too happy to be even a little bit pessimistic. I continued refilling his glass as his toasts became more and more frequent. Being the observant, well-practiced bartender I was, I noticed Jake had stopped drinking after a few shots of whiskey, and Harper was still nursing his second rum and Coke. Sanchez and the guys chatted, lounging in the wicker chairs that were scattered along the wraparound porch. They paused periodically, watching Sarah and me with amusement—I was intoxicated, but Sarah was just plain silly.

"Can we have pink ones next?" she begged, and I conceded, giving in to her every whim. In turn, *I* became less coherent. I knew I'd need to slow down if I was going to make it to sunset.

Putting a CD titled "Songs that Rock" into the stereo, I pressed play. I wasn't shocked when I heard the high-pitched voices of a pubescent boy band emanating from the speakers.

"Oh my God, Sarah, this is hilarious," I barked, laughing. "I can't believe this is one of your 'songs that rock'."

"I *love* this song!" she exclaimed, the white-washed boards of the porch creaking under her feet as she danced around. I was gasping to catch my breath in between bouts of laughter, trying not to pee my pants as the songs continued—each more ridiculous than the last, just like Sarah's dance moves.

Eventually Biggs zeroed in on me, tugging on my arms and trying to pull me up from my perch on a chaise. "Come on, Zoe. You haven't danced all day!"

Resisting, I said, "Thanks, Biggs, but I'm not drunk enough to start dancing. Especially not to this. Sorry, buddy."

"Nope, no more excuses. Sarah told me you ladies used to go

out dancing, so come on!" He continued pulling on me, and as my drink sloshed in my glass, I relented, if only to avoid a spill.

"Uncle, uncle!" I conceded, but Biggs kept at it. "Okay! One second!" Downing what remained of my drink, I set the glass aside and followed him over to where a completely sober Sarah flailed and sang.

With each unsteady step, I realized how drunk I actually was —I swore that I was done drinking for the night. The sun was low, and the sky would be full of vibrant colors soon…I hoped I would make it that long. As we started dancing, I stumbled, barely catching myself before falling. Biggs threw me around, attempting his own rendition of swing—he was three sheets to the wind, so our movements may not have qualified as dancing, exactly.

When I flashed a "please rescue me" glance at Harper, he smiled, getting out of his chair and sauntering over to us. "Mind if I step in?"

Biggs shook his head and returned his attention to Sarah.

As Harper gathered me into his arms, a classic rock song blared from the speakers, and his eyes lit up. "This was my sister's favorite song," he said.

"You have a sister?" I'd sort of expected it. As much as he flirted, he was also protective and brotherly.

Twirling me, he said, "I have three, actually…or I *had* three. All younger." There was sadness in his voice I understood too well.

"You've never mentioned them," I thought aloud.

"I know. It's hard to talk about life before."

I nodded and rested my cheek on his shoulder.

"You surprise me, Baby Girl," Harper whispered.

Lifting my head, I cocked it to the side and studied his face. "What d'you mean?"

He chuckled. "I thought you used to be a bartender, but you aren't holding your liquor as well as I'd expect."

Feeling defensive, I tensed. "We've been drinking for, like, five hours or something. I'm not a linebacker, you know."

"Calm down. I'm just saying…" He watched me curiously, and I scowled in return. "And it's been more like seven hours," he added.

"Oy," I muttered. "I rest my case."

Smirking, Harper said, "You're funny," before tightening his hold on me. Again, I leaned my head on his shoulder and closed my eyes, feeling like I might float away as we swayed to the rhythm of the music.

"I'm sorry I didn't tell you," he said guiltily.

I instantly knew what he was talking about, and in my intoxication, his sincere apology was all I needed to forgive him.

He pulled away so he could see my face. "I would've wanted to know too. I didn't think about it like that. I know you would've told me, and I should've done the same for you."

I nodded, trying not to get emotional in my drunken haze. "It's okay," I slurred, repositioning myself in the comfort of his arms.

After a couple more songs played, I decided it was best to extricate myself from Harper's hold—before I got too comfortable and passed out standing up. Opening my eyes, I saw Jake watching me. I smiled shyly at him before turning my head to face the opposite way.

I was glad no one else in our group could feel people's emotions and see their memories like I could. I couldn't imagine someone glimpsing into the unruly depths of my consciousness.

After giving Harper a peck on the cheek, I took a step back. The world spun a little as I turned and walked down the porch steps. The music was giving me a headache, and the serenity of the lake seemed like the perfect solution.

"Where are you going?" Harper called.

"Just taking a breather!" I yelled back as I wandered down the path and disappeared into the trees.

46

ZOE

Dizzily, I trudged to the lake. The crickets were silent as I walked, only resuming their chirping song when I settled myself on the end of the dock. I pulled my legs up against my chest and looked out at the ripples in the water, wondering what lived beneath the lake's surface. *If Dani were here, she'd be daring me to jump into the frigid water. Not a chance*, I thought drunkenly.

I was glad I'd lasted long enough to see the sunset—burnt orange and pink filled the sky as the sun sank behind the hills, its rays casting a glowing haze over the forest. It was strange to think that the same sun had shone in the skies over Fort Knox. So much had happened at the base, it seemed like a lifetime had been folded into mere weeks.

A gust of wind shook me from thoughts of darker times, and I hugged my legs closer. I was in no state of mind to go back to the others, so I rested my head on my knees and closed my eyes, hoping the forest would stop spinning around me.

Unfortunately, my solitude was disrupted by the sound of two-by-fours creaking under slow, heavy footsteps.

"You doing okay?" Jake's voice rumbled.

My eyes flew open, but I didn't move. "Fine. Just thought I'd get some air," I said, hoping the extent of my drunkenness wasn't completely obvious.

"Are you sure you're fine? I watched you wobble out here."

I looked back at Jake, who'd stopped a few steps behind me, and gave him an evil stare before refocusing on the gently rippling surface of the water. I reminded myself not to be distracted by his alluring ruggedness; I was still hurt he'd withheld such alarming information from me.

It was silent for a moment before he spoke. "So you heard."

"Yeah," I said. "You should've told me." Although I didn't want to have such an important conversation in my jumbled state, I was curious about the truth.

Jake took a step closer and crouched down beside me. "Do you think that would've made a difference?"

"Um...*yeah*!" I blurted. "I can look for trouble better if I know it's coming. How does no one see that?" I leaned back, uncoiling from my warm ball of body heat.

Jake remained silent for a moment, then sullenly said, "I didn't know if it was true. I thought it was...crazy...until I actually saw you. Then..." He stalled. "I still couldn't really believe it. I didn't want to tell you beforehand because you'd worry all the time, and I was still trying to figure out what I should do when..."

His ambivalence toward me from the moment we met—the first time he saved my life—suddenly made sense. "That's why you stayed after you killed Jones and Taylor?" I asked, looking over at him curiously. I was secretly surprised I'd connected the dots after so many drinks. "You told me you were leaving, but you stayed."

There was something thoughtful about his demeanor as he stood and looked out at the lake. *Is he searching for the answers he thinks I want to hear?*

"Just be honest with me," I pleaded softly.

"I didn't know what the hell to do," he said roughly. I could feel his uncertainty and frustration. "I didn't know how you'd die or how I'd cause it. I thought the whole thing was ridiculous. But if there was any truth to it, I didn't know whether I should stay…or just leave." He looked down at me attentively. The light reflecting off the water's surface brightened his usually shadowed features. "Then you said you were going to Colorado on your own, and I knew that was a bad idea. I told Sanchez everything. I hoped she could change your mind, but she didn't know what to do either."

I still didn't understand. "What do you mean you'd 'cause' my death? Who told you that, anyway?"

Shoving his hands into his coat pockets, Jake looked back out at the water. "'She'll die because of you'," he said forcefully. "'The woman with the long black hair and teal eyes…you'll save her, but she'll die because of you.' That was the last thing my sister said before she died."

Hearing his words, I felt sick to my stomach. I closed my eyes, trying to forget the feeling of impending death—both during Taylor's attack and during the poisoning.

Sitting up, I sighed heavily and massaged my temples. "I still can't believe I didn't *see* any of this."

"I told you you're not very good at reading people." He looked down at me, smiling playfully.

I was surprised by his attempt at humor, and I couldn't help but grin. "So, do you *always* joke at my expense or am I just lucky to be around when you're in such a good mood?"

"You're just lucky, I guess." His sexy smile made my insides flutter.

"Your sister was like Harper," I said, abruptly changing the subject. In my intoxicated stupor, it had taken me a moment to process Jake's earlier words.

He nodded. "I didn't know what was wrong with Becca then, but *they* said they'd seen cases like hers and could help us." I knew he meant the military people I'd been introduced to through his memories. "She must've seen what they were gonna do to her."

I became lost in thought, wondering what future horrors Becca had viewed that would make killing herself seem like the best option.

Jake's eyes turned imploring. "I'm *not* going to let you go there alone. I know we aren't sure the same people are involved with the Colony, but why take the chance? Think of what they might do to you if they find out about your Ability."

Instantly, I was furious. He had no right to tell me what to do. "You're not gonna *let* me? I'm going…and I'm going alone. Nothing's changed," I told him, but the moment I said the words, I knew they weren't true, and Jake's expression confirmed it.

"Right." He shook his head and stalked passed me, back toward the shore.

I struggled to stand. "Just because you saved my life doesn't mean you get to tell me what to do!" I called after him, surprised by the desperation in my voice. The sound of Jake's footsteps on the dock reinforced the distance growing between us—our relationship seemed to be unraveling before it even started.

"Fine," he said, and my heart seemed to constrict at the coldness of that single word.

Shit. My head was a jumbled mess of wishes, desires, and frustrations…and drunkenness. Stumbling after him, I yelled, "What exactly do you want from me, Jake? You want honesty? You want me to tell you that I want you? That I need you? Well it's true, and it drives me insane." My breathing was ragged.

"You want me to go back to pushing you away? Done," he said flatly and continued walking.

"Really? Just like that? You act like it would be so easy—"

He stopped and turned, glaring at me like I'd slapped him in the face. "It won't be *easy*," he said heatedly. "But you're either so busy worrying that *nothing* will work out, or too scared that it *will*, that you're not even willing to try. If not having me in your life is easier for you, then fine." He started to walk away again.

I knew he was right, but I didn't like him calling me out so easily. I ran after him, but after only a few steps, my feet were moving faster than I could manage and I tripped. Instinctively, I thrust out my hands to break my fall as my knees hit the dock. "Shit," I hissed as the rough boards scraped my palms.

Even in my drunkenness, embarrassment burned inside me. I sat back on my heels and stared down at my stinging palms, wishing everything with Jake had been easier from the beginning. Instead, since we'd met, we'd been pushing each other away—because of prophecies, stubbornness, and fear.

"Zoe." I hadn't realized Jake had stopped walking away until I heard the boards creak under his feet again. "Are you okay?" he asked, his voice a mixture of anger and concern.

"Yeah, I'm fine," I said pathetically, refusing to look up him. "Just leave me here…maybe the animals'll drag me away."

He laughed despite his anger. "That's not overly dramatic or anything." Crouching down in front of me, he gripped my arms. "I'll help you up."

"Let me, please. I'd at least like to keep *some* of my dignity intact."

Jake let go and took a step back, letting me rise on my own.

Straightening, I looked into his eyes. They radiated an urgency I'd never seen in them before. I tilted my head, trying to decipher the meaning behind his intense expression, and began to feel extremely self-conscious.

"Please don't look at me like that," I pleaded quietly. I balled my hands into fists at my sides but couldn't stop them from trembling. Yearning and despondency floated in the air between us, and I was unable to distinguish his emotions from my own. Mentally exhausted, I closed my eyes and sighed.

"Nothing's changed, huh?" Jake's tone willed me to think about everything that had transpired between us during the past few weeks. When I opened my eyes he reached for my hands and examined the minute scrapes on my palms. The heat of his touch swept through me, banishing rational thought.

"For whatever reason, I know you don't want to let me in…or maybe you just don't know how." He released my hands as he spoke, and I reluctantly let them fall to my sides. "I can't read *your* mind, and I don't understand you half the time…but I know what *I* want." His voice sounded calm—confident—but I could feel both fear and hope welling within him.

Jake's vulnerability jump-started something inside me.

He moved closer, and his jaw clenched. "What are you afraid of?" I could feel his growing impatience.

"Jake, I—"

Swiftly, one of his hands grasped the back of my neck, tangling in my loose hair, and his lips pressed against mine, fierce and hot. Surprised, I stumbled back, but Jake slipped his arm around my waist, holding me against him. His kiss was greedy, and I drank in his desire. His overwhelming need awakened such an intense thirst in me that I couldn't get enough of him.

I clutched handfuls of his jacket to steady myself as he backed me up against the nearest piling. Frenzied, he began to explore my body—his mouth savoring the sensitive skin on my neck and under my jaw, while his hands drifted down my back and lower. A pleasurable ache throbbed between my thighs as he nudged his leg between mine.

My hands ventured up his broad chest, over his shoulders, and combed through his short hair. I crushed his lips harder against mine. As we kissed, lustful images from his mind began to invade mine.

Us, panting in unison. My nails digging into his bare back. His teeth grazing my collarbone, and both of us crying out in pleasure.

A deep groan vibrated in his chest as the images flashed through his mind. I wanted—no, needed—him more than I'd ever needed anyone before. Impulsively, I reached for his belt, fumbling with his buckle.

Jake froze.

Our lips lingered together for a moment, and as he pulled away, I whimpered in protest. I could still feel our combined desire humming through my body, willing me to kiss him again.

Confused, I looked up at him. "Why are we stopping?" I asked through swollen lips. He took a step back, and my heart seemed to stop completely. "Um, excuse me. Where are you going?"

Jake shook his head, taking another step backward as he tried to control his breathing. "You're drunk."

I scoffed. "I'm not *that* drunk. Besides, most guys would…" I stopped talking as his eyes flared with warning—Jake wasn't most guys.

Running his hand over his hair, he reeled in the excitement rolling through him. "I'd like you to remember this tomorrow," he said, sexual frustration apparent in his tone.

Although I felt slighted by his comment, I let it go. There was no way I could ever forget a moment like that, no matter how many drinks I'd consumed. Knowing what it felt like to have his body pressed against mine made me crave more. I needed to be closer to him, in any way possible.

"I came out here to bring you into the house," he said with an amused smile. He walked over to the edge of the dock and sat down.

"I'm *glad* you came out here," I said, plopping down beside him.

He glanced at me and lifted his arm, allowing me to nestle against him. I was surprised by how easy it was to be affectionate with him. He was right, a lot *had* changed.

My fingers explored the waistband of his pants as my mind drifted to heady thoughts of kisses and nakedness and… "What's this?" I asked, feeling something hard and leather strapped to his belt. "Your knife," I answered for him. Momentarily distracted, I unclipped it from his belt.

Jake watched me as I examined it.

"It's really cool. I like the wood handle." I held it up in the moonlight. "It looks old. Where'd you get it?"

Jake stared at it for a moment. "Someone gave it to me when I was a kid." I saw an image of an older man, a grandfather perhaps, flash in his mind. I could tell the knife meant a lot to Jake.

"I like it." I flipped open the blade and turned it over on my palm, thinking about how useful a knife would've been during the past few weeks. "I should get one." It was compact enough to store in my pocket, but the blade was menacing and sharp. "It could really do some damage," I said, slicing it through the air.

"Not a bad idea," Jake said, reclaiming the knife and putting it away. "But maybe you should wait to practice your slasher moves until you can at least walk without falling." He glanced over at me with a rueful grin.

"You're hilarious," I deadpanned and once again rested my head on his shoulder.

"You ready for bed?" he asked. As he spoke, I could feel his stubble brushing my forehead.

I giggled. "Is that an offer?"

"You're feisty when you're drunk," he mused.

I shrugged and snuggled closer against him. "Yeah well, you bring out the best in me, what can I say?"

He chuckled. "So, shall we do this the easy way…or the hard way?"

"Do what?" My breath caught as I considered the possibilities.

"I'm taking you inside."

"Excuse me?" I pulled away and locked eyes with him. "What if I'm not ready to go in?" I asked, pretending to be offended.

Jake shook his head. "Fine, have it your way." Before I knew what was happening, his arm wrapped around my waist, and he tossed me over his shoulder.

"Jake, put me down!" I ordered. "I can walk just fine!"

"Yeah, and you've got the scrapes to prove it."

"Is that why you're out here—to make fun of me?"

He said nothing and continued up the tree-lined path toward the house.

I began flailing. "Put me down, Jake. This is ridiculous!" My stomach churned. "Ugh…I think I'm gonna be sick."

"You better not be," Jake said.

I wiggled and cussed as he held the backs of my legs down with his right hand.

I continued to struggle against him. "Jake, seriously, put me down. I don't want to puke on you."

"Then don't. Stop being so squirrelly." His voice was full of amusement.

Jake carried me through the French doors, into the kitchen, and passed by the living room toward the stairs—everyone else was in the living room, listening to music and chatting.

Amidst my wiggling, Sarah skipped toward us, laughing. "Oh wow, this is priceless," she said.

"Oh shut up," I snapped.

"I guess I'll see you tomorrow," Sarah said, shaking her head and waving.

"I'm not going to bed! He's being absurd." I smacked Jake's butt. "Put me down!" I demanded.

"Say goodnight, Zoe," he ordered.

"This is pointless, I'm just coming back down here," I claimed, but he ignored me. Jake lugged me through the foyer and up the stairs in silence. "I'm serious, Jake!"

"Okay," he said placatingly, both of us knowing I definitely wouldn't be coming back down.

My stomach started churning again. "Oh God…you better hurry." Opening my bedroom door, he took me into the bathroom and set me down on the tile floor. I braced myself against the counter, wishing my head would stop spinning.

"You okay?"

I glared at him in the darkness. "Dandy. Thanks."

The rest of the night passed by in a blur. All I remembered was crawling into bed—Jake's fully clothed body curled up beside me.

The next morning, I woke to the slamming of the front door and frantically looked around the room. My palms were sore and rough from falling on the dock, snagging on the comforter wrapped around me. As I stretched in bed, my knees felt achy, and I figured giant bruises colored them.

I abruptly sat up, pieces of the previous night flashing in my mind. Stunned, I touched my fingers to my mouth at the memory of Jake's lips on mine, of his body against mine. I glanced over, expecting to see him, but I was in bed alone.

Hearing the slamming of the door again, I crawled out of bed. My head was pounding, and I needed some water…immediately. I trudged into the bathroom, brushed my teeth, and half-heartedly fixed my hair, but I quickly gave up on making myself look more presentable. I slid my slippers on, headed out into the hallway, and stood on the landing. Confused, I took in the chaotic scene below me.

In the front yard, Sarah was screaming at Biggs—I could hear her through the door—while Sanchez and Harper hustled around in the library, Cooper following them excitedly. I watched them in confusion, uncertain what all the fuss was about.

"Is everything okay?" I called down to Harper as he hurried across the foyer.

"Oh…hey, Baby Girl. We're leaving." He smiled and wriggled his eyebrows, knowing I'd be happy to hear the news.

My mood brightened instantly. "For Colorado?" I asked hopefully.

He nodded and continued into the piano room—Biggs's makeshift communications center.

"Wait, what can I do to help?" I asked, running down the stairs, completely forgetting my headache and sore body.

"You can start by getting properly dressed. You look like you just rolled out of bed," he called from out of sight.

I stood at the foot of the stairs, evaluating my attire. "I did." Before I could head back upstairs to dress and pack, Jake walked in through the front door, his face drawn. Sarah and Biggs were still shouting at each other in the front yard, and I could tell not everyone was happy to be leaving.

Jake seemed like a different person than he'd been the night before. He had dark circles under his eyes, like he hadn't slept at all, and his shoulders hung under the weight of his anxiety. I could feel it emanating from him and knew he was dreading returning home.

Timidly, I approached him, unsure what to say. I wanted to console him—to tell him everything would be fine—but I knew I couldn't promise such a thing.

"Hey," I said dumbly.

"Morning." He managed a weak smile, but he was clearly distracted. He looked at his nonexistent watch. "You slept in."

"Yeah, I guess I did."

Jake was more intimidating without the liquid courage flowing through me. I recalled his concern from the night before—that I wouldn't remember the kiss—and hoped the heat in my cheeks and my shy grin told him otherwise.

I met his eyes. "So, H told me we're leaving," I said to break our silence.

Jake only nodded.

"I'm assuming you're coming too?"

He smirked, finally showing some of the playfulness from the night before. "I told you I can't let you get yourself into more trouble without me being there. You're a magnet for it, you know?"

Although he was teasing me, there was truth in his words, and I was grateful to him for skirting around wounding my pride.

The door flung open, and Sarah stomped into the foyer, Biggs trailing behind her. "It's a horrible idea, Riley, and you know it!" she yelled.

Biggs stopped in his tracks and looked down at the marble floor.

When Sarah heard his footsteps come to a halt, she took a deep breath and turned around. "Look, I understand you want to leave with your team. I don't want them to leave us any more than you do, but we have a baby to think about now. We have a pretty good idea of what we'll come up against out there, and I don't want to chance anything. Do you?"

As the scene unfolded, I felt completely out of place. But I stayed anyway.

"And what'll we do here?" Biggs argued. "We'll be alone, Sarah. Is that what you want? To sit here and die alone? Eventually that could happen you know? We haven't even been to the city yet, who knows what condition it's in. We're living in a bubble. We can't stay here forever."

Biggs walked to Sarah as some small semblance of understanding registered on her face. "I'm only one person, and we have our whole lives ahead of us. We have a baby that's going to need to be delivered by someone who knows what the hell they're doing. We can't stay here out of fear. What if something happened to me? What would you do, alone…with a baby?"

Wiping away her sudden tears, Sarah cleared her throat. "Nothing will happen to you, and we have plenty of food here," she said, grasping for anything that might change his mind. I could tell that the thought of never seeing her home again was heartbreaking to her.

"Yeah, maybe for a while. But do you really want it to be just you and me for the rest of our lives? I love you, Babe. I really do, but it'd be nice to have someone else to talk to, a family to share our memories with, and friends to laugh with and help us when we need it."

The tears continued to run freely down Sarah's face, and Biggs wiped them away with his thumbs. "I don't *want* to go." Her voice was weak as she gasped for air.

"I know, Babe." He pulled her into a hug, gently rubbing her back and whispering reassurances in her ear. He bent down, gathered her up into his arms, and scaled the stairs toward her bedroom.

I looked back at Jake as he walked out the front door, rubbing the back of his neck as memories of Gabe and Becca flashed in his mind. Cooper whined, his tail hanging low as he trailed behind him.

47

ZOE

After a day of planning and packing, we loaded our clothes, food, medical supplies, and everything else into the two vehicles. Once Sarah had taken a moment to say goodbye to her childhood home, she locked the doors for the final time and joined Biggs in Dave's truck. Finally, we were headed to Colorado… unsure if we had enough fuel to make it.

Riding in Dave's truck proved to be too difficult for me because of the memories it provoked. The scratch on the center console reminded me of the many times Sammy had scampered between the front and back seats, and the miniature stuffed Wally —the mascot for the Red Sox—swinging from the rearview mirror made me think of Dave winning it at the Suffolk County Fair. Although I remembered the happier times we'd shared, my thoughts continuously circled back to our rocky relationship near the end…before his death. *Did he suffer? For how long? Was he with Stacey?* An hour into the journey, I opted to switch vehicles and ride in the van with Sanchez and Harper.

"I never asked you what led to the sudden decision to leave," I said to Harper as we drove through the middle of nowhere, otherwise known as Kansas. "Did something happen?"

Harper considered my question too carefully before answering. "I had an unsettling vision."

"About…?" I prompted.

"About Clara, so…Sanchez and I thought it'd be best to leave." For what seemed like the hundredth time in only a few minutes, Harper glanced into the rearview mirror.

The mere mention of Clara's name made me feel like a million invisible spiders were scurrying over my skin, and I rubbed my arms. "What was in the vision? I mean, what happened?"

Harper's eyebrows drew together as he tried to make sense of what he'd seen. "She was in a dark room, smiling evilly. She was leaning over someone I couldn't see, and she said something like, 'When I'm done with you, you won't remember anyone…you won't even know who you are.'" His grip tightened on the steering wheel. "I knew she was going to hurt whoever it was, and the hatred in her eyes worried me…I thought it might be you. When I told Sanchez about it, we decided we should keep moving." Harper's frequent glances in the rearview mirror were starting to make more sense. "There's strength in numbers," he said and then shook his head. "…at least there used to be." I thought of Cece and all the trouble she'd caused. *It didn't work out so well for Dani and Jason.*

By the time we'd reached Garden City to look for Harper's uncle, Curtis—who was nowhere to be found—the van had run out of fuel. Unable to find more, we shuffled all of our belongings from the van to the truck. Wanting to get off the main road and set up camp, we all piled into the truck—Jake, Cooper, and Harper riding in the bed—and drove along Highway 50, following the Arkansas River over the Colorado border.

We thought our fuel would last the rest of the way, but we ran out about a hundred miles from our destination and were forced to continue on foot. We sorted through all of our things, separating what we were taking from what we would leave behind. We eventually distributed the food, medical supplies, and camping gear among us, adding whatever personal items we could fit in our packs. Because we'd lost most of our belongings in the fire, we didn't leave much behind.

After a week of walking in the cold, we arrived in Pueblo, a city south of Colorado Springs filled with ample food, medical, and hygiene supplies, plus weapons. It didn't escape our attention that Pueblo was completely abandoned. Although we thought it strange that there were no survivors to speak of, not even Crazies, I wasn't complaining. Jake, however, became increasingly wary—I could feel his apprehension grow the closer we drew to the Colony. Thankfully, he knew the surrounding area well, and after a long discussion, we agreed to wait for Dani and my brother, whether they were together or apart, south of Colorado Springs in a valley near an old mining town called Cañon City. I was too busy worrying about how Dani or Jason would find us to pay much attention to the conversation.

It was on our third day of trekking through the valley, looking for the perfect place to set up camp, that we stumbled upon a ramshackle ranch. We all agreed the abandoned barn would be sufficient in serving as our new, temporary home. Although the rusted tack and rustic farm tools made it seem like the place hadn't been used in years, the new, nearly finished roof and an unfinished foundation a few hundred feet away indicated otherwise. Inside, the weathered, red barn provided enough stalls that each of us could convert one into our own sleeping quarters—hay bales for seating, sleeping bags, and our few belongings were all that filled them.

Uncertain of what to expect over the next few weeks, we preserved our nonperishables by living off the land as much as possible. Jake and Cooper continued their hunting efforts as needed, and I fished for trout in the creek's brisk waters.

Most nights, the six of us sat around the campfire, feasting on a freshly caught dinner with beans or boiled vegetables. We'd found an untended winter garden behind an old farmhouse outside of

Cañon City, providing us with an assortment of roots—carrots, potatoes, and turnips—to cook with.

I had an inkling of what the average day for a settler on the Frontier might have been like—hunting, gathering berries and firewood, washing clothes in frigid water, and roasting game over a fire. The Zoe who'd worked at the gallery wouldn't have recognized me at all.

As the days went on, we settled into a daily routine of hunting, training, scavenging when needed, and practicing our Abilities. And, we watched Sarah's belly grow at an unnatural pace—after two weeks it was noticeably larger, and after three weeks she could no longer wear her jeans. Biggs acted like she might burst at any moment, insisting Harper examine her every time she yawned, burped, or frowned.

Although Harper didn't know what to make of the unprecedented progress of her pregnancy, he'd had enough nieces and nephews to know her symptoms were more or less normal. When Biggs wasn't coddling her, she spent her time eating obscene amounts of food, napping, and watching from the sidelines as I got my butt kicked during training.

I was learning to embrace my Ability—it felt more natural and fluid every day. I no longer struggled to tune out people's feelings and memories, and if I wanted information about someone, it was there. Anything and everything about that person was scattered in my mind like a broken stained glass window, only I couldn't figure out how to piece it together to get the answers I was seeking.

Early one morning, I was sitting by the fire with Harper, half asleep and trying to focus.

"There's just too much to sort through," I explained.

"Try to control what you're seeking, Baby Girl," Harper said. "Are you thinking of something in particular, or are you just jumping in to see what you can find? Maybe it's overwhelming because you're not searching for something specific. For instance, you think about the ocean and hundreds of memories and feelings will pop up, but if you think of the East Coast, there will be fewer to wade through because it's a smaller part of your life. Try it."

"Yeah, but that's me, *my* memories. If I don't know someone, how will I know what to look for?" I whined, tired of practicing so early every morning. I could feel Harper's patience growing thin, and I flashed him a "please forgive me" smile.

"Really, Zoe? I know you're not a morning person, but you're not even trying. I thought you were sleeping better…doesn't that help?"

"Meh," I said. I was still having the recurring nightmare about my mom and her car accident.

Harper shook his head. "Deciding what to look for in a stranger is probably the easiest part. Think about it. You're walking out by the river and you come across someone. What's the first thing you want to know?"

"If they're a Crazy," I muttered.

"Exactly. If you ask Sanchez what she *really* thinks of your chili and she brushes you off again, what do you look for?"

Sanchez passed at that moment, eyeing us with a wry smile on her face.

"The truth." The answer seemed like a no-brainer.

"Precisely. So…be specific when you're searching someone's mind. Now try it on me," he prompted, looking out at the woods encircling the ranch.

It was easy to think of something I wanted to know about Harper. Ever since I'd seen Sanchez's memory of the two of them in bed together, I'd wanted to learn more about their relationship. So, as Harper and I sat by the fire, I decided to find out for myself.

I couldn't help but smile at what I saw. His mind held tons of memories of them—working together *and* sleeping together. Sometimes his arm was around her, and she'd fling it away. Other times, she was nipping at him and batting her eyelashes, trying to get his attention. They laughed and argued like friends always do. I also saw them having enough sex to fully awaken my body from its morning stupor.

"How long have you and Sanchez been sleeping together?" I asked Harper.

His eyes widened, and he burst into laughter. "I knew you stumbled onto something good with that giant-ass grin on your face." Whistling and slapping his thigh, he said, "A while."

"As in…years?"

"Yeah. We've known each other for a long time, but don't tell her I told you…or I'll say you were snooping."

"But what about your *very* public proposition to me at the cabin?" I asked, recalling the constant, severe expression Sanchez had worn the first few weeks I'd known her.

Harper waved away my question. "It's nothing serious."

I just snickered and buried the knowledge with all the other information I was never meant to know.

Like the days, most nights passed rather routinely, with all of us playing cards or telling stories. I spent most of my free time sketching and documenting what we saw and experienced. I mapped out the paths we took and the landmarks around the valley. I hoped that if I was able to contact Dani at any point, I'd have enough information to make sure she could find us.

I also documented the different types of Crazies we ran into: the slow movers we deemed the "AW's" or the "Aimless Wanderers", and the violent "Grunts" who mostly dwelled in more populated areas, among others. Everything I was learning about myself and my surroundings went into my sketchbook, and when I ran out of pages, I started a new one.

"How many of those things did you bring?" Jake asked me one night, cleaning his rifle while I was sketching the campfire's jumping flames.

"Enough." I smiled and leaned back against his chest. "I've been gathering them up wherever I can." I flipped through the pages of the sketchpad, showing him my own personal post-apocalypse field guide.

Curiosity piqued, Jake read through my entries. I immediately felt his mood change when he saw Clara's name:

Classification: Manipulator (Clara)

Species: Homo sapiens

Region: All

Origin: Infected by Virus; Survived

Symptoms: Easily agitated; Conceals aggressive intentions and behaviors; Uses victim's psychological vulnerabilities to determine effective tactics; Willing to use sufficient level of ruthlessness and cause harm to the victim; Generally covert and sneaky.

Dwelling : Groups of survivors (more targets to choose from)

Weakness: Entitlement—greedy and moody leading to irrationality and unexpected outbursts that expose them for who they really are, oftentimes giving them away and turning their followers against them.

I tried to ignore the negative emotions that cycled through him as he read, still blaming himself for what Clara had done to all of us.

His arms wrapped around me, and I happily abandoned my sketchbook and snuggled closer to him. Being in Jake's arms was as surreal as everything else we were going through.

"I want you to have something," he said. He held his knife out in front of me.

"I can't take that, Jake." Although I didn't know the story behind it, I knew it was probably the most meaningful thing he owned.

"I want you to have it. You've been training hard, and I think it's time you had a weapon of your own—something small enough to hide, but sharp enough that you can do a lot of damage." He gave me a wry, crooked smile. "I'm sure you'll need it."

"But what will you use?" I asked, eyeing it carefully.

"I have others; this one's just the best."

I looked back at him, not sure what to say because "thank you" seemed inadequate. "That means a lot to me," I told him. "I promise I'll take care of it."

He nodded.

"Will you tell me the story behind it sometime?"

He nodded again and returned his eyes to my sketchbook, to Clara's name.

Feeling him retreat back into his dark thoughts, I elbowed his leg and whispered, "Hey."

Jake blinked, and his eyes slowly found mine, relieved but disconnected as he resumed cleaning his rifle. I could feel his uneasiness and wondered if he was thinking of Harper's prophecy about Clara.

When Jake excused himself to talk to Harper, I left my post by the blazing fire and headed for the barn. I situated myself in the sleeping bags in the corner of our stall, knowing they wouldn't be the only things keeping me warm for long—Jake had slept beside me every night since we left Sarah's house. Remembering the images of Harper and Sanchez having sex, I blushed. I wished we were still back at Sarah's so Jake and I could find someplace to be alone; the barn was far too cozy for intimacy.

When Jake finally crawled into our joined sleeping bags, I savored the warmth of his body. After only a moment, he sat up, and his hands wandered down the length of my leg. "What are you doing?" he asked.

The feeling of his fingers moving over my sweatpants made my eyelids spring open. "What do you mean?"

"With your feet…" His strong fingers closed around my toes as they wiggled back and forth.

"It helps me fall asleep," I said, realizing I'd been rubbing my feet together.

"Cute," he said quietly, lying back down and wrapping his arms around my waist. "And when did you start wearing a beanie to bed?" he whispered, his breath brushing gently across my cheek.

I giggled reflexively, smoothing some flyaway hairs back into place before pulling the knit cap over my ears. "It's freezing…my ears are cold."

"Really?" I heard a purr in his voice, and as I opened my mouth to reply, his lips were on the sensitive skin behind my ear. I welcomed his hands as they traveled over my hips and down to my thighs, pulling me back against him. I suddenly felt way too hot.

"Are you warming up yet?" His voice was husky, saturated with the same desire that smoldered within me.

"You're killing me," I groaned.

He playfully bit the side of my neck, and his mouth lingered near my ear for a moment. "'Night, Zoe," he said. Under the covers, his grip on my thighs loosened, and he ran his fingers over my hip like he was memorizing its contours. I shuddered.

Hearing Harper and Biggs's hushed voices only feet away, I knew nothing would really happen.

Taking a long, deep breath, I sighed. "Night, you tease," I said and pressed my backside against him, eliciting the exact response I wanted—a deep groan. *Two can play this game.*

48

DANI

"Oh…ooooooh!" I screeched as I dumped frigid river water over my head to rinse soap from my naked body. The purple bar of lavender-scented suds had become my all-in-one body wash, good for everything from my hands to my hair. Salon shampoo and conditioner, specially designed to control my wild curls, were a thing of the past.

I poured a second canteen full of water over myself and nearly slipped off my platform—a two-foot-wide, smooth, flat river stone. It was large enough that I could stand comfortably, and low enough to the water's surface to make my bathing needs possible—and my bathing needs were *needs*. Since the disastrous encounter with Mistress Mandy nearly eight weeks back, we'd been avoiding nearly all houses and buildings…and the people they might be sheltering. It had been four days since we'd last seen piped-in water, and I was out of patience—thus the part where I was bathing in a creek in the middle of Utah…in the winter.

"Ooooh!" I exclaimed one last time, doing a little dance to shake off as many of the chilly droplets as possible.

Hearing a deep chuckle from the creek bed, I turned and glowered at Jason. "This isn't funny! It's cold! Like, COLD cold!"

"I just liked the shimmy. It was a *really* good shimmy." His eyes glinted in the rich afternoon light as he reclined against a mossy, fallen tree.

"I'm sure it was," I grumbled.

"Hmmm…much as I'm enjoying this, you're turning blue. It's fire time. Let's go, Red." Jason stood, crunching the underbrush, and held out the towel he'd been keeping warm under his shirt.

I hopped from stone to stone across the river, slightly hunched over with my arms crossing my chest. It was sunny and unseasonably warm, but I was still frozen to the core. I would've been embarrassed about being in front of Jason, naked and shaking with cold, if he hadn't already done the same. Cold water could turn even the toughest man into a whiny, little boy. Plus, the weeks of hard travel and living off the land had trimmed and hardened my body—where once it had been petite with soft curves, my body was now a composition of lean muscle and smooth lines.

"I think…I'm ready…for spring," I mumbled through shivering lips as Jason wrapped the towel and his strong arms around me. Like me, living in the changed world had altered him, making his body more compact and lithe, quickening his reflexes, and sharpening the angles of his face. Though he'd lost much of his excess, bulky muscle mass, he was far more lethal than he'd ever been before.

"No kidding," he said. He dried me off quickly while I trembled, then tossed item after item of cold-weather clothing at me, enticing me to dress. I didn't complain. "You're lips are purple," he said, leaning in for a slow kiss.

"I'm not surprised," I said when he pulled away. "I think I have permafrost."

"That's not a medical condition."

"Thank you *so much* for that enlightening information."

"You know what'd warm you up?" Jason slipped his hand under my layers of tops to tease the chilled skin of my lower back.

"Stop it! I just got dressed!" His touch made a brand new set of goose bumps cover my skin.

Jason laughed. "What? I was thinking jumping jacks. Damn Red, get your mind out of the gutter."

"You're a huge butthead, you know!" I wasn't the least bit ashamed of my immature insult. He'd earned it.

All he did was chuckle.

"Oh shut up. C'mon," I said, grabbing his hand. "I'm sure everyone else wants their chance to wash up."

"You're bossy…I like it."

I laughed softly. "That's what Zo says. It was one of the first things she told me when we became friends."

"That she likes you being bossy?" he teased, and still smiling, I shook my head. When he was around me, and only me, Jason shed some of his austere shell…*some*.

"Just that I'm bossy."

"Yeah?" he asked, evidently interested. "How'd that happen anyway…you and Zoe? I mean, one day you were just…there."

It seemed an odd question, like he should've already known how Zoe and I began. But then I remembered that Jason had always been distant, and that the story of Zoe and me and the fortuitous start of our friendship wasn't something we'd made public knowledge. In fact, it was a little embarrassing.

Groaning, I said, "It's no biggie…just a little playground incident."

Jason grinned and his eyes lit up. "Come on, Red. Spill."

I cringed and readjusted my hand in his. "Well…it was in fourth grade. I'd been cornered by a couple of girls behind one of the soccer nets during recess. They were teasing me about my hair, calling me 'carrot head'…it was oranger back then…"

"I don't think that's a word," he commented.

I glanced at him sideways. "It was *oranger*…and I was too small to do anything but glower and try not to cry. Zo found us and yelled something like, 'What the hell are you doing you fat trolls!'

I'd never been good at standing up for myself, so I was completely in awe of her. I remember thinking that she looked like Xena with her long, straight, black hair and angry, blue eyes." I smiled at the memory.

"Anyway, the other girls got mad, and one tried to push Zo, but she was too quick—maybe because she'd had practice dealing with you. She dodged, and the girl stumbled and fell flat on her face and started crying. Zo and I ended up getting in trouble; the other girls tattled, saying we'd pushed and bullied them, but it was worth it."

After I didn't say anything else for several breaths, Jason pointed out, "That doesn't explain the bossy thing."

I flushed. "Oh, right. I, um, made Zoe take me home with her after school that day so I could tell your dad what really happened. I thought it was the most unfair thing in the world that *she'd* been punished for helping me. Then I made her play a game we invented and eventually called 'Beat the Bully'. So dorky, I know. We practiced being the bully and coming up with insults so we'd be prepared next time. I think we ended up crying and laughing hysterically like a million times doing that. But anyway, it was after that second demand that she told me I was bossy."

Laughing softly, I looked askance at Jason. "You know, when I got offended by what she'd said, she told me it wasn't really a bad thing. She said her brother was *way* bossier."

Jason shrugged, accepting the decades-old judgment with little concern.

"Ever since that day on the playground, we've been inseparable…more like twin sisters than just friends. I'm sure a psychologist would say it was because we both have 'mommy abandonment issues' or something." I held up our clasped hands and nudged my sleeve to reveal the black tattoo on the inside of my wrist. "That's what this is all about—the bond between sisters, not the abandonment thing. We got 'em on Zo's eighteenth birthday."

Jason looked at me with an odd expression on his face, like he'd just solved a complex puzzle. "Huh," he grunted. "I thought it was just something to do with your grandma. Since she was Irish and all that…"

"You didn't know your sister has a tattoo?" I scoffed.

He shook his head. "We're not exactly close…we haven't been for a long time."

Yet again, I mentally noted how similar Zoe and Jason were, and they didn't even know it; they barely knew each other. I also thought again about how Zoe was going to react to finding out about me and Jason. Sometimes, when we were younger, my infatuation with her brother had really irritated her. *How's she going to feel about it now? Will she be confused? Happy? Disbelieving? Worried? Jealous? Pissed? Disgusted?* I was unsure about the rules for getting romantically involved with friends' siblings.

Seeing my frown, Jason asked, "What is it?"

"Nothing important," I told him, forcing away my frown. "You have a second chance now, you know, to get to know her."

"Yeah. If we could figure out where the hell she is. She could be at that 'colony' place…she could be somewhere else…" The frustration in his voice amped up my own worries. All routes of communication were completely and utterly dead. On top of that, trying to use my telepathy to find her mind had proven akin to searching for a needle in a haystack, except each piece of hay weighed a hundred pounds and shuffling through even a handful left me exhausted.

I chewed on one side of my lower lip for a few seconds, and then took a deep breath. "I have an idea…but you're not going to like it."

"What?" he asked flatly. Good old Jason, not one to pussyfoot around uncomfortable issues.

"Well, if I could talk to MG, I could ask him to visit her dreams, and he could find out where she is and where she's planning to be by the time we get near the Colony. He's the only person I know who can definitely find her. But…"

"But you need me to let him in." He didn't sound happy.

"Jason—"

"I don't like it. I don't like him being in your head. I don't like him being somewhere I can't protect you."

"He's not going to hurt me."

Jason grumbled, "I don't know if I can even make myself turn it off, not if I really don't want to."

"Don't you want to find Zo?"

His sideways look told me he thought the question was ridiculous—not even worthy of an answer. Jason and Zoe may not have been close, but he'd always been protective of his little sister.

"Well then, he's our only shot, aside from combing every square inch inside and around Colorado Springs. You should *want* to stop blocking him so I can talk to him. He can find her for us—I know he can." My voice was tight, reflecting the edge I was teetering on with Jason and his jealousy and protectiveness.

With a deep, angry sigh, he growled, "Fine." Relief relaxed my shoulders and loosened my grip on his hand.

Later on, when the full, golden moon glowed near the horizon and nocturnal predators sang their eerie, lonely melodies, Jason and I lay entangled in our joined sleeping bags, panting and completely satisfied. Over the past two months, the mountain sounds had transformed from disturbing to comforting—they currently mingled with our heavy breathing to create a peaceful, hypnotizing lullaby.

"Mmm…," Jason rumbled softly. His body still covered mine, slick with sweat despite the cold, and I basked in the warmth the moonlight illuminated in his eyes.

"'Mmm' is right," I purred.

After a slow, lingering kiss—one that made me wonder if he

was starting round two—Jason said, "If you're going to talk to this guy, we should probably call it a night."

A few minutes later, I was clothed in sweats and falling asleep in the safety of Jason's arms.

"Are you sure this'll work?" I mumbled, momentarily shaking off the lure of sleep.

"Yes, Red, I'm sure. As soon as I can control it, I won't block the bastard at all." For some unknown reason, Jason always lost complete control of his Ability after we had sex—nulling every nearby Ability for a good fifteen minutes. Teasing him about it amused me to no end.

"Hmmm…" I snuggled against him happily and succumbed to unconsciousness.

I was sunbathing on my favorite stretch of Northern California beach. I'd been dreaming of something else—something that worried me. I thought maybe I'd been swimming, looking for something under violent swells of frigid ocean water. I was also sure that I was still dreaming, and confusion overwhelmed me as I thought about dreaming while I was dreaming.

Suddenly, my confusion cleared. MG.

It had been so long since I'd seen him—since I'd experienced the odd feeling of sleeping awareness—that it hadn't made sense at first.

Where is he?

"Dani," his smooth voice intoned as a long shadow suddenly shielded me from the sun. "It's been a while."

I stood and faced him, allowing a small smile. I really was glad to see him. "Uh, yeah. Sorry about that. I'm back with my people, and it turns out that one of them can sort of block other people's Abilities. I think you guessed that before…you were right. Yay for you…" My words sounded lame, even to me.

"Right," he said dryly. "I tried to get through. Can't your friend control his Ability at all?"

"He's getting better at it. Stronger."

"So has the wall that's been keeping me out," MG retorted.

I didn't know what to say. I couldn't really tell him that my boyfriend was blocking him on purpose and that, until tonight, I hadn't asked him to stop. I just hadn't thought...

"It's nice to see you," I said sincerely.

MG sighed dramatically and then grinned. "You too, Dani."

"So...how've you been?"

He glowered for no apparent reason. "I've been better."

My eyebrows rose of their own accord. "Okaaaay...Um, MG?"

"Yep?"

"I was wondering if I could ask you a big-ish favor."

"Which would be...?"

"I'm looking for someone. We're headed to the Colorado Springs area, and we're trying to meet up with a friend, but we don't know exactly where she is." Or if she even made it, I thought sullenly.

"And what exactly do you want me to do?"

"Well, you can find pretty much anyone's dreams, right? Something about finding them based on the type and strength of their Ability?" I asked hopefully.

"Er...yes."

"The person we're looking for is Zoe, the woman you saw in the badminton dream. You know, gorgeous with long black hair and super blue eyes?"

"Yeah, I remember."

"Well, she can feel people's emotions and sometimes see their thoughts, or maybe their memories. And she should *be near Colorado Springs. Do you think—could you look for her dreams and ask her where she is? You're our only hope." I added the last bit hoping the damsel in distress thing would ping his macho side and persuade him to help.*

MG chuckled, and I held my breath. "Oh, little Dani, you are so adorable sometimes."

I just smiled, unsure of how to react.

"I'll do it," he finally said. "Give me a moment..." Abruptly, he disappeared, and with him the dream faded around me.

For what felt equally like minutes, hours, days, and years, I floated from dream to dream, from ocean to forest to desert, completely unaware of myself. Only when he returned did I become aware of my wanderings.

Sitting across from me at Grams's kitchen table, MG said, "Found her."

"Found her?" I asked, still shaking off the remnants of my mind's subconscious. I'd been in a desert—digging a hole, but the sand kept slipping down the sides, negating my efforts.

"Your friend. Zoe. Who you asked me to find," he reminded me.

As always happened in his presence, clarity returned, and I remembered the conversation we'd had earlier. "That was fast...or slow. I'm not really sure actually."

MG nodded. "Don't worry about it. That's normal. It took a couple hours...not too long."

"Oh? So where is she? She's okay, right?"

"Yeah, she's fine...with some other people, I guess. She said they came with her from Fort Knox."

"Really? Good!" It was a relief to know she wasn't alone.

"Right," he said dryly. "They're southwest of Colorado Springs, in a valley on the outskirts of the San Isabel National Forest, just north of Cañon City," he informed me.

"San Isabel National Forest...Cañon City—got it. I can't believe you found her! I mean, I knew you could...but...thank you! You're the best ever!" I squealed, unabashedly excited at the nearness of my reunion with Zoe. I gave MG a quick, enthusiastic hug and was surprised to find him looking decidedly forlorn when I pulled away. "Um...Are you okay?"

"What? Yeah, it's nothing," he said, brushing off my concern.

"If you say so. Do you know what time it is?"

"Almost six."

Tapping my mouth with my pointer finger, I pondered sleeping another hour but thought better of it. "Would you mind waking me up?"

"Sure...see you later." He sounded so despondent that I didn't have the heart to tell him Jason wasn't likely to extend the nullifying reprieve for another night.

"Right. Bye. And thanks!" I smiled as MG and the familiar surroundings of Grams's kitchen faded around me.

"Oh!" I exclaimed, sitting up suddenly in the tent. "That was abrupt."

"Mhhmff?" Jason asked incoherently.

"Wake up, Jason," I said, poking his shoulder.

"Arrghhmph," he groaned and rolled away from me. The sun had yet to crest the horizon, which meant Jason was nearly impossible to wake.

"I said, 'Wake up'," I sang softly as I curled my body around his backside. I kissed the side of his neck just under his jaw bone and repeated the command.

"Mmmm...," Jason murmured as he turned over and slipped his hand under my t-shirt.

I giggled, thinking his reaction was so completely Jason, and tried to ignore the yearning ache elicited by just that small touch. Softly, I said, "I know where she is."

The hand slowly moving up my side stilled, and Jason's eyelids opened, revealing his stunning, if sleepy, gaze. "What?"

"I know where Zo is. It's sort of far, but I think we can get to her in a few weeks."

MARCH

49

ZOE

Gathering more firewood in preparation for what I hoped would be a long, fun-filled night of laughing, drinking, and catching up, I lugged it to the fire pit Jake and Harper had created in a clearing of trees. It was close enough to the barn that we never had to leave our "home" unattended—our supply of food, weapons, and booze was *very* important to us—but far enough to not disturb Sarah during her many naps.

Dropping the wood at my feet, I busied myself with the unnecessary task of sorting through it. I'd been antsy with anticipation and excitement for the past few days, every minute passing as fast as a two-legged turtle climbing up a hill…against the wind. According to the information I'd received from MG when he'd entered my dream a few weeks ago, Dani's entire group should arrive any day now. I couldn't stand still.

"Hey, Zoe," Sarah chirped, making me jump. "You okay?"

"Yeah, the anticipation's just killing me, that's all," I said with a quick laugh. "I can't believe this might finally be happening, you know?"

Sarah smiled and nodded, but I could feel her eyes on me as I continued working. Forcing myself to stop, I looked up at her. "Are *you* okay?" I asked, although I already knew the answer—I could feel her anxiety every time she rubbed her swollen belly.

"Umm, yeah, I'm just worried about this little guy." She pointed to her belly. "What if it's a mutant or something? It's *huge*."

Noticing her belly *had* grown a bit larger, I suddenly felt scared for her. I moved closer and wrapped my arms around her, squeezing her the way a mother might. "I know it's scary, but I just have a feeling everything'll be okay." At least, I hoped it would. "Maybe someone in Dani's group can help us figure all this out."

"Yeah, maybe," she said with little conviction.

"We're all here to help you, Sarah." She nodded again, and even though I felt her body sag slightly with relief, I knew she wondered how things would change once Dani arrived. "And I'm not going anywhere," I reassured her. *Well, at least I don't think I am.*

She brightened at my words and offered to help me get dinner started. Jake was carefully cleaning the day's catch at the makeshift fish cleaning station—a metal door resting on top of two saw horses. Harper and Biggs were hunched over the fire pit, arranging kindling into a teepee shape in an attempt to start the evening's fire. Like clockwork, Sanchez was jotting notes as she sat on a hay bale beside the fire pit, cooling off from her final workout of the day.

Sarah and I were gathering lemon pepper, salt, and other seasonings for the food when Cooper suddenly growled. I jumped and glanced over at him; his posture was rigid and he was staring into the trees at the edge of the pasture. His tail drooped momentarily before picking up in a half-hearted wag.

Looking up from his freshly filleted fish, Jake peered out at the woods.

I grinned. "I think they're here!"

A deep, relentless barking grew louder as a large German Shepherd emerged from the tree line. *Jack*! I stepped forward, following Cooper as he trotted toward the other excited dog.

"Wait," Jake said, gently grabbing my arm. "What if—"

"It's D's dog," I said, pulling out of his grasp to continue on toward the tree line. I couldn't believe this was really happening. Dani and Jason were here. They were *really* here.

Jake and Sarah followed me, and I could hear the others coming up behind us. We watched the two dogs yip and sniff as they circled one another curiously.

Suddenly, Jake stopped short, and I turned to him. Confusion wrinkled his brow as his eyes darted around us. Unprovoked, he said, "Ummm, what?" He looked over at me, perplexed. "I think someone's looking for you."

From behind me, I heard Sanchez say coolly, "I'm definitely *not* Zoe."

"Zo? Is that you?" Dani inquired…inside my head. *Wait, what? Is she like Sanchez?* Turning back toward the woods in excitement, I searched for her in the trees. Everyone watched me as I swiveled around, my smile so big I no doubt looked ludicrous.

A small herd of horses and goats broke through the dense pines beyond the dogs. My eyes instantly fixed on Dani's bright, auburn hair as her Paint horse galloped closer, ahead of the rest.

"D!" I yelled, running to her. She was immediately accompanied by a large, dark-haired man sitting atop a chestnut horse much larger than Dani's mount. *Jason. He looks…different.*

"ZO!" Dani called.

Momentarily forgetting about my group, I jumped up and down in uncontrollable excitement as the horses stopped mere feet from me. I watched Jason jump out of his saddle and reach for Dani just as she swung her leg over to dismount.

"No you don't, Red." Gripping Dani's hips, my brother eased her descent. I could feel his concern diminish the moment her feet safely touched the ground. *Wow, protective much?* Jason dwarfed my petite friend, making her appear more fragile than I knew she was.

Dani slipped out of his grasp and ran to me, shrieking and giggling. "Zo!"

"D!" I screeched and grabbed her hands. Frantically, we hopped in a circle until she suddenly paused and flung herself into my arms. Feeling her body tremble and her mind fill with overwhelming happiness and relief, I hugged her as tightly as I could. When I heard her heaving sobs, I pulled away, unable to resist smiling as I soaked up her quintessentially Dani reaction. Losing control of my own emotions, I let tears slide down my cheeks.

"You're making me cry!" I whined and tugged her closer again. "I'm *so* happy to see you," I said. "I can't believe you're finally here."

A quiet, unintelligible response squeaked out of her, and I suddenly realized everyone was watching our soggy reunion. The rest of Dani's group had dismounted and were making their way toward us.

My eyes fell on Jason, standing behind Dani. Shock blanketed his face as he stared at something behind me.

"Jason?" Sanchez's voice was filled with awe.

Feeling Dani stiffen, I let go. Curious, we simultaneously turned to watch Sanchez approach. Her eyes were locked on my brother, narrowed in disbelief and showing a vulnerability I rarely saw in her. Moving quickly, she threw her arms around him, muttering words I couldn't discern.

The dream of them at the bar…it was a memory!

Jason looked pleasantly surprised and returned the hug loosely. Out of the corner of my eye, I noticed Dani take a hesitant step toward them. When Jason looked at my best friend, his face blanked, and he gently pulled away from Sanchez.

I was confused, wondering what exactly was going on between Dani and my brother, but only for a moment. Dani's memories invaded my mind, and I saw Jason heatedly gazing up at her while kissing her bare hip.

"Oh. Fuck." I couldn't stop the words from escaping.

Looking back at me, recognition registered on Dani's face, and she instantly turned red. My head whipped to my womanizing brother. "Jason!"

"Zoe." His face and voice were expressionless.

I pointed at him and then at Dani. "We're talking about this later."

"No, we're not."

Rolling my eyes in exasperation, I turned my back on him. *Now I remember why I can't stand him.*

Almost everyone was carrying out the age-old tradition of greetings and introductions. An older man stood off to the side of the group, watching, but my attention locked on the blonde woman beside him. *That must be Chris.* A sense of gratitude overcame me as I approached her.

"Chris?" I asked.

"I am," she said, smiling. She extended her hand in greeting. "And you're Zoe. It's a pleasure to meet you. I've heard so much about you from our girl."

I took a step closer, wrapping my arms around her strong shoulders. "Thank you for taking care of her," I whispered.

She patted my back, and I gave her a squeeze before pulling away.

"It wasn't easy, but I did my best," she said with a smirk.

I noticed a young man standing behind her, and I could feel his discomfort as I approached him. "Hi," I said, offering my hand. "I'm Zoe."

He seemed hesitant as he accepted my greeting, but was also filled with curiosity. I had no idea who he was. "I'm Carlos," he said, averting his gaze.

"Carlos joined us a few days after we left," Chris added, putting her arm around him. "We had a little run in with a mind-controlled cult. I'll let Dani tell you the whole story."

"Miss Cartwright?" asked an older man.

Recognizing his sharp eyes as he drew closer, I realized it was Mr. Grayson. *What the hell is* he *doing here?* "Mr. G?" I pointed to his impressive mountain man beard. "I like the new look." I leaned in to hug him, receiving an uncomfortable side hug in return.

"Oh, yes, well we haven't had much time…traveling, you know," he explained, moderately embarrassed.

"No really, I like it," I said reassuringly.

An athletic-looking Asian man walked up behind Mr. Grayson, a mischievous smile playing on his lips. "Stop hogging all the ladies, Old Man."

"Oh—" Mr. Grayson began, but the younger man interrupted.

Outstretching his hand, he introduced himself, "Ky."

"Zoe," I offered, trying not to blush at the desirous emotions dancing through his mind.

"Hey guys…whatcha talkin' about?" Dani asked, suddenly appearing at my side. But before either of us could answer, Dani said, "Ky, why don't you go meet that Sanchez chick?"

I couldn't help but laugh at Dani's jealousy and wondered how serious things were between her and Jason. *Maybe I don't want to know.*

Surveying the group for Jake, I found him standing beside my brother, talking. My heart practically stopped. In my entire life, the only time my brother ever actually acted like a brother was when he turned unbelievably protective around any guy who showed any interest in me. *This is going to be…interesting.*

I looked at Dani in both anticipation and horror.

She grinned wickedly. "Who's that? He's yummy."

I smiled, only half distracted by her comment. "That's Jake, and I don't know if I want him talking to Jason alone." I grabbed her hand. "Let me introduce you," I insisted.

Hustling over, we overheard their stilted conversation.

"So you're the guy that saved my sister's life," Jason said.

"Yeah, I guess you could say that."

As we reached them, I rested my hand on Jake's arm to get his attention. I tried to ignore the excitement and curiosity building in Dani, and focused on the two men.

"Jake, this is Dani," I said, introducing them. Glancing back at my friend, I could tell she was trying to control the avalanche of questions threatening to explode from her mouth. Leaving Jake to be ensnared in Dani's bubbly, conversational pandemonium, I turned to my brother.

"I'm…glad you're okay," he said, surprising me with the honesty in his tone.

As I took in the sight of him and felt his relief, my own emotions flared up again. I could only nod as I tried to control the tears welling in my eyes. I hugged him, and he squeezed me tightly. Worried he'd vanish into thin air if I let go, I held on to him, barely able to control my sobs.

"I mean it, Zoe. We have to stick together now."

At first, I reveled in his hold, not wanting to let go, but out of nowhere, an alarm rang in my head, and a burst of negativity shot through me. I pulled away from Jason. Scanning the group, my blurred vision fell upon Harper and Dani as they separated from an introductory hug. His masculine features were scrunched with worry.

What did he see? I wondered, knowing he'd probably just had a vision and that it couldn't be good.

"Zoe," Sarah said meekly, just as Dani frolicked toward me, shouting, "Zo!"

Taking a step back, I continued wiping the moisture from my cheeks.

"Have you two met yet?" I asked, and Sarah shook her head bashfully. "Sarah, this is Dani," I offered. "Dani, Sarah."

"So, wow…you're pregnant!" Dani noted and then brought her hand up to her mouth. "Oh! Sorry, that was rude."

"It's okay," Sarah replied, her hand instinctively going to her belly.

"Er…congrats?" Dani offered with a crooked grin.

Awkwardness settled over us as Dani and Sarah stared at one another. I was instantly thankful to see Harper and Sanchez helping Jason and Carlos unsaddle the horses. I gestured in their direction. "We should probably help them unpack."

The three of us started to join them, but Dani caught my wrist, stopping me mid-step. "Wait, Zo. There's some stuff I need to tell you…"

50

DANI

I snuggled closer to Jason, staring into the fire and wondering if it was the best night of my life. We'd found Zoe. She was safe. We were together—all of us. I sighed. I would have been completely content if the news I'd delivered regarding Zoe's dad wasn't the reason for her puffy eyes and frequent remote looks.

Standing, Zoe called out over the roar of the far-too-large bonfire, "Who's ready for another?" She was tending an impromptu bar she'd set up on a long, table-like boulder a dozen feet from the flames, and seemed to find comfort in the task. The volume and variety of alcoholic beverages her crew had gathered were astounding, including a cornucopia of wines, liquors, and beers.

"I'll take one," Jason and Jake called out in synch and then exchanged uncomfortable glances.

Meeting Zoe's eyes, I stifled a giggle and patted Jason's knee. Watching Jason and Jake interact throughout the evening had been absolutely hilarious and predictably awkward. Once Jason had realized his sister and Jake were *involved*, he'd taken on the usual protective, disapproving brother role.

I studied Jake, who was sitting beside Zoe's vacant spot on a tarp-covered hay bale. He was rugged and reserved, which was surprising. Zoe usually went for clean-cut, sporty, generally douchey guys. But Jake, though definitely athletically built, was none of those things.

"So, Zo," I said, intruding on her thoughts while she fiddled behind the rock bar. *"Jake sure is something. I'm…surprised."*

Zoe looked up and grinned, then masked it with a false glare. *She'd accepted my telepathy without fuss, though she did seem to be having a hard time with some of the finer details.* "Well what'd you expect?"

"OMG shut up! You don't have to speak out loud! Hello… secret conversation here!" I screeched in her head. Jake and Jason were already staring at her for the random statement, as were a few of the others.

I watched as Harper, lean and muscular with a really great derriere beneath his fatigues, approached Zoe and asked for a top-off. He was drinking the same Scotch as Mr. Grayson, something from a simple and very old-looking bottle. Cocking my head, I appreciated how appealing he looked leaning his elbows on the boulder, swirling his plastic cup.

Zoe laughed at something he'd quietly said, and I smiled at seeing her entire face light up. She had a habit of shielding her emotions around almost everyone, but Harper had definitely weaseled his way into her heart. Admittedly, I felt a pang of jealousy. For years, I'd been the only one she would really open up to —or so I'd thought before I found out about the stupid box—but I truly was happy she'd expanded her circle of trusted confidantes. Just so long as I was always first, of course.

"So, he's also kind of amazing to look at. What are you, like, a hot guy black hole or something?" I asked.

"That's definitely not true. And what about you? Ky's easy on the eyes. Not to mention that the sexy, ominous voice belonging to a certain mystery man in my dreams a few weeks ago was nice too…"

"Oh, right. Pot and kettle, eh?" I said and grimaced. *"But, back to your men—you and Jake, have you two…you know… knocked boots…made the beast with two backs…gotten jiggy with it…?"* I wiggled my eyebrows.

At my flippant teasing, Zoe rolled her eyes in irritation.

"Okay, sorry…didn't mean to pry," I said, feeling a little hurt.

"No, it's not you. I haven't had the privilege yet…unfortunately. There's been too much going on, and we haven't really had the opportunity. Well, not unless we want an audience—close quarters, if you know what I mean."

I thought back on the two months of close quarters Jason and I had been sharing with our companions—and how little that had stopped us—and blushed profusely. *"Um…yeah. I know what you mean. Right…"*

Zoe shook her head in disbelief, or possibly disgust, and tried to hide her amusement as she said, *"Normally I'd say, 'spill'…but, I* really *don't wanna know."*

"Yeah, probably not," I said, and my face heated even more. Unintentionally, I remembered the time Jason had pulled me away from the group during a lunch stop. He'd practically dragged me into some nearby woods, braced my hands against a tree trunk, yanked down my pants, and—

"Could you stop thinking about having sex with my brother, please!" Zoe squeezed her eyes shut, trying to block the images I was unintentionally shoving into her brain.

I grimaced again. *"Well…not really, no. SORRY! I know this must be* so *weird for you, and I'll try not to think about it, I swear, but—"*

"I get it! Just…stop there, please." Obviously trying to hide her discomfort, Zoe picked up the two cups she'd finished preparing for Jake and her brother, and carried them to where they sat by the massive fire.

I still didn't really know how Zoe felt about my relationship with Jason, but I was certain she didn't appreciate being bombarded with my memories of our time together. I wished I knew how to keep them contained. *"Zo, I'm—"*

"Oh!" I gasped as the connection between us instantly disappeared. Turning to Jason, I scowled. "Hey! You said you wouldn't do that anymore!"

Zoe, handing a glass of whiskey to Jake, watched us curiously from the other side of the fire.

"And you said you wouldn't use it to carry on long, private conversations when it wasn't necessary. You know what happens…," Jason said, trailing off when he realized he might be revealing too much to people we barely knew.

"Well, there are *some* things I wanted to know that aren't polite to ask when everyone can hear, thank you very much!" I snapped, but my irritation was deflating rapidly. I was already worn out from using my telepathy to find Zoe and her people, and Jason didn't want me to end up shivering and passing out again.

"Dani…," Jason warned.

"I know, I know," I grumbled, pouting.

Shoving Jason's drink at him, Zoe interrupted, "Wait, you passed out from using your telepathy?"

I looked at Zoe suspiciously. "How'd you know—are you in my head!? Zo! Get out!"

"You were just in *my* head!"

"That was completely different. I couldn't see your memories! You could be keeping all kinds of secrets, but I can't just scoop them out of your brain. Like with the—"

"Secrets?" Zoe asked, her dark eyebrows drawn down in confusion. Abruptly, she shifted her gaze to glare at her brother. "Is that you? Are you—seriously? You're blocking me? *Really*?" She wagged her pointer finger at Jason and me. Narrowing her eyes, she said, "You're not telling me something." Hands on her hips, she fixed her penetrating stare on me and waited for a response.

I shrank back, huddling into myself. I hadn't seen this side of Zoe for years. She was one of the strongest, most determined people I knew. She could be downright terrifying when she wanted something, and at the moment, she definitely wanted something —information.

Jason cleared his throat and nudged me with his shoulder.

"I need another drink. Care to join me?" I asked Zoe with fake perkiness. Inside, my stomach roiled uncomfortably.

We trudged over to the array of alcoholic beverages, and Zoe started concocting something with a half-dozen ingredients. "Um…I was just gonna have more of this," I said holding up my nearly-empty, red plastic cup of wine.

"This one's for me," she said, holding up the drink shaker. She handed me the bottle of Pinot Grigio so I could refill my cup, and continued on with her task.

Sighing, I blurted, "Zo, I know about the box—your dad's box. Jason has it." When her eyes snapped up excitedly, I added, "He hasn't opened it." I paused, studying her expression. "He said you've been obsessed with it for, like, ever. Why didn't you tell me about it? Why'd you keep it a secret?" My voice sounded small, lost.

Zoe's eyebrows drew down in confusion, wrinkling the skin between them. Slowly, understanding smoothed her expression. "It wasn't a secret. Well…not really," she said, hesitating. "It's embarrassing, D. I mean, what would I have said, 'my dad has a secret box, and I want to know what's in it so badly I've stayed up thinking about it almost every night since I can remember?' It's sort of ridiculous, don't you think? I don't understand why he hid it from us." She paused again. "What if there's something really horrible in there?" she asked quietly.

I was taken aback, more than a little ashamed of my inability to put myself in her shoes. Not that they'd fit, but still…

Zoe mixed her super complicated drink in the shaker and stared at the surface of the flat boulder.

I suddenly felt like a really crappy friend. "Zo…I'm sorry. I didn't think. I just kept wondering why you'd hide it from me.

Maybe like how you wondered why your dad hid whatever's in the box. I thought maybe you didn't really trust me, not completely. I thought…I don't know. I thought stupid things, and I'm *really* sorry."

"I'm sorry I didn't tell you, D. It's not personal, I promise. I thought about telling you…but I guess I was sort of scared. I still am—like knowing what's inside somehow changes everything—even though none of that really matters anymore. Jason's the only family I have left."

Seeing the raw emotion painting her face, tears welled in my eyes for the second time that day. "Zo…I'm…I'm just so…so…," I said, but I started crying before I could finish the sentence.

"Why are you crying?" Zoe asked. I hadn't realized she'd come around to my side of the rock until I felt her arms wrap around me. Resting her chin on my shoulder, she teased, "All this crying is excessive—even for you, D."

Laughing despite my sniffles, I replied, "Oh my God, I know. It's getting ridiculous. I'm like a hormonal pregnant woman." As Zoe stiffened behind me, I hastily added, "Which I'm not. Absolutely, definitely not. No way. Yikes!"

As if on cue, we burst into peals of laughter, nearly collapsing on the ground.

"Oh. My. God. It feels so good to laugh," Zoe said, attempting to catch her breath while she held herself up with one hand on the boulder's surface.

"Ah! I know!" I agreed. My face was tired and twitchy from smiling so hard, and I felt like I'd done about five thousand crunches. "My stomach hurts!"

"You need another drink!" Zoe returned to her side of the bar and refilled the cup I'd unconsciously drained during the emotional conversation. Noticing she was starting to make another complex drink for herself, I didn't feel so bad about downing my previous one.

"So…" I took a sip of the crisp wine and wiped the residue of my tears from under my eyes. "What'd you think of MG? You said you just heard his voice? You didn't actually see him?"

"No, his voice just sort of appeared as I was having a delicious dream about making out with Jake. It was awkward, to say the least. Once I realized who he was and what he was doing, I tried not to freak out. I felt really vulnerable having him in my head, but it was also sort of interesting. It was surreal to be aware but asleep at the same time."

"I know, right!"

"He sounds hot though."

"I know, right!" I agreed with a giggle.

"Ladies," Ky cut in. Leading Sanchez and Ben, he sidled up to the bar and plucked a few clear shot glasses from a stack. Setting them down, he filled each to the brim with top-shelf tequila and handed one to his brother and one to the gorgeous, exotic woman at his side.

"Bottoms up," Ky said. They clinked their shot glasses together and gulped down the deceptively fiery liquid, all three taking the burn like real men. But it was *very* obvious that Sanchez was a woman. Ky quickly refilled the shot glasses, and they headed back toward the fire.

"That's not a very pretty face, D. Do you smell something foul or what?" Zoe asked, and I realized my facial features had twisted into an undoubtedly ugly sneer.

"Something like that," I said. "What's the deal with her and Jason anyway?"

"I'm not sure exactly, but they obviously know each other from before."

Feeling an odd mix of hope and dread, like when opening a college acceptance letter, I asked, "Well, have you, um, *seen* anything? Were they…involved? I mean, she seemed really happy to see him, and he seemed sort of happy, too…I guess."

"At the time I thought it was just a weird dream, but I saw a memory a while ago. They were together, but not romantically—at least, not that I could tell. They were with a group of friends…at a bar maybe?" Zoe shrugged. "I'm not sure." Glancing at me mischievously, she smirked. "Do you want me to find out for you?"

"You mean, like, brain spy?" I thought about the offer—really thought about it—and shook my head. It was unbelievably enticing, and I felt bad that Zoe had to deal with the temptation to delve into people's minds, to discover their secrets, every second of every day. "No. I don't really want to know anyway," I lied. And I knew Zoe knew; she could read me like her favorite, dog-eared, well-worn book—Bob Ross's biography.

"Okay. Let me know if you change your mind," she said, then leaned across the bar and conspiratorially added, "I don't think you have to worry anyway; Jason hasn't taken his eyes off you all night, and Sanchez and Harper have been going at it for years."

"What?" I squealed, then covered my mouth and bounced up and down on my toes. "Oh wow," I giggled. "That's *so* freaking juicy!"

Zoe allowed a moderately wicked laugh to escape her lips as she rounded the boulder, drink in hand, and linked her arm with mine. "Come on, I'm cold."

Reaching back for my cup of wine, I exhaled with relief and let my best friend pull me back to the fire. *We're okay.*

"You know what I said about Harper's visions?" she whispered near my ear as we slowly walked back to our designated seats next to our respective men. "I think he had one when he hugged you earlier…his face looked really worried, and I could feel how upset he was."

"Really?" I asked, surprised by her words…and by the way she bypassed both of our empty spots.

"Yeah. I wonder if we can get the details out of him."

She led me to a vacant bench that was so rickety I was surprised it didn't collapse when we sat down. *No wonder nobody's sitting here.* Chris and Harper shared the adjacent hay bale and were locked in conversation.

"So you *do* agree with the H1N1/09 theory…that only those who'd been infected with *that* virus had the antibodies to survive this later version," Chris stated.

"Well, not exactly," Harper said, frowning. "I still don't think it all adds up."

"So you disagree?"

He shrugged and took a sip of Scotch. "I'm really not sure. Are you positive that those people on your base knew about the Virus and everything before the initial outbreak?"

"The more I think about it," Chris said, "the more sure I am. I watched them prep the special yellow-banded uniforms *before* the first infections were reported."

"If you're right…"

"I know. Surviving the Virus might be just the beginning. If I *am* right, then somebody orchestrated this whole thing—all the death, the insanity, *and* the Abilities. But why? And how?" Chris tore her gaze from the handsome medic and studied the towering flames. "I hope I'm wrong," she said quietly.

Zoe and I exchanged worried glances, and I figured she'd abandoned her mission to weasel info about Harper's vision out of him.

The remainder of the evening passed too-quickly, filled with developing friendships and decreasingly tentative conversations. I was pleasantly surprised by how well our two groups blended together, finding camaraderie in the shared experience of surviving in the Virus-ravaged world.

Late in the night, I stood alone before the fire, the benches and hay bales abandoned. The others were all either acquiring another beverage or relieving themselves of the ones they'd already consumed. I shed my jacket, overwhelmed by the heat of the towering fire, and stared into the hypnotizing dance of flames and air and embers.

Without a word, Jason came up behind me, almost touching but not quite. "You look like some sort of fire spirit," he whispered, his lips mere inches from my ear. "Watching you like that—savage and glowing—damn, Red, I want to bury myself inside you…right now."

I leaned back into him, closing the miniscule distance between our bodies, and was pleased by his obvious state of arousal.

"I set up our tent a little ways away from the barn. I thought we'd need the privacy," he said, slipping his arm around my middle.

"Really? I wonder why?" I asked, feigning confusion.

He grazed his lips along the side of my neck and whispered, "You know why."

Twisting in his hold so I could see his face, I said, "I'm not sure…you may need to remind me."

Jason's answering grin was wolfish and hungry. He immediately led me away from the fire and into the woods beyond the barn where everyone else would be sleeping. As we hurried along, I could barely contain the anticipation humming through me.

Wiggling into sweatpants was difficult considering that all of my muscles—and possibly some of my bones—had recently been turned into quivering gelatin.

"What are you doing?" I asked Jason as he sat up on top of the sleeping bags and reached for his boxer briefs.

"Coming with you."

"No. Don't. I'm just peeing. I'll be, like, a minute." Seeing the concern still creasing his brow, I added, "I'll be fine, really. I'm a big girl."

"Anyone could be out there," he said, but remained seated. "At least wait until my Ability works again."

"Oh," I said, laughing and shaking my head. "I'm not holding it just because you turn into a super null every time we have sex." He scowled, and I smiled.

As I unzipped the tent's door, I assured him again, "I'll be fine."

51

ZOE

Loosening my hair from its braid, I idly combed through it. I couldn't shake the heavy uncertainty I'd hoped to shed once I saw Dani. It still tugged at me, gnawing on my consciousness.

The sound of the barn door sliding open and then shut was followed by Jake's footsteps. As he changed into sweats, I crawled into the sleeping bags, devouring the sight of him in the candlelight.

His brow furrowed slightly at my whimper. "You okay?" he asked.

"Perfect," I admitted as I wiggled further into the sleeping bag, imagining the warm pressure of his body against mine. "Just admiring the view." Picking up on the husky tone of my voice, the corners of his mouth pulled up in a smile. "There are definitely perks to getting into bed first," I added.

"Yeah? Like what, hogging the sleeping bags?" he teased.

I nodded. "Yeah, that's exactly what I was talking about."

Pulling the hem of his sweatshirt down, Jake crouched down and appraised the space beside me.

"What's wrong?" I lifted myself up, resting on my elbows.

Glancing at me, he said, "It's interesting how someone your

size needs so much space." He gestured between me and the stall's wall a couple feet from me. "And I only get this." He looked down at the small space to my right. "Between you hogging the bed and your scattered clothes all over the place…I'm wondering if I should find somewhere else to sleep."

"Sorry," I said, scooting over a smidge.

As Jake crawled into the sleeping bags beside me, I curled into his sheltering arms. My thoughts were shadowed by the night's festivities, and I expelled an exhausted sigh. *Why am I anxious? Dani and Jason are here. They're safe.* Although I'd been ecstatic only minutes earlier, I still felt…wrong.

"What's wrong?" Jake whispered.

"Nothing," I lied. "Why do you ask?"

"You keep sighing."

"Oh." I hadn't noticed. I rolled over, facing his inquisitive, warm, brown eyes. They scoured my face. "I think I'm sort of in shock, actually."

The events of the evening replayed in my head. "It's so strange to have everyone here. I don't know what to do with myself. It's like there's nothing to worry about anymore, and I feel a sort of emptiness…or something." And that was exactly what it felt like —a hole I didn't know how to fill. I no longer had to fret about how and when I'd reach Dani and Jason. They were finally with me.

Brushing a loose ribbon of hair from my eyes, Jake stroked my cheek. Involuntarily, I thought of Dani and Jason together, and the hole I felt immediately filled with concern.

"I don't know what to do about my brother."

"You mean him and Dani," Jake said. When I nodded, his eyes focused on me intently. "You don't think they should be together?"

I grunted, my emotions a mix of excitement for Dani and distrust in my brother, and rolled onto my back. "It's not that. I'm just worried about…you don't understand. Cam just died, and my brother's a heartbreaker. He always has been. And Dani's been in love with him her entire life…" I paused, imagining her devastation when Jason eventually decided to move on.

Will he break her heart? I thought of how careful he was with her, how taken he was by her mere presence, and I wondered if that was even a possibility. "He seems to really care about her…at least he believes he does, I know that much." I just hoped his interest in my best friend wasn't as changeable as his mood always had been.

Jake's thumb traveled to my face, grazing my bottom lip. "Jason seems…serious enough. I don't think he'll hurt your friend if he really cares about her."

"You're right," I admitted. "He's an ass, but I don't think he'd do that to her. She's not just some random girl. She's Dani."

"You two talked a lot tonight," Jake said idly as his fingers trailed down my belly, eventually playing with the elastic waistband of my sweatpants.

I smiled, remembering my conversation with Dani about Jake and Harper. "Yeah," I said, but my smile faded as I realized I'd forgotten to ask Harper about his vision.

"Zoe," Jake whispered, his lips suddenly hovering by my ear. His suggestive tone caught my attention. "Stop trying to find something to worry about. You've been waiting for this day since I met you." He pulled back, and his eyes latched onto my lips before moving slowly up to my eyes. "I think we should celebrate."

A smile splayed across my lips once more, and I shuddered as his warm breath caressed my face.

"You're so bad. Four people are, like, seven feet away," I admonished quietly, barely able to contain my anticipation.

"I don't care anymore," he growled, unbridled lust emanating from him. His mouth lingered over mine, his eyes waiting for an invitation to consume me in all possible ways. I giggled in consent, and he pulled me closer with a determination I had no interest in protesting.

Leaning down, Jake gently brushed his lips against my neck and then my jaw before capturing my mouth. A delicious heat swept through me as he ventured lower, kissing the swells of my breasts that protruded from the top of my scoop-neck shirt. Wrapping his leg around my thighs, he pulled me under him. His hips rested over mine, and I could feel his arousal.

Desire throbbed between my legs as I liquefied beneath him. I coveted the sheer weight of his body pressed against mine. "God, I want you," I moaned. My hands clenched around the hem of his sweatshirt, pulling at his clothes impatiently.

Breathing raggedly, I heard a sharp cry shatter the stillness of the night, interrupting the pounding of my heart.

"Shhh." I grabbed Jake's arms, waiting for my breathing to slow. Fear washed over me as another scream pierced the quietness. I froze in absolute terror.

That's Dani's scream!

"Dani!" I yelled, pushing Jake away like he was nothing. Jumping to my feet, I ran to the door. "Dammit!" I shouted as I struggled with the latch. "Dani!"

Finally, I opened the latch and pulled the door open. I barely heard Jake calling after me as my sock-covered feet carried me out into the frigid darkness.

"DANI!"

EPILOGUE

Dani

Waking, I attempted to open my eyes and assess my surroundings. A searing white light stabbed into my skull, and I snapped my eyelids shut before the glare could make my pounding headache any worse. *What the hell happened?*

"She's awake," I heard an unfamiliar female voice say softly.

A large, warm hand slipped into mine and squeezed.

I groaned. "Uh…Jason? Zo? What…?"

"Dani?"

At the deep, familiar tone, all thoughts of headaches and bright lights momentarily subsided, and my eyes snapped open again. I turned my head on the pillow and caught my breath when I saw the man sitting there…beside *my* bed…holding *my* hand.

"Um…am I dreaming?" I asked hoarsely.

Looking disheveled and wearing pale green scrubs, MG pressed his lips together and shook his head. "No. And call me Gabe."

The End

Thanks for reading After The Ending! This marks the end of the book, but not the end of Dani and Zoe's post-apocalyptic adventures. The adventure continues in Into The Fire.

Keep reading for a preview of book two - Into The Fire.

INTO THE FIRE

THE ENDING SERIES BOOK TWO

PROLOGUE

MASE

JANUARY 5, 1AE

"I'm just sayin' the General freaks me the fuck out, Mase, and..." Carter stopped talking—for once—as he shifted the beam of his flashlight to shine down the next aisle. "D'you hear that?"

Carter could be dense, but if he thought he heard something, there was something to be heard. Thanks to the Virus, the guy had the ears of a dog.

Mase lifted his left arm and made a fist, and the other two members of his fireteam froze behind him. Ahead, Carter stood, head cocked to the side. As one, they listened. Mase barely caught it—whimpering. After giving Carter a curt nod, he signaled for all three men to follow him, raised his M4, and crept closer to the noise.

Patrolling the supply warehouses had been their duty for over a month, ever since the Virus had wiped out almost everyone, and they'd yet to find an intruder. General Herodson's standing order was that only select personnel could enter the warehouses to guard, inspect, and distribute food and other supplies. Unless Mase was grossly mistaken, they were the only patrol on duty at Warehouse F until the shift change at midnight, which was still hours away.

It looked like they'd found their first intruder.

As they crept down the aisle between two towering metal shelving units stuffed with pallets of shrink-wrapped supplies—paper towels, toilet paper, plastic cups—they swept each side with the lights attached to their rifles. Halfway down the aisle, huddled on the cold cement floor, was the intruder. The girl was hugging her knees and hiding her face like she was trying to disappear. Mase scowled.

Slowly, the girl raised her head, and when Mase saw her dirt-smudged face, his breath hitched. It couldn't be *her*...not in the Colony. Her long, dark hair was ratted and clumped, tear tracks trailed down her cheeks, and confusion filled her eyes. Mase knew they were hazel from memory, even if he couldn't see their color in the darkness.

"Stand down," Mase said to the other soldiers before turning his attention to the young woman. "Camille? What are you doing here? Are you hurt?" His voice was always deep, gravelly, but concern or maybe fear made it even harsher. Hesitantly, he took a step closer to her.

Camille flinched, becoming an even tighter ball of folded limbs and tangled hair on the dirty cement floor.

For the first time in his two years as a Ranger, Mase regretted spending so much time lifting weights. She was afraid of him. But he *knew* her. He had to help her.

Clearing his throat, he put on what he hoped was a comforting smile and took another step closer.

"We won't hurt you," he told the teenage girl as he knelt down in front of her. "I promise." When he touched Camille's arm, she flinched again. "I promise we won't hurt you," he repeated. Intruders were to be taken straight to headquarters—to General Herodson—but he couldn't do that. They tended to disappear after that. Of course, if the bastard found out Mase had disobeyed his orders, Mase would disappear himself . . . but it was Camille.

When she finally peered up at him, Mase did his best to look less intimidating by hunching his shoulders, hanging his head, not scowling. She watched him carefully, blank curiosity filling her face.

"What are you doing here, Camille?"

She opened her mouth to speak, but no sound came out. She tried again. "Who—who is Camille?"

Surprised, Mase sat back on his heels and studied her. *It is her, isn't it?* She was older—more a woman than a child, unlike the last time he'd seen her. Camille was a few years younger than him, so now she had to be at least seventeen. She still looked like a perfect little doll, though. There was no question in Mase's mind that he was staring at the young woman he'd lived next door to nearly his entire life.

"You," he said. "You're Camille. And I'm Mase." He remembered the day her parents brought her home from the hospital…the afternoon she fell off her bike and chipped her tooth on the sidewalk…the Valentine's Day she gave him a card made out of pink and purple construction paper…the day he taught her how to coast on his skateboard without falling…the night she ran away crying after meeting one of his girlfriends. But if Camille could remember any of that, she was hiding it well. She just stared, not responding, and began to shiver.

Mase heard his men whispering and shuffling around behind him. He ignored them. "It's okay, Camille," he said, doing his best to soften his voice. "We're friends. We were neighbors, remember? Back in Minneapolis? I used to look after you when your parents—"

The other men chuckled, Carter bursting into open laughter. Mase flipped them the bird over his shoulder. They only laughed harder.

"You..." Carter couldn't stop laughing. "You...you used to *babysit*?"

Rising, Mase spun and pointed threateningly at Carter. "Shut the fuck up." He glared at each of the men, warning clear in his eyes, until they quieted. "Nobody touches her. Nobody says a fucking word about this. Forget you ever saw her."

Their amusement vanished, and they stared back at him with identical expressions—fear mixed with pity and regret. They knew what had to be done.

"Mase," the nearest said. "We have to turn her in. The General's standing orders are to—"

"I know the orders," Mase snapped. "Fuck them. She's not going anywhere near Herodson. Forget. You. Ever. Saw. Her."

After a brief hesitation, all three men nodded.

Letting out a relieved breath, Mase turned back to Camille. She was watching him with eyes widened in interest, not fear. He knelt in front of her and explained, "It's not safe for you here. You're going to have to hide until I can get you registered as a Colonist."

Surprising him, Camille reached out and touched the side of his face with her fingertips, frowning when he flinched. "Where am I?" she whispered.

Mase glanced back at his men, silently warning them to keep their mouths shut. If Camille didn't have any memory of the Virus—of nearly everyone dying—he didn't want to be the one to tell her. At least not yet. "You're in the Colony. It used to be a military base. You'll be safe here as soon as I get you registered." He hesitated for a moment. "You have no idea how you got here?"

Quietly, Camille said, "No. I have no idea." She studied him with eerily calm eyes.

A metallic bang stole Mase's attention, and then the overhead lights flared to life. Someone else was in the warehouse. While the others stood nearby, rifles raised, Mase helped Camille hide between two pallets of paper towels. She was barely out of sight when the newcomers rounded the far end of the aisle. Mase's stomach dropped when he saw *him*.

"Atwell! How is your patrol going this evening?" asked the man leading a dozen soldiers. Dressed in his usual officer finery, General Herodson strolled down the aisle toward Mase…toward Camille.

"Nothing unusual, Sir," Mase reported, stepping away from Camille's hiding place before the General was close enough to see her in the shadows.

General Herodson inspected Mase and his fireteam closely. "So it seems," he said, giving Mase an instant feeling of *holy-fucking-shit*. Casually, the General glanced around, his gaze lingering near Camille's hiding spot.

"How are the Ability transfers going?" Mase asked, hoping to distract him.

The General looked at him with cold, gray eyes.

Mase returned the man's stare, refusing to look away. "Have there been any new developments? I know some of the men would like to get outfitted with regeneration or telekinesis."

General Herodson bared his teeth in a smile. "Not yet, no. However, we *have* had an interesting breakthrough on another project. We're calling them 'Re-gens'—they're reanimated corpses, more or less. They even retain their Abilities, though they're altered somewhat from what they were during their first lives." He paused, glancing up at the lights thoughtfully. "But the process wipes their minds completely clean, making them *very* easy to influence." He rubbed his hands together briskly. "No need to deal with pesky memories or morals."

Reanimated corpses. It took effort for Mase to keep his expression blank.

Abruptly, General Herodson said, "As you were," and turned to leave.

Mase watched him walk away, reluctant to move. Why had the

General told him about the Re-gens? Why had he come into the warehouse in the first place? Something wasn't right.

As they neared the end of the aisle, General Herodson and his guards halted. "CL-one," the General called out as he turned to face Mase again. "Come here, CL-one."

Shocking the shit out of Mase, Camille wriggled out from her hiding spot and hurried to General Herodson's side.

Mase clenched his jaw, realizing he'd just signed his own death warrant.

"CL-one is a particularly amazing Re-gen, don't you agree, Atwell? We just finished her the other day." General Herodson watched Mase like he was gauging every minute change in his expression. Mase kept his face hard and cold, like the General's. "Take their weapons, my dear," Herodson said to Camille.

Even at a distance, Mase could see the confusion on Camille's face. "Why, Father?" she asked softly.

The General stiffened. "Because I told you to, *my dear*," he said with strained affection. "These men must be arrested and put on trial. They broke the law. *My* law."

"Oh," Camille said, sounding sad, or maybe confused. "What will happen to them after the trial?"

It seemed to take a conscious effort for General Herodson to suppress his simmering anger. The man hated being questioned. "The other three will be banished from the Colony," he said through gritted teeth. "Atwell will be executed and turned into a Re-gen."

"Okay," she said, smiling contentedly. She took a deep breath, then shut her eyes. Her mouth thinned to a flat line.

As Mase looked from her to General Herodson, hatred flooded his veins, quickly followed by adrenaline. His muscles vibrated with the unnatural strength that had increased steadily over the past two years. He was the strongest, fastest person he'd ever heard of —not that it would help him now. The General knew about his Ability. Mase figured that was probably the only reason he wanted to bring him back as a Re-gen: to be used...owned. Mase ground his teeth together and tried to think of a way out of this clusterfuck.

Suddenly, his M4 tugged out of his hands and floated upward. He tried to yank it back down, but it continued to float higher. Moving quickly, he untangled his arm from the rifle's strap before it forced him up onto his toes. From the sounds of his men cursing behind him, he knew they were being remotely disarmed as well. Mase watched as their weapons glided into the hands of the General's guards. His attention was drawn to Camille, who was still concentrating. *She* was doing it.

She opened her eyes and left the General's side, a coy smile curving her mouth. Mase watched her approach him, frozen in remorse at what he'd caused. His men wouldn't be "tossed out of the Colony"—they would be executed, regardless of what the General had claimed.

It felt like minutes, but finally Camille reached Mase. She caught his gaze, a spark of sharp intelligence lighting eyes that had once been hazel but were now gray. Almost inaudibly, she whispered, "Do not be afraid, Mase. I will take care of you, just like you used to take care of me. And with my friends, we will take care of Father."

Mase barely registered her robotic intonation. He couldn't believe what was about to happen. Soon, he would die, only to be brought back as something else. As some*one* else.

The reanimated young woman stood on tiptoes and lightly touched her lips to Mase's cheek. "My friends *really* do not like Father."

MARCH - 1 AE

1

ZOE

MARCH 14, 1AE

N*o! No! This can't be happening!*

"Dani!" My voice carried throughout the eerily quiet field as I sprinted along the pasture fence, away from the barn and toward Dani's bone-chilling scream. Jake was right behind me, the light from his flashlight dancing around my bare feet. Each breath was so loud, so raspy, it was like I could hear nothing else.

My mind started to feel odd, momentarily distracting me as I ran, but I ignored the feeling along with the frigid air biting at my skin and the jagged rocks poking the bottoms of my feet. My eyes blurred with unshed tears, and I stumbled over something, barely catching myself before colliding with the unyielding ground. I shook my head, trying to dispel the disorienting fog that was steadily creeping into my mind.

In the darkness a few yards ahead, I could see Jason's shadowy form. His flashlight and gun were pointed in front of him as he swept into the forest with Jack, Dani's German shepherd, leading the way.

I slowed, hesitating at the edge of the forest. Seeing Jason's pistol raised scared the shit out of me. *Did he find something? Who's in there?* What's *in there?*

"D!" I cried out.

In an instant, a strong hand wrapped around my arm. I whipped my head around to face Jake. "What—"

"We *have* to be quiet, Zoe." His voice was low and severe. He pointed into the woods, and I realized all I could hear was the sound of flapping wings and a hoot from an owl off in the distance. Jason wasn't calling out for Dani; there were no voices.

I nodded, feeling stupid, but I still wanted to call for her. I needed her to know that we were nearby…that we would find her. *Why is this happening to us? Why can't we catch a goddamn break!*

Turning back to the woods, I concentrated on controlling my breath and regaining some clarity. *Why can't I focus?* Sanchez, Harper, Chris, and Carlos passed me, bouncing flashlight beams lighting their way into the dense forest. I vaguely noticed Biggs, Ben, and Ky following them, Biggs muttering curses under his breath. My head started to throb under the massive influx of foreign emotions. I shuttered myself against the onslaught and rushed into the woods, hardly feeling the scraggly branches poking and scratching me.

"What was she even doing out here?" I rasped. I stopped inside the tree line, wishing I had been levelheaded enough to grab a flashlight and a pair of boots like everyone else.

Jake stopped beside me, but Cooper trotted passed us, his nose skimming the ground for a scent. He locked on to a trail and began to follow it. I heard a barrage of whispers around me before everyone broke off into groups, but I focused on the dogs; they were following two different scent trails.

After what felt like an hour of following, searching, and waiting for Jack or Cooper to find some sign of Dani, both dogs' trails converged at a narrow, jagged tree stump. Jack whined, and Cooper sniffed the pine needles around the base of the stump. The dogs had found something. Instinctively, my gut balled into a knot.

Ben, who was helping to keep his brother upright, began to say something. "I think—"

"Here," Harper said, aiming his flashlight at the exposed roots of the stump. Crouching, he shifted a fist-sized stone and picked something up.

Chris stepped up behind him and peered over his shoulder. "Jason," she said ominously, glancing at my brother.

He moved to her side, and hesitantly, I followed. I stopped almost instantly. Jason's dread washed over me, a wave of nausea making my insides lurch, and I had to close my mouth and hold my breath to avoid vomiting. Every hair on my body stood on end at the thought of what they'd found. "What is it?" I croaked. *Please don't say a body part…*

Stiffly, Jason squatted beside Harper, taking whatever Harper had found from his hand. *A yellow piece of fabric?*

"It's just like the ones we saw back at Lewis-McChord," Chris said quietly. Rising from his seated position next to Jason, Jack stretched out his neck to sniff the cloth and whined.

Chris glanced around at our confused faces and explained, "It's an armband, or at least part of one. Some of the personnel were wearing these when they put our base on lock-down." She shook her head. "We stole a few; it was the only way we could get off the base. The people wearing these"—she snatched the armband out of Jason's hand and clenched it in her fist—"had something to do with the Virus."

"I've seen those before too, on people from the Colony," Jake said. He'd been trying to convince us that the supposed safe haven was dangerous since we first met up with him at Fort Knox. "It must've been them…"

An image of his sister's dark hair and violet eyes flashed through my mind. He was remembering her. He was remembering the men who'd promised to help her, the men who had frightened her enough that she'd taken her own life before *they* could.

Everyone looked at Jake, including my dangerously quiet

brother. "Why would they take Dani?" Jason asked as he rose and took a menacing step toward Jake. "How would they even know we're here?"

I didn't like Jason's accusing tone, but Jake didn't seem to notice. Never taking his eyes off the yellow armband, he answered, "I don't know how they knew we were here, but if they wanted her bad enough to kidnap her…their resources are—were…" He paused. "It wouldn't have been difficult for them to take her." The images of his sister's final breath played through his head… through mine. A gut-wrenching feeling of loss took root in the pit of my stomach.

"You seem to know a lot about them," Jason probed, taking another step toward Jake. "Maybe you know more than you're letting on. Maybe you—"

"You think I'd save Zoe's life back at Fort Knox just to put her in danger again? You really are a piece of—" Jake inhaled and then emitted no further sounds, like he'd decided holding his breath for a while was the safer option. He was probably right.

He met Jason's challenging stare a moment longer before turning his angry gaze on me. "I warned you not to come here." His words stung with truth.

"Then how the fuck did they find us?" Jason's voice was damning, his glare focused solely on Jake. I didn't like it and felt a sudden desire to punch my brother in the face.

"How the hell should I know?" Jake snapped. "We've been here over a month and nothing. You get here and now they know where we are."

Jason made a noise that was part exhale, part growl. "How *exactly* do you know so much about them?"

"Because they tried to take my sister, and now she's dead," Jake replied hotly.

The two men were standing less than two feet apart, Jason's rage barely contained. He didn't lose control often, but when he did…I shuddered, recalling the worst of the fights between him and our dad. Jason cracked his knuckles, an ominous sign I was all too familiar with, and I feared my brother wouldn't be able to rein in his temper.

I stepped between them. "It's not Jake's fault, Jason, so back off!"

My brother ignored me, instead turning his aggression on Chris. "Stay the fuck out of my head," he ordered, obviously feeling her cerebral fingers trying to manipulate his mental state into something more stable.

Jake and Jason weren't the only ones on edge. Biggs was worrying about Sarah and their unborn baby, and Ky was in pain, practically folding under the weight of our collective panic. Ky's Ability to feel volatility—to sense and internalize everyone's destructive emotions—was physically debilitating him. He reached for the flask in his pocket without a second thought. Abandoning Jason, Chris ran to Ky's side.

The weight and amount of negativity Ky was picking up on frightened me; it was as if he wasn't just sensing our group, but all of the fear and hostility surrounding us. *From Cañon City? From the Colony?* Like Ky, I was pulled in all directions by the mounting unease and fear of everyone around us, as though I were being emotionally drawn and quartered. I wanted to scream.

The looming fog seemed to thicken in my brain, tangling with the barrage of emotions. *What the hell's going on?* I searched my convoluted mind for something I could grasp on to—something other than anger and fear and resentment. I'd been so fucking naïve to think everything would be okay once we found each other. *Keep it together, Zoe, Dani needs you.*

Closing my eyes, I took a deep breath, inhaling the scent of the forest—the sharp smell of pine needles, damp soil, and wood. The fog continued to spread its tendrils through my mind in a horrifyingly familiar way. I felt trapped in my own head, unable to escape the encroaching numbness. The only other time I'd felt such an overwhelming loss of mental control was when my mind had been invaded by Crazies in the hospital back at Fort Knox. *What if we're wrong? What if it isn't the Colony?*

Feeling a sudden jolt of panic, I opened my eyes. I could see the lichen coating the tree trunks in the dim moonlight, like spots on a leopard. But there were no snarls or howls or voices beyond our group. There were no fiendish sounds of Crazies cackling in the distance. There were no signs giving me cause to think anyone was there at all.

But someone *took Dani.*

A bolt of anger shot through me, jostling me from my statue-like state. I took a step toward my brother. "What the hell was she doing out here, Jason?" He'd always been big, bad, protective Jason—so why had he let Dani go outside, alone, in the middle of the night?

In the faint moonlight dappling his face, I could barely make out the hard set of his features. "Peeing," he answered lamely.

"Peeing? Alone? In the woods?" My anger flared, fury consuming my disbelief and fear. "I can't believe you, Jason! I just got her back, and now you—"

"Fuck you!" He pointed at me in warning, his eyes glinting silver in the darkness. "She was just peeing," he muttered.

"I can't believe someone was just standing here," Biggs said and began pacing. "Were they just waiting for us this whole time? Sarah...the baby..." He looked up at Sanchez abruptly. "We need to get out of here," he said evenly. "It's not safe here anymore. We've—"

"Do what you want," Jason growled. "I'm going after Dani."

"You think you can just walk into the Colony and get her? We need a plan first," Jake said, facing Chris and Sanchez. "We need—"

"Need to what? To wait for them to hurt her? To do worse?" Jason's tone was scathing as, once again, he took a step closer to Jake.

"Calm down, Jason." I placed myself between them again. "We

need to come up with a plan first. I mean, what if it's Crazies and has nothing to do with the—"

"It's *not* Crazies," Jake and Jason said at the same time. They exchanged an irritated glance.

I rolled my eyes. "If it *is* the Colony, they'll outnumber us and—"

"Then you stay here and *plan*," Jason said with a smirk. "I'll go find Dani."

"Get over yourself already!" I seethed. "You think I'm not worried about her? Like I haven't been waiting to see Dani for months? Like I haven't been worrying about her since all this bull-shit started? Like suddenly I don't care about her anymore because *you're* in the picture? She's my best friend, remember? Or did you forget that, since everything's always about you?" My voice was riddled with bitterness and jealousy, and my words were laden with twenty-six years' worth of resentment.

To my surprise, Jason remained silent.

Sanchez cleared her throat. "Look," she said deliberately. "If we want to find your friend, we need to be rational. So grow the fuck up and stop arguing, and then we can come up with a plan that *won't* get us all killed."

"We can't do much else in the dark," Harper said, his voice breaking through the tension. "The sun'll be up in an hour or so, then we can continue searching for signs of what happened."

"I'm not finished looking for her," Jason muttered and turned toward his tent.

"I wasn't implying that any of us were finished looking for her," Harper clarified, but Jason continued stalking away. The rest of us dispersed, some making their way back to camp, but Jake, Harper, and I stopped at the edge of the forest, watching…thinking.

"Look how close they were to us," I said with a shaky breath. I gauged the distance between where we stood and the barn. Although far away, I could see the dim embers of the night's fire and the outline of the hay bales and chairs surrounding it. I watched the dark figures of my companions as they moved around the camp. "We never even heard them."

Suddenly, as if my skin had become animated, creeping over my bones and muscles, I shivered. The thought of never seeing Dani alive again after everything we'd been through—journeying across the country, surviving homicide attempts and Crazies—caused a rogue tear to roll down my cheek. *Determination, Zoe,* I told myself. I hurriedly wiped the tear away.

With my brother out of earshot, I turned to Harper. I recalled the fleeting look of unease that had flashed over his dark, handsome features when Dani had arrived the day before. Whatever he'd seen was startling enough to have made his green eyes flare with apprehension.

"You had a vision earlier...yesterday, when you were hugging Dani, didn't you?" I knew I wasn't going to like his reply the moment he closed his eyes in...*regret*?

Harper didn't look at me when he spoke. "I saw her in darkness," he said quietly. "I don't know if she was sleeping or—"

"Unconscious," I finished for him, refusing to hear him utter the word "dead."

2

ZOE

MARCH 15, 1AE

I sat on one of the hay bales arranged around the campfire and brushed off the bottoms of my feet to pull on my socks. My eyes drifted to Dani's cup from the night before, sitting on the makeshift table Jake had made. It still held about an inch of white wine. Then my gaze moved to the empty liquor bottles and red plastic cups stacked on the boulder a few feet away. The sight was enough to make me sick to my stomach all over again. I couldn't believe how stupid we'd been…how careless. We weren't safe, and we never *had* been.

Cooper licked the back of my hand, and I looked down. He was watching me with downtrodden eyes, his tail moving in a half wag. "Thank you for your help, Coop," I said, rubbing his velvety ears. I hadn't seen Jack in a while, but I assumed he was still in the tent with Jason.

"What if whoever took Dani is waiting for you guys in town?" Sarah said to Biggs as he, Harper, and Sanchez noisily readied our weapons behind me. "I mean—"

"They won't be, baby," Biggs said, trying to soothe her. "They have better things to do than wait around for the likes of us." His voice was cool and easy, and I wondered if Sarah believed him. *I* wanted to believe him.

I glanced over my shoulder in time to see Biggs give Sarah a kiss on the forehead. She smiled, rubbing her bulging belly anxiously. Their unborn child had grown so much in the past month that Sarah was limited to sweatpants and loose shirts, a look that was so out of character for the former fashionista, I almost smiled.

"Are we at least moving camp?" she asked him, practically pleading. "I mean, what if they come back and take someone else?"

"Dani might come back," I interjected before Biggs could formulate an answer. I knew he wanted to leave. "Besides, they could've hurt us last night if they really wanted to. They're not interested in the rest of us." At least, I assumed they weren't.

Sarah tucked a strand of curly hair behind her ear and absent-mindedly chewed on her fingernails—a new nervous habit she'd adopted within the last couple months since learning she was pregnant. Realizing I was watching her, she focused on me and lowered her hand from her mouth. "I guess that makes sense," she said and wrapped her arms around her belly. It was like she was protecting the rapidly growing fetus from the gloomy shadow that had settled over us all.

As Sarah retreated into the barn, an image of her house in St. Louis flashed through her mind, and I knew she was missing her home. She hadn't wanted to leave, but she'd done so for Biggs… for me. A fleeting pang of guilt gave me pause, but there was little I could do. I turned back around and picked up my right boot. *Dani's out there somewhere, in the hands of…who knows. That* was my focus.

Three miles to the east, Cañon City was the closest place to search for maps, plans, and anything else that could help us come up with a way to get Dani back. Jason didn't like waiting, but most of us agreed we needed to be strategic if we were going to have any chance of rescuing her. *Assuming she's still alive.*

"I think we should assume these 'Colony' people want something specific from Danielle," Grayson said, practically reading my mind. He sat on a hay bale on the other side of the dying fire. Although his face was grim and his weathered skin seemed particularly pinched around his eyes, his presence provided a sense of comfort. I couldn't quite pinpoint why. Maybe it was because Grayson reminded me of home, of my past.

I thought of my dad and Jason, of how they used to be, but that only conjured a mess of unsettling memories. *I can't believe Dad's really gone.* Then, I remembered the box Jason had brought from Bodega Bay—our dad's box. I glanced toward Jason's tent on the edge of the woods, assuming it was in there with him.

In my peripheral vision, I spotted Grayson watching me. I looked down at my boot instead of meeting his knowing, apologetic eyes. Satisfied that the laces were tied well enough, I pulled my pant leg down and raised my other foot to tie my left boot.

"They wouldn't have gone to all this trouble," Grayson continued, "just to kill her, or—"

I swallowed another wave of nausea. Once the sun had risen, we'd searched the woods surrounding our camp for what felt like endless, heart-wrenching hours, only to be left with nothing but broken twigs indicating there'd been a struggle, the torn yellow armband, a cigarette butt, and five sets of boot prints, not including our own. We'd wasted the early hours of the morning getting nowhere. It was difficult to remain hopeful when I could feel everyone's concern and even some of their doubt.

I gathered my hair behind me and started weaving it into a French braid, wondering what was taking Jason so long to get ready.

"—saying. They knew what they were after, and they must have planned it ahead of time." Grayson leaned forward to stoke the fire with a scrap of cardboard.

"If they were after *her* specifically," Harper said, drawing my attention to him, "they must've known about her 'Ability'." He was rifling through an ammo-filled duffel bag behind me. "It's the only thing that makes sense."

"But what would they want with her Ability?" Carlos asked as he, too, joined us, donning his leather jacket. Though the sun was up, it was chilly. "A lot of you have an Ability, you know, so why take her instead of…" He shrugged.

Grayson nodded thoughtfully and scratched his brow. "True. There are other, more accessible victims they could've taken." He glanced at Sarah as she waddled out of the barn, her cheeks packed with the last mouthful of her second breakfast.

Carlos tossed a piece of straw into the fire. "And…how'd they know about *her*? How'd they know *anything* about us?"

"Well, I suppose the first thing we need to consider is who, outside of us, knows anything about the people in our group." Grayson reached behind him, pulling a couple saddlebags up into his lap, and he began packing them with water and granola bars.

Carlos crouched down near the fire, his eyes squinting from the brightness of the sun. "Hmmm…"

Sarah stopped at the edge of the campfire and tossed her paper napkin and plate into the pit. The flames grew. As I leaned in toward their heat, I scrubbed my face with my hands and took a deep breath. I watched the dancing flames until they died back down, recalling the weekend bonfires Dani and I used to have on the beach back home.

The beach… The memory of a dream flickered to life.

I was lying on an incredibly soft mattress, candles glowing all around me, illuminating the fire burning in Jake's eyes. "I'm going to do things to you, Zoe," he whispered against my cheek with delicious promise. His fingertips skimmed across my belly, lingering at the waistband of my boy shorts, and his lips were soft and moist against my neck as he kissed me. I closed my eyes in anticipation.

"I'm definitely *going to do things," he said again.*

"Yeah?" I giggled. "What sort of things?"

"I'm going to..." His warm breath caressing my skin turned into a chilly breeze, and the heat of his body against mine vanished. A bright, blinding light seared through my eyelids. Instinctively, they flew open, and I sat up. Wait...what?

I was lying on a beach—a seemingly familiar beach that Dani and I spent long summer days lounging on back home—and I was suddenly wearing a purple bikini. I closed my eyes and sighed. So much for a salacious dream tonight. *I stretched out on my towel in resignation.*

"Hi, Zoe."

I opened my eyes and sat up with a start. Dani was sitting on a green towel beside me, her legs crossed and her hand raised. She waved casually. Her hair was poofier and redder than usual, and she seemed more subdued.

"Uh...hey, D." I flashed her an awkward smile, and then realized she wasn't the only thing in my dream that seemed off. The cypress tree up on the ridge to my left was too small, and the ocean stretching out in front of me was too blue, too vibrant.

"Hey, Zoe." Dani said again, and I looked back at her. Her grin suddenly grew...too big. I frowned.

Is there a glitch in the matrix or something? *I plastered a tolerant, perhaps sad smile on my face.* It would be nice if any of this was real. *"Hey, D."*

Dani donned a pair of sunglasses that appeared out of nowhere and lay down on her towel, her strangely too-red curls fanning out behind her. As she adjusted her bikini top, I noted she was much curvier than in real life.

I started chewing on the inside of my cheek. "This dream is really creeping me out."

The breeze died down, and Dani suddenly vanished.

"That's my fault," a man's voice echoed around me. "I was

trying to recreate a scenario that would be comfortable and familiar to you."

Startled, I scanned the beach. There was no one there. "Who are you, and what the hell are you doing in my dream?" My eyes narrowed as I again scanned the endless beach, expecting to see someone walking toward me.

He chuckled. "I think you know who I am."

It was strange having a conversation with someone I didn't know...and couldn't see. "Do I?" At first I wasn't convinced, but when he chuckled again, I thought about the mystery guy from Dani's dreams. Is it possible he's real? *"MG...?"*

"According to Dani, yes, that would be me."

"And you're in my *dream because...?"*

"I'm doing a favor for our mutual friend."

Relieved, I smiled. "Really? Then she's okay?" I hadn't heard from her in weeks, not since she'd gone off on her own. "Is she still alone?"

"Yes, she's okay. She's with her friends, and she wants to know where you are. They're on their way to meet you, but it might take them a while...they're on horseback."

Ignoring a fleeting feeling of distrust, I told him where we planned to set up camp once we made it to Colorado. Dani was alive, and I knew MG was the only hope I had of finding my best friend and my brother.

"I knew I shouldn't have trusted him," I spat.

Six heads whipped in my direction.

"Trusted who, Baby Girl?" Harper asked.

"The bastard from her dreams. Mystery Guy or MG or whatever she calls him," I said. In my moment of clarity, I'd bitten the inside of my cheek too hard, and I could taste salty blood welling in the break of my skin. "I told him where Dani could find us... where we'd be." I lowered my face to my hands. "I can't believe I was so stupid! It had to be—"

"But he helped bring us together," Carlos reminded me. "Why would he do something like this?"

"He was playing us," I snapped. "He's the only one who knew we were here. And, outside of us, he's the only one who knows about Dani's Ability." I shook my head, still staring into the fire pit, which was once again a smoldering mess of embers and weak flames. "Why was he in her dreams to begin with? How did he even find her?" *Was he* hunting *her?* Herding *her to the Colony?*

"Wait." Still crouched, Harper pivoted to face me. "Didn't Dani *ask* him to find us, to find you?"

Carlos stood up defensively. "She did. And he helped her learn how to use her Ability. He's her friend."

The reminder made my skin crawl. *Was he grooming her? Molding her into a toy, something he could play with?* I groaned. Not knowing what MG wanted with Dani filled me with dread.

Understanding widened Harper's eyes. "He had to have known we'd figure it out eventually—"

"Right, and now that we know who he is…we still don't know who he *really* is," I bit out, wanting to scream. "It's fucking perfect."

"Which is why we need to leave," Biggs said forcefully. "He knows we're here, and if he's got the whole Colony to back him, we can't protect ourselves if he comes back for us."

"But he could've killed us already," Harper argued. "He could've killed us, taken Dani, and never given us a second thought. I mean, it makes sense that he's the one who took her, but the repercussions of letting us live…" He shook his head.

"We're nothing to them. There are only a dozen of us and only half are trained to fight." I counted to five and then to ten, trying to breathe away the tremors of outrage.

Jake strode over from the stable, oblivious to our collective realization. "You ready?" He dropped a pistol holster next to me on the hay bale. "This one straps to your thigh," he explained. "Chris had an extra. It'll make lugging your duffle bag around easier."

I gave him a weak, grateful smile, loving his thoughtfulness and the way his warm, brown eyes made me feel a little less pissed off. "Thanks."

Sanchez cleared her throat and we turned to her. She was focusing on the small, fold-up map in her hands. "I know the Colony is set up at Peterson, but what about this other base—"

"They were going to take Becca to Peterson," Jake said. "Dani's situation doesn't seem so different."

"What happened to her—your sister, I mean?" Carlos asked. I could feel his growing fear.

After a moment, Jake shrugged. He was as exhausted as the rest of us, and naturally, he wasn't eager to relive the moment his sister died in a bloody heap in his arms.

"We need to know everything we're up against," Grayson told him.

Jake's expression was blank, but he nodded slowly. I reached for his hand and pulled him down to sit beside me. He started by telling them that his sister was like Harper, that the Virus had changed the way her mind worked, and that she had visions of the future.

"But I didn't know it was real. I thought she was losing her mind." He paused and looked down at his hands, picking idly at the callouses that had formed on his palms. "Gabe—my best friend—was a contracted geneticist at Peterson. He swore he could help her, that he could fix her."

Jake continued, his natural reserve making it difficult to speak openly about what was easily the worst night of his life. His words faded to a steady hum in my ears as his memories of the events surrounding his sister's death played out in his head, drawing me deeper into his mind. His remorse cloaked my own emotions, and I could feel the excruciating depth of his emptiness, his crushing regret. Feeling Jake's pain helped fuel my determination to make sure Dani's fate wouldn't resemble Becca's. Unbidden tears accumulated in the corners of my eyes, and I blinked them away.

"Becca saw what the people at Peterson were going to do to her, and she chose death instead." Jake ran his fingers through his short, dark brown hair.

With the exception of a hawk screeching somewhere in the distance and the crackle of the dying fire, it was completely silent.

After a long moment, Sanchez said, "We should probably go or we'll run out of daylight before we get back."

"He's gone!" Chris called from behind me. I turned around to see her jogging back from the stable. "Jason's not in his tent and his horse is gone." She glanced out at the woods. "So is Jack."

Carlos jumped up from his seat on the other side of the fire. "He left?"

"I should've known," I muttered. "He's going to try and get Dani…on his own. He's going to get himself killed, and then Dani's going to blame herself for his death, just like she did with Cam." Terror jolted through me, and I stood and started pacing. *My brother is going to get himself killed.*

Carlos hurried over to Chris. "We have to go after him. We have to—"

"We can't go after him," she said sympathetically. "We don't know how much ground he's covered or which route he took. We have no idea where he is, and even if we do find him, he won't come back with us." She squeezed his shoulder. "Jason knows how to take care of himself. We need to stick together, and we need to focus on getting Dani back." She turned her attention to Sanchez. "I'll stay here and wait for Jason in case he returns. Get to Cañon City. Find out everything you possibly can about Peterson, and get your asses back here."

"I'll finish getting the horses ready," Carlos offered, jogging toward the stable.

As I turned to follow him, Jake's strong fingers entangled with mine, giving me a momentary wash of comfort. I peered at him, a tired but grateful smile spreading across my face, and he glanced toward Jason's tent. "He'll be back," he said, trying to reassure me.

No he won't. I knew how my brother was, but I nodded without arguing and continued on to the stable.

Wings stood out among the group of grays, chestnuts, and bays. I smiled. Of course Dani would ride the most vibrant paint horse I'd ever seen. Wings's colors were rich and pure and bold, like her owner. Taking a slight detour, I stopped by a galvanized tub that held a few small apples and snatched one before heading over to introduce myself to my new riding companion.

"She's all ready for you," Carlos said as he double-checked the cinch around Wings's belly.

I unwound her leather reins from the metal railing. "Thanks."

Carlos gave me a quick nod and started toward the barn, toward Chris.

"You're not coming with us?"

He shook his head. "I'm gonna wait with Chris."

I shrugged and turned my attention back to Wings. Thoughtfully, I looked into her watchful, pale blue eyes. They were inquiring and cautious. "Hey, girl," I whispered. I couldn't communicate with animals like Dani, so I was left to my own devices to win her favor. I placed my palm below her velvety nose so she could smell my scent.

Wings's nostrils flared as she studied me. Slowly, she lowered her head to my palm. Her ears—one white, one coffee-brown—angled toward me, and her head bobbed a little, almost like she was nodding with approval.

"I know I'm not Dani, but I like horses, too. I'll take good care of you for her," I promised, stroking her chin and patting her thick, mostly-white neck. I held out the apple and offered it to her in my flattened palm. Eagerly, she reached for the treat with her lips, pulling it into her mouth. When it was gone, she nudged me. Wings suddenly seemed excited to have me as a riding partner, and I couldn't help but grin at my small but very important victory.

"Ready?" Jake asked, his deep voice interrupting me from my celebratory moment.

"Yeah." I smiled, stroking Wings's sleek neck once more before moving to her side and climbing up into the saddle with surprising ease—I hadn't been on a horse in years, but walking would take too long and cars weren't a viable option. Carlos had gauged the length of the stirrups perfectly. I pulled back on the reins ever so slightly, backing the mare away from the hitching post and positioning her toward the rest of the group.

"You're pretty good at that," Jake said enviously as he struggled with the reddish-brown horse he was riding…or trying to ride.

Grinning, I observed his valiant attempt at horsemanship. I was no expert, but I'd taken enough riding classes with Dani to have some know-how. "Your reins are too tight," I offered, stopping Wings beside him. "Give him some slack and he'll like you more." I lifted mine to demonstrate.

"I need to give him an apple so he'll like me more," he muttered, and my grin widened. Jake loosened the tension of the reins so the horse could move his head in stride as he walked, and then his gaze met mine, a playful glint in his eyes. A slight smile curved his lips. He opened his mouth to say something but closed it again when Harper guided his horse up beside us.

"Let's go," he said, waving for us to follow him.

Still sitting atop our mounts, we paused in the cover provided by two houses, grateful to have reached the outskirts of Cañon City. The ride had taken just under an hour, but my butt was paying the price.

"Downtown's a little ways that way," Jake said, pointing to the southeast through a ritzy suburban neighborhood that stretched out ahead. He continued to speak, but I was distracted. I couldn't tear my eyes from the serrated, snow-covered peaks of the Rocky Mountains to the north and west of us. I had been surrounded by their majesty for over a month, but the sight of them still enthralled me. Colorado was untamed and beautiful—so different from the colonial grace and sprawling greens I'd left behind in Salem.

Sighing, I threw my leg over Wings to dismount.

"What're you doing, Baby Girl?" I glanced over my shoulder to see Harper's eyebrows raised in curiosity as my boots hit the ground with a thud.

"Getting off my horse so whoever's here doesn't hear us clomping in a mile away." I walked Wings through a gate into a large, overgrown backyard. She followed me happily, eyeing the tall, untended grass. I waited for everyone else to follow suit. When I looked back at them expectantly, they dismounted from their horses—some with more ease than others—and did the same.

We secured the horses and unloaded what supplies we needed before heading toward downtown. After almost an hour of mostly silent slinking around, ducking under windowsills and crouching behind delivery trucks, we spotted the row of stone and brick buildings lining Main Street. It was easy to imagine the city in its heyday, booming with miners and cowboys in the decades after the gold rush. But now, windows were shattered, neon graffiti colored century-old brick walls, and cars were covered in dirt and grime, the only remnants of the season's final snow.

With the exception of our footsteps and hushed exchanges, Cañon City was quiet. There were no barking dogs, no Crazies mumbling incessantly, and no soldiers patrolling the streets. *This seems a little too easy.* My gaze veered up to the rows of windows on the second floor of the buildings, suddenly sinister and foreboding. *Where are all the Crazies?* That was one thing we'd come to expect.

"Something's not right," Sanchez said inside my head, and I assumed she was speaking telepathically to the others as well. Even though her Ability wasn't as strong or multifaceted as Dani's, it was still useful. *"Where are the Crazies?"* she asked, echoing my thoughts.

"There are worse things than no Crazies," I offered, not wanting to give the others too much time to consider turning back.

My companions exchanged apprehensive glances before we continued on to Main Street.

Staying true to our usual, cautious methods, Jake and I paused in an open, brick alley between two buildings, waiting for Harper and Sanchez to scout the nearby parking lots and shops. The cinderblock museum and history center, the most promising place to search for useful information about the Colony's layout, was a few blocks further down the street.

A gust of wind whooshed through the empty, stinking alleyway. The brisk air bit at my skin, and I shivered. My sweatshirt wasn't cutting it, especially since I'd stopped walking. Sunlight reflected off of a storefront window ahead, and I squinted in the glare. An antique shop was nestled between a pool hall and bridal shop.

"Ready?" Jake asked, looking back at me. He nodded across the street in the direction Harper and Sanchez had gone, but I was focused on the figures in the antique shop's display window. Sunwashed mannequins posed—one wearing a 1950s floral-print, halter sundress, the other in faded blue jeans and a vintage, olive-green bomber jacket. Its distressed leather looked worn and soft and enticingly warm. It looked so comfortable, I was practically salivating. I glanced up at the hand-painted sign: *Alice's Attic*.

"Hey," Jake nudged my shoulder with his. "What's up?"

"I'm cold," I said, glancing up and down the street. I looked over at Harper and Sanchez, who were moving toward the antique shop. "Where are we going?" I asked, happy to be moving closer to the shop that held the jacket and my potential warmth, but confused to be headed to the right, away from the museum.

"Pit stop," Jake said, pointing to the sign that hung three stores down from the antique shop. *Tommy's Gun Exchange*, read bold red and orange letters. *Perfect.*

Jake reached for my hand, entwining our fingers, and we

hurried across the street toward the others. Sanchez was already inside *Tommy's*, rifling through what remained of the store's stock, while Harper waited just outside the entrance, his sidearm drawn and aimed as he scanned up and down the street for movement.

Once we reached Harper, I pointed my thumb over my shoulder in the direction of *Alice's Attic* and said, "I'm going to grab a jacket."

Stopping a few steps inside the store, Jake glanced back at me with an agitated smirk.

Harper chortled. "Why am I not surprised."

I shrugged, equally annoyed with my inability to withstand the cold, and flashed them both an innocent smile. "Sorry," I mouthed.

"Jake," Sanchez called from the back of the store. "Bring me that bag, would ya?"

Harper looked from Jake to me. "I'll go with her." He nodded toward *Alice's*. "Come on, Baby Girl," he said with a nudge and started down the sidewalk, rifle drawn and each footstep light and calculated.

I glanced back at Jake, who nodded hesitantly. "Be quick about it."

Harper and I reached *Alice's* in less than a minute. The glass door was shattered, allowing us to slip into the shop easily.

I climbed up into the window display, unnerved by the antique mannequins, whose eyes were too wide and animated and whose mouths were too small for their heads. With a scrunched face, I unzipped the jacket, hoping the sleeves would be long enough for me. Harper helped me maneuver the plastic person's arms, jerking it toward me a few times, clearly entertained each time I recoiled. It was just…creepy.

Finally, I freed the jacket and shrugged into it. The moment I zipped it up—the bottom snug around my waist and the stand-up collar closing around my neck—I sighed. It fit perfectly. Unzipping the pockets, I stuck my hands inside and posed. "How's it look?"

Harpers eyebrows waggled in playful interest, and he flashed me a killer smile. “Not too bad,” he said with a wink. “Alright, let’s get this show on the road.”

He was making his way for the door just as the rumble of an engine echoed down the street. We were hugging the shadows on the walls in milliseconds, my body tense and my heartbeat quickened.

“Shit,” I hissed. Harper reached for my hand and pulled me closer to him.

The engine noise grew louder until a military Jeep sped past and continued through downtown.

“Damn, they’re in a hurry.” Harper whispered. “Let’s move before—”

The sound of roaring engines grew louder, and another truck passed the antique store and stopped somewhere not too far down the street. Hearing the engines turn off and the doors creak open, I prayed the newcomers weren’t planning on hanging around. We shuffled closer to the door and watched five men unload their things and settle into a store a few buildings up from us on the same side of the road. *Shit.* They had duffel bags and thermoses of what I assumed was coffee, or possibly booze, to warm their insides and help alleviate their boredom. *So...not just a quick stop then.*

With the soldiers out of sight, Harper and I hurried down the street to the gun exchange. Once inside, the four of us fell into a heated debate over whether we should stay and keep searching for helpful information or go back to camp.

“What other options do we have? We need information...*something*, otherwise this trip was pointless,” I said anxiously. We’d come so far and now they were considering turning back. “There are only four of us. There’s gotta be a way we can get to the museum without being seen.”

Sanchez and Harper considered it for a moment, and finally

Sanchez nodded. "Fine, but we need to stay off the main road. We'll go in from the back."

"There's probably an alley," Jake said, and he found my hand and led me to the back of the gun store. He unlocked the back door and slowly opened it. Loosening his grip on my fingers, he let go and leaned out for a better look. A moment later, he closed the door. "The back alley runs along all the buildings. If they stay inside, it's doable."

Sanchez took a deep breath. "Let's get this over with," she said bitterly.

Within minutes, we were darting behind the buildings, crouching and ducking wherever we could. We were getting close. Just as Jake and I slipped behind an enormous delivery truck, a screen door flung open. It was the back door to a café—crates of coffee filters and paper cups were piled beside the dumpsters like they'd been unloaded but never delivered. Sanchez and Harper were up ahead, but Jake and I were stuck behind the truck, waiting for whoever had come out of the café to go back inside.

"I thought we were giving her a few days to get the intel," a man with a lisp said. Curious, I peeked through a slat in a stack of empty crates behind the truck just in time to see him unzipping his pants. I shrank back. The man—a soldier wearing green fatigues with a black armband wrapped around each sleeve at the biceps—had dark hair and a goatee. I could smell the tobacco smoke from his cigarette amidst the other rank smells of rotting food in the dumpsters.

"I mean, I don't get it," he said. I could tell by his muddled words that he was holding the cigarette between his lips as he used his hands to pee…at least that's what I assumed he was doing. "Just seems a little excessive, don't you think?"

"Apparently she's something special. He wants her back sooner," another man called from inside.

"She better be great in bed for all this trouble we're going to. I thought he had a thing for the doctor, but I guess he can get away with more than one piece of ass." The man cleared his throat. "Either way, I heard his newest flavor is a redhead." He groaned. "I love redheads."

A redhead...that could be Dani! So, who's the "he"? MG? The soldier's second groan made me want to walk over and kick him repeatedly in the groin, especially when the men inside the café only laughed.

"So, the raid's moved up to tomorrow night?" After goatee zipped up his pants, I heard him take a deep drag on his cigarette and cough.

"Roger that. We've got to get his toy home safe and sound, though. God, have you seen that bitch naked? I swear, I've never gotten a chub so fast."

"Hey, fuck-wad," another man called. "Are you taking a piss or a dump? If you're taking a shit at least shut the fucking door!"

Goatee laughed. "Shut up, dickhead, I'm done. Don't get your panties in a bunch."

Once the screen door slammed closed, I looked at Jake. The dread I felt was mirrored in his eyes. *A raid?* Assuming Dani was the "redhead," I couldn't help but think they were likely talking about us.

"A raid? Tomorrow?" I mouthed.

Jake shook his head, not wanting to think about an impending catastrophe while we were in the middle of another.

Carefully, we continued on toward the museum. Once we were inside, luck seemed to throw us a much-needed bone—a regular post-apocalyptic miracle. The museum contained ample information about Peterson Air Force Base.

We rummaged through the mini-exhibit and gathered a few maps of the base—they were vague and had obviously been created for tourists, but helpful nonetheless—a few history and general information books, and some black-and-white photos that had been taken on the base.

After nearly an hour, we cautiously found our way back to the horses, hoping that the café outpost was the only one we needed to worry about. It was another hour before we made it back to camp, leaving us with only a few hours before dusk.

Chris was the first person we saw as we rode up behind the barn. She'd apparently been waiting for us.

"I was starting to worry," she said, then let out a nervous laugh. "I never thought I'd be so happy to hear Sanchez's voice in my head." She surveyed our group, her eyes assessing, and I figured she was making sure we'd all made it back in one piece.

Jake's boots hit the ground with a dull thump, and he started unloading the duffel bags and backpacks of weapons, ammo, books, and maps. I dismounted and patted Wings on the neck, thanking her for being so steady and fast.

"We saw soldiers…I'm assuming from the Colony. They had trucks and were wearing armbands, but these ones were black instead of yellow." I frowned, feeling slightly ill as I recalled the perverted comments they'd been making. "We overheard them talking about a redhead…and, well, they mentioned a raid that's supposed to happen tomorrow," I told Chris while, around me, the others were unsaddling their horses. "We think the raid's gonna be here."

"Great," Chris breathed.

"Seriously. We were talking on the way back and we think we should leave. We can't take any chances. Especially with Sarah so—"

"Carlos is gone," she blurted.

I froze, my mouth gaping open. "What?"

"I'm sure he went after Jason."

"Jesus," I muttered, resting my forehead against the side of the barn.

Chris ignored my melodramatics. "So…Ky and Ben went after Carlos. Ky felt responsible, since Carlos must've ridden right past him." Her eyes drooped with exhaustion, and she shook her head. "This is such a damn mess."

I could sense there was something else she needed to tell us.

"What is it?" I groaned, straightening and dropping my hands to my sides. "What else happened?"

"A woman showed up this afternoon. She's not a Crazy, but something's not right about her. Her mind is…off, somehow. Cooper heard her walking around in the forest and…" Chris shook her head again. "Anyway, she was unarmed, confused, and seemed like she hadn't bathed or eaten anything in a while. Sarah and I got her cleaned up and fed her."

Sanchez took Wings's reins from me, and Chris matched my stride as I headed for the campfire.

"She seemed so lost and helpless," Chris added.

As we rounded the corner of the barn, I slammed into Jake's stiff, motionless body. "Jesus, Jake…" I half expected him to turn around and reach out to steady me like he'd done so many times before, but he didn't move. I righted myself and glared at him. He was completely unfazed that I'd just crashed into him. "Good thing I'm not as delicate as I used to be," I muttered tartly, but he didn't notice. Shock and horror—*his* shock and horror—trumped all preceding thought, and goose bumps prickled my arms.

I shifted my eyes in the direction of his to find the woman Chris had mentioned—our uninvited guest. The duffel bag Jake had flung over his shoulder slid to the ground with a heavy thud.

"Oh my God," I rasped, and Jake said, "Becca?"

Want to read more of The Ending Series?

Visit www.theendingseries.com for purchase information.

OTHER NOVELS BY THE LINDSEYS

THE ENDING SERIES

The Ending Beginnings: Omnibus Edition

After The Ending

Into The Fire

Out Of The Ashes

Before The Dawn

World Before: A Collection of Stories

NOVELS BY LINDSEY POGUE

A SARATOGA FALLS LOVE STORY

Whatever It Takes

Nothing But Trouble

Told You So

FORGOTTEN LANDS

Dust And Shadow

Borne of Sand and Scorn

Wither and Ruin (TBR)

Borne of Earth and Ember (TBR)

NOVELS BY LINDSEY FAIRLEIGH

ECHO TRILOGY

Echo in time

Resonance

Time Anomaly

Dissonance

Ricochet Through Time

KAT DUBOIS CHRONICLES

Ink Witch

Outcast

Underground

Soul Eater

Judgement

Afterlife

ATLANTIS LEGACY

Sacrifice of the Sinners

Legacy of the Lost

ABOUT AUTHOR LINDSEY POGUE

Lindsey Pogue has always been a sucker for a good love story. She completed her first new adult manuscript in high school and has been writing tales of love and friendship, history and adventure ever since. When she's not chatting with readers, plotting her next storyline, or dreaming up new, brooding characters, Lindsey's generally wrapped in blankets watching her favorite action flicks with her own leading man. They live in Northern California with their rescue cat, Beast. You can follow Lindsey and her writing adventures on social media and www.lindseypogue.com.

ABOUT AUTHOR LINDSEY FAIRLEIGH

Lindsey Fairleigh lives her life with one foot in a book—as long as that book transports her to a magical world or bends the rules of science. Her novels, from post-apocalyptic to time travel and historical fantasy, always offer up a hearty dose of unreality, along with plenty of adventure and romance. When she's not working on her next novel, Lindsey spends her time trying out new recipes in the kitchen, walking through the woods, or planning her future farm. She lives in the Pacific Northwest with her husband and their small pack of cats and dogs. www.lindseyfairleigh.com